BEHEMOTH 2

MICHAEL COLE

SEVERED PRESS
HOBART TASMANIA

BEHEMOTH 2

CHAPTER

1

Vertical gusts of wind pounded the Atlantic water, already rippling from the remnants of the storm that had passed through. Five hundred feet above, three Sikorsky SH-60 Seahawk helicopters accelerated northward in a triangular formation. Bluish-gray in color, sixty-four feet in length, and a loaded weight of over seventeen thousand pounds, the two trailing Seahawks kept at a three-hundred yard distance from the leader in front. All three were fully loaded, with armaments including three Mark 46 torpedoes, four Hellfire missiles, and an M60 machine gun mounted within the sealed cabin. Etched into the steel above the weapons pylons were the words *United States Navy*.

The normally blue water appeared more like a liquid charcoal, reflecting the grayish black clouds above. The clouds still blocked the sun, giving an eerie grayish appearance to the horizon, as if the choppers were flying over a graveyard. The rain was reduced to a steady shower now after hours of torrential downpour.

This was fine by Ensign Matt Riggs. Harnessed into the fine leather pilot seat within the cockpit of the lead Seahawk Helicopter, he led the small unit north. He replaced his aviator sunglasses, previously having removed them after visibility was compromised by the intense rain. To his amazement, his co-pilot, Lieutenant Sherman, never removed his glasses. He stared dead ahead, with a soulless mechanical expression on his face. Although Riggs had been through plenty of missions, he still got nervous when conditions got bad. Sherman, however, never broke a sweat. It certainly made an impression. Riggs almost wondered if Sherman was, in fact, machine.

"We have a new reading. Target has descended fifty meters. Continuing to move rapidly," a voice spoke into his headset. The traffic was heard by all crew in each chopper. They all knew the voice.

Colonel Richard Salkil sat in the cabin, eyes glued to a computer screen. Normally dressed in an officer's uniform, the Colonel was outfitted with a blue combat jumpsuit, as if prepared to jump into action himself. And prepared he was. It was quite a sight, even to the two soldiers seated with him in the cabin. Unshaven from two days of tracking his Moby Dick, he intently watched the red blip on the radar monitor. The tracking device installed onto the target was still functioning, although it would glitch every so often. He was so intent, he didn't even notice Sergeant Mike Logan standing nearby, watching the monitor. Built like a tank, he also watched the monitor. Small red letters flashed with the blip; *IP-15.*

What does that stand for?

Logan was well versed in most acronyms and codes used by the U.S. military. But *IP-15*, he had no clue. It was also odd to see the Colonel so intent on finding the target. Riggs felt the same, although he didn't know the Colonel so well. Even Lt. Sherman, though nobody could tell through his expressionless face, felt a bit odd about the scenario.

When told to scramble, the only information given to them regarding the target was that it was a killer shark. Of course, they followed the orders without question, as they were trained to do. But each man and woman of this Navy unit felt the same bizarre sentiment. A Naval Destroyer, patrol ship, and fully armed Seahawk helicopters, to take out a shark?

For Logan, it wasn't the first time he had been called upon to hunt a deadly sea animal. Two years prior, a great white was believed to be the cause of death for two surfers up along the Jersey Coast. His unit happened to be close by, so rather than the Coast Guard, he was called upon to hunt the creature down. And all it took was a Navy hull boat, launched from the *USS Hurricane*, a patrol vessel.

Logan stuck his head into the cockpit and looked ahead. He could see the Destroyer, the *USS Freedom*, closing in from the north. Down at the console, the blip at the pilots' radar monitor. They were nearly over the supposed shark. Riggs glanced up at him and cupped his hand over his microphone.

"You think the boss is just really hungry for shark-fin soup?"

"I don't know what this is about," Logan said. "It's real hush-hush. All they'll say is that it's something they want dead."

"A cover-up?" Riggs asked.

"SHH!" Sherman suddenly hissed. It was the first movement from his face in hours, it seemed. He leaned toward his co-pilot and spoke very softly. "You realize he can hear you. Knock off the chatter and just focus on the mission." Sherman then sat up straight, and returned to his expressionless, statue form.

Salkil could hear them. Years of Marine combat and survival training, and years of applying his tactics, enhanced many of his natural senses. One of which was the sense of hearing. It became useful when detecting enemy troops nearby when sabotaging narcotic operations in the jungles of Columbia and Ecuador. He trained himself to hear the shallow breathing and light footsteps of a passing enemy. Now, in the present, that ability never wavered.

It wasn't the first time he overheard confused conversation about the mission. He understood that it was most unusual, and wished there was a better story he could give them. But the U.S. Government had given the military strict instructions to keep this operation as quiet as possible, and because he had knowledge of the situation, Col. Salkil was in charge. In addition to destroying the target, the military instructed him to eliminate further loose ends of the failed *Warren Institution* experiments.

What was supposed to be a simple inspection had become a nightmare.

It was only days ago when Salkil had arrived at the *Warren Institution*, called in to inspect the project and possibly approve further funding. The facility was an enormous underwater lab, which provided an artificial habitat for the bizarre experiments taking place. There, he met Dr. Isaac Wallack, the geneticist in charge of the project.

Salkil was given a tour of the facility, only aware that its purpose was to create a new kind of weapon for the U.S. military. What Salkil found fascinated him, and simultaneously, disturbed him.

Through a process of genetic fusing, Dr. Wallack had created an army of hybrid beasts. The first was a new breed referred to as *Isurus Palinuridae*...a disturbing genetic fusing of Mako Sharks and Spiny Lobster. Wallack was convinced that, with the help of technology, he could command these creatures to go into warzones and eliminate enemy personnel and sea craft, while the hardened shell would protect the creatures from enemy fire. Adamant that he could control anything he created, he had revealed his ultimate creation: *Architeuthis Brachyura,* a sixty-foot crossover of a giant squid and a crab. In what seemed like a twist of fate, the beast proved Wallack wrong while this meeting was taking place.

The Behemoth tore through the steel siding of its chamber, flooding the laboratory. The event was so unexpected, there was no time to seal off the chamber. Water ravaged much of the lab's interior, overflowing the pools containing the other hybrid specimens. This was only the beginning of the problems.

The hybrid creature had made its way to the island chain called Mako's Ridge. There, it made a habitat in the rocky island of Mako's Edge. There, it attacked fishing boats, and eventually killed a Coast Guard diver sent to investigate a sinking. The United States Coast Guard investigated, but didn't locate the creature, as it was hiding in an underwater cave. However, it did not take long for more tragedy to strike. During a marlin fishing competition, the hybrid went on a bloodthirsty rampage, sinking several vessels and devouring many people, including members of law enforcement. It eventually made its way to the beach, where it killed more, and maimed many others.

Matters were made even worse when Dr. Wallack took his own initiative to capture the beast. With a small team of mercenaries, he had kidnapped a local fisherman, Rick Napier, to commandeer his vessel to capture the creature. Others kidnapped were Napier's daughter, her boyfriend, the local police chief, and an off-duty Coast Guard diver.

The plan to capture the beast proved unsuccessful. It killed the mercenaries, as well as Wallack, the very man who gave it life. Napier and his friends were able to make it out alive, thanks to a nearby Coast Guard cutter. With several shots of the seventy-millimeter gun, *Architeuthis Brachyura* was destroyed.

That solved the issue of the creature being on the loose. However, many more problems were created as a result. There were many eye witness accounts of the hybrid beast, including an exclusive report featuring Rick Napier regarding the events surrounding him, and what he learned of Dr. Wallack and his experiments.

Worse yet, an inventory of the remaining specimens revealed that one was at large. One of the *Isurus Palinuridae* hybrids had escaped as a result of the breach and subsequent flooding.

Salkil was notified to tie up any loose ends. Immediately, he sent officials to Mako's Ridge to take care of the devastation taking place. More importantly, he was to track the escaped hybrid. Each one had a tracking device installed, but the tech was glitching, possibly due to damage during the incident. Under no circumstance should this creature be allowed to escape.

The bottom line was: nobody else was to know of the existence of these creatures, and there must be nothing linking these incidents to the government. Already, cover stories were being cooked up regarding the attack at Mako's Center. Salkil also knew, that after destroying this surviving specimen, he would have to pay Rick Napier a personal visit.

"This is Admiral Joel Ford of the USS Freedom. We have a reading of the target. Colonel Salkil, are you copying this transmission?" The Colonel pressed his finger to the microphone attached to his headset as he spoke.

"Yes, Admiral," he said.

"As I said, we have a reading on your fish. I'm sending in three hull boats to draw it to the surface. Once it comes up, they'll spray it with some shark-repellant fifty-cal. Easy-peasy."

Logan had taken his seat in the cabin as the call came in. It was then when he noticed the slightest twitch in the Colonel's expression. Most people would have missed it, but he had been around enough higher-ups to recognize the subtle clues to what they were thinking. Salkil's facial muscles constricted briefly before returning to form.

"Negative, Admiral," he said. "I have authorization to use necessary force to eliminate the threat. I want to lock Mark 46 torpedoes on the target."

"For a fish? Negative!" The Admiral spoke.

"Sir, this isn't..." Salkil was about to follow with *any ordinary fish*, but managed to stop himself. Even to higher ranking officers, he couldn't even hint to the identity of the creature. "Sir...I must insist on the most direct method on destroying the target. We can destroy it with the torpedoes and be complete."

"As I said, negative," the Admiral said. *"I'm not wasting explosives on a damn fish. Our guys on the Zodiac crafts will draw it up with chum, and eliminate it. That's how it's going to be."* Salkil's face tensed once more.

"Copy," he said through gritted teeth. He moved the microphone away from his mouth. "Goddamn," he mumbled. It was another case in which he was expected to get a task done but had so many obstacles that impeded his progress. For this plan to work, it would mean the sailors aboard those ships would likely get a visual of the creature; which was exactly what he was trying to prevent. In addition, Salkil wasn't convinced that plan would work. He was aware of the creature's exoskeleton, and how Dr. Wallack had designed it to withstand gunfire. However, to his understanding, there was no field test conducted. And what did Wallack know of military weapons, anyway?

He could only hope the shell wasn't thick enough to withstand gunfire.

"Target ascending twenty yards," Sherman spoke through the comm. There was a pause of nearly twenty seconds. *"Target is also decreasing speed. We're nearly above it. Colonel, we'll have to reduce speed or we'll be past it."*

"It probably senses the presence of the *Freedom*," Salkil spoke into his microphone.

4

"*Zodiacs are en-route,*" another voice spoke. The Colonel stared at the monitor intently with unblinking eyes. He could see the large blip representing the *Freedom,* and the blips for the Zodiac boats approaching *IP-15.*

"Salkil to *Viper 4* and *5*... form a perimeter around the target area. Be ready to provide support if necessary."

Riggs looked over at Sherman, curious to see if the Lieutenant was as confused over the situation as him. Sherman maintained the same stone like expression, though he found the order bizarre. Then again, this whole mission was bizarre. There was no question that the Colonel knew something they didn't.

Salkil felt the cabin tilt toward the right as the Seahawk turned. His eyes went to the door as Logan slid them open and propped an M60 machine gun. The black nose of the weapon protruded through the open doorway, while a blast of cool ocean air swarmed the cabin. Salkil propped himself up and looked down toward the water. Three black Navy Zodiac boats, spaced two-hundred feet from each other, splashed through the rippling current below. Several hundred yards across were *Viper 4* and *5,* appearing like black dragonflies against the gloomy sky. He could almost see the guns pointing down toward the water.

"*Viper 4 in position.*"

"*Viper 5 in position.*"

Salkil watched the boats. The one in the center carried a large red tub. He could see one of the sailors pop the top off and dip a large scoop into the murky red chum mixture over the sides. In a few short minutes, there was a large red stream of fish guts trailing the boats. On the radar screen, the target maintained position, possibly confused by the commotion in the water. It slowly ascended, but only slowly. Salkil worried that the presence of the Destroyer had made the creature wary.

At this moment, another voice spoke through the comm.

"*This is Lieutenant Hendricks from Unit One calling for Colonel Salkil.*"

The Colonel looked down toward the boats. He could see the Lieutenant in the center boat, holding the microphone extender. "Go ahead."

"*Sir, as you well know, we've commenced the operation. Exactly how big a fish are we talking about, here?*"

Salkil recalled the documents he had seen before the creature was revealed to be missing. Fifteen Lobster-Shark specimens were in containment. The first three were measured at twelve feet. The following eleven had grown between fifteen and eighteen feet in length. Then there was number fifteen... which had grown to be the largest of the specimens. And it was the one at large.

"Twenty-three feet," Salkil said. Logan glanced over his shoulder, saw that twitch in the colonel's expression again.

"Big ass fish," Lieutenant Hendricks said to himself as he replaced the microphone. *Not really big enough for a friggin Naval ship.* At six-foot-three and a solid muscular frame, he stood at the helm while his two shipmates, Private Dunn and Corporal Meyer, stood at opposite sides of the boat. With the red tub in front of the Fifty-Cal., they shoveled loads of chum into the water. The red trail quickly zigzagged with the uneven currents. Hendricks looked over his shoulder at the trail, hoping they would luck out and the shark would come up at the most convenient place to shoot it.

He briefly scanned the sky, drawn to the sight of the three Seahawks up above. The drone of the twin turbine engines of each one created an endless howl in the grim afternoon sky. The Destroyer held at bay five hundred yards south. In each hull boat traveling parallel, a man stood at a mounted Fifty Cal. machine gun.

They really want this shark dead. It was odd, indeed. During his career, even when going after Somali pirates or drug smugglers did they sometimes not use so many resources. And this was only a shark. There had been plenty of times when he didn't have the full scoop when undergoing a mission. When infiltrating a Columbian drug smuggler's yacht, little did he know that he was actually exterminating an informant who was giving U.S. secrets to Iran. When instructed to open fire on, and ultimately sink, a cargo ship approaching the Gulf of Mexico, it was under the guise that it was carrying deadly diseases from a south Atlantic island. Only later did he find out that the ship was actually carrying a mercenary group that conducted operations starting in Northern Egypt and worked their way through the Mediterranean. To this day, he never knew what they did, but it was so Top-Secret, the U.S. Government wanted them eliminated to preserve the secret. With that knowledge in mind, Hendricks did not want to know.

What he did know, was that the government wanted this animal dead. Though it was only a fish, or so he was told, the principle remained the same. It contained a secret that the Feds did not want exposed. What that would be, once again, he figured it was best not to know.

"Hurry it up, boys," he said to his team. "We don't know how long the weather will hold up. Might be another front moving in. I don't want to be caught in it."

"Tell it to the fish, sir," Corporal Meyer jabbed.

****

All the creature had ever known was the controlled environment in which it was imprisoned. Every aspect had become familiar, down to the food, the smell, the sounds, even the sensation of the water against its rigid shell. Now everything was new. It had to fight against the motion of currents and allow its eyes to adjust to the differing changes in light. Then there was the temperature, which was much lower than what the shark was previously exposed to. This initially slowed its movements, until its body eventually adapted.

At six thousand pounds, it glided with graceful freedom as it explored its new surroundings. Its blood red color contrasted sharply with the surrounding blue water. With a solid shell plating its entire body, the creature was split into segments; the head, body, and tail, which itself had multiple segments for flexibility. Each swing of its tail forced water through its gills, oxygenating its blood. For a while, this was all its system required as it migrated. Its only purpose was to swim endlessly.

However, the inevitable drive that was hunger soon brought new purpose. Not only did it need to replenish spent energy from swimming, the colder water temperatures sped up its metabolism. It used its sense of smell to detect blood in the water, and extended its two thin antennae, positioned near its nostrils, to scavenge for any stray sources of sustenance.

Its hunt came to a brief halt. Its senses were overloaded with the presence of multiple objects in the water above it. One of which was immensely large, and its presence caused the creature to pause. Pores located in its rigid snout, *Ampullae of Lorenzini*, flooded its brain with the detection of electric movements from nearby. Then its nostrils flooded with a much-desired sensation…the smell of blood. Suddenly the ocean had become full of it.

The creature turned upward toward the surface. The scent did not seem to point at any of the objects above; rather it seemed spread out, as if any one or all of the intruders were bleeding. Its eyes locked on the one most directly ahead. Then, it swiped its tail, generating the massive speed of its genetic parent, the Mako. It did not yet bare its jaws, as it would ram its target like a torpedo to stun it. Afterwards, it would tear away flesh.

The distance closed. Its eyes rolled backward, covered by an eyelid that acted like a protective shield.

****

Salkil's heartbeat felt like a shutter as the depth reading changed on the monitor. A moment ago, the target was fifty meters deep. In less than an instant it was thirty meters…twenty. Logan saw the change of expression in Salkil's face. It was no subtle twitch. His eyes had opened wide, and his jaw dropped ever so slightly, in a way that expressed alarm. In that same moment, the Colonel propped the microphone to his mouth.

"Boating units, use evasive maneuvers! Target ascending!"

Only the first half of Salkil's transmission came through, as all eyes went to the most easterly boat. Hendricks looked to his left, and watched the enormous eruption of water. Impacted from an overwhelming force from underneath, the boat lifted several feet and flipped in mid air. All three sailors aboard, mentally stunned by the surprise and physically stunned by the impact, were flung from the twisting craft. Transmissions quickly filled the radio waves.

"*Unit Two, come in!*"

"*What in the hell was that?*"

"*Units One and Three, respond to Unit Two's position!*"

"*Viper Four has a visual on the target! It's…What is th…*"

Lt. Hendricks didn't waste time waiting for orders. As soon as he saw the surge, he redirected the craft in its direction. Water splashed his face as the bow sliced the surface. The wind kicked up and tugged at his uniform. He slid protective goggles over his eyes to protect against the dreaded salt water sting. The other sailors on his boat did not need to be told to seal the chum tub and take position. Corporal Meyer stood at the Fifty-Cal., while Dunn placed the strap of his M4 over his shoulder, and stood ready to haul in the men overboard. After only a few short seconds, they had closed the gap. Unit Three was close behind.

The black bow of the Unit Two Zodiac pointed upward. Though the boat was mostly submerged, Hendricks was able to identify some of the damage. The solid hull was breached, and the starboard inflatable tube had completely ruptured. The other tube seemed to be currently losing air as well. Splashing in the water beside it were two sailors. No sign of the third. Hendricks pulled the boat alongside them. His teammate on the side reached down, grabbed the nearest sailor by the wrist, and pulled him upward. Corporal Meyer scanned the water with the sights of the machine gun. Soaking wet, exhausted, and still staggered by the sudden impact, the sailor collapsed to the flooring. The second man overboard swam toward them.

"Where's the third guy?" Hendricks said.

"I don't know..." the exhausted sailor said, spitting water onto the floor. "I'm not even sure what happened. It's like we were hit by a semi-trailer." Hendricks snatched up the radio.

"Viper Four! You said you had a visual? Where is it?"

"We've lost sight. It dove. The reading shows...hang on...wait...it's coming back up."

Dunn leaned far out over the gunwale for the other sailor, who reached back. They locked hands, and Dunn shut his eyes for a moment as his muscles contracted with the upward pull. He opened them, just in time to see the red shape emerging behind the sailor. A massive set of jaws opened, baring rows of jagged white teeth. The sailor saw nothing but the darkness that overtook him as he disappeared into the creature's mouth. The jaws clamped down right onto Dunn's forearm. Teeth seared his flesh and grazed his bone. What was left became lodged in the closed jaws. The monster dove with its prey, dragging Dunn over the gunwale.

There was no time for Hendricks to save the Private. He only heard a loud splash, followed by a brief shriek. By the time Hendricks turned, Dunn was already overboard, and a red triangular fin cut the water before diving. In the moments that followed, the ocean around him turned dark red.

"Son-of-a-bitch!" he shouted. "Meyer! Point that thing over and put the hurt on this thing!"

"Sir? Private Dunn is still..."

"Dunn's dead," Hendricks said. He picked up the radio. "We have men down. Does anyone up there have a visual on the thing?" Suddenly the boat shook with the rapid shutter of the fifty-cal. Meyer clenched his teeth as he fired a stream of bullets at the oncoming swell of water that approached. Beneath that grayish water was the red shape of the creature. The fin emerged, as if taunting.

Empty cartridges peppered the bow. In the few seconds in which the creature approached, Meyer had unloaded fifty bullets onto its hide. Each one was as useless as the next, crushed against the solid exoskeleton. Rapid fire from the third Zodiac struck the beast all along the side of its body.

The creature's eyes went black with the protective lids that peeled over. Its nose struck the bow. Tremor of impact shook the Zodiac. Meyer fell to his knees, still clinging to the weapon. Hendricks fell forward against the console. Machine gun fire from the other boat ceased to avoid friendly fire. For the briefest of moments, it seemed that the shark had dived once again. That moment was quick to end as the boat shuddered a second time. Hendricks pulled himself to his feet and attempted to operate the controls. He put the boat in reverse. The engine moaned, and the propellers twisted, but the boat failed to backtrack. Then there was a loud burst, followed by a sizzling sound. Propping himself up, he looked ahead of the bow. The shark's red body twisted and turned. With each motion, it shook the boat. Clenched in its jaws was a mouthful of the inflatable tube. He snatched up the radio.

"Unit Two, smoke this son-of-a-bitch!" Luckily, there was no argument regarding him being in the line of fire. The sailor at the 50 Cal. depressed the trigger. Bullets zipped through the air, momentarily visible as bright yellow streaks. They pelted the side of the shark. Though they inflicted no damage, they were successful in acquiring its attention.

Sensing the presence of another attacker, the creature released its grasp on the 'wounded' opponent. In a single quick motion, the shark whipped its body around to turn toward the other boat. And in that same motion, it swung its tail to generate a burst of speed.

Just before it did so, Meyer squeezed on the trigger, sending a haze of bullets down at it. Bullets tore at the water around it. The swinging tail smashed hard against the steel hull. The Zodiac rolled in the water. As it did, the machine gun pointed toward the sky, bullets still discharging from the barrel.

"Jesus!" Riggs said as bullets struck near the cockpit. The pounding sound of metal echoed through the aircraft, as if someone was pressing a jackhammer to the hull. Emergency warning lights flashed. He pulled back hard on the controls.

Colonel Salkil grabbed his seat as the chopper banked hard. It tilted to the right and dipped suddenly. As it did so, the pilots briefly lost control. The chopper fishtailed. The rotating tail blades sliced air vertically and horizontally during multiple complete spins. Even through the sound of the twin turbine engines, rotator blades, and warning beeps, he could hear the sharp slicing sound of bullets as they passed by. Logan braced himself against the door as the chopper descended. The other soldier, caught off guard, lost his footing. He fell backward, only to be supported by Colonel Salkil, who reached out and grabbed him by the uniform while still seated. Amazed by the immense strength the Colonel possessed, the soldier gave a quick salute as a thank you, and regained his footing.

The chopper leveled out. Riggs and Sherman both went over the systems and readings to assess the damage. During this time, the radio was still blaring with alarmed voices of Navy personnel as the conflict ensued.

"*Viper Three, Status Report!*"

"*Unit One is capsized.*"

"*Dispatching rescue units. Unit Two, report status.*"

Hendricks filled his lungs with air as his life vest pulled him to the surface. He looked around to gain his bearings. He was immediately drawn to the sound of gunfire from the remaining Zodiac behind him. It had ceased as he turned around. The boat was a dozen yards or so away. His first instinct was to swim to it, but a glance at the sailors gave him pause. He watched their eyes and the barrels of their rifles. Each were pointed at the water, scanning the immediate area near their boat, meaning the creature had either already attacked them, or could be circling.

Self preservation took over. Hendricks reached to his thigh holster and snatched his waterproof Sig Sauer P226 and scanned the water. To his left, the starboard side of his Zodiac floated. Floating several feet from what he believed to be the stern of the craft, was Meyer, face down in the water. Hendricks spat bitter salt water from his mouth as he paddled toward the Lieutenant. Meyer bobbed in the water, with little swells splashing against his vest.

"Meyer!" Hendricks called out. There was no answer. Meyer drifted motionless, his head pointing toward the Lieutenant. Hendricks arrived and grabbed him by the vest. "Hey, Mac!" He lifted to turn Meyer over. The Corporal's face was frozen in a horrified expression: jaw slack, eyes open, one wider than the other. His skin was pale white, as if all the blood had been drained. Hendricks moved him to check his vitals. With uneven weight, Meyer dunked and rolled over, and his waist emerged over the water.

Below the waist was nothing but a string of entrails.

Hendricks shrieked and pushed himself away from his brother-in-arms, who had been bitten in two. Machine gun fire drew his attention back to the other Zodiac. He searched for the fin near the vessel, until he realized the .50 Cal. was aimed several yards off. Just as he measured the location of the weapon's aim, he heard the sailors call out for him.

"Look out!"

Hendricks saw the swell, then the fin. The head emerged, like a giant red cone. Then the mouth opened, like the compartment door to a landing craft, only this one was lined with three-inch teeth. Hendricks kicked his feet and paddled his one free arm, while pointing his Sig Sauer at the oncoming beast. He only managed to fire off two quick shots before the creature passed over. The swell had nearly bounced him out of the way, save for his wielding arm. The jaws closed down, and the creature's tail thrashed to pull away.

In a single instant, Hendricks felt the multiple, but individually unique sensations of tearing flesh, twisting bones, snapping tendons, and searing cartilage as his arm was torn off by the roots. Blood filled the water around him. The shark glided along the surface, swallowing the stolen appendage. It turned toward the remaining enemy.

The sailor at the .50 Cal. yelled as he fired the weapon at the approaching monster. The other two shouldered their M4s and started blasting away, shocked and confused that their weapons had no effect on the strange creature. The red shark moved in like a guided missile and slammed into the starboard hull. It did not stop nor slow down. Like a relentless force of nature, it passed through. The boat flipped, sending all hands into the water.

The cold temperatures numbed the immense wound where Hendricks' arm used to be. As consciousness faded, he could hear the screams from the other Navy men as the beast slaughtered them one-by-one.

"*It took out Unit Two!*" a voice called out over the radio. Riggs and Sherman had just leveled out the helicopter, just in time to witness the horrific event unfold beneath them. The red fin could be seen below, cutting away at the water as the shark sped away in an easterly direction. It quickly dove beneath the waves.

Salkil emerged through the doorway between the cabin and the cockpit.

"Get after it!" he barked. Sherman, still stone-faced, looked up at him.

"Sir, we have a fuel leakage, and possible rotor damage," he said. "It's best we land on the *Freedom*, and allow the other units to…"

"I said get after it, goddamnit!" the Colonel yelled. He then grabbed a radio extender. "All airborne units, pursue the target!"

"*Sir, we have men in the water,*" one of the other pilots said.

"You have your orders, now move!" He slammed the radio down and moved back into the cabin. Riggs shook his head in discontent and adjusted the controls. The radio blared with transmissions from the Admiral.

"*Colonel Salkil! What the hell is this thing?!… Colonel?… COLONEL!*"

The engine groaned, and warning lights flashed as he pushed the chopper forward. Riggs gave a quick glance at the Lieutenant, whose stone face was now tense with a foreboding dread.

The Seahawk hauled after the fleeing shark, followed by the two support units.

CHAPTER
2

The wind kicked up, and the ash colored clouds above turned a darker shade. Inside the Seahawk, red lights blinked on and off. A hydraulic alert came on, along with an engine pressure warning. Riggs' eyes repeatedly glanced down at the alerts on the console. Both he and Sherman believed a bullet penetrated the exterior of one of the engines. This was further evidenced by a small stream of smoke that trailed their chopper. They switched off the overhead warning light, which only served as a nuisance at this point.

To Salkil, these problems paled in comparison to the tracking device. Moments after the creature had engaged the Zodiacs and fled, the signal failed and the creature disappeared off the tracking monitor. The radar had difficulty tracking it as well, possibly due to changing depths. Logan could feel the frustration brewing within the Colonel. He stayed silent, ready at the M60 as instructed. Above him, a cloud of smoke billowed. It had gradually thickened as they continued the chase.

"*Viper Five to Viper Three. Condition of your engine appears to be worsening. Must advise for you to turn back and reconvene at the Freedom.*"

Salkil spoke into the microphone, "We're resuming pursuit." Riggs leaned to the side to call through the opening. Normally, he'd speak over the radio, but there was no sense in having the other units overhearing the conversation.

"Colonel, sir…if our condition worsens, we may need to make an emergency landing. And begging your pardon, sir, but we have nowhere to land. The other two units can continue pursuit." By the time he finished, Salkil had emerged through the opening.

"We are going after that thing and seeing through the mission." Riggs reactively flinched as the Colonel raised his voice. Most other people wouldn't get under his skin so easily, but this was a Colonel, and an authoritative one who could easily dampen his military career. He knew best to shut up and keep flying.

Several long minutes passed, and the pilots adjusted their direction based on the infrequent blips on the radar screen. The creature was still on the run and did not appear to be slowing down. Salkil tried to adjust the signal from the tracking monitor.

"Those bastards had all this technology to build a lab and create these things, but couldn't manage to create a decent tracking device," he growled. It was likely the device suffered further damage during its encounter with the Zodiacs. Once again, a voice blared over the radio.

"*Viper Three, I must insist that …*"

"Understood!" Salkil cut him off. At that moment, Sherman spoke into the radio.

"*Sir, when we get a positive ID on the target, how do you propose we eliminate it?*"

"If it's near the surface, I want everyone to lay some hellfire missiles into it," Salkil said. "I want the bastard vaporized."

Sherman replied with a simple, "*Copy.*" Twenty minutes ago, the order would've seemed absurd. However, it was clear that this was no ordinary shark. More to the point, it was something that the Colonel wanted to keep under wraps.

The chase ensued further out into the Atlantic. Finally, as the pilots watched the surface, the undeniable red shape emerged.

"*Colonel, we have a visual,*" Sherman said through the comm. "*Target is surfaced...appears to have reduced speed.*" Salkil stepped into the cockpit. He looked down at the hybrid experiment with a feeling of disdain, but simultaneous satisfaction. In a few moments time, it could all be over.

"Perfect opportunity," he said. "Rain hell on the bastard right now." Riggs and Sherman began activating the weapons system. They positioned the damaged Seahawk to fire all four hellfire missiles.

At this moment, Sherman noticed a new reading on the radar monitor. Something was approaching from the northeast. He scanned the horizon. In the grayish reflective ocean, he could see the sparkling white hull of a sailing yacht unknowingly approaching the kill zone. His eyes returned to the shark.

In the blink of an eye, it changed direction and gained speed. Its pointed head, like an arrow, was pointed directly at the approaching yacht. Salkil saw this as well. With binoculars raised to eye level, he quickly scanned the side of the oncoming vessel, reading the name printed on the hull.

"*K. McKartney,*" Sakil said the name to his pilots. Sherman grabbed the radio unit and changed the channel to a civilian frequency.

"This is Lieutenant Sherman of the United States Navy, calling civilian yacht *K. McKartney.* Please redirect your course immediately. You are entering a dangerous area."

There was no answer. Riggs was starting to sweat. They increased speed to keep pace with the creature, but it was nearing the unsuspecting yacht too quickly.

"It's getting too close," Riggs said. "We can't fire the missiles without endangering the civilians."

Salkil slammed his fist against the wall with frustration and anger.

****

Dressed in an Hawaiian shirt and blue shorts, thirty-two year old Gene Aeilts was stepping down in the companionway when he heard what sounded like a distant droning sound. It steadily grew louder over the next few seconds. His attention was drawn to it further when his younger brother, Frank, yelled from the bow hatch.

"Gene! Come out and look at this!"

Gene dropped what he was doing and hurried on deck. He could see Frank poking out past the mainsail. A skinny man, Frank pointed off the starboard bow. At first, the helicopters appeared like little black dots in the grey sky. However, with speed and a few moments time, they took definite shape and a greater magnitude in their perception.

Standing near the tiller, Gene held his hand over his brow as he watched the three military choppers approach. Grabbing the guardrail, he made his way around the cabin to get a better view. Frank looked over at him, displaying confusion and amazement, then returned his gaze toward the sky.

"What the hell's going on?" he said.

"I have no idea," Gene said. Over the wind and the sound of the helicopter blades, he could barely hear the crackling of the radio unit, back by the outside helm. He moved along the guardrail to get to it. As he arrived, he managed to hear the audible words, "*Dangerous area. Alter course at once.*" He grabbed the speaker to reply. Before muttering any response, he shuttered at Frank's vociferous voice.

"Oh Christ! Gene! Look!" his voice sounded as alarmed as it was astonished. It was enough to have Gene more concerned than to reply to the radio. He dropped the speaker and hurried back. His eyes instinctively went to the choppers, but there was nothing different, save for the shortage in distance. He then realized his brother was looking below them, pointing with a trembling hand.

Gene sucked in air as he saw the red fin coming straight at them, preceded by rapid swells generated by the creature's mass. He did not find it strange that it was dark red and had jagged spines protruding from it. He didn't have time for such thoughts. His brain could only process the size of the beast, and how it was moving fast; faster than even the choppers.

Straight towards them.

For the second time in under a minute, Gene hurried back to the stern. He reached for the helm with the intent of redirecting course. His hand barely touched the maple wood when the boat shifted backwards in a violent shaking motion. Water sprayed and metal groaned as the creature collided headfirst into the starboard bow, like Moby Dick against the ill-fated *Pequod.*

The hybrid did not stop its forward motion after the collision. For what seemed like endless moments for the Aeilts brothers, the creature pushed the boat back, digging its head into the hull like a screw. Frank fell forward over the frame, his upper body laid over the forward hatch. Gene hugged the helm, barely keeping himself from hitting his head on the deck. The flat transom pushed back large surges of water as the boat was thrust backwards.

Finally, the shark eased up. Its tail cracked the surface as it angled down for a dive, leaving the yacht bobbing with the waves. The starboard hull was crumpled inward like tinfoil, with a large jagged crack that ran vertical like that on an egg shell.

Gene leaned off the helm and found his footing. He looked for Frank and saw him crawling from the hatch. Frank made eye contact with him, and without speaking, understood what Gene wanted him to do. Frank went to the bow rail and looked down. He suddenly felt a wave of nausea and adrenaline, not at the sight of the crushed hull or the water gushing in, but at the sudden sight of the shark as it sped upward toward their boat.

14

After making a brief dive, the creature had readjusted its position, and angled for an attack from beneath. Its eyes rolled back as its solid head smashed into the underbelly of its target. A thunderous echo reverberated through the surrounding sea, followed by an outward shockwave.

For an instance, the yacht was not touching the ocean, as it had been lifted several feet out of the water from the intense impact. Gravity pulled it back down, resulting in another great splash. The boat rocked hard and bobbed up and down. Frank was lifted clear off of his feet, hitting his head on the guardrail on his way down. As the boat settled, he laid on the deck as blood gushed from a gash near his right temple. Gene had fallen backwards, directly down the opening of the companionway. By luck, it was a perfect backwards summersault that didn't result in any severe injury.

There was no time for recovery. The shark hit again, again along the starboard side. The boat, which was already tilting heavily to port, gave way to the pressure. The yacht rolled like a spit over a fire. The mast struck the water and snapped, and the ocean quickly consumed the deck. Frank's senses were barely coming back to him as gravity pulled him off the deck and into the water. His natural instinct of breathing had come to a stop when water gushed into his nostrils. Though weak and disoriented, he started paddling until he broke the surface.

Gene threw his hands over his face as water raced into the cabin. The overwhelming force threw him backward once again. He quickly got on his feet, bringing his head above the water level before it completely flooded. He sucked in a deep breath, and the water completely flooded the interior. With arms reached out, he found the entrance and started working his way back out.

Though flooding, the boat maintained a level of buoyancy. Bits of hull, decking, and various belongings bounced in the water around it. Frank, still disoriented from his head injury, clawed along the deck in an attempt to find the surface. Pain throbbed in his head, and was only worsened by the adrenaline rush. His brain couldn't figure whether he was upside down or swimming parallel to the deck.

Finally, he opened his eyes. Fighting through the sting of the salt water, he could see his own air bubbles race toward the surface. He realized that as he blindly "climbed" along the deck, he was actually driving himself deeper. He corrected his position and kicked his way to the surface, trailing a small stream of blood.

After tearing away chunks of the vessel, *Isurus Palinuridae* had determined that its inorganic enemy had been neutralized. It started swimming off, in search of another enemy to destroy. Before it could make much distance, its nostrils picked up the most desired scent: the trace of blood. The creature curved its body and turned. It felt the electrical impulses of the injured target struggling near the yacht.

Gene emerged from the cabin entry and shouted for his brother. He lifted his hand for the guardrail, now a foot above his head, and lifted himself up. Balancing on the gunwale, he scanned the water for Frank. It didn't take long to spot him. Frank was down a ways, trying to grab onto anything to stay afloat. On his hands and knees, Gene worked his way over to his brother.

A sharp gust of wind swept downward and a massive shadow blanketed the wreck. Gene looked up. Directly above him was one of the helicopters. Out from the side door descended a rappel line, and a pararescue quickly began working his way down. Through all the chaos that had unfolded in the past few minutes, finally there appeared to be a way out. He turned and reached his arm out for Frank, floating horizontally as he clung to the boat.

His hand had barely extended out when the large red shape emerged. Jaws hyperextended, engulfing Frank up to his upper torso. Teeth punctured through the breastplate and trapezius muscle as the jaws came down on him. There was no time for Gene to react, or for Frank to endure the pain. As the shark snatched its prey, it did not slow its course.

It immediately collided once again with the yacht. Frank's head, still exposed from the creature's mouth, was smashed into the deck, instantly caving in his skull. Bits of debris sprang from the point of impact like shrapnel. The yacht spun in the water like a fan. Gene fell headfirst into the water. After twisting and turning, he emerged at the surface, just as the bow swung in his direction. Caught up in the swell, he struggled to keep his head above the water. Finally, the boat settled. Only a few yards from it, he quickly made his way back.

He bent his fingers around the edges of broken deck and slowly climbed upward. Behind him was the sound of swishing water. He dared to look back. The terrible red fin had surfaced again, and just a few feet ahead of it, he could see the pointed head of the shark coming toward him.

Just a few feet to the right was the forward hatch. He reached and grabbed the frame. He drew a breath and pulled himself through the three-foot opening into the cabin unit. Gene had barely cleared the frame as the beast smashed through. Wood and fiberglass exploded inward, making way for the shark's six-foot girth. Its jaws snapped, desperate to get to Gene, who backstroked to the back of the cabin. He found the door, which led to the interior hallway. He opened it, only to make the horrible discovery that the walls had caved the hallway in. There was no way out, and the only oxygen he had remaining was in his lungs.

After its failed attempt to devour Gene, the creature's brain alerted to the imperative need to oxygenate its blood. With its head caught in the yacht, it could not swim forward to fulfill this need. And it could not swim backward, due to its imperfect physical design, not only by its creator, but nature itself. It attempted to twist itself and wiggle free, but it was pressed tightly within the ravaged enclosure. It was stuck. The beast lashed its tail from side to side, trying to wiggle free of its entrapment. The entire vessel shook from the creature's force, which continued to break it apart.

****

From up above, it looked as if the ocean was quaking from an underwater earthquake. Salkil solemnly watched the shark's tail flap in the air. They could hear the loud creaks as the boat steadily broke apart. Ripples expanded around the carnage in near perfect rings. Above, the pararescue was hoisted back into the chopper, which then swerved around to join the other two in formation. Exhaling sharply, Salkil leaned in toward the pilots.

"Do it now," he said. Both Riggs and Sherman looked up at him. To Riggs, the expression on the Colonel's face was almost as bloodcurdling as the slaughter taking place below.

"Sir?" Riggs said. Salkil turned his gaze toward him.

"You heard me, Ensign! Fire the missiles," Salkil said. He looked at Sherman. "Lieutenant, don't waste any time! Destroy it!" Sherman didn't say anything, as if battling the mental dilemma in his mind. Never before had he had to fire on a civilian vessel.

"Sir!" Riggs said. "We cannot fire! We still have at least one civilian in the kill zone!" Salkil grabbed his head by the helmet. Riggs felt a crack in his neck as the Colonel forcefully turned his head to look at the shark.

"Look down there, pilot!" Salkil snarled. "Those people, as far as we know are DEAD! If not, there's no saving them! We already tried! But that fucking shark...if we don't kill it here and now then it will kill more! You want more days like today? There's no stopping it...except here!" He let go of Riggs' helmet. There was a brief, uneasy pause between the pilots. Lt. Sherman pressed the transmitter to speak to the other pilots.

"Viper Three to Four and Five..." he said. He took a breath, "Civilians are dead. Colonel Salkil's orders are to fire all hellfire missiles at target. On my mark, all units fire." He released the transmitter and hoped his lie would bring ease to the other pilots. Riggs clicked a few switches, equivalent to switching off the safety feature on a firearm. They gazed down at the fish to set their aim. Its rapid motion caused the boat to rotate again, facing the hull toward them. They could not see the shark directly, but the constant shaking of the boat confirmed its presence.

The shark twisted with all its might, further ravaging the hatch frame that it enlarged after penetrating the cabin. Its jaws snapped viciously, not out of hunger, but as a result of the shark flexing every available muscle to free itself. It tilted its head up and down and side to side, while flapping its tail.

In a twisting, corkscrew motion, the shark caused further splintering of the sides. Bits of the entrapment broke away, and the shark managed to simply drift from the hole due to the backpressure in the boat. It tilted down to dive.

"Open fire!" Sherman said. Boosting flares ignited at the rear of several rockets, launching them at the yacht. In less than a moment, the yacht was transformed into one enormous fireball. A mountain of fire rose above the water like a big orange cloud, as if a volcano was letting loose its fury. Unrecognizable bits of burning debris arched thousands of feet in the air before crashing back down. Smoke billowed and twisted into various shapes as it climbed into the grey sky.

Salkil looked down at both the pilots' monitor and tracking screen. There was no reading of the creature, nor the boat itself. He stood straight, maintaining the posture of an officer, and placed his hand gently on Riggs' shoulder.

"Good job gentlemen," he said in a soft tone. He didn't wait for a response. He knew the feeling of rout within them. He stepped back into the cabin and took a seat. He stared past Logan, out the open window, where he could still see the smoke filling the sky. Logan watched the Colonel, noticing how his demeanor returned to being normal and collected.

Unknown to Logan, Salkil, though he wouldn't show it, was weeping inside from the order he had no choice but to give. Thought it was not the first time civilians of any nation had perished under his command, it was he who had directly issued an order resulting in such tragedy.

The radio blared, *"This is the USS Freedom approaching. Please relay any updates on the pursuit."*

CHAPTER

3

The black tornado of smoke had thinned to a grey, see-through vortex. Most of the fire had quickly died down, both from sea water extinguishing it, and from the flammable material being burnt out. The floating remains, smoldering from the heat, drifted apart from each other, while the disintegrated bulk of the yacht sank to the ocean bottom, where the current would further ravage it.

Salkil watched salvage crews aboard life rafts inspect the wreckage, while he stood at the edge of the starboard bow on the *USS Freedom*. Patrol boats roamed the waters around them, to provide protection in the unlikely event that the threat still lurked beneath.

That threat is what bothered Colonel Salkil. In his mind, he knew there was very little chance that the creature survived. Eight missiles had rained down on the yacht, four of which from his chopper, while the others fired two each. That would be enough to turn a freighter into an unrecognizable heap, much less a simple shark of twenty-three feet.

Except it was no simple shark. Even the Colonel was shocked that .50 caliber bullets were incapable of penetrating its shell. How well could it have protected against explosives? Even in this case, it seemed implausible that the creature survived. Yet, Salkil would not be satisfied until presented with physical evidence that it was dead.

Clangs of approaching footsteps drew Salkil's attention behind him. Marching toward him was Admiral Joel Ford, accompanied by the ship's Captain, and a few MPs who stood guard, like Secret Service to the President. Dressed in his whites, with his ribbons of decorations pinned to his left jacket breast, the fifty-three-year old Admiral was no man to be trifled with. And Salkil, to his disenchantment, was forced into a position to do such a thing.

"Colonel, you'd better have a damned good explanation for this!" The Admiral barked. The Colonel postured and presented a salute.

"With all due respect, sir," he said, "none of this would have occurred had you listened to me in the first place." He kept his tone neutral and non-antagonizing. However, as he always did and always would do, he would speak the cold hard truth. Admiral Ford stopped three feet in front of him. He stared at the Colonel with angry, fiery eyes that would kill if able.

"Colonel, if you had properly informed me of what this creature was, I would have listened. But because of your secrecy, several of my men are dead and injured. You better be damned sure that I'll be presenting to Washington with this case, and ..."

"Again, with respect, Admiral," Salkil interrupted him, "Washington was who sent me out here, and presented you orders to assist. It is you who ignored my instructions, and thus, soldiers and civilians are dead."

"Excuse me, Colonel," the Admiral said. "Are you suggesting this is my fault?"

"If there is fault, I would place it with the individual who created this abomination. I can't mention his name, but you might be pleased to know he's no longer around."

"As in deceased?"

"Aye, sir," Salkil said. Ford took a step forward.

"I never delight in death," he said. "Not even for those who deserve it. Now, I deserve an explanation of what happened. You informed me that we were chasing a shark. Needless to say, that was no ordinary shark."

"No," Salkil said. "It wasn't." A shout from one of the salvage boats drew his attention back to the wreck. The boats had piles of debris loaded up. Bits of metal, wood, fiberglass, and floatable accessories were piled up on the deck of the three boats. Using a net, they hauled a large object up over the side. Salkil lifted his binoculars to see. It was red, over two feet across, with black burn marks, at least three inches thick. He lifted his portable radio. "Bring that over here."

The boat quickly drew near the Destroyer. Salkil looked down at the sailor who lifted the object up toward him, providing the best view. No doubt, it was a portion of shell.

"Be sure to isolate that from the other wreckage," Salkil informed him. "That'll be all." The boat returned to the salvage operation. Seeing the piece of shell brought mild relief to the Colonel. Yet, it just wasn't enough. He desired more, something more definitive. "We're going to need submersibles out here."

"Why?" the Admiral asked. Salkil returned his gaze toward him.

"To check the ocean floor for a body," he answered. The Captain, standing next to the Admiral, spoke up.

"Colonel, the odds of finding anything are extremely low. This is a very deep area, and the current sweeps out to the northeast, into deeper waters. Finding a needle in a haystack would be a more desirable scenario."

"You bombarded it with missiles, Colonel," Ford added. "You're still not convinced? Is there anything more about this creature you've failed to inform me about?"

"I never failed to inform anything," Salkil said. "I gave as much detail as permitted by powers above either of us. In regards to my wanting to locate the carcass; I just prefer to be thorough. Nothing more than that, sir." He gazed past the Naval officers toward one of the helicopters. They had just finished refueling one of them. "If you'll excuse me..." he gave the Admiral a salute and proceeded to walk past him. The Admiral turned around.

"Colonel," he shouted, "you do realize you'll have to make a report explaining this whole thing. When the media hears about this..."

"When they do, you'll be commended," Salkil said, looking back at Ford. "It was good work of you, locating that band of terrorists who hijacked a sailing yacht, killed its crew, and used it to sneak a bomb into our coastal waters. Of course, there was no other way to stop it other than to use Seahawk helicopters to destroy it with hellfire missiles."

"You expect to make a cover story of all this?"

"Not my choice," Salkil said. He turned and stepped into the cabin of the refueled helicopter. The two pilots boarded, as if already aware he wanted transporting. They took their seats and placed their headgear on.

"Off to Mako's Center, sir?" one of them said.

"Affirmative," Salkil answered. He buckled himself into the seat, and felt the blades begin to rotate. Soon enough, they were airborne, going southeast where Salkil would oversee the operation to ensure there be no word of a hybrid monster attack.

****

Its last movement was a downward arch, and a single swing of its tail. Weak and motionless, the injured creature sank in a slow, spiraling motion to the bottom of the ocean. A trail of blood, appearing like red clouds of fog in the water, seeped from the large wound behind its left gill-line.

The creature had no conscious memory of the fiery explosion that nearly engulfed it. Nor did it understand what it was at the time. The shockwave came sudden and unexpected, like an invisible force that penetrated the water, and fractured its nearly impenetrable shell. Stunned by the paralyzing blow, it was unable to contract its muscles. The ocean darkened as it sank beneath the reach of sunlight, causing it to see nothing but black. Its sense of smell was flooded with its own blood. Its heartbeat slowed with the loss of blood, furthering its weakness. The rapid loss of blood slowed the process in which its platelets could seal the wound. The shark, although it had no conscious understanding of it, was well near death.

The shark hit the dark ocean bottom headfirst. With the pull of gravity, it rolled motionless on its side. There it would lie, motionless and with a complete lack of energy. It could not even muster the strength to generate enough motion to push water over its gills. Minutes passed, and the brain began to shut down from insufficient oxygenation.

As if determined by fate, a gush of water suddenly flowed into its mouth, circulating through its gills. Its brain cells lit up, replenished. Its heart, while slowly, continued to pump blood through its veins. Life would not fade just yet. The ocean current lifted the hybrid shark by mere inches, and slowly carried it out into deeper waters. The hybrid made no effort against this; it simply didn't have the strength.

Over the next few days, the current gradually moved it along, bumping it against rocky formations and hills, rolling it like a log, and occasionally gliding it a few feet above the ocean floor. The hybrid continued to barely cling to life. The current fed water over its gills during this time, providing just enough to keep it alive. But the creature was still weak, and its brain was ready to shut down at anytime. Like the last ember in a fire, it struggled to function.

Finally, the current brought it to a canyon. Lodged by some underwater rocks, the hybrid lay flat on the ocean bottom. It still found itself unable to move itself. Weakness and fatigue plagued its muscles like a disease. The creature even seemed to lack a will to live. It laid there in wait for the likely inevitable death.

21

Its Ampullae of Lorenzini picked up nearby movements in the water. Its lateral line could pick up a heartbeat. Something lurked nearby: something alive. Though the hybrid could not see, it could sense the motion of two snakelike tentacles slithering over the rocks toward it. Behind those tentacles was the bulk of *Architeuthis Dux*. With red leathery flesh, the giant squid pulled itself nearer, curious to see the possible meal that had floated its way. It flapped its fins at the end of its twenty-foot mantle, helping to lift itself with the aid of its eight regular arms. It extended its two longer tentacles toward the strange lifeform. The clubs grazed the rigid side of the hybrid, as if studying it. Suction cups squished against the shell, only to retract from the spines. In an automatic response, the shark wiggled. It was a small physical motion, and it settled back down. The squid's interest piqued. There was no doubt this strange object was alive and would likely provide great sustenance.

The shark could feel the leathery tentacles dig between it and the earth, ultimately scooping it up. The tentacles rolled the shark toward the hungry squid. Its meal offered no resistance. Other tentacles, lined with subspherical suction cups, reached out, snagging the creature by the tail and fins. Teeth from these suction cups clawed at its prey, but only scraped against rigid shell. The squid was not concerned; it was not the first time it slaughtered prey with solid exoskeletons. Tentacles curled around the tail, body, and head, properly securing it. The squid snapped its beak, like that of a parrot, and pulled the shark in towards it.

In a scissor-like fashion, the white beak bit down near the head. The squid's whole body jerked, as it was unable to penetrate. The squid tried a second time, only to have the same result. The squid rolled the shark to the side and attempted to bite just ahead of the dorsal fin. Once again, it could not break the exterior. The squid was hungry enough to continue. It attempted biting at various other spots. Its tentacles squirmed over the hybrid, searching for any weak spots.

One of the red, flexible arms pressed over the scabbing wound on the hybrid's side. Neurons fired in its small, donut shaped brain, as it sensed the vulnerable spot. It manipulated the shark to bring the injured area into view. It pressed its head into the crevice in the shell. The beak bit into soft flesh. Blood erupted from the reopened wound. The squid's radula, a tongue lined with razor sharp teeth, drove tiny bits of flesh into the esophagus.

At that instant, nerves flared within the hybrid. Its heart started pumping incessantly, as if injected with adrenaline. Like a rebooting computer, the creature's brain kicked on. It was struck with consciousness and a sense of pain. That activated a sense of alert, and thus, the instinctual drive for survival.

The shark, previously motionless and weak, now twisted and turned. The squid, nearly caught off guard, tightened its hold. This was a natural course of action. In this case, it was a mistake.

The tentacles curled around the shark's body and tightened. The shark then rolled like a wheel. As it did, the splintering spines along its body tore into the leathery flesh of the tentacles. It was equivalent to holding on to barbwire. Flesh was ripped and ravaged. Nociceptors lit up along the damaged arms, signaling the brain of the damage. The shark writhed. The tentacle around its head, after being sliced in several places, uncoiled and slid down near the nose.

This was the second mistake.

The hybrid's nostrils picked up the sense of blood. The visceral need of self-preservation was now conjoined with the lust of hunger. The hybrid snapped its jaws. Teeth seamlessly sank into the arm. The squid had hardly any time to react. With its jaws clasped onto the tentacle, the hybrid swung its head side to side, like a canine shredding a chew toy. Flesh tore, and the tentacle quickly detached. The hybrid swallowed a portion of meat.

The squid quickly learned that this meal was not worth further injury. It loosened its grasp and attempted to slide away into the darkness. It hardly gained any distance as the hybrid turned to face it, and quickly bit down on another of its arms. After seizing the squid, the hybrid then turned and started swimming back, dragging its flailing meal along. The squid writhed in pain. Blood oozed from the various wounds. In the dark depths, the cloud of blood was as black as the surrounding water.

The squid, distressed and eager to escape, tried to release itself from the shark's powerful grasp. It reached two of its tentacles toward the jaws, and attempted pulling them apart. It did not work, as the shark only tightened its hold. Finally, in an act of desperation, the squid pushed itself away. The tentacle in hold went taut. The tears created by the teeth incisions widened as the tentacle pulled away. Flesh ripped and blood spurted, until finally, the tentacle was torn clear of the squid's body.

Free from the deathly clasp, the squid flooded water into its mantle cavity. In a single strong motion, it flushed the water through the siphon, jet propelling the squid into the distance. Blood and ink trailed the creature as it fled.

While its eyes proved useless in this darkness, the sense of smell worked perfectly. The Ampullae of Lorenzini detected the fluttering movements of its enemy as it made distance. The shark swung its tail in large rapid movements. Like its genetic ancestor, the Mako, it shot after the squid like a bullet.

The squid was caught off guard yet again. It barely detected the shark's rapid approach. The hybrid hooked slightly upward, eventually curving down until it collided with its target. Teeth sank into the mantle just above the right eye. Its downward force drove the squid into a bed of rocks beneath it. Pointed rocks tore into the soft underside. Dust and gravel formed a mucky cloud.

In sharp, vicious motions, the hybrid tore into the mantle. Pieces of pink innards joined the cloud of ink and blood surrounding the titans. The squid sprung its remaining arms at the shark in an attempt to peel it off.

The hybrid momentarily stopped its ravaging of the mantle to fend off the eel-like arms. It quickly tore one away, and then another. One of the arms constricted around its mid-section like an anaconda, but the hybrid instinctually corkscrewed. Spines sliced through the tentacle, forcing it to release. The shark turned and darted downward. It attacked the same mantle wound. Each chomping bite tore away pounds of flesh. The tentacles writhed, like that of an enraged demon. Eventually they slowed, swaying like pink stalks of kelp in the ocean current. Soon, even these motions came to an end, and the remaining tentacles fell into coiled positions around the squid's lifeless carcass.

There was no sense of victory for the shark. It continued tearing away at the mantle, swallowing mouthfuls of flesh. Soon, the squid's body had lost all distinguishable form.

As if finished its vicious assault, the Ampullae of Lorenzini picked up new movements. Something approached behind the shark. Territorial aggression kicked in, and the hybrid turned and lashed forward in a single rapid motion.

After detecting the scuffle between the hybrid and the squid, the cuttlefish hoped to feast on the scraps of the loser. When it realized the danger, it reacted with lightning fast reflexes, jet propelling away. Unfortunately for it, its reflexes were surpassed only by the swift advance of the hybrid.

Teeth tore into flesh. Water swirled in a large circular motion, kicking up dust and debris. Blood spurted from many wounds. Within a few brief heartbeats, it was over. Bits of flesh swirled in the water after much of its mantle was swallowed by the creature.

Blood still leaked from its wound as the hybrid explored its new environment. The injury was of no concern. Eventually, it would molt its shell and form a fresh one, thicker and more solid than the last. Food here was plentiful. Soon, its eyes would adjust to the darkness. Like a submarine patrolling new waters, *Isurus Palinuridae* stayed close to the ocean floor. After slaughtering the deep's most notorious predator, it had established new territory.

CHAPTER
4

THREE YEARS LATER

Golden rays of sunlight pierced through the blue, cloudless sky and cast upon an equally blue sea. The Atlantic Ocean, vast and superior, seemed flat and undisturbed. Any passing waves were so gentle and slow, they hardly seemed noticeable. The wind was nothing more than a soft breeze.

The stillness in the water was perfect for the large flock of gulls. Resembling a large white sheet in the blue water, the gulls settled in, floating like little white canoes. Chirps and squawks echoed through the crowd, as if the birds were casually chatting to each other. Some dipped their heads to catch little fish that lingered too close, while others drank salt water from the sea they rested on.

Soon, a whirring motor noise filled the atmosphere, along with screams of joy and merriment. The noises drew closer and louder. The water began to vibrate, and the flock of gulls spread their wings and fled skyward. A speedboat, towing two people on jet skis, passed through the cloud of birds at a maximum speed of thirty knots.

Standing at the helm, Adam burst with laughter as he deliberately drove the Atlantic 670 open speedboat through the flock. Some of the slower gulls bounced off the hull and dipped into the water, before flapping their wings to take off. Others, too injured, simply floated. He kept one hand on the wheel, while clutching a can of beer with the other. After they cleared the flock, he tilted the can into his mouth and gulped a mouthful of beer. He wiped the suds off his scruffy face onto his forearm, which he proceeded to wipe on his exercise shorts. He let out a loud belch and proceeded to chuckle and listen to the cheering from the two skiers behind him.

Over the cheers came the inevitable scolding from his girlfriend, Elaina, sitting in the rear seat.

"Jesus, Adam! That was horrible!" Adam sighed heavily. *And...it starts...* In his mind, there was nothing he could do that she wouldn't criticize. *You didn't cut the grass! That's not the tile we agreed on! You spent eight hundred bucks on a motorcycle when the roof's leaking?! Why didn't you tell me you were gonna be out late?*

Of course, he didn't bother to consider he might have deserved criticism for most of those things. In his mind, there wasn't a care in the world. He glanced back at Elaina. Normally, he'd be checking out her slim athletic body in that blue bikini. But, unfortunately this time, her angry gaze pulled him away from all that. He retracted his attention to the path ahead.

"Relax babe, they're just birds," he said. He cut the wheel to port, steering the speedboat into a tight circle. He looked back at the skiers in tow. Both of them, lady friends of Elaina, successfully held on to their ski handles and leaned slightly to the left. With Elaina being in his line of sight, he couldn't help but notice she maintained that angry glare. "You know, it'd be helpful it you'd keep an eye on them so I can drive this thing," he grumbled.

"You're a dick," she said. She adjusted in her seat and looked at the endless reach of ocean, as if to avoid looking at Adam. He rolled his eyes and focused back on his driving.

"God!" he exclaimed, under his breath. He completed several more circles before maneuvering into a different path. He curved the speedboat into an S-shaped course. He glanced back at the skiers, who remarkably managed to hold on. Usually by now, someone took a spill. Elaina reached over to the cooler, seated next to her, and grabbed a beer. As she opened it, she repositioned to face her boyfriend.

"So, when do I get a turn?" she asked. Her voice lacked the annoyed tone it previously had. Rather, it sounded pathetically friendly. This was another common thing Adam had grown used to: attitude changes to obtain a particular want. Adam ignored her and took another swig of his beer. "Hey," she said, "don't blow me off. When do I get a try?"

"Babe," he said, while keeping his eyes forward, "you ALWAYS fall off. I barely accelerate two knots before you take a dive."

"I do not!" she exclaimed in a high-pitched voice.

"Yeah…you do," Adam said. He curved the boat to the right, then back to the left. He could hear Elaina stand up and step up behind him. Reaching around his shoulders, her hands caressed his chest and abs. She pressed herself against his back, an effort to entice him.

"Come on," she said. The words were long and drawn out. As if in direct response, Adam released a loud gurgling belch. His whole body reverberated with the repulsive action, and the air was briefly ranked with foul odor before the wind brushed the air away. Elaina pushed herself away, aghast and disgusted. With a frustrated sigh, she sat back down.

"You're disgusting," she remarked, and crossed her arms.

"More where that came from," Adam quipped. Elaina groaned, exaggeratedly expressing her displeasure. She grabbed her beer from the cup holder and sipped on it.

God, I'll be hearing about this all evening, Adam thought to himself. He tipped his beer into his mouth, bottom up. After draining it, he dropped the can and stomped on it, releasing another belch. He looked over his shoulder.

"Get me another one, will ya?" he asked Elaina. She scoffed, nearly spitting suds from her beer. The burning glare that followed already provided the answer, and moments later, the verbal translation came out.

"Really?" she said. Adam shrugged his shoulders. "Unbelievable." She crossed her arms. "Get it yourself!" Adam glanced at the cooler, just out of reach.

"Oh, come on! Are you being serious?" he complained. The silent treatment followed, and Elaina simply sat and watched the passing waves. Adam felt his temper slipping away. His mind warped through a scroll of things he wanted to say, none of which were friendly. Eventually, he resorted to the old teaching; *If you have nothing good to say, then don't say it.* Considering what he wanted to say, he figured it was a course of action.

Holding on to the wheel with one hand, he reached back as far as possible with the other. His fingers could only just touch the sides.

"Damn!" he groaned. He repositioned briefly at the helm and straightened the boat from its zig-zag course. With the boat moving straight, he quickly turned to reach inside the cooler. With the first step, he landed on the crushed can, nearly sending him to the floor. He caught himself by grabbing onto the edge of the seats. As he straightened himself out and reached to the cooler, he inevitably noticed Elaina's pathetic attempt to ignore him by looking away. She had been looking to the left, but now he was in her line of sight, so she redirected her gaze to the front of the boat.

That's when her expression lit up with shock and fright. She jumped in her seat, pointing her finger straight ahead.

"LOOK OUT!"

Adam swiftly turned. The enormous black hide of the whale was unmistakable. It rested along the surface, directly in their path. Its rounded bulk was raised a couple of feet over the waterline. Adam shrieked and tried hurrying to the helm.

It was too late. The hull beneath the bow hit the whale just behind its left pectoral flipper. The twenty-one-foot speedboat skidded over the creature and went airborne, as if speeding off a ramp. Adam ducked, and Elaina let out an ear-piercing scream. With the bow pointed slightly upward, the boat came down. Both ends of the boat bounced, creating a forward/backward rocking effect.

The two skiers barely had any time to react. One managed to let go of her handle. She dipped beneath the surface, but the forward momentum still drove her forward until she crashed into the mammal. Ribs cracked along her left side. Her life jacket pulled her to the surface, where she floated with the wind knocked out of her.

The other did not let go in time. Her legs hit the whale, and the momentum sent her flying literally head over heels until she crashed down along the other side of the whale. She emerged, numb to her broken legs.

The water was red with the creature's blood. The whale, clearly in pain, flapped in the water. Its tail rose and crashed down several times, driving it several yards forward. It let out a bellowing cry, and then settled down again.

Adam slowed the boat to a stop, in shock from what had just occurred. After several deep breaths, he looked back. The sixty-foot whale rested, almost motionless, along the surface. Its flipper flapped, splashing up water.

That sight of moving water suddenly worried Adam. He moved around the console onto the bow deck and looked over the gunwale. From what he could see, there didn't appear to be any breach in the hull. He turned around, and remembered the skiers after seeing them in the distance, struggling to get to one another. In his line of sight was Elaina, giving him that ever-critical stare, as if she wasn't fazed at all from the incident. Before he could react, she stood up and shouted at him.

"Aren't you gonna help them?!"

****

Dr. Julie Forster had just stepped through the front entrance of her house when she felt the familiar buzzing in her side pocket. She grabbed the vibrating phone and flipped the screen towards her. She sighed upon recognizing the number. She held her thumb over the red *decline* button, but ultimately touched the green one instead to answer.

"Dr. Forster here," she said.

"*Hey, Julie. It's Joe,*" answered Police Chief Nelson. He usually referred to himself by his first name. "*Sorry to bother you. I know you tend to get home around this time.*"

You don't say.

"*...however, I kind of need your help, and it's urgent.*" Julie dropped her bag and tossed her mail onto the kitchen counter.

"What can I do for you, Chief?" she asked. Despite his insistence, she almost never called him Joe. Through the line, she could hear a siren wailing in the distance, along with the sound of splashing. Then she heard him yell at someone nearby. His voice was muffled, as if he was pressing his phone against his jacket.

"*Guys, what did I tell you?! Just keep your distance!*" The sound of his breathing then filled the line, as he had lifted the phone back to his face. "*Sorry about that,*" he said to her. "*There's been an accident out here, a quarter mile west of the Milan Reef. Some knuckleheads on a speedboat crashed into a whale.*" Dr. Forster's interest piqued, though mixed with a bit of bewilderment.

"They *hit* a whale?" she asked.

"*Yes, ma'am,*" Chief Nelson answered. "*The thing is alive, but it's definitely injured. There's a big gash from where they hit it, and well... it's just floating here.*" He paused a moment, as if waiting for a response. Forster scrunched her face in displeasure at the realization of what he was hoping she'd do. Finally, he asked, "*Would you mind coming out here?*" Forster wiped her eyes and yawned, holding her phone away.

"Yeah, just uh," she took a breath and tried to hide her disappointment, "give me about twenty minutes. I'll be over."

"*Yeah, you'll see our lights. It'll be hard to miss,*" Nelson said. "*Thanks. See you soon.*" As he hung up, Forster could hear him start to yell at somebody else. She looked at her phone with disdain, as if it itself was responsible for her day continuing to get crummier. In addition, she felt like a physical mess. Her red hair had dried up all stringy, with bits of dried salt from the ocean water stuck in it. Plus, she smelled like dead fish from feeding the marine animals she cared for.

She walked through the living room into her kitchen and took a quick seat. She leaned back and rested her eyes for a brief moment, but instantly felt the urge to fall asleep rapidly approach. To prevent it from overwhelming her, she stood up.

Her eye noticed the name above the return address on one of her mail envelopes. *Dr. Jacob Wren.* It was a former colleague during her studies at the University of Texas, before she moved on to study at University of Maine. When

28

she rotated back to University of Texas to complete her doctorate, this colleague had already moved on. This was the first time since then, she had heard from him. She quickly opened it. The letter was hand written, mostly in cursive.

Hi, Julie.

Been a long time. Since you moved away, I've always wondered what new heights you would achieve. After all, you were at the top of every class we shared. I figured you'd be exploring the bottom of the ocean, making new discoveries. That was the dream, right?

Then I see your name on the news...

After this line, Forster felt her stomach tighten uncomfortably.

It comes as a shock and a disappointment that you've settled for Felt Paradise. So, the person who bragged about how much she loved the ocean is working for a rich schmuck who took money from Wan's Industrial Company. They're still pulling out the crap that they've been dumping in the ocean.

At least the other person had the guts to get out. How much is he paying you? I gotta say, what a waste of talent and potential.

I'm not usually one for writing these kinds of letters, but I can't contain my shock and disappointment. Save what decency you have left, and jump ship. Otherwise, everything we thought you were was a lie.

Sincerely,

Dr. Jacob Wren.

Forster crumbled the letter into a ball and tossed it toward the trash. Naturally, it bounced off the edge and ended up on the floor.

Just what I needed, a crappy letter to bookend a crappy day.

That day started at *3:00* a.m., when she woke up to an unexpected phone call, asking her to report to the aquarium. There, she spent the entire day with a dolphin suffering from toxic poisoning. For hours, she worked on getting it to eat and take antibiotics. The aquarium, which was designed to be a main attraction for the island resort, now was starting to serve as a marine hospital. It was the latest attempt by her boss to improve public relations after the controversy involving Wan Industry dumping toxic waste into the ocean. After her partner had resigned a week earlier, she was the only marine biologist working at Felt Paradise Aquarium and Resort. This promoted her to primary caretaker of all the animals. The job only sounded nice. The duties were something else entirely. Long hours, little sleep. Only one reliable assistant. Hardly any social time. She was always on an on-call status. The worst part was, it was all she could ever have.

It was a long eight years of college, rotating between the University of Texas and Maine, to achieve her doctorate in Ichthyology, with additional education in Marine Geology. Since being a child, she loved the ocean, and always had a dream of exploring the depths. Being a straight-A student, she graduated high school early, and started college at the age of seventeen. Her father, who worked all his life as a manager in an assembly plant, saved away every spare penny to save for her education. It was something she wouldn't appreciate enough until it was too late. A heart attack ended his life prematurely, leaving Julie Forster alone in the world.

But it seemed the dream was realized. Graduating at the top of her class, Forster was accepted into a program for deep sea exploration. The program was titled BRIZO, named after an ancient Greek goddess who was the protector of sailors. The goal of the mission; to discover possible minerals at the ocean floor in hopes of creating a new viable energy source. While her goal was to study sea-life, this was a great start. A year-long training period followed for her and the seven other cadets. Forster had already trained on submersible piloting during her two-year study in Maine, so naturally she came out once again as head of the class.

Then came the moment aboard the research vessel when she discovered a fellow cadet preparing a dose of cocaine. Forster reported the activity to the program director, leading to a brief suspension of the program pending an investigation. The investigation was a tedious process, with each cadet needing to conduct a new full physical exam and blood test, as well as subject their belongings and quarters for searching.

Evening came one day at Monterey Bay, and Forster was spending time outside near one of the submersibles. The calm and peaceful evening went awry when the cadet confronted her about reporting him. First there was the sob story, of how stressful the position became, and the psychological burden of eventually being miles under the water, protected by only a few inches of steel. She didn't budge on her position. Then an angry flood of insults came her way, which she managed to ignore. There was no point in arguing with a drug addict, much less one careless enough to start his habit in the middle of a training camp for deep sea diving. She figured it was time to walk away.

She figured a moment too late. She had just turned her back and taken the first step when the cadet made the remark, "*I bet your dead daddy would be really proud of you, ratting out your friends.*" For a moment, Julie Forster disappeared, and someone more sinister took over. It resulted in two broken ribs, missing teeth, and a concussion. Sadly, that wasn't the worst part. The cadet's fall resulted in him accidentally hitting his head on the edge of a cement step, resulting in a skull fracture. The cadet survived, though he would be confined to a wheelchair for an undetermined amount of time.

This led to a whole different investigation. With her admitting to her actions, in addition to camera footage, it was rather swift. So was the judgement. Dr. Forster found herself booted from the program, after thousands had been spent on her training. There was a charge of assault and battery, which she agreed to settle on a reduced sentence of twenty-four months behind bars. The black mark on her record was worse than anything. Upon being released after serving thirteen months at Lowell Correctional Institution, she found it impossible to find work in her field. Universities rejected her, as did private research institutions.

Then came William Felt, a business owner of several resorts. He was completing the construction for the addition to his resort on the island of Pariso Marino, located north of the Florida Keys. He was in town, requisitioning for additional workers for the park. Among the list of jobs was animal caretaker.

With a nearly empty bank account, she was desperate for anything. Felt took an instant liking to her. It was nothing inappropriate as physical appearance. Rather, it was the black mark. The job did not specify pay, which allowed him to offer a cheap wage. He quickly offered her the position. Just as quickly, she accepted. It was a job after all, and did have the perk of subsidized housing.

As the financial misery ended, a whole new misery began. After several months working at Felt's aquarium, a discovery had taken place. A business partner of Felt's, Maria Wan of *Wan Industries*, was caught dumping toxic waste into a deep region several miles north of Pariso Marino. The investigation revealed that miles of open water were contaminated. Fish had to be destroyed, and other forms of marine life were suffering from toxic sickness. The news was released that Felt had accepted money from Wan, after the costs of his new park skyrocketed. Rumors began to circulate that he had deliberately turned a blind eye to Wan's illicit activities in return for the handouts.

This created a large rift in the island population. Fishermen and Felt employees were at odds with each other. The fishermen blamed the loss of catch, and subsequent income, on Felt's role in the scandal. It was as if each employee had a red mark on them. Forster could hardly go out in public without being battered with harsh insults from local residents.

And now, even people she considered friends were calling her out. Uncertainty flooded her mind. Her conscience told her to leave, but what would she do? No employer would accept her already, and with the scandal, she felt she had another black mark on her record...for something she wasn't even a part of. She did the only thing she could think of: pretend Felt wasn't aware of the dumping. Still, she felt trapped and miserable. It seemed almost everyone hated her.

Nothing compared to the unanswered question; *what does my father think of me?* It was something that plagued her. He supported her passions and dedicated his entire life to see her succeed. At the time of his death, she was on track to being a renowned marine scientist. Now here she was, reduced to being an ex-con, rejected submersible pilot, and now a caretaker of fish and dolphins, as if she worked in a zoo.

In her mind, she failed him.

She nearly dozed off again. She caught herself and stood up. She went into a closet and found her wet suit. She then grabbed her cell phone and made a call. The line rang twice before someone answered.

"*Hello?*"

"Hey, Marco," she said to her assistant. "Hey, are you still at the dock?"

"*Yes sir, I am, ma'am!*" he quipped. She rolled her eyes, though he wasn't there to see it.

"Could you get the *Neptune* ready? Chief Nelson needs our help with something. I'll be heading over there shortly."

"*You betcha!*" Marco said.

"Thanks. See you in a bit," Forster said. She hung up and started changing into the wetsuit.

CHAPTER
5

Located forty-two miles east of the Georgia coast lay the island of Pariso Marino. From high above, it resembled a speck of green against a light blue background. Plant life flourished with trees such as the well-known Sabal Palms, Coccothrinax argentata, the bushy Swietenia mahagoni, and Jamaican Dogwood, formerly believed to be native of the Florida Keys.

The waters around the island ran deep, occasionally exceeding four hundred feet. One particular exception to this was an atoll that rested about a mile-and-a-half to the southwest. About seven-hundred feet in diameter, the atoll was simply a large, barren structure. Under the water, it resembled a small mountain.

The island's overall shape resembled that of a fried egg, cooked sunny side up. The center of the island contained the town's general business area, featuring a grocery market, restaurant area, and bank. But the primary local source of revenue on the island was the fishing market. The southern side of the island contained several ports, as the local community was one comprised mainly of fishermen. Residential homes lined the interior of the island, with some along the west beach.

The outer perimeter formed a near perfect circle, except for the north side, which formed two peninsulas. The eastern peninsula, rounded in shape, was the primary location for Felt's Resort and Spa. The west peninsula was more pointed in shape, and was the base for the 'park' section of the resort. In the water-filled valley between the peninsulas was Felt's Aquarium. On the shore was a large, cylinder-shaped building containing large aquariums full of fish, crustaceans, some turtles, and other aquatic creatures. But the biggest attractions were the outside pens. Metal enclosures, rectangular in shape, extended over one hundred-and-fifty feet out into the ocean water. In the first one was a great white shark, the first in history to be kept in captivity. More impressively, it was a twenty-three-foot great white. Even experts were baffled to see one so large be contained, though it still had limited effect in improving the resort's reputation. Huge signs lined the artificial cement ledge where the pen protruded from, reading *Great White Exhibit*. The other pen did not yet have a dedicated tenant. Currently, it was intended to house sick dolphins.

Several feet beneath the ledge was an enclosed viewing area. Designed like a small movie theater, the area sported several seats facing a large plate glass separating visitors from the interior of the pen. This underwater viewing area allowed visitors to get a spectacular clear view of the attraction within the pen. Encircling the whole pen was a walkway that elevated above the waterline, allowing visitors to view the shark from different angles. From above, it just appeared like a simple, rectangular dock.

Close by the aquarium was the private harbor. Two wooden docks protruded from the silver-gray sand. Along one of those docks was a twenty-foot workboat used primarily by the maintenance crew. The other dock ran a lot further out. Alongside it was the thirty-eight-foot research model 38-18 Munson boat, titled the *Neptune*. Water-tight, self bailing decks made of heavy duty aluminum plates sparkled in the bright sunlight. The deck was twelve feet across, containing plenty of work and storage space. A small crane for loading and unloading heavy objects was folded into place on the portside. At the front of the square bow was a watertight dropdown bow door. Underneath was a V-hull, made for slicing through waves. Designed for rough seas, this model was efficient for smooth rides.

Inside the wheelhouse, Dr. Forster stood at the helm. She had just finished loading waterproof bandages and disinfectants, with the help of her assistant Marco, who climbed up on deck by ladder. Fourteen-by-twelve feet, the wheelhouse looked like the car of a train. Several square windows lined all the sides, except the bow-facing one. Inside were numerous tables with all sorts of electronic equipment stored on them. Several large computer monitors lined a table on the starboard side. Each screen was linked to feeds from underwater cameras installed onto various locations along the hull and gunwale.

Dressed in a white shirt and grey cargo shorts, Marco clapped his hands. He had just finished fueling the boat, in addition to assisting Forster with loading the supplies. He turned toward the wheelhouse and waved. Forster glanced at him. As usual, she couldn't help but notice that his bicep was nearly about to rip through his sleeves. He was an extremely well-built man, almost ranked with the physique of a professional bodybuilder.

"All set and ready to go," Marco called to her through the cabin's open doorway. Forster replied with a two-finger salute from the helm. She inserted the key into the ignition. The engine started up. With a gentle push of the throttle, the V-hull cut the water as Forster steered the boat clear of the resort's private harbor. Water splashed against the bow before making way for the vessel.

As they made distance, more of the resort came into view behind them. Marco crossed his arms along the side as he looked to the east. The east peninsula seemed to take shape. He could see the cove come into view, where much of the casual resort was. He could see people relaxing along the beach, while many others splashed in enclosures in the cove, simply referred to as pools. Some tourists were busy getting massages by professional masseurs on beach tables, and many others sat at circular bars that lined the beach.

Loud whirring mechanical noises, like tracks on a train, pummeled the air to the west. Shouts of excitement quickly followed as the roller coaster initiated its run. The car, full of tourists, dipped from its high peak mid way up the west peninsula, and sped down the steep slope. It hooked upward, grazing the water just enough to generate a large splash, before performing a loop and speeding away to the remainder of its run.

As Dr. Forster steered the vessel out, the park came into more complete view. The rollercoaster extended far out into the water, except for its starting point. The Ferris wheel rolled at a steady pace, the merry-go-rounds spun, and other rides dipped and moved along. The park area extended out into the bay, where prize games were floated on large decks. Long wooden docks, intersecting into perfect square shapes, led way to each of these games, some going hundreds of feet out. It was like a huge wooden checkerboard over water.

Though it seemed that there were a lot of people, attendance was actually at an all time low. It was particularly substandard for an opening year. Felt's Paradise had been fully booked for the summer, with only a few vacancies in the fall months. This changed after the news was released of Mr. Felt's collaborations with Wan Industry, and the rumors that followed. Like rats fleeing a ship, the resort experienced an exodus of reservations as people withdrew. Within weeks, attendance was cut down to nearly half, and still dwindling. This loss of revenue, combined with the massive expense of the facilities, brought an immense level of anxiety to Mr. Felt.

After clearing the peak of the peninsula, Forster turned the boat west and drove it south along the other side until she reached the Milan Reef, midway down the protrusion of landmass. In the shallow region near shore, the water almost appeared to glow in a rainbow of colors. Coral reef creatures of all shapes and sizes lined the seabed. It was a peaceful sight that always had a soothing effect on Forster's mind, even on the most stressful of days. She followed the reef out into the blue open ocean. Out there, she saw a different array of lights, these ones not so pleasant.

A quarter mile out, red and blue emergency lights flashed. Multiple police vessels formed a perimeter. As they moved toward it, one particular set of flashing lights moved in their direction. After a minute, an orange and white Fire/Rescue vessel passed by. The sirens blared throughout the salty afternoon air. Marco squinted as his ears felt like they would burst. He looked back as the boat turned south toward the nearest dock.

"Good lord, you'd think they were on the highway," he said. Even after several months of working together, Forster still expected an accent each time he spoke. He was a man of Brazilian descent and looked every bit of it. However, he was completely American, having been born in Utah of all places.

"The Chief had said it was a boating accident," Forster said. "If they hit a whale, I wouldn't be surprised if the whale wasn't the only one busted up."

"You think the whale attacked the boat?" Marco asked. "Like, retaliation? Thinking they were attacking it, maybe?" Forster thought about it.

"No," she said, although her voice sounded unsure. "At least, that's not how the Chief explained it to me. In fact, he was concerned for the whale itself." Marco scratched his chin.

"Hmm. They must have hit it hard, then," he said. "They had to, to severely injure the thing and themselves." This sparked a thought in Forster's mind.

"What I want to figure out is how they hit the thing," she said.

"I thought you pointed out that they rammed it along the side, behind its flipper or..."

"No," Forster interrupted him. "I mean, how did they even manage to make contact? Whales have pretty good reflexes, and usually a good awareness of what's around them. Most would have steered clear of that boat, especially if it was moving at that speed."

"Hmm," was Marco's only response. Although he was her primary assistant, he didn't have much knowledge in the behaviors of most sea life in terms of their natural habitat. The only ones he really understood were those he helped care for in the aquarium. It was simple; feed at certain times; certain species do not mix with others; some are more aggressive than others; keep the water circulating; and very importantly, don't touch the glass.

They drew near to the police perimeter. Four black boats, with stripes of white that ran horizontally down the sides, tried to maintain a square formation. In the middle of that white stripe read *Pariso Marino Police*. Off to the side was the twenty-one-foot Atlantic speedboat, with its two occupants sitting with their arms crossed. The *Neptune* dwarfed the twenty-foot patrol vessels as it approached. Forster slowed the boat to a crawl and looked at the middle of the perimeter, where the fifty-foot humpback whale floated. She angled her direction to align with it.

"*Excuse me! Nobody is permitted beyond this point!*" a voice, blaring through a bullhorn, called out to her. Surprised, and slightly irritated, Forster stopped the throttle and stepped out onto deck. The nearest police boat moved toward her. An officer stood at the bow deck, with the bullhorn still raised, even though they were right next to each other. Forster planted both hands on her hips and scowled.

"Excuse ME," she said, "but I'm Doctor Julie Forster. Either you're an idiot, or they didn't pass on to you, I'm here at Chief Nelson's request. And I'm not on payroll, so fuck off and get out of the way." The officer stood speechless for a moment. Naturally, he wanted to respond with an audacious remark, but professionalism would prevent him. His radio crackled.

"*Harrison, I told you she was coming! Get out of the way.*" The officer tried not to let his embarrassment show. He looked down at his transmitter.

"Aye-aye, Chief," he said. By the time he looked back up, he was face-to-face with Forster's middle finger. Worse than that was Marco's intimidating stare, like that of a Goliath ready to stomp on the little man who angered it. And angered he was. Forster re-entered the wheelhouse, gritting her teeth as she slowly steered the boat near the whale. The officer was clearly playing the whole event as a misunderstanding, but she and Marco knew better.

The controversy of William Felt's dealings cut deep into the reputation of anyone who still worked there. Even members of the police department seemed to harbor resentment. The fishing industry, which had gone on since the founding of Pariso Marino, had been impacted hard from the poisoning in the water. Plankton and small fish were the most directly affected, and the creatures that fed upon them either died off or became so badly infected that they were inedible upon catch. Before this, the local economy was booming. However, local incomes were dwindling, and taxpayer dollars along with it. Prices at the markets went up, making matters even worse. With less local taxpayer income, government employees were beginning to fear for their positions. This included the police department.

With the burden on the island increased, so was the resentment Forster felt. Even with officers, such as Harrison giving her grief, it was clear that few people had a favorable opinion of her as long as she worked for Felt. It was hard for her to even fill her car up with gas without getting a rude stare. As if she was marked; everyone seemed to know who she was. She was clearly at odds with the island population.

She stopped alongside the whale, keeping a distance of about twenty feet. After dropping anchor, she stepped on deck and looked at the animal. It was motionless in the water. There was no air moving in nor out of its blowhole. The lifeless eye seemed to stare past her, with its eyelids half closed. The flippers seemed to move with each ripple of the water. The whale was dead.

She looked at the wound. A red indentation of flesh creased nearly a foot into its hide behind the flipper. From what she could see above the water, the slice appeared to be a few feet long, running up onto its back.

Odd, she thought. It certainly was a severe injury, and the whale would certainly have suffered significant loss of blood.

But fatal?

Then she looked down, where the injury had dipped below the water line. She realized the wound dipped down into its belly. She leaned over the side to get a closer look. From what she could see, the wound was widened, as if that's where it had taken the brunt of the impact.

She looked back at the red speedboat. Though it was hard for her to see, the boat appeared to only have some indentation on the hull. It was floating on its own okay, so it was not taking in water. The bow was in perfect form, otherwise.

One of the police boats pulled up alongside, blocking her view of the speedboat. Standing on the deck was a tall man in his early forties, with salt and pepper hair. Chief Nelson gave her a smile as they made eye contact. He had both hands placed on the rail bar as he leaned against it. His eyes were almost as glassy as hers, longing for a full night's sleep.

"Is this how your monkeys usually behave?" Forster remarked, tilting her head toward Officer Harrison's boat. Nelson's smile quickly faded.

"Come on, now," he said. "I'll take care of that issue." He watched Forster look back at the dead whale. "Yeah, it stopped moving a little after our phone conversation." Forster looked back at him, then pulled her phone out of her jacket pocket. She looked at the screen. No missed calls or text messages. He noticed her gaze turn back toward him, and it wasn't friendly.

"How nice it was for you to call and let me know," she said. Chief Nelson quickly ran a hand over his eyes. It was clear he was tired and feeling a bit scatterbrained. Forster's harsh attitude had caught him off guard, as the two usually were very friendly towards one another. He felt foolish for being surprised; he was aware of the stress in her life, as well as the unrelenting demands in her work schedule; and after all, he was the one who interrupted her day.

Lately, he had been experiencing similar things. In his six years as police chief on the island, he had grown used to the simple quiet life it provided. There was just enough going on in the community to keep him and his department occupied, but it rarely was anything severe. After fourteen years as a police officer in Atlanta, he was perfectly fine with that life. Things had taken a turn in the past several months, however. Animosity between local fishermen and resort employees sparked a series of incidents. It was as if two tribes had formed and were warring against each other. Often, these incidents would occur late at night.

Off duty workers would go into town, and subsequently get testy with local residents. Despite having seen the worst in society, it still came as a surprise to Nelson to see the community take such a drastic turn. He had found himself getting called in the middle of the night by his staff regarding incidents. Six years ago, he had been perfectly used to it. Now, he had settled into the seven-to-three realm, and he was having a hard time readjusting.

"Yeah, I apologize about that," he said. "I should have given you a call, it's just that..." his voice trailed off, as if he was trying to figure out what to say.

"I'm sensing a request," Forster said. Nelson felt slightly nervous, worried that what he was about to say was going to trigger an unfriendly response.

"Well I, um," he muttered, then cleared his throat. "You have a tow line, right?" An unsoundly *'ugh'* sound echoed from Forster. The answer was yes, although she wouldn't yet say it.

"Dude, do you need coffee or something? Just spit it out!"

Yes, please! You offering?

This was the reaction he feared he would get. Now Nelson was feeling foolish for not properly notifying her.

"I'm sorry, Julie," he said. "Look, I notified the Coast Guard. They're gonna be by to pick this thing up. It'll be a couple of hours. Since you were already on your way out, I didn't bother calling you again, but I realize I should have. Your boat's much sturdier than anything we've got. Could you tow this thing to a more appropriate spot for when the Coast Guard arrives?"

Forster turned her eyes out and scanned the blue ocean. There was hardly anything around, except for a small fishing boat out to the northwest.

"Because this is such a busy area?" she sarcastically asked. Nelson struggled to maintain his friendly demeanor. He pretended to itch his face, while actually blocking the brief tensing of facial muscles from her view.

"These are fishing lanes," he said. "With everything that's going on, I really don't want to deal with the complaints. Aside from that, we don't want it to wash ashore." He mentally braced for her unkindly reaction.

"Alright," she simply said. Her voice was calm, without irritation. She went into the wheelhouse, emerging a few moments later with flippers, an air tank, and goggles. Nelson waited as she got ready. He was simply grateful that the awkward conversation was over.

Forster slipped the air tank on and tested the airflow. She tucked her feet into the flippers and spat into the inside of the goggles. While she did this, Marko prepared the towing harness. He attached the cable to the crane, and slowly winched the harness into the air, while extending the arm toward the whale.

Forster stepped to the ladder by the starboard aft quarter with the heavy-duty towing rope in hand. After shoving in her mouthpiece, she splashed down. For a moment, there was nothing but water in her sight. Under the surface, it was slightly darker than how it appeared above. There was a slight cloudiness to it, likely from the whale's blood. She swam over to the whale's fluke, which angled a few feet down. She rested on the tail and used hand signals to help guide the crane arm. Luckily, the whale had drifted a bit closer during the conversation, so he didn't need to adjust the boat. He placed the harness down behind the fluke.

Forster got to work on getting it all the way around. She clipped the end of the towing rope to the metal ring on the harness. She submerged to hook up all the metal clips, and made sure they were tightened properly. After a few minutes it was all done. She surfaced and turned toward the *Neptune*, giving a thumbs up to Marco.

Before she took the first paddle, she suddenly became consumed with curiosity of the whale's injury. She figured she had time to examine; Marco would currently be busy adjusting the towing rope to the cleats; and hell, it wasn't as if she was on any payroll anyway. She swam over and dove to get a proper view.

The portion of the wound that expanded down to its belly was much wider, and was also deeper. To her surprise, much of the muscular tissue was missing, exposing the deeper innards. Intestines were exposed, as well as the edge of one of its ribs. She examined the edge of the wound. The meat around the edges seemed mangled, with tiny bits flapping in the water. It didn't look like the result of a puncture wound from the bow of the speedboat. Instead, it looked rather as if the flesh had been torn away. Behind the edge were a few small slits, as if a dozen knives had been sunk into the skin.

Tooth marks? she thought. *No way that boat did this.* She pondered the possibilities. Possibly a feeding frenzy occurred. The blood certainly could have attracted several sharks. But then, where were they now? The police boats wouldn't have scared them off. Or perhaps, the boat simply did ram the whale, and when they pulled away, it caused additional tearing of the flesh. Except, that would guarantee the bow would be completely ravaged, and it was in relatively decent shape.

The sound of muffled conversation disrupted her theories. She quickly emerged, and immediately saw Marco yelling and pointing. She followed the direction of his finger and the sound of shouting that interloped with his. That fishing boat she had seen earlier had pulled up nearby. Standing outside the cockpit was a skinny man in his fifties, dressed in a ragged flannel shirt and jeans, both smothered in grit and bait. Even his cap couldn't prove immune from the muck. He pointed back at Marco and shouted back. The only dialogue she could make out were the yells from Chief Nelson. He had pulled his vessel up in front of the *Neptune*, providing a separation between it and the fishing boat.

"Marco, stop just a second," he said. He looked back to the fisherman. "Hal! I'm not going to tell you again. Get a move on." He seemed much clearer and more well spoken. Apparently, the current situation had stimulated his groggy mind. Hal started reaching for his shirt pocket, but stopped short. Clearly, there was a bottle of whiskey tucked in there. He looked down at Forster in the water.

"So, lady! Did killing fish get old for you guys? Figure you'd get around to killing whales too, aye?" He shouted down to her. She felt her temper already starting to let loose, despite being caught off guard by the situation. Marco shouted again.

"Old timer, you better shut that trap before I do it for ya!" he said. He held onto the stern rail. He looked poised and ready to spring over it and the police boat, and strangle the fisherman. Nelson looked back at him again.

"Marco, I told you to knock it off!" he commanded.

"Then get this old hack out of here!" Marco shouted back at him. Forster quickly swam to the boat and climbed up the ladder.

"What the hell's going on?" she asked while grabbing a towel.

"Same old shit we've been dealing with," he said. "This duck fucker decided to pull up and accuse us of killing the whale." Overhearing them, Hal lit up like a fire cracker.

"What's that, boy? I'll give you a lesson!" Nelson, having had enough, put his hand near his cuffs.

"Alright, Hal," he said, "I've already told you; you're trespassing on a police barrier. Leave this instant, or we'll arrest you and confiscate your boat. Which is it?" Hal stared him in the eye with disdain, ultimately deciding to comply. His gaze passed over Forster and Marco, the former had taken the opportunity to flip him the finger. He sneered like a crazed animal before returning to his wheelhouse. The boat engine groaned as it moved off.

Nelson took some deep breaths, worried for a moment that Hal wouldn't have complied.

"Good lord!" he exclaimed. "You guys alright?"

"Nothing we're not used to," Forster said. It was just another reminder of the island's disdain for the resort and all its employees.

"Well, Hal's always been a piece of work," Nelson said. It was a way of putting it mildly. Hal had been locked up in the past, usually for starting drunken bar brawls. Other times, he would be picked up after wandering the streets intoxicated, and sleep it off at the jail until morning. Forster was already over the ordeal.

"Where do you want us to tow the whale?" she inquired. "Or, where would the lovely *fishermen* prefer?" Nelson ignored the remark.

"We'll escort you to the atoll," he said. "It's shallow enough over there. We can beach the thing on the rock, and the Guard will have an easier time getting their own tow cable on it."

"No need for an escort," she said.

"Oh, yeah there is," Nelson said. He moved on, while the other officer moved the patrol boat out of the way. Still dripping wet, Forster moved into the wheelhouse, while Marco winched in the anchor. The engine reverberated as it kicked on. With a nudge of the throttle, the boat moved forward. She kept it slow as the tow line gradually tightened.

For a moment, the engine groaned as it struggled to tug the massive weight behind it. Eventually, it was able to gain forward momentum, and drag the massive whale by the tail. It could only move up to half-speed without stressing the engine too much. Luckily the atoll wasn't too far away.

The three patrol boats moved back toward the island, along with the speedboat. Nelson's vessel traveled parallel to them, obviously as a deterrent for any other fishermen desiring to start a confrontation. Forster kept her eyes on the horizon, focusing on the beauty of the ocean. As always, it was soothing, a real diversion from the misery she was almost constantly feeling.

Marco stepped through the open doorway. In his hand was a cell phone, and on his face was a puckered brow. Forster instantly knew what was in store.

"Felt?" she asked, already knowing the answer. Marco nodded. She took the phone. "This is Dr. Forster."

"Hey Julie, I need you to come in," Felt said. *"Someone found another sick dolphin. We're gonna move it into the aquarium, and we need your help."* Forster felt her grip tightening around the phone.

"I'll get there as soon as I can," she said, faking an upbeat pitch.

"I appreciate it," he said. Without saying *goodbye,* he hung up. To Forster it was no loss. She let the phone fall to the dashboard.

Story of my life.

CHAPTER
6

The engine coughed smoke from its exhaust pipes, as the *Brisk Cold* proceeded further west. The boat reverberated with the quaking of the engine. It had been too long since its last oil change, and the engine likely needed to have its filter and plugs changed. Additionally, there was something wrong with the prop, which added to the vibrations. Inside the small wheelhouse, Old Hal hardly seemed to notice his vessel's dire need of maintenance. It wasn't a lack of awareness as much as it was general laziness. When going to his usual hangouts at night, his fellow fishermen and drinking buddies would tell him, "Listen bud, if you don't take care of that boat it won't take care of you."

Hal often blamed his failure to fix his boat on the current economic problem, although it was a blatant lie. Even if he was doing well, more likely than not he would ignore the problem. Much of his money went to cigarettes and booze, and occasionally a hooker if he went to the mainland...as long as they weren't repulsed enough by him.

He pulled his whiskey bottle, half-full, from his shirt pocket. He angled his jaw so his remaining front teeth would align, and bit down on the cork. It came out with a typical popping sound. He spit the cork and chugged a mouthful before wiping his mouth on his sleeve. Over the next couple of minutes, he downed the rest of the bottle, all while groaning about his recent encounter.

"Damned newcomers, think they own the damn place," he mumbled. A few incoherent slurs followed, full of foul language. Any voice of conscience that would've considered the fact that he caused the little bout was silenced by the flood of alcohol that coursed his veins. He downed the last of his whiskey and simply dropped it to the floor where it joined the rest of the garbage. The wheelhouse was rank with trash, from burnt cigarette butts to empty whiskey bottles, even crumbled balls of tinfoil used to package sandwiches. Belching, he looked back to look at his trawl net. It dragged behind the boat, down about thirty feet. He knew it probably wasn't catching much.

It wasn't meant to, as it was purely for show. Hal just wanted to be sure if anyone saw him, that they would think he was just trawling. The reality was that he was making way for a buoy a few miles west. This buoy marked the location of two large traps. They had been lawful up until a few years ago after the reveal of negative environmental effects. Many of the less sturdy traps would break apart, eventually riddling the ocean floor with broken wire, wooden planks, nails, and other hardware. All that was now allowed was lobster pots, and solely for that use. To Hal, laws didn't fill his wallet or subsequently his flask.

Finally, he saw his buoy, round and black like a bowling ball, jiggling in the small ripples. It was a specific area that ran especially deep. With fish becoming harder to come by in his usual places, he decided to move further out past the jurisdiction of the island police. Of course, he would have to look out for the Coast Guard.

Hal stepped out on deck and anchored the boat. Hal scanned the surrounding water. So far, not a boat in sight. Still, he knew it was best to keep an eye out. He grabbed a long wooden pole and stepped to the transom at stern, where the buoy floated about ten feet out. He reached out with the pole, trying to hook the line attached under the buoy. After a few tries, he finally got it, and he pulled it up on deck. Attached to the line were the two cables. He hooked the first one up to the winch, then pressed the lever to reel it in. The machine groaned as it slowly rotated. A bit of thin grey smoke puffed from the joints, in need of grease. Hal spat on it, growing impatient.

"Come on, you little bastard," he said, as if the machine was listening. It quickly built up speed and reeled up the cable. As it did, Hal scanned the surrounding water. So far, not a boat in sight. Still, he knew it was best to keep an eye out. When his eyes returned to the line, the trap was just emerging. He opened his jaw in stunned silence, revealing the tips of his jagged teeth. The trap was completely destroyed.

"The hell?" Hal mumbled to himself. He pulled it on deck to examine it. The sides were crushed, with broken wires frizzing in every direction. The small wood planks that made up the frames were busted up, splintered at the middle. The metal frames were bent entirely into tight 'v' shapes. In contrast, the entire top side was ripped outward, with the torn wiring creating a jagged funnel shape, as if someone had been tugging on it with a huge pair of pliers. The rest of the trap was crushed inward, like a crushed pop can.

"Well, I'll be goddamned," he said. "Nothing down there can do this; rip through metal wiring and crush these frames. I bet it was some bastard from that asshole resort." Of course, his drunken mind didn't conceive the fact that any of the people he suspected would simply report him, which would cause him further trouble. He hooked up the other cable to the winch and reeled it in.

The second trap was in similar shape. The sides were all busted inward, while ironically, the top appeared torn out. Hal kicked the side of the boat. After a foul-mouth tantrum, he unhooked the traps. They fell into the water, disappearing behind a huge splash as they sank to waste at the bottom. Hal had no use for them in that condition, and he had nowhere to store them.

He brought the anchor in and started up his boat. The engine spat, and nearly died, before finally catching a spark. Hal stood at the helm and throttled, while steering the boat back toward the island. He reached in a cabinet and pulled out a fresh bottle of whiskey. After taking a slug, he pulled a phone out of his pocket and pressed a contact name. The call was answered.

"*Yeah?*"

"Hey, Bob! Meet me at the shed," Hal said. "I'm gonna need some parts to build some new traps."

"*Tonight?*"

"Yeah, tonight! Something happened to mine, so I want to get new ones out before the night is over."

"*Get someone else, Hal. I might have a date tonight!*"

"Gimme a break, Bob! She'll turn tail at the first sight of ya," Hal said. "Just bring me the parts, and I'll take care of the rest."

"*Like you have room to talk. Alright, let me see what I can do,*" his friend answered.

"Works for me," Hal said, and flipped his phone shut. He tucked it in his pocket and drank another mouthful of whiskey, ignoring the thickening exhaust fumes trailing behind him.

CHAPTER
7

The one small bit of good luck in responding to Chief Nelson's call was that Julie Forster had already geared up in her wetsuit. She walked in the large circular pool, with water up to her chest, holding the sick dolphin by the pectoral fins. Its head hugged her side, relying on her to stay afloat as it took shallow breaths through its blowhole. The dolphin, found washed ashore on one of the island beaches, was suffering from severe dehydration and malnutrition, likely the result of toxic poisoning. For the past hour, she had been walking it in the twenty-foot diameter pool, located in a restricted room in the aquarium's top floor.

As much as Forster loved the water, she had grown plenty sick of it today. The chill temperature was starting to wear on her, despite the internal sublimation inside the wetsuit. Being busy nonstop for sixteen hours with hardly any sleep was wearing on her, as it had steadily been doing for months now. Her eyes felt foggy, and the lightweight sensation from the water did not help.

She completed another lap. She felt the dolphin take some deeper breaths. The Dimercaprol that she had administered seemed to be having a mild effect, enough to make a visible difference.

"You finally ready to try your cubes, huh?" she asked it. Interestingly, the dolphin wiggled its flipper. She smiled, envisioning the dolphin to be answering yes. "Alright, let's give it a try." She led it over to the side, where one of her aids stood by a table.

Though Marcus was her main assistant, the aquarium aides also served as helping hands in caring for the biological attractions. Most of them were young and eager to learn. However, they contained no training nor licensing, possibly exactly what Felt was looking to hire in order to save a buck. Forster did what she could to give each of the aides a crash course in the care of marine life. Essentially, these aids were the CNAs of the aquarium.

The aide opened a cooler. Inside was full of ice, and on top was an ice cube tray, full of frozen meaty squares. Forster referred to these as protein cubes, designed to give an emergency supply of iron, calcium, protein, along with various other nutrients. The dolphin had been refusing them in favor of being walked.

The aide handed her a cube. Forster held it over the dolphin's beak. It didn't open, and the dolphin tilted its head away, like a child refusing to take its dinner.

"Oh no you don't," Forster said. She held the cube in front of its eye. "Come on, it's not broccoli. Don't make me stay in here all night." She moved the cube back to the crease in its mouth. It opened ever so slightly, just enough for Forster to slip the cube in. It disappeared into the back of its throat. "That's a good boy." She gave it another cube, which it accepted with increased interest.

After several minutes, the whole cooler was cleared out. Forster turned to the aide, who was dressed up in thermal clothing for the evening shift.

"I think we'll start to see improvements by morning," she said. The aide nodded and climbed into the pool.

"If its condition worsens?" he asked.

"There's no good answer," Forster said. "We'll have to contact the Clearwater Marine Aquarium in Florida. They have a better suited staff." The aide took the dolphin and started walking it.

"If I may ask; why don't we just take it there?" he asked. Forster climbed out of the pool, feeling much lighter. She grabbed a towel, while shaking her head with displeasure for the answer.

"It's one of Mr. Felt's publicity stunts," she said. "Attendance is dropping because people think he's partly responsible for what's been happening to the water. The EPA couldn't find anything to prosecute him on, but they're pretty sure he was aware of what Wan Industry was doing. This, what we're doing, is just an effort to win the public's heart back." She wiped her face with the towel. The warm air in the room embraced her, worsening her drowsiness. She collected her wallet and watch and went into a nearby locker room. After changing back into her regular clothes, she stepped out and headed for the door. "I'm done in for today. Have a good night." The aide waved goodbye and continued walking the dolphin.

Forster took the elevator down to the first floor, watching the numbers count down in the upper left monitor. As the doors opened up, she could hear the commotion of what seemed to be a large crowd outside. She stepped out of the elevator and looked to the entry to the right, where the noise was coming from. Through the glass double doors, she noticed workers moving about, appearing to be setting something up near the Great White Exhibit. She glanced back at the back doors, which led to the employee parking lot. An imaginary voice in her mind yelled at her to just go home. However, curiosity got the better of her.

Stepping out the front entrance, she saw a crowd of guests taking seats on a multi-level set of metal bleachers. The bleachers were facing the great white's aquarium. The sight of them caught Forster by surprise, as they weren't there a couple of hours prior. With the pool being ground level, the bleachers were able to provide a clear view inside. Stray pieces of popcorn and cotton candy already littered the cement as people piled on. Young children hugged their prized stuffed animals as their parents guided them up the steps. Standing around the bleachers were staff workers. Forster could see the sweat, exhaustion, and frustration in their faces.

It suddenly became apparent where the bleachers came from. Forster realized they were taken from the concert stage. Forster waved to one of the workers, who approached. His white uniform shirt and khaki pants were smothered in grease and dirt, while beads of sweat dripped from his brow.

"What's all this?" she asked him.

"Orders from the boss," he said. "The stage event for tonight got cancelled. I guess U2 knew they were better off not to waste their time here. Or rather, they wanted to avoid the bad press. So, Mr. Felt had us move the bleachers over here for some impromptu event he has in mind." Forster looked at the bleachers again. They were at least thirty feet across, and ten rows high.

"Wait…" she said… "so you had to move these…how were you able to…?"

"We had to disassemble them, drive them over, and put them back together," he said. Now the dirt, grease, and sweat made sense. He pulled a ragged handkerchief from his pocket and wiped it over his face. It didn't do much good; the rag was also covered with dried dirt and grease. A frustrated sigh breezed from his lips. "Now, we're just waiting for this thing to be done so we can do it all over again, to return them to the stage."

Forster understood his misery. He and his fellow workers were visibly exhausted. With how impressively fast they assembled the bleachers, they had to have been hustling. The ninety-five-degree heat certainly didn't help their situation. She looked at the crowd, and then looked back at the pool. Along the starboard side, she saw Marco standing on a hydraulic lift attached to the adjacent dock. She noticed a long wooden pole, and a four-by-three-foot plastic tub on the metal table. A few feet off to the side stood William Felt. Six-foot-two with balding hair, dressed in his normal grey suit jacket and trousers with a white shirt underneath, he supervised the set-up. That suit used to fit him perfectly, when the forty-two-year-old businessman was much rounder around the mid-section. Over the past couple of months, he had slimmed down significantly, undoubtedly from the constant stress he was facing. Now, the jacket looked too big on him.

Forster looked back at the worker, "What is he planning?" The worker shrugged his shoulders.

"I heard somebody say something about a '*National Geographic* experience in the flesh'; something about feeding the shark. I don't really know."

"I see. Thanks," Forster said. She started to turn to walk away, but stopped for a moment. "Hey, upstairs, there's a bunch of water bottles in the employee lounge, in the fridge. Run up and get some for yourself and the others."

"I most definitely appreciate that," the worker said. He happily embraced the air conditioning as he entered the Aquarium Building. Forster then marched over to Felt. He noticed her approaching. He gave his normal, business grin.

"Hey, Julie! How's the dolphin doing?" he said.

"There's mild improvement, but someone's gonna have to be with it all night. I've already got people scheduled."

"Oh, good," he said. He looked up at Marco. Forster looked up as well, and couldn't help but notice the noose at the end of the pole, and the red drippings secreting from the edge of the purple plastic tub.

"What's going on here?" she asked Felt. She didn't bother concealing the concern in her voice. Felt maintained his upbeat demeanor, although he was growing anxious inside.

"We're putting on a demonstration for our guests," he said, with the naïve hope that the vague answer would end the questioning. The next question was as he predicted.

"What demonstration?"

A brief shudder followed. He brushed it off, pretending to cough.

Felt mentally berated himself. *She's YOUR employee, idiot. She can disapprove all she wants for all you care.* He cleared his throat, then pointed up at Marco.

"See that tub there next to Marco? There's some big slabs of beef in there. Got it fresh from the local butcher's market in town. Marco's gonna put a slab on the hook at the end of that pole there, and hold it down. Hopefully, we can get the white to breach and grab it. Just like something you'd see on *National Geographic*."

If this were any other person, Forster would be starting a riot. Looking at the equipment, particularly the hydraulic lift…with no safety bars along the table, she knew this was not a proper set up to conduct this type of feeding. Unfortunately, this was her boss, a reality that he preyed on.

"Mr. Felt, sir," she said…thinking of a proper way to talk him out of this. "This…this probably won't work. See, I had instructions for the great white to be fed at *4:30*. It probably won't be hungry."

"Oh, I know," Felt said. "I saw your feeding schedule. So, I just told the aide to not feed it today. So, don't worry, it'll be plenty hungry."

Forster couldn't be more worried.

"Mr. Felt, this thing isn't a trained circus performer. It's a wild animal," she said. "It won't simply abide by your rules."

"Oh, it'll be fine," Felt said. "Just a quick show, and it'll be done. I promise."

"Sir, this isn't a proper setup," she said. "It's not as simple as what you watch on TV. To do this properly, we need a crane, or at least a large pulley, from which we can hang the bait over the water without putting someone in danger. Let's just put the show off for a bit, until we can get the proper equipment." Felt chuckled.

"Excuse me, but take a look back there," he said, pointing his thumb behind him toward the bleachers. She took a brief glance, seeing them packed with guests. "You think I'm gonna tell these people, 'Hey, folks, sorry. Show's over,'? Hell no." There was a sense of urgency in his voice. He knew that if this went well, it could possibly lead to good word-of-mouth reviews of the resort. Anything to boost interest in his business, even the smallest thing, was desperately needed. "This thing is happening. Like I said, it'll be fine." Although he maintained his smile and spoke in his usual friendly fashion, Forster could read between the lines. There was nothing more she could do, except nod and hope that nothing went awry.

Marco knelt at the tub to remove the lid. He noticed Forster watching him. Over the past six months, he'd come to recognize any disapproving body language. He wanted to say something such as, 'I don't have any say in this,' or 'Felt instructed me to do this.' He didn't need to say these things. The doctor was already aware.

"Just be careful," she said to him. Marco gave her a thumbs up.

"You've got it, boss," he said.

"I'm serious!" she said. Her tone was higher pitched this time. "You don't have any rail barrier. The shark could easily yank you over the side by accident, so let the pole go if you have to."

"Oh, he'll be fine!" Felt cut in. "Besides, if he ends up in the water and the big guy moves towards him, all he has to do is punch him right in the nose. Everybody knows that."

Everybody believes that.

"Actually, what you want to do is…" she started to correct him by stating the eyes and gills are areas that are more sensitive, but Felt turned and walked to the bleachers, clearly disinterested. Marco lifted the hydraulic table, until it was about eight feet above the dock. He reached into the tub and pulled out a large chunk of beef, which dripped with blood. He tightened the noose around it. As he expected, blood splattered onto his shirt.

Great. Now looking like the victim in a slasher movie, he waited for Felt to give him the instruction to begin.

With a good view of the pool, Forster decided to wait until everything was over. The nervous adrenaline caused the drowsiness to temporarily subside. After this was all over, it would come back with a vengeance.

Mr. Felt grabbed a handheld microphone. He tested it by tapping the round grey end, which echoed a loud thumping noise. The seated audience heard this and quieted their commotion, knowing the show was about to begin.

****

Out in the bay drifted a fishing vessel, the *Omega*. It was an old boat, with more rust than metal at this point. It wasn't for lack of funds for repairs and replacements. At least, this was what its captain, Scott Hamilton, claimed. Dressed in a black long sleeve shirt and dirty blue jeans, sporting a *Florida Gators* ball cap, he stood at the bow deck. He was a skinny man of thirty-nine, although he looked a decade older, and like his close friend Hal Pepper, he favored the bottle. Binoculars were raised to his eyes, pointed toward the aquarium.

"Hey, I think that's the chick there that Hal ran into today," he said.

"That's the doctor lady," his first mate responded from the port quarter deck. Ben Carlton was ten years younger, and a much more muscular fellow; possibly because he did the vast majority of the heavy lifting on the job. He wore no hat to cover his head, and his bald scalp was almost completely red from constant exposure to the sun. He also had binoculars to his eyes, watching the same event. "You think she wrecked his traps?"

"That's what Hal told us," Scott said. "It was her, or somebody from this circus. I tell you, there's nothing down there that can bust those crates like that."

"Should we go in and teach them a lesson?" Ben asked. Scott only responded with a barely audible "hmmm." Their original goal was to raise hell as a form of retaliation, although they never truly had a plan.

These two, along with Old Hal, were considered the local low-lives of the island. Good manners and general morality seemed to be absent to this bunch. They cheated buyers when selling their catch to market; they often would make a ruckus at bars, and had no problems using illegal means to catch more fish. Most of the fishing community didn't have much respect for them, nor did the general population. But with the growing animosity between the community and Felt's

48

resort, there was hardly any disapproval toward whatever discord these agitators caused toward the workers.

"Let's wait a bit," Scott said. He had watched the fellow on the hydraulic lift elevate it, then place what appeared to be a chunk of meat onto a noose on a pole. "I want to see what's going on here first. Drop the anchor so we don't drift off." Ben complied, and the two watched the event from a distance.

****

Mr. Felt stood proudly in front of the crowd and raised his microphone to his mouth.

"Thank you everyone for gathering over here at Felt's Paradise. I am William Felt, the owner. What you are gathered here to see is the one and only great white shark in captivity." He paused for effect and looked back to the pool. It was a cue for Marco to dump a couple of scoops of blood into the water. Marco noticed the subtle signal and bled a scoop down into the water eight feet below him. The dark red, coagulated blood splashed down and quickly divided into several loose strands and shapes, like red ghosts.

A few moments later, the familiar grey dorsal fin emerged. The audience saw the triangular shape, cutting through the water like a sailboat. Under it, they could see the massive twenty-three-foot body of the great shark. The clear water provided great detail. Its rounded head turned as it followed the tasteful scent of blood. Its fin turned along with each motion of its body, which followed in a snake like pattern.

The audience applauded. There were even a few cheers. Felt's business smile became one of genuine happiness. It was just the reaction he was hoping for. People held out their iPhones and snapped pictures and digital video footage of the amazing fish. It reduced its speed as it swam through the cloud of blood. It dipped down, them emerged again, searching for the source. Finding nothing, it started to curve away toward the back of the pool.

"Just take a look at that," Felt shouted with the enthusiasm of a rodeo show host. "Now, we're going to give you a demonstration of its awesome power! Marco, our aquarium assistant, will lower a little enticement of beef, and you will see the amazing power of the great white as it snatches its meal. These sharks have the most powerful jaws of any species of fish! Its bite is so powerful, it could easily crush a John Deere lawn mower like a soda can!"

Forster quietly shut her eyes and took a solemn breath.

Ugh, not even close. Her thoughts naturally went through her education. Bull sharks' bites actually contained a much stronger PSI measurement than great whites, whose bites weren't nearly as strong as Felt's exaggerations. Though the bite force was powerful, the teeth were what really caused damage to its victim. Like a good employee, she kept her mouth closed, and allowed her boss to entertain his guests.

Marco listened as Felt finished his monologue on the shark's strength. Finally, Felt turned toward the pool again, glancing up at him. Marco sat on his knees and lifted the pole. The forty-pound slab of beef weighed heavily on the other end. Luckily, Marco's muscular frame was able to handle the unbalanced weight. He extended the pole downward, holding the meat just above the surface, just a few feet from the thick glass wall. With no safety barrier, he was forced to lean a bit over the side. The meat, slung in the noose, dripped fresh drops of blood.

The fresh scent attracted the shark. It turned back, much to the delight of the spectators. It moved ever gently closer, guiding itself along the wall of the tank. Forster watched from the deck. Her heart rate increased with anxiety. So did Marco's. Suddenly, he felt stupid for agreeing to do this favor for Felt. Not that there was much choice; Felt didn't really ask him.

Forster wanted to give him tips, such as 'let the pole go if the meat doesn't come free,' but she knew all that would do was break his focus. She kept her hands behind her back, keeping from making a nervous posture.

The shark's six-thousand-pound bulk broke the surface. Its head tilted up slightly, and its black marble eyes identified the meat. Having not fed in a while, its body was aching for sustenance. With a slash of its tail, it lifted itself higher, enough that its pectoral fins cleared the surface. Its eyes rolled back for protection, and its jaws extended. Inch-and-a-half long serrated teeth sliced onto the meaty end of the slab, and the fish pulled down violently. The meat pulled clear of the noose. The pole instantly became forty pounds lighter, causing Marco to nearly fall back.

The shark crashed back down with its meal. Water crashed over the pool walls and onto the concrete flooring. The audience erupted with applause. Joining them was Felt, who was equally impressed by the stunt he had orchestrated.

Forster exhaled a strong sigh of relief, followed by a smile. She looked up at Marco, who was equally happy of how well the demonstration went. He gave her a thumbs up, which she returned.

"Alright, good job," she said. "Now, let's get you down from there."

"I agree to that," Marco said. He began the process of collecting the items with putting the lid back on the plastic tub. At that moment, Felt spoke into his microphone with excitement.

"So, what did you think of that?" he shouted to the audience, who promptly responded with some cheers. "That's what I thought! You know what else I think?... I think you lovely people would love to witness that one more time!" A bigger eruption of cheers answered him.

Forster swiftly turned toward Felt with questioning eyes. That relief she had felt instantly started to subside. Drunken by the thrill of the stunt and the audience's positive reaction, Felt looked up at Marco, who was slightly surprised.

"Hey son," Felt called up to him with the microphone. "There should be another slab of beef in that tub! Let's get that thing on the stick. That shark is hungry!"

That's what I'm afraid of.

Marco reopened the container and lifted the heavy piece of raw meat. He loosened the noose and slipped the cord over the bleeding beef. He groaned after accidentally smothering more of it on his shirt. Once the noose was tightened enough, he lifted it clear of the tub, taking no notice of a small fist sized square of meat that dangled freely by a thin strand of fat. As before, he dumped a scoop of blood into the water.

It took a few seconds longer this time, but the familiar fin soon emerged. As soon as he saw it, he lowered the heavy end of the pole downward.

"Oh, here it comes, just as hungry as before!" Felt's voice carried on, as if narrating the event.

Marco mentally blocked out the annoying audio and focused on the task. The shark moved a little slower, possibly because it had already consumed forty pounds. However, especially having been deprived of its previous meal, it was likely still hungry. Its torpedo shape became clear beneath the pure water it swam in. Marco dipped the pole further, just touching the bottom of the meat to the surface.

Unbeknownst to him, the loose chunk of meat broke away with the contact of water. With not enough fat content to keep it afloat, it sank down, trailing a thin stream of blood. The great white's lateral line picked up the faint water distortion. It dipped downward, submerging its dorsal fin, and scooped up the tiny bit of meat in a single effortless motion.

"What the hell?" Marco said to himself as the shark unexpectedly dove down. He could still see its large bulk under the fading red blood cloud. It leveled out and started to circle back. His eyes briefly went to Felt, who was suddenly struck with unexpected confusion. Understanding his boss' concern with satisfying the crowd, Marco leaned a bit more forward. He plunged the large chunk of meat into the water. Its jacket of blood lifted into a stringy cloud.

The scent flooded the nearby shark's nostrils. As instant as it picked up the scent, it turned and lashed forward. Its jaws stretched open and quickly closed down on its prey. Teeth sawed into the red lifeless bait, and immediately the shark pulled away with its prize, still bound by the noose.

Marco's brain barely comprehended the sudden response from the fish. He was still clinging to the pole when it was yanked into the water, taking him with it. He fell in a forward rolling motion, nearly hitting his head on the side of the pool.

Marco had barely hit the water when the audience reveled in a concurrent gasp. People jumped to their feet, eager to see the worker and the shark. Workers rushed to the guardrail barrier of the pool, yelling for Security on their radios. Even Felt gasped, accidentally made audible by his microphone.

A sudden sense of urgency flooded Marco's nerves. Spitting salt water from his mouth, he swam to the surface. He emerged at the surface and turned. A high-pitched shriek drained his lungs as the shark's tail whipped toward him. The white had bumped into the glass after it grabbed the bait, which nearly caused it to lose the food. It grabbed it again and turned violently to swim off. Its tail slapped into his chest, knocking him several feet backwards. Marco saw nothing but a series of blurry images as the wind was blown from his lungs.

"Marco!" Forster yelled as she watched her friend get knocked around like a bowling pin. She quickly got control of herself and focused on the shark's position. She could see its fin starting to circle back. It had finished consuming the beef and was now coming back... straight for Marco. Its approach was slow, but there was no doubt its Ampullae of Lorenzini were detecting his weak, injured motions.

He floated in the red bloody water, stunned and disoriented. Many of his bodily senses malfunctioned. He couldn't hear anything except assorted garbled sounds; and his vision was blurred with watery images. His chest felt like a hundred-pound weight had been planted on him. He was conscious, but barely so, and he had no awareness of the shark's approach.

Workers climbed over the guardrail, ready to jump into the pool. Each of them froze at the sight of the dorsal fin. Marco was too far away for them to simply reach for, and there was nothing they had to extend out to him.

Forster quickly analyzed the situation and her surroundings. She turned toward the hydraulic lift. Its table was elevated roughly two-and-a-half feet over her head. She took a couple of steps back, then dashed toward it. She jumped and reached high like a basketball player doing a slam dunk. Her hands clutched the side of the table, and she pulled herself up in a chin-up motion. She rose to her feet, and turned to face the pool. Marco had floated about ten feet out, and the shark was closing in. As her eyes locked in on it, it had just begun to increase its speed. She could see the jaws beginning to extend under the water. There was no opportunity to time her rescue attempt. It had to be done now.

Forster took a single running step and leapt from the edge of the lift. While she was momentarily in midair, she kicked both her feet down toward the fish. The heels of her boots struck the middle of the gill line as she came crashing down.

Nerves lit up like an electric shock that zipped through the shark, and it swiftly jerked to the side. Its crescent shaped caudal fin brushed over Forster, missing her by inches. She twisted underwater in the powerful current it created, which lasted for only a second. She kicked to the surface and drew a breath. Turning back, she saw Marco and swam towards him. She swam to his side and tucked her left arm under his. She kept an eye on the dorsal fin as she paddled back, with the two-hundred-forty-pound assistant in tow.

"Who'd ever think I'd be the one saving your ass," she remarked, spitting out water with each word. Each paddle was a strain, but with each one they closed the distance. Security officers in blue uniform shirts ducked under the guardrail and reached out. Forster and Marco were successfully pulled from the water. Forster rested on her knees for a moment, while Security checked Marco's vitals. The distant echo of an ambulance gradually drew closer. Dripping wet, Forster stood to her feet. At that same moment, Marco weakly lifted his hand and gave a thumbs up.

A sense of relief brushed over the crowd, who complimented all those involved with an applause in recognition of the successful rescue. Forster stepped through the gathering of security and workers and looked down at Marco.

"You'll be alright, bud," she said.

"Oh, I've been through worse scraps than this," he jokingly muttered, although painfully. He was lying of course in a humorous attempt to sound manly. Forster smiled at him then started walking away. Marco called back to her, "Hey Julie?" She stopped and looked over her shoulder. "Thanks," he said. She smiled again.

"Don't mention it," she said. As she started walking away, the flashing red ambulance lights came into view. It parked near the crowd, and EMTs stepped out of the box with a stretcher.

As she walked away, Forster looked down at her dripping clothes and wished she had stayed in the wetsuit. All the contents in her pockets were now soaked. Luckily, she kept her phone in her car. At this point, she didn't care. All she wanted was to go home and lay on her couch. And that was exactly her plan.

As the crowd gradually dispersed, William Felt stood with his microphone, simultaneously shocked and grateful. However, the feeling that overshadowed both was a sense of dread. As people went about their way, he could see many visitors uploading images and videos onto their social media accounts. Curious, he turned on his own iPhone and brought up *Twitter* on his screen. Almost immediately, he started getting hits for headlines such as *Shark nearly eats handler at Felt's Paradise.*

Felt's hopes for promotion through social media backfired. Now, he had yet another controversy on his hands. His mind raced for new solutions, but came up short. The resort was coming up short in revenue, and the dread of foreclosure was starting to seem more like a horrible reality. With the millions invested in it, his career in business would come to a halt.

He felt his stomach tighten, and beads of sweat run down his temple...and it wasn't because of the heat. He felt every desire to leave, but knew the public eye was still on him. Thinking quickly, he hurriedly walked to Marco, who was being tended to by the EMTs. He stood on the toes of his shoes to look at him.

"Hey, Marco. You doing alright?" he asked. Marco tried to smile, but the pain in his chest was setting in even worse. The EMTs had removed his shirt, revealing the early signs of bruising on his chest.

"Yeah," he said with a weak voice. "It's just that my chest really..."

"Oh, that's great that you're feeling better!" Felt said. He swiftly turned and walked toward the aquarium

His heart raced in his chest, coupled with an overwhelming anxiety. He angled for the nearest restroom, but changed direction seeing a small crowd of visitors. He located an employee-only stairway to the second floor, and walked toward it, pretending to be casual. Hopefully, nobody would notice that his face and neck were now soaked in nervous sweat. As soon as the door shut behind him, he sprinted up the stairs. Luckily, the second floor had private unisex bathrooms. Again acting casual, he locked himself in one. As soon as the latch slammed home, he yanked off his expensive suit jacket and threw himself onto the toilet and vomited.

****

After a loud fit of laughter, Scott and Ben pulled themselves together. It was a sick sense of enjoyment watching the near-tragedy from the safety of the bay. Scott wiped the tears of laughter from his face and shoved a pinch of chewing tobacco into his mouth. Ben cracked open a beer.

"Stupid bastards," he cackled. He swallowed a mouthful of suds. "So, what should we do?"

"We wait," Scott said. He spat a stream of brown residue into the water. "I think I have an idea. Who knows, knowing the moron who owns this place, we'll probably be saving lives."

"I'm not catching on," Ben said. Scott pointed out toward the pool.

"You see the far side, there," he said. Ben lifted his binoculars. "See, that wall facing out has a set of mechanical double doors. That pool was originally built as a rehabilitation tank for small whales."

"Oh," Ben said. He thought for a moment until he realized Scott's idea. "OH! You mean you want to…"

"Oh yes," Scott said, sporting a wicked smile. He then spat another wad of tobacco juice. "If they want to mess with our property, we'll mess with theirs."

"When do we do it?" Ben asked, while draining the rest of his beer.

"When it gets dark," Scott answered. "By then, there'll only be a few night time employees. There's a control console for the pool. I'm sure I'll be able to figure it out." He chuckled to himself, like the villain in a spy picture. He went onto the main deck and reeled in the anchor. "In the meantime, let's get out of here." After the anchor was winched aboard, he went into the wheelhouse and started the engine.

CHAPTER
8

As night fell over Pariso Marino, maritime activity came to its usual end for the day. The fishing boats had returned to their ports, and the evening police shifts normally kept to the island interior. The crystal blue quality of the water ceased with the daylight, and it now reflected the black night air with some silver streaks of moonlight.

It provided the perfect cover for Hal, who had just set out west in his fishing vessel. He kept his lights down to a dim. There was no curfew for fishing vessels to be out; however, he did not want to be seen with the two large metal traps he had recently constructed. He and his neighbor, Bob, had spent the last few hours constructing the crates. They had to be handmade, as there was nothing suitable that could be purchased legally on the island.

As Hal predicted, Bob's date did not go well, so he had spent the wasted evening in Hal's garage. Several hours, and three whiskey bottles later, they managed to construct eight crates. In his impaired mindset, he was completely convinced somebody from the resort was responsible. Hal wanted to spread them out, and not make it too easy for his assumed adversaries to locate them all and sabotage his unlawful livelihood. With only enough room on his deck for four crates, Bob reluctantly agreed to go out on his own boat, *The Thrice*, and deliver the rest.

Two crates splashed down in the first location, attached to a fresh cable and buoy. Standing at the transom, Hal watched the water fizzing from the splash, barely visible in the moonlight. The black buoy bounced a couple of times until the water settled. After that, the only noise to be heard was the coughing of the *Brisk Cold*. The black fumes were invisible in the night air, and Hal ignored the odor.

He stepped back to the helm and started throttling to his next location, where he would meet up with Bob. Despite having hardly any visibility, he knew exactly where he was. Being on these waters all of his life, he could travel with his eyes shut.

Hal pulled a crumpled cigarette from his shirt pocket and stuffed it into his mouth. In the same hand, he held a lighter and a whiskey bottle. He fumbled to ignite his cigarette, eventually succeeding, and washed the first draw with a mouthful of booze. He stuffed the bottle back in his pocket and grabbed his cellphone. He dialed Bob's number, with intent to let him know he was on his way to the red buoy. He figured Bob would have a hard time finding it, even with the installed GPS.

The phone rang, but there was no answer. At first, Hal thought there just wasn't any signal. However, that theory went to dust when his phone started vibrating from an incoming call. The contact name was *Scott*, his other favorite drinking buddy.

"I've been waiting to hear from you," Hal answered the call.

"*Hello to you too, dickhead,*" Scott replied. "*You have the traps unloaded yet?*"

"On my way to meet up with Bob," Hal said. "Won't take long. These traps are sturdier. Any jackass from that aquarium will have a hell of a time busting them up. I bet it was that chick. Probably did it to protect the fish. She seems the real 'love animals' type."

"*How do you figure that? She works for Felt. Still does, after everything's been turning up dead,*" Scott said. Hal tried to think for a moment. His booze-flooded brain had trouble comprehending his friend's logic, as well as his own. With everything he was doing, he was acting on impulse. The crates, which he claimed were sturdier, were actually built very sloppily. Screws were fixed in at inept angles, and in many cases the wrong size was used. One of the traps was uneven in its shape, with the top grate screwed to the planks at a slight angle. For the other, the flap door where the fish would enter required a bit of force to get inside.

"I uh, uh…"

"*Speaking of fish, did you hear about that thing with their great white?*"

"I did. Hilarious."

"*Well, I'll be heading over there again with Ben. We have a plan for their little fish.*" Hal thought for a second, once again unable to figure out what Scott was getting at. "*We're gonna let it loose!*" Scott finally said, realizing Hal wasn't catching on.

Hal's cigarette burst from his mouth as he laughed.

"That'll piss them off," he said.

"*Better yet, after we do, I plan on catching the thing. I know a guy on the mainland that specializes in shark meat! I'll make a killing…so to speak.*" He broke into laughter.

"Make sure I get a cut of that!" Hal said.

"*Uh, yeah…try no!*" Scott said. "*I'm doing you a favor as it is.*"

"You sound like my ex-wife," Hal said. This led to an awkward pause.

"*As long as I don't look like her…*" he shuddered in disgust. "*Anyhow, you'll be even with them. Who knows, we might be heroes in the animal rights world.*"

"Except you're planning on catching the shark afterwards…" Hal said.

"*Yeah, but they don't know that. I'll let you know how it goes.*"

"I'll hear about it somehow or another. Anyhow, I'd better go. I should be coming up on the next buoy in a few minutes. Have fun with the fish."

Before Scott could say his farewell, Hal hung up the phone. He had a habit of ending his phone calls abruptly. He traveled for several more minutes until finally turning on his small GPS monitor. The screen showed that the buoy was less than a quarter mile south. He adjusted the *Brisk Cold*'s direction.

He had already activated the night blinker, more for Bob's benefit than his own. Watching through the windshield, he kept an eye out for the blinking red light. He quickly spotted it, nearly three hundred yards ahead. In the dark, it was impossible to miss.

He squinted as he scanned the water around the buoy. Even in the dim moonlight, he knew he should have been able to see Bob's boat. He tried calling once again. He pressed the contact button, only to have a dead dial tone beep in his face. This time, the call wasn't even getting through.

"Where the hell is he?" Hal said to himself. He went to use the radio, only to remember it wasn't functional. Just another repair he had failed to complete. Not that he cared; hardly anyone ever addressed him on the radio.

The flashing red light grew brighter as Hal brought his boat to a stop alongside the buoy. He stepped onto the deck and anchored, then reached out to the buoy with a pole.

A few more minutes passed and he hooked the new traps to the cable. He splashed them down and reeled the anchor back in. Another scan of the water revealed no obvious sign of Bob's boat. Knowing Bob, he'd likely be traveling with his interior lights on at least, which would stand out in the night. But there was nothing.

"Whatever," he said to himself. He returned to the wheelhouse to begin his return trip. He turned the wheel and leaned in on the throttle. The engine groaned heavily as the propellers pushed it along. Hal stuffed another cigarette in his mouth and fumbled in his pocket for his lighter. He held the flame to the tip.

Hal flinched as the entire boat shuttered. The cigarette fell from his mouth, and he stuffed the lighter back into his pocket. The engine kicked a few more times, coupled with the sound of grinding metal. It all silenced as the engine died.

Hal took a quick slug of his whiskey to relax his nerves. He tried starting the engine again. The gears twisted a few times, but to no avail. He went to a hatch at the rear of the cabin. He opened it, revealing a cloud of grey smoke. He coughed and brushed the air with his hand. He fumbled around for a flashlight, finally locating one in the mess of a wheelhouse, and shined it into the engine.

The smoke was too thick for him to identify the specific problem. He crawled inside for a closer look. He felt a rush of heat from the warm engine room, which instantly drew sweat from his brow. Holding his breath, he inspected the engine. There appeared to be a crack in the cylinder, as well as some damage to the camshaft. The spark plugs were blistered from overheating.

Hal didn't consider his lack of maintenance to be a factor. Boozed up and self-entitled, he cursed at the engine, believing that luck was down on him.

"You little piece of shit, useless machinery!" he yelled. His voice amplified in the tight space. He kicked the engine, causing small rusted pieces of metal to sprinkle the floor.

Almost immediately, more rusted pieces fell after something bumped the hull. Something tapped against the boat from the outside.

"Oh, what now?" Hal groaned and hurried to the deck. He leaned over the portside gunwale to look into the water. His flashlight illuminated a jagged object, which appeared to be a piece of wood. It bumped against the side of his boat as it bobbed in the water.

Just a piece of wood. Who cares? He started turning away to return to the engine, but stopped after he caught the glimpse of something further out. He shined his flashlight back down. As he aimed it further out, he saw a couple more objects floating about. He suddenly realized they were pieces of decking. He aimed the light further.

The ocean was covered with floating pieces of wreckage. Bits of hull, rubber, decking, gradually drifted apart from each other. Hal shined his light on a large piece of rounded steel that floated about twenty feet from the stern. It was about twelve feet long and had enough buoyancy to keep it on the surface. He noticed a few white letters printed on it: *he Thr*.

The letters went from one side to the other, clearly the middle of a word. Hal's took a heavy swig of his whiskey upon the realization he was looking at the wreckage of *The Thrice*. Anxiety seized control of him. He didn't bother comprehending what happened to the boat. It didn't require any imagination to realize something horrific had recently taken place. He just wanted to get out of the area. He rushed to the wheelhouse and tried starting the engine.

As before, it turned a few times before quitting. He took another drink and set the bottle down on the countertop. With a shaking hand, he turned the key again, only to produce the same result.

"Start, you piece of shit!" he cursed it, while hammering his fist on the helm. He twisted the key in the ignition again. This time, the starter didn't even initiate. All he heard was a faint click, like a car with a dead battery.

He grabbed a small toolbox and hurried down into the engine room. He shined the flashlight to inspect it. The smoke had cleared, giving him better visibility. It wouldn't make any difference, however, as he was by no means a skilled mechanic. While he had learned much about fishing over the years, he retained nothing about maintaining a boat.

He looked at the crack in the cylinder, then fumbled in his toolbox. In doing so, he dropped his flashlight, which switched off upon hitting the floor. In complete darkness, he got on his hands and knees and started tapping the floor in search of it. Finding nothing but floor, he swept his hands around to cover a wider area. He felt his fingertips bump the handle, knocking it to the side. He quickly reached over to the sound of the rolling tool.

"Ah, fuck!" he yelled after smacking his forehead against the engine. He rolled backwards, knocking his toolbox over. Tools scattered across the room, nearly invisible in the dark. Anger now joined the anxiety and desperation. "Son...of...a...bitch!" He pounded the floor with each curse. It was as if the boat was directly punishing him for not repairing it.

As he clambered about inside the boat, Hal was left completely unaware of the creature circling the *Brisk Cold*. Twenty-four feet in length, it searched desperately for sustenance. Prey was becoming difficult to come by, and its previous encounter had resulted in only a meager meal. It had searched the wreckage it had created, hoping to scavenge anything edible. But the material was all inorganic.

Now it had a fresh new target. It was like the one it had encountered previously. This one was motionless, however. It circled the boat, deciding on whether or not to attack. Hammering sounds from within it echoed throughout the water, spiking the creature's curiosity. The vibrations seemed to originate from inside the 'underbelly'. It was like detecting the heartbeat of a wounded animal.

Memory of its recent attack on the other vessel reminded it that these inorganic floating objects carried edible prey. The beast made distance and lined up with the side of the vessel. In less than a second, it burst into a speed of a hundred miles per hour. Its eyes and jaws clamped shut, keeping its cone shaped nose pointed forward, like the head of a spear.

Hal fumbled along the floor, tossing aside various tools. Finally, he grasped the rounded flashlight handle. He leaned against the engine and pressed the button, shining it against the side wall. The red paint of the rusty wall came into view.

That caved in towards Hal in a sudden motion. The metal siding pressed inward into a bizarre cone-like shape, then breached. Flaps of metal peeled apart like flower pedals. Water burst into the room, preceding the snout of the enormous red shark that penetrated the vessel. Hal didn't have time to notice the irregularities, such as the protruding antennae and rigid exoskeleton. He only saw the black eyes open and close again, and rows of teeth bulging from red gums. Hal jolted in fright and yelled out, dropping his flashlight. It spun in the swishing water, illuminating both Hal and the beast in brief circular flashes.

It bit down on his torso. Teeth tore into his wrinkly flesh, drawing blood. Hal squirmed in its grasp. His yells were ceased as the entire room flooded with water.

With its prey in its mouth, the shark twisted its body violently until it shook itself loose from the breach. It opened its mouth and chomped down, creating a hundred more simultaneous puncture wounds. It repeated this motion, until Hal's body broke into several bloody parts. The shark swallowed each one.

It circled about, making sure it didn't leave behind any bit of its meal. It determined there was nothing left and swam off in search of more sustenance.

The *Brisk Cold* continued filling with sea water until the added weight overcame its buoyancy. Water flooded the cargo hold, causing the stern to dip first. The bow tipped up and slowly lowered at a forty-five-degree angle, tilting to starboard.

Many of the loose items in the wheelhouse fell toward the back with the pull of gravity. On the countertop, the opened whiskey bottle, Hal's last prized item, fell on its side, spilling its contents.

CHAPTER
9

Golden brown whiskey splashed down into the three-ounce glass, leveling off at the rim. Forster held the glass up, eyeballing her tiny reflection. She sat by herself at the far side of the counter in a bar called *Lionfish*. Brown lights hung from the ceiling, mixed with yellow lights to produce a gold-like shine. This detail annoyed her. Assuming the place was named after the fish of the same name, they had the colors wrong. Lion fish were more red and white than brown. She had seen the owner slip in and out of the back hallway, where she presumed his office was located. The only employee present otherwise was the bartender, who kept to himself as he cleaned the counter. She ignored the drive to bring the inaccuracy to his attention, but immediately realized doing such a thing would be foolish.

She drank the whiskey. The burn down her throat was another reminder that she was no longer a drinker. She only managed to get a third of the glass down before stopping. She chased it down with some water, then checked her watch. It was approaching *11:00*. Her instinct screamed at her to return home and get some desperately needed sleep before getting up the next morning. However, this was a rare moment she was feeling truly relaxed and wanted to savor it. With last call being at midnight, she knew she had some time.

The bar was mostly empty, typical for a Monday evening. A few people sat at the booths, while a few more huddled at the bar. Night owls and retirees, most likely. As long as they didn't bother her, Forster didn't mind. Getting out in town was rare, with the tension between local residents and resort staff being so high. They most likely didn't recognize her as a resort employee. Whatever the case, she was just happy to be left alone. She slowly downed the rest of the glass, while trying not to think of the failures in her life that led to this misery. Day in and day out, her mind would fixate on the assault that ruined her career. She fantasized about somehow being able to travel back in time and do things differently. Of course, that fantasy only made the mental agony worse.

All I had to do was walk away. Her mind scolded her with this alternate choice. Sometimes it sounded as if her father was talking to her. It was those moments that made sleep hard to come by.

A slight buzz started setting in. It provided a small escape. Being a light weight drinker was helpful in this regard. It allowed her mind to drift away, although there was the mindful thought of how much whiskey she should consume. She recalled celebrating her doctorate, where it seemed to take a fifth of Bourbon to get her wasted. Prison certainly set her back. Now it seemed a few shots did the trick. But she didn't mind, as she appreciated the quick timing.

She heard the ringing sound from the front entrance, as a man entered the bar. She only saw him in her peripheral vision and didn't pay much attention beyond his basic looks. He was a well-dressed man in his forties, with a black shirt tucked into blue jeans. She heard him walk up to the bar. He didn't take a seat, rather he put both hands on the counter. She tilted her gaze toward him, curious. He didn't appear aggressive, but distressed. The bartender recognized him.

"You okay, Jeffrey?" he asked. Jeffrey shook his head.

"Do you know if Luke got my resumé?" he asked.

"I believe so," the bartender said. "I don't know what the status is. I don't think he's looking to…"

"Can I please speak with him?" Jeffrey said, cutting him off. The bartender paused, clearly unsure of what to say.

"He's a little busy at the moment. He's about to leave for the night."

"I just need a minute with him," Jeffrey said. His tone was very insistent. Realizing there was no quicker way to satisfy the individual, the bartender stepped around the corner to the hallway. Forster casually watched as he returned, followed by the manager. By the way the top few buttons of his dress shirt were unbuttoned, it seemed that the bartender wasn't lying when he said he was getting ready to leave. Forster finished her glass, unable to keep from overhearing the conversation.

"Hi Jeffrey, what can I do for you?" the manager asked.

"Hey Luke, I'm here to follow up on my application," Jeffrey said.

"Jeffrey, I told you before, I don't have anything for you, man," Luke the manager said. His voice displayed sympathy, but also a frank attitude. Subtle hints of desperation began to present in Jeffrey's body language; most notably, a small nervous shudder. It was not the answer he wanted.

"Luke, listen, Sir…" he paused, trying and failing not to sound desperate, "Listen, I haven't been bringing anything in to market. The fish just aren't there anymore. Now my wife received news that she might be getting laid off from the grocery store. I can do anything. I can even just do a few hours a week in back stock." Luke scrunched his face and shook his head.

"Listen, man, I'm sorry," he said. "Believe me, I want to help ya, but there's nothing here. I've already cut down the hours of most of my steady staff. Full time employees are now working part-time. If I add you in, it'll cut into their hours. You see how there's only a few people here? Business is down by a third, because people are in a similar predicament. I'm sorry." There was a slight nod from the bartender as he proceeded to wipe things down. Understanding there was no chance of finding work with the bar, Jeffrey backed from the counter.

"I understand," he said. "Thanks."

"I'm sorry, Bud," Luke the manager said. He left to return to his office. Jeffrey stood defeated for a moment. He turned to the door, then suddenly looked back, doing a double take at Forster. She could feel his eyes burning into her temple. She felt herself become suddenly alert. He slapped a hand down on the counter near her. She barely managed not to flinch. It was not her first unfriendly encounter with local residents. She looked up at him, more annoyed than confused at his actions.

"Can I help you?" she asked. She noticed his polite demeanor was gone, replaced by a hostile stance.

"I know who you are," he growled. "You're the marine biologist lunatic, who supposedly loves animals, who works for somebody who helps kill them. I saw that video of you kicking a shark today. Very friendly of you. What are you doing here?" Thirty seconds ago, Forster was feeling sympathy for the man. It had quickly rescinded.

"I *was* enjoying some peace and quiet," she said. "Something I don't seem to get very often."

"Good," he said. "'Cause you got no business being here. You assholes are the reason our fishing community is falling apart."

Normally, she would respond to these accusations by explaining that she had no knowledge of Felt's affiliation with Wan Industries, and equal knowledge of the illegal dumping of toxic waste until after it was discovered. But she had grown tired of explaining this to people who continued to hold any Felt employee responsible. Now it was instant anger when approached on the subject.

"Seeing that I can at least afford a drink, I'd say you're the one with no business being here." Hostility radiated from both of them. All eyes in the bar turned toward them. Jeffrey straightened his stance and creased a smile; it was not a friendly one.

"Oh, you have real nerve," he said. "Before you came to this island, I was doing great. My wife and I were bringing in decent incomes. Then your buddy gives Wan a place to dump her garbage, in exchange for a few extra bucks to build his so-called paradise." He held up his hands to mimic air quotes. "Now, we might have to foreclose our new house." He stopped and looked at the other patrons. He raised his voice as he spoke to the room. "Hey, guys! Everybody! You see this person here?! Are you aware this person works at Felt's Paradise?"

Some people didn't respond, intending to keep out of the quarrel. A few others, however, called out some derogatory comments toward Forster. Her temper gradually slipped away. The difficulty to find sleep did not help, nor did the intake of bourbon. She could feel her hands starting to shake from the adrenaline. She steadied herself and simply tried to pour another glass, hoping that Jeffrey would grow bored and go away.

"What? No more classy remarks?" he said. Clearly, her plan was not going to work. She turned her head slightly toward him, just enough to look him in the eye.

"Listen pal, I'm sorry about your situation," she said, "but if you don't move along, it's gonna get a helluva lot worse." A mocking "Oooooooooh" sound echoed across the room from many of the patrons in unison. The bartender was the only person who appeared particularly uncomfortable. He moved over to Forster's end of the counter.

"Listen, guys, can we please break this up?" he asked. He looked up to Jeffrey. "Jeff, come on man, I know she's just a…" he cut himself off for a quick moment, though Forster already knew he was going to say something unfavorable toward her. "It…it's just not worth it, man. Just go home, alright?"

Forster started to sip on her glass. Jeffrey reached down and slapped it out of her hand.

"Hey! I'm talking to you, bitch…."

A hard left cracked his front teeth, quickly followed by a right to his stomach. Jeffrey found himself bent over as if about to puke, with a hand covering his bloody mouth, and another on his bruised gut. He barely had time to groan as Forster lifted her right knee into his face. It nearly flattened his nose, and put him on his back. He hit the edge of a square table on his way down. It crashed down, sending a full pitcher of beer falling down on his head.

In a manner like *déjà vu,* the memory of the assault on her teammate came flooding back. The blood on his face, the painful yells, the hands covering his injured areas. Then there was one last thing; the inevitable group of people who immediately responded to the fellow's aide.

Many of the patrons stood up and marched over. A couple went over to Jeffrey, while others stood across from Forster, seemingly in a standoff. The manager burst from his office and saw the chaos unfolding.

"What the hell's going on here!" he yelled.

Forster eyeballed the many people who stared her down. Clearly, they didn't care for the circumstances of the incident. They instantly took sides with their fellow fisherman. A few women stood behind the group of men.

"Get her out of here," one of them said, pushing her man forward. With fists clenched, Forster looked him in the eye.

"You next?"

****

Images of red and blue flashes seemed to burn into Forster's eyes as she sat in the back seat of the blue patrol SUV. The flashers illuminated the side of the building, alternating between red and blue while a couple of deputies stood outside the vehicle. She had watched them take statements from multiple patrons. While they did so, she couldn't help but heckle each one to herself, knowing they were giving a sob story of how the nice, poor fisherman, who is down on his luck because of the fishing crisis, was viciously assaulted by the mean Felt employee. She was already aware of the high probability that everybody was giving a biased account of the incident. Her only concern was that some of these deputies might possibly be just as biased, and choose to believe them. There was nothing she could do but sit, with her hands cuffed behind her back.

She glanced to the right of the vehicle, where an ambulance was parked close by. Inside its large square box, Jeffrey was being looked over by two paramedics. On his way in, she clearly heard him lie, flat out, that she assaulted him 'out of nowhere'.

Forster kept quiet, and also kept calm. With it not being her first time cuffed in a police vehicle, she had a good idea of what to do. Her main relief was that Chief Nelson was on scene, speaking with Luke the manager inside the bar. She witnessed his animated antics as he shouted at the Chief about the damage she caused. The phrase that stood out the most was his desire to press charges. That didn't bother her so much as the expression on Nelson's face when he realized that she was the suspect. It was a combination of shock, displeasure, and worst of all, disappointment. Though he was only twelve years older than

Forster, it still made her think of the disappointment her father likely would feel. That was worse than any jail sentence or fine.

For what seemed like forever, Nelson conducted his interviews inside the bar. At first, Forster was anxious to find out what was going to happen. Now, in a police vehicle of all places, she found herself starting to drift off. Images of dreams started glimmering, intermingled with sights and sounds of real life. Then, finally, she snapped back into reality after hearing Chief Nelson exiting the bar. He was anything but the bumbling, confused cop she had helped earlier. His very presence exuded authority. The manager stepped out after him, stopping just outside the entrance as Nelson proceeded down the steps.

"Okay fine!" he called down. "But still, she is not permitted in my business! I own this bar, and I reserve the right to refuse service to anyone I choose! We don't serve her kind!" Nelson scoffed, not bothering to look back at him.

"Alright, I'll let her know," he said. The manager stepped back inside, slamming the door behind him. Nelson walked to Forster's side of the vehicle and opened the door. She looked up at him.

"I guess this wouldn't be a good time to call you Joe, huh?" she remarked. He didn't laugh. Forster realized the humor was not going to do her any good. She shrugged her shoulders and sighed. Nelson gestured for her to step out. She planted her feet on the ground and stood out of the car. Her knee still ached from the fight. "So, what's going on? Am I getting charged, or what?" Chief Nelson stepped behind her and removed her cuffs.

"Believe me, that's all he wanted," he said. "Same with Jeff. Thanks to me, that's not the case. I had him show me the video feed." What he omitted was the manager's initial refusal to show the footage, knowing it would display the truth of the matter. Only when Nelson insisted that he needed to see it in order to complete an investigation, did the manager reluctantly comply. "I looked at it, and I saw the whole thing. The guy touched you first. Simple as that."

Forster moved her wrists to ease out the strain from the cuffs. "Well, I guess that's that." Chief Nelson raised a finger.

"Oh yes, he wants me to tell you…"

"I'm not allowed here anymore," Forster completed his sentence. "Yeah, I heard him. Interesting decision considering he insists his business is losing money. But whatever." She looked around for her car, until she remembered she parked at the end of the lot. She turned to Nelson. "I'm assuming I'm free to go?" Nelson nodded. "Sorry for the trouble. Thanks for your help." She started walking away.

"Hey, Julie?" Nelson called back to her. She slowed down and looked back, allowing Nelson to catch up to her. They both continued walking down the lot. "So, what the hell were you thinking, hanging out over here tonight?" She grimaced.

"What do you mean?"

"Gimme a break. You know exactly what I mean," he said.

"What? Am I under house arrest, or something? Is there some law against me going anywhere other than home or work?"

"No. But with everything that's going on, did you not think that anything was going to happen?" Forster stopped and faced him.

"You want to know why I was here? First, I haven't been here before, so I thought I wouldn't be recognized. Second; my phone doesn't get a signal over here. I couldn't sleep at home, because every half hour I would get texts or phone calls from either Felt, or one of the aides at the aquarium. I can't get any sleep."

"You think I don't know what that's like?" Nelson said, pointing at himself. "Why do you think I'm here right now? I was finally getting some decent sleep when I get a personal call from Luke in there," he pointed back to the bar. Both a pro and con of being an island police chief, every person knew him almost on a first name basis and knew how to get in touch with him personally.

It was a reversal of earlier that afternoon. Now, for the first time, Nelson spoke to her with exasperation; something she was not used to. Normally, whenever they encountered each other, it was laughs and good times. But the stress of both their lives had caught up with them.

Forster slapped her hands against her sides.

"What do you want from me?" she said. "I get your life has gotten more miserable on this island, like everyone else apparently. You think I'm having a blast? I can't get out of my house without getting in some sort of trouble. I can't stand my job right now, and I definitely hate being here. But I can't leave, not without getting myself a welfare plan. I'm stuck. What can I say?"

"I just want you to take care of yourself," he said. "I'm not convinced you're just here to get away from work and home." Forster shook her head, acting confused.

"I don't know what you're getting at…"

"You've told me about your dad, and I know of the ups and downs in your life," Nelson said. "I can put two-and-two together. You could've turned your phone off at home. I think I know what your idea was, coming here." Forster took a big step back. Another angry grimace creased every corner of her face. How dare he even consider that she would try and drink her problems away. Whether it was the truth was irrelevant.

"You know what…get a life…*Joe*," she said. She turned and marched to her vehicle with large strides. Nelson didn't bother following her. His concern grew. When reviewing the footage, he was able to watch her for several minutes until the brawl started. She was by no means an alcoholic, but he knew how these things often began. After all, he'd been there himself. And he had no doubt Forster was miserable and depressed enough. Her tires screeched as she sped out of the parking lot, and her rearview lights faded from view as she drove down the road.

Finally, he turned back and walked toward the ambulance to have his talk with Jeffrey.

CHAPTER
10

Security Officer Patrice completed his seventeenth tour of the park and aquarium. The front main entrance was his start and end point. He put his hand to his mouth to shield a yawn, then felt foolish for displaying good manners with nobody around. There were only two other employees who regularly worked during the night: a building maintenance worker and a custodian.

Patrice checked his watch. *4:13* a.m. Under three hours until shift change.

Working the midnight shift was about nothing but repetition. When he first started working at Felt's Paradise, a single tour around the facility took over fifty minutes. It helped with making the time go by. However, learning the area took a little extra time. Four months after his hire, it now only took him thirty minutes. Now the shift was a drag.

He eyeballed the front doors to the aquarium. Another coffee was in order. It served two purposes; keeping him awake, and to kill more time. In addition, the employee lounge had computers with internet. Since his iPhone couldn't connect, it was an additional incentive.

Patrice removed his key from his belt loop and let himself through the front entrance. He took a left turn to the nearest stairwell, and hurried upstairs to the employee lounge.

"Alright, he's inside!" Ben said, lowering his binoculars from his eyes.

"Shhhh!" Scott swiftly turned toward him, rocking the twelve-foot johnboat. "Not so loud," he said in a whisper. Hidden in the dark, they had waited in the small boat for two hours, waiting for a proper opportunity to sneak ashore. Rowing the boat from around the peak of the East Peninsula took almost another hour. It was the only available alternative to the noisy engine of Scott's fishing boat.

"His last two breaks inside the building were roughly thirty minutes," Ben said. They had watched the guard make his rounds, timing each one out as well as the occasional pass from any other crew.

"Hopefully that's as long as he takes this time," Scott said. He took a breath. Hopefully they would time their sabotage just right. Dressed in black sweatpants and long john shirts, they looked as if they were trying to dress as ninjas. Completing the image, they pulled black sock masks over their faces, knowing they would likely be caught in the security feed. Scott was aware of their pathetic appearance, but his eye was on the prize: releasing that great white and subsequently catching it. "Alright, bring us in. And keep it quiet."

Ben tapped the oars into the water and pushed them toward the deck. The dim walkway lights cast a small reflection on the metal bow. Pulling up near the deck, they wrapped a line around one of the posts. Ben was the first to climb out, causing the boat to rock back and forth.

"SHHH!" Scott hissed again. Ben whipped back toward him.

"Will you knock it off?! Your 'shush' is louder than anything I'm doing," he hissed back. It wasn't often Ben would talk back to Scott. When it did happen, it effectively silenced the latter, despite being the employer. Scott climbed onto the deck. Ben took a step forward, and then stopped nervously. Normally, the slight creaking noise from the boards would hardly be noticeable. However, in the dead of night...and in the midst of a crime...it might as well have been an air raid alarm. Ben looked, keeping an eye out for any employees. Losing his patience, Scott nudged him along.

"Come on, go," he said. Ben took each step, barely separating his foot from the deck until they were on the cement. They looked out into the pool, wondering if they could see the shark. The dark kept it out of view, which meant they would be unable to tell whether it exited the pool once they'd opened it. Scott anticipated this, and had brought along some bloody bits of chum to help coax it out once they got the doors open.

That, however, was the initial challenge. The doors, as well as the entire enclosure, were made of solid metal over eighteen inches thick. There was no way they were going to break through them, which immediately voided their backup plan. This left their initial plan of using the control panel. The panel was located just inside the railing, looking like a high-tech podium. Ben, who was the savvier of the two when it came to technology, walked up to it.

"Suckers," he said. "Of course, they would conveniently have this thing right next to the pool."

"Well, it's supposed to be a rehabilitation tank, designed for whales. That was the original intent when they got this shark," Scott said. "At least, that's what I heard from someone. I guess animal rights nutcases don't usually try to break into these kinds of centers."

Scott moved the plastic cover, designed like that of an outside grill to protect it from water splashes, and observed the control design. It was similar with a computer keyboard, with a small screen on top which immediately read *Loading...*

The time it took for the system to load seemed like forever. Ben nervously looked around again. So far, nobody was nearby. Every so often, he'd jump at a slight noise, only to discover it was a couple of seagulls hopping about near the drop-off. Finally, the system indicated it was ready. Ben examined the buttons again. He brushed his finger over several different commands; *filtration cleansing; circulation flow; elevate floor level; Water Pump OFF/ON*. Finally, he located a button that simply read *door*. He pressed it, and the screen listed various commands for the door. He tapped the top left button on the touch screen.

Please scan ID card.

"Son-of-a-bitch!" Ben cursed. Scott stepped over to him.

"What? It won't let you open it?" he asked.

"No," Ben said. He sighed heavily. "It needs an ID card in order to open it." He pointed at a black card swipe located on the side of the panel. A small red light blinked, indicative of its demand. "I don't know what else to do..." he stopped and thought for a moment. A malicious idea came to mind...one that could get them into deeper trouble than what they possibly had signed up for. He faced Scott to express his idea. However, he recognized the look in his boss' eye.

"You thinking what I'm thinking?" Scott asked. Ben nodded.

"You sure you want us to do this? If this goes south, this could land us in real deep…"

"This fella I know is willing to pay big bucks for this fish," Scott said, with heavy emphasis on the word *big*. It was a lie, as he had never spoken to his associate on the matter. In fact, Scott had no clue of the delicacy of great whites, but figured they had to be a top dollar menu item. At this moment, already in the act of committing a burglary of sorts, he deliberately allowed the wishful thinking to take over. "So yeah, I'm damn sure. How much longer until that guy should be coming out?"

Ben looked at his watch, "Based on our guess, probably fifteen minutes." He looked around for anything to use as an instrument. His eyes went to the boat oars. "Ah-ha!"

****

Officer Patrice downed his second coffee for the break; fifth overall for the night. He turned his eyes off his *eBay* account and looked at his watch. *4:42.*

"Oh, shit," he said to himself, realizing he once again let time get away from him. He grabbed his paper log and jotted down that he was beginning his next tour. After grabbing his jacket, he rushed downstairs and came to those double doors. He pushed one open and stepped outside.

Immediately he saw a man, dressed completely in black, standing up ahead to his one o'clock. Patrice froze for a brief moment as he absorbed the sight of the masked individual.

"Hold it right there," he said, pointing a finger at the intruder. He reached for the mobile phone attached to his duty belt. Just then, another image came to view. A momentary flash of wooden brown, oval in shape, crowded his vision. He barely felt the oar slam into his face, as he was instantly knocked into unconsciousness.

Ben stood over the downed guard and raised the oar over his head, as if posing to a stadium audience.

"Oh! It is out of here!" he exclaimed.

"Dude, knock it off!" Scott scolded him again. Ben froze, realizing how audible he was. "Get his tag," Scott ordered. Ben rolled the guard onto his back and tore the tag from the shirt pocket. He removed it from the plastic cover and slid it through the swipe on the control unit. The tiny red light turned to green.

"Yes," Ben said to himself, throwing his arms victoriously in the air again. Even Scott allowed himself to laugh a bit. They could hear a few mechanical sounds as the gears started to push the door open. Then a large yellow light flashed on both far corners of the pool, joined by a loud beeping sound like that of a back-up beeper. The mechanical gears grew louder as well, and the doors separated. Scott and Ben quickly stopped their celebration, and simultaneously looked at each other. Each was as alert as the other. Without saying a word, they hurried to their boat before somebody would hear the device.

It didn't take long. The building maintenance person rushed from the park area. The brief sprint already had the overweight worker out of breath, but it got worse once he came around the corner and saw Patrice laying on the ground.

"Oh Christ!" he yelled and rushed to the guard's aid. Though bleeding from his mouth and nose, Patrice was breathing fine. He began moving his arm as he slowly stirred awake. The maintenance worker had just knelt by him when he realized what the flashing yellow light meant on the pool. The doors were all the way open at this point. "Oh shit! Oh, no!" He ran to the panel. "No! No! No! No! No!" One was said with each step. He ran to the panel and instantly started tapping the button to close the door. "Come on, come on!" He tapped the button relentlessly, then realized the red flashes on the swipe. He tore his tag off of his shirt and ran it through the device. The buttons turned to green, and the doors slowly started to close.

It was then he realized he was too late. The flickering yellow lights cast a shine on the huge dorsal fin as the fish made its way out into the bay. The worker ran to the dock, trying to get a better visual of the shark. As he looked further out, he noticed the slight reflection of something in the water. He realized he was looking at the stern of a small metal boat. He drew his flashlight and pointed it out. It was dim, but he could just see the two men in the boat, dressed in black, looking back at him.

"Hey!" the worker called out. There was the sound of a motor starting up, followed by the droning sound of the propellers going into gear. Soon the boat and its occupants were out of view.

He returned the light to the water. He barely caught a tiny splash from the shark's tail as it traveled out. Digging into his pockets, the worker pulled out a phone and hurriedly dialed some numbers. He hit *send*, cursing repeatedly under his breath as he waited.

"Come on, come on! Pick up! Pick up!"

CHAPTER
11

Repeated vibrations from the iPhone drummed against the wooden dresser. Forster lifted her face from her pillow and blindly reached for it. Through her blurred vision, she read Felt's name on the caller ID. The call ended just as she went to answer it.

"Shit!" she said. A box appeared on her screen, showing four missed calls, all by Felt. She worried that she overslept until she read the time. *6:08* a.m., only seven minutes from the time on her alarm clock. The phone started ringing again.

"Hello?" she answered.

"Hey, what took you so long to answer your phone?!" Felt said.

"Well, sorry, it was on vibrate and…"

"Never mind," Felt interrupted her. There was urgency to his voice. *"Not important. I need you to come here right away!"* Forster fell back into the bed, already feeling frustrated.

"Oh, don't tell me you picked up another damn dolphin," she said.

"The shark escaped!" Felt said. Forster sat up, suddenly feeling completely awake and alert.

"What?"

"It escaped! It's gone!" At this point, he was practically in hysterics. *"Some guys came in through the bay and opened the pool!"* Forster stood up and immediately started getting herself ready to leave. She snatched up some clothes from the dresser and threw them on the bed, then rushed to the sink and slapped some cold water to her face, all while still on the phone.

"Alright, relax," she started to speak. Felt cut her off almost immediately.

"Relax?! How can I relax? If that thing injures somebody, we're certainly going to be held liable."

"Re-lax!" she emphasized each syllable. "First of all, shark attacks on humans don't happen as frequently as you might believe."

"Oh…well uh," Felt fumbled for something to say. The urgency in his voice was still there. Forster knew what the real concern was; Felt believed that the great white had become the main attraction in the resort, and was worried about increased drop in revenue.

"Listen," Forster said. "First, get a grip. Second, is the tracking device still functioning?" There were several moments of silence.

"Tracking device…uh," he mumbled, clearly having no clue of what she was talking about. Felt was strictly a businessman, good with numbers. But when it came to the actual inside work, he was clueless.

"The shark had a tracking tag installed when we first acquired it," Forster said.

"It does?" his voice suddenly contained slight composure.

"I'll get on the research computer on the *Neptune*, and I can track it. Let me get my act together and I'll be right over."

"*Hurry up,*" Felt said, and he immediately hung up. Forster tossed the phone onto her bed and went back to the sink. She dipped her hands into the water. Her knuckles on her left hands, scraped from where they chipped two front teeth, stung from the water's touch. It was a fresh reminder of last night's encounter, which itself was a reminder of her constant misery from which there seemed no escape.

She didn't waste time thinking about it, nor did she waste time showering. She tore her clothes off and changed into some white Softshell pants and a black hoodie. Though it was likely going to be another hot summer day, she knew she would be out on the water for most of it.

After grabbing some on-the-go items, she hurried out the door.

I've been awake for ten minutes, and already I'm in for a shitty day.

****

The sun had fully peaked as Forster arrived. Cars flooded the lot as employees rapidly arrived to start the day. Tourists were making their way about the resort. The rides were just starting to open up, and the main doors to the aquarium should have been unlocked by now. This early in the morning, the majority of tourists normally would dine at the restaurants or relax at the pools. However, it would only be a matter of time before they made their way to the aquarium, and subsequently the Great White Exhibit. Forster could only imagine the public reaction to the news of the shark's escape. Undoubtedly, it was something on her employer's mind.

She stepped out of her car to find two police units nearby. When she arrived to the Great White Exhibit, she immediately noticed the barriers that had been put in place. A large sign read; *Great White Exhibit temporarily closed for Maintenance.* Clearly, Felt didn't want it made public that the shark was gone. Forster knew that lie wouldn't last long.

The first face she saw was Chief Nelson. He stood by the barriers and immediately saw her, as if he was waiting specifically for her. He looked as tired and irritable as she was. Most likely, he had slept just as well, and was probably awoken under the same circumstances. He held two coffees, one of which he sipped out of. As she approached, he extended the other out to her.

"Checking up on me now, are you?" Forster remarked. The stone-like expression on Nelson's face conveyed no sense of humor.

"Give me a break," Nelson said. "I'm obviously here for the…"

"Relax, Chief. I'm just busting your chops," Forster said. She took the coffee. "Thanks."

"No, problem," he said. "And, uh, sorry." He suddenly felt embarrassed. "Had to get here so fast I didn't have time to make a pot. Figured you had the same predicament. Cream and sugar, right?"

"You've gotten to know me well," she said. She took a sip. *Oh, very well!* Judging by the sweetness, it was loaded with extra sugar. Exactly what she needed. She started walking toward the dock, and Nelson followed. "So, did the security feed show anything?"

"Two guys came in by boat. Knocked out the guard, took his tag, opened the pool, and took off. Nothing to ID them, unfortunately. They were dressed in black, with masks. So far, we've found no prints. It appeared they were wearing gloves as well. We've sent the tape to Forensics, but I'm sure they'll have the same luck." They arrived at the *Neptune*, and Forster climbed onto the deck. Nelson remained on the dock as she readied the boat, figuring it was best if he stayed out of the way. "If I may ask, what are you planning to do?"

"Felt expects me to track the shark and bring it back in," she said. She dipped into the wheelhouse and came out with a long pole. At the end of it was a hypodermic needle. Nelson felt mildly nauseous at the sight of it.

"How do you plan on tracking it?" he said, gulping his coffee.

"The shark was initially brought in as a rescue animal. Anything we rehabilitate that's over a hundred pounds usually gets a tracking device so we can monitor its status once it's released. Not that Felt expected me to actually track the thing, but it looked good for the papers." She checked some vials, and moved some containers off to the side. She went into the wheelhouse and started digging about. Nelson downed the rest of his coffee and finally climbed aboard.

"You need any help?" he finally asked.

"No thanks," she said. "I have my own way of doing things here." Nelson realized his first instinct was correct, but decided to remain on deck. "Anyways," she continued, "we were able to get authorization to keep the shark because its fins contained irreversible injury from the net it had been caught in. Really, it was nothing that prevents the shark from performing properly, as demonstrated yesterday. But Felt managed to exaggerate its condition to Wildlife Control, and they gave the green light for it to be contained indefinitely. So, it's Felt's property, and I have to go get it."

"All by yourself?" Nelson asked. Forster nodded.

"No choice. My assistant was injured last night and is still in the hospital." She started wondering how Marco was doing. She shook the thought from her mind. "So, I don't have anyone else."

Nelson felt a flood of concern. Forster going out on her own? Of course, she seemed to know what she was doing, and appeared to be okay with it. But then again, she acted like she was okay with a lot of things, and Nelson knew that wasn't truly the case.

"You know, maybe you should…" he stopped as William Felt climbed up onto the boat. He had his usual insistent demeanor, as he had all morning.

"Ah, Julie, there you are!" he exclaimed. "I'm glad you're here. Things have been chaotic here." His attempt to be sincere was as pathetic as it was false.

"Tell me about it," Forster said in a dry tone. Felt clasped his hands together at his waist and stood silent for a moment. Though she didn't look directly at him, Forster could read his body language. He wanted to ask her something but seemed hesitant. "What is it, Will?" she said.

"Uh, well I, uh…. I was just curious when you were planning to ship out?"

"As soon as you get me some bait," Forster answered without skipping a beat. Felt stood dumbfounded. She noticed this, and looked at him directly. "You do realize I need that to draw the shark in?" Felt made a nervous smile.

"Of course!" he said. "I was just getting someone to head over to the butcher. The white certainly liked that beef yesterday." His nervous chuckle ended when he remembered that yesterday's incident wasn't funny. Rather than risk saying anything more foolish, he simply climbed down. Nelson quickly followed him down.

"Mr. Felt?"

"Yes, Chief?" Felt answered, continuing to walk to the aquarium building.

"Do you have any other assistants for Julie? She's planning on going out on her own, and I don't think that's safe."

"I don't believe so," Felt said. Each word was long and drawn out, as he knew Nelson wouldn't like his answer. "The aides are only trained in caring for some of the animals here, but none have any nautical training. At least, not to my knowledge."

"Not one?" Nelson asked. "And you're okay with just sending her out there? It's a two-person job at least." Felt stopped and turned toward him. His face expressed severe irritation.

"You telling me how to run this business, Chief?" he growled.

"No, sir," Nelson said. "I'm just advising you of the situation."

"Listen, Chief, it is not your concern. Ms. Forster is a very capable woman, and I have the utmost confidence she will successfully return the shark to my facility. Rather than worry about that, you should be focusing on who broke into my park last night."

"We're already working on it, Mr. Felt," Nelson said.

"Good," Felt said. "Now if you'll excuse me…" without finishing his sentence, he turned and walked away. Nelson saw him speak to an employee, likely giving instructions to go into town and pick up some bait for Forster.

A thought came to mind: *Maybe I should tag along.* Today was not a busy day in terms of administrative schedule. No meetings or seminars. Although he didn't consider himself a seasoned sailor, he understood how to work on a boat. Most importantly, he could make sure she'd be safe.

He returned to the *Neptune* and climbed up on deck. Forster had just stepped out of the wheelhouse.

"Well, hell," Nelson said. "You shouldn't be going out there alone. Just let me finish up here, and I'll head out with you. I know my way around a boat." Forster chuckled; not quite the response he was hoping for.

"Yeah? What are you gonna do? Arrest the shark if he doesn't agree to come in?" She laughed. Nelson didn't. "No offense, Chief, but I tend to work better by myself."

Nelson didn't trust that she was telling the complete truth. He suspected she was avoiding possible conversation regarding last night's incident. However, he felt adamant that she should not be out by herself.

"Listen, I'm no Marine Biologist, and I've never worked on a research boat. But, looking at all of this, you're gonna need somebody to drive the boat at some point, or look at the monitor. Or just to do the heavy lifting. Or you might need somebody to…" he fumbled for things to say, "Okay, I don't know what I'm talking about. But, obviously you would normally take Marcus along. Just pretend I'm him."

Forster searched for reasons to say no. However, what he said was actually true. Although she would love the peace and quiet of being on her own, it wouldn't be so peaceful once she sedated the shark. At the very least, she would need somebody at the helm while she applied the tow line. Still, she was tempted to say no.

It was nothing personal against Nelson. In fact, in this entire island, he was probably the only person who truly gave her respect. It meant more to her than she would show. Deep down, she was worried she would do something to screw that up. Hence, she was still upset about the previous night.

But it was more than that. This assignment was just another reminder that she was doing something far below her potential. 'High tech monkey work,' is how she thought of it. It was another torture for somebody who wanted to research and explore; to make a real difference in the world of science. Instead, she was basically wrangling a zoo animal, whose condition had so improved that it really ought to be in the open ocean. And it would be if not for a technicality brought up by Felt. She was working against her own belief system in a job that didn't live up to her standards.

Having Nelson on board to witness her misery just made it seem more real. But at the end of it all, she had to face reality. It was a job that needed to be done, and the *Neptune* was a large vessel. She would need help of some kind.

"Wouldn't it be imposing on you?" she asked.

"I've got nothing going on," Nelson said. "We'll just consider this a police escort." He made a small joking laugh. Forster made a small grin as a way of accepting his offer.

"We'll be shipping out once Felt gets me the bait," she said. "You'll probably want to dress into something different." Nelson looked at his uniform and understood her point. It would be a shame to get chum all over his trousers and shirt.

"Give me twenty minutes," he said.

CHAPTER

12

It was forty minutes when Nelson had returned. He had timed the trip home and back almost perfectly, until he realized he needed to pick up Dramamine. Luckily, it had taken that long for Felt to gather the items that Forster needed. Dressed in jeans and a thin sweater, he helped with loading the tubs of bait on deck while Forster tested the crane. Shortly after, they were off.

The *Neptune* cut through open water with the ease of a rocket through space. Nelson found the endless stretches of blue very peaceful. According to Forster's computer, the great white had already traveled a few miles out. Pariso Marino looked like a thin grey bump in the distance behind them.

Forster alternated her gaze between the bow and the monitor. She hadn't exchanged many words with Nelson since they cast off. A headache had set in from lack of sufficient sleep, and there were still the awkward leftover feelings from the trouble he had gotten her out of last night. She focused heavily on the task at hand, more so for the benefit of getting it out of her mind.

"It's about a mile out now," she said. "Northeasterly direction." Nelson looked in that direction, off the starboard bow.

"Is that the green light to start chumming?" he asked. Forster stepped from the helm and peeked out the door.

"You sure you'll be okay with that?"

"I promise, I'm fine," he insisted. Forster was used to people getting nauseous around the chum. While the sight was unpleasant to say the least, it was usually the smell that drove assistants over the edge. For Nelson, however, it was nothing compared to things he had seen in his fourteen years in Miami PD. Gang violence was not uncommon, and often hits would be carried out at the target's private residence. Bodies would usually be found after baking in the Florida heat for numerous days, and as a cop, he would have to preserve the crime scene. This would mean spending hours with a foul, rotting corpse until it was cleared to be taken to the morgue. Compared to that, chilled fish guts did nothing.

Forster brought the boat to a stop then stepped out to the bow deck to drop anchor. She stepped back into the wheelhouse and brought out two computer monitors. One displayed what appeared to be a radar image, with their boat in the middle and a blinking dot to the upper right corner. The other one showed a dark image from one of the underwater cameras. She placed both laptops on a table, and secured them to it with clamps. Nelson watched her do this and then walk toward the crane. She rolled up her sleeves and opened the large metal storage container. She reached down and groaned as she lifted the heavy piece of meat. Nelson stood up for a moment, instinctively to help.

"I can get that…"

"I'm fine," she said. She strung a rope to it, which itself was clipped to the end of a cable. Nelson continued chumming.

"I know I'm oblivious to shark hunting," he said, "so could you tell me what the plan is?" He threw a scoop out into the water.

"With that chum, you're going to draw him in," she said. "When he gets close, we're gonna dip that beef into the water, just enough to force him to raise his head high enough to bite it. Basically, the proper version of Felt's stunt, yesterday. When he comes up, I'm gonna hit him in the mouth with this." She grabbed a black pole with a long syringe needle at the end. Nelson winced at the sight of it.

"Won't that piss him off?" he asked.

"He won't even feel it," she said. It didn't make Nelson feel any better. Looking at the pole, he realized it was the size of a broom handle.

"Still," he said, "you'll have to reach out pretty far with it."

"I'll be fine," Forster said. Judging by her tone, she had heard the same thing from other people equally uneducated in her field. "The tranquilizer will take effect fairly quickly afterwards."

"That sounds easy enough, then," Nelson said.

"That is the easy part," Forster said. She put down the pole and started walking back to the wheelhouse. "Afterwards, I have to dive down after it and secure the towing harness. Sharks sink when they're not moving. If I don't act fast enough, it'll drown." This time, Nelson's eyebrows lifted. That feeling of worry crept back up, and he had to fight the near irresistible urge to ask her why she would do that. He already knew the answer she would give him. He just hoped it wasn't anything else.

Forster stepped back into the wheelhouse. She shut the door behind her and closed the blinds over the front windshield and windows.

Minutes later, she came back out, dressed in black scuba gear. In her hand was a compressed air tank. She quickly tested the airflow and checked her goggles before setting them next to her flippers. She then grabbed the control unit for the crane. She lifted the beef and gently swung it over the portside, just over Nelson's head. Nelson ducked when he saw it pass above. He then felt stupid, realizing it was at least ten feet above him.

"Nice one," Forster said. She adjusted the crane until it held the package just above the bloody water. For the next couple of minutes, she watched the monitor nearby. The blip remained in the same general location. It would probably take a bit of time for the white to become interested. "So…were you able to get any sleep last night?" It was the type of question to spark small talk and fill the dead air. Nelson just wished it was a different subject. Forster did too. She had simply asked the first thing that came to mind.

"Not much," he said. "I had to write a couple of reports. Get Jeffrey to settle down, and then get his wife to settle down. She was more pissed than he was, I think. Then of course, I wake up to a phone call around five about these guys who let this shark out. So, no, I'm operating on coffee mostly." Forster now felt foolish for being tired. At least she got a few hours in. Also, there was shame, as she was part of the reason Nelson got almost none. In addition, here he was helping her when he should be home.

"You should've gone home, then," she said. "Taken a sick day." Nelson just shrugged his shoulders nonchalantly and mouthed 'nah'. "Seriously," she said, "I would've been okay. Why were you so eager to come out here?" Nelson stopped chumming and looked at her questioningly.

"I just didn't think you should be doing this alone," he said. "It just sounded like dangerous business."

"Is that what it was?" she said. He could tell she suspected an alternate motive. He felt an uncomfortable apprehension as to what thoughts were going through her mind.

"Yes," he said.

"It's just that you seemed awfully eager to come out here with me," Forster said. "After what happened last night...sorry, I just am getting the feeling you're keeping tabs on me." Nelson stood up to face her.

"Let me switch it around; why were you so anxious to come out here all by yourself?" Forster stared him down.

"Probably because...I'm the only one who can capture the shark? Didn't we discuss this?"

"Not really," he said. "Not thoroughly, anyway. You do realize the Coast Guard would've been able to pick it up, right?" Forster didn't answer. "I just worry that you had something else in mind, coming out here alone. That's all."

"And what would that be?" Forster questioned. He could see the anger building up in her eyes. It was a very specific body language that he recognized in people undergoing severe depression and exhaustion. He wasn't sure if he should give an honest answer in fear that it would light a fuse. Unfortunately, even the silence seemed to worsen her temper. "Come on, spit it out."

"I think I'll get back to chumming," he said.

"Oh, no," she walked over to him until she was almost nose to nose. "Tell me. Come on, I dare you."

"Don't do it," he said, and took a step back. Forster looked at him, almost puzzled as to what she meant. Then finally she saw her own clenched fist. She had balled her hands unconsciously, blinded by her own irrational anger. The anger gently subsided, and disbelief took over. She didn't even feel herself doing this.

"I, uh," she loosened her hands. "Chief, I...I wasn't going to..."

"Oh, yeah you were," he said. Her eyes welled up, and her mouth quivered. She backed away until she nearly fell into a seat, shocked at the extent of her rage, the lack of control she had, and how quickly she allowed it to escalate. She took a deep breath and regained control.

"I'm...I'm sorry, I..." she struggled to find a sentence. Nelson walked over to her.

"It was your dad's birthday yesterday, wasn't it?" he said. She looked up at him, slightly surprised that he knew, and nodded. "You told me," he answered her unspoken question. "That's why you were at the bar." It wasn't a celebration. She intended to get drunk, with a goal to forget it all. Nelson didn't bother explaining this, as they both already knew. "When we get back, I think you should tell Felt that you're gonna take some long overdue vacation. Take a boat to the mainland. Get out of here for a few days. You're exhausted, pent up, and stressed. Way stressed."

He was correct, and his suggestion sounded very good indeed. She knew she could certainly use some time away. However, she was uncertain it would become a reality.

"I like that idea," she said. "But I don't think it'll happen. I'm the only biologist working at that aquarium, and I don't see Felt approving the time. Besides…" she trailed off. Nelson knew what she was thinking of.

He went back to the chum bucket. "Tell you what, kid; when we get back, go to Felt and demand the time off. If he refuses, then I'll be sure to make his life a living hell."

"I guess I could stand a vacation," Forster said. She stood up from her chair, and for once, she felt as if a small weight had lifted. "Any suggestions on where I should go?"

"Anywhere but here," Nelson said. He tossed a scoop of chum into the water. "Probably somewhere with a nice beach. St. Simons, maybe. They have good fishing, though I don't know if you're into that." Forster made a smile, which suddenly went away as her eyes went towards the monitors. The blip on the tracking monitor was rapidly nearing their location. She then looked at the feed from the underwater camera. The image was blurry from the red dissipating cloud of chum, but the image of the white's caudal fin was unmistakable as it brushed past.

"Speaking of fishing…" she said. Both she and Nelson looked toward the water. The triangular dorsal fin pierced upward, and slowly guided along the surface like a sail.

CHAPTER
13

It had been over sixteen hours since the white had fed. A massive fish of twenty-four hundred pounds, it needed to consume approximately three percent of its body weight each day to survive. Free from its confinement, it spent greater amounts of energy in the past several hours than it had in the past several months combined. The burning of energy increased its need to supplement through sustenance intake.

The smell of blood would have been considered great timing if the shark had the intellectual capability to think so. It turned southwest and quickly neared the source. It stopped when it detected the presence of a larger object, but it quickly determined that the boat was not a threat. The great white darted through the blood cloud, swirling bits of fish through the water as it searched. It swallowed stray bits of flesh and entrails, but nothing nearly sufficient for its survival.

Then it sensed a disruption in the water above it. Its nostrils simultaneously picked up added scent of blood. It tilted its cone shaped head upward, and its round eyes saw the meaty bulk. It was partially suspended over the water, but it gave the white no concern. It moved upward, and bared teeth to tear away its meal.

With all of its senses being so focused on the target, the great white was completely oblivious to something else traveling in the water. Thirty feet below it, *Isurus Palinuridae* zipped viciously into the chum, looking for any injured organism. Unable to find anything, it analyzed the boat, as it had learned these objects carried suitable prey aboard. The greater capacity in size didn't bring disinterest, rather the hybrid considered the possibility of greater numbers. Its interest was slightly waned when it detected the displacement from the white. The hybrid kept a distance as it analyzed the shark. It was a creature of nearly equal size, but with flesh much softer. The beast knew it would provide much more adequate sustenance.

It held position and analyzed the great white's movements, just as it would for the targets its creators intended it for. If it could detect a pattern, it would launch a more effective attack.

****

Forster reeled in the winch just as the white breached. Water sprayed on deck as its pointed head lurched toward the beef. Its jaws snapped shut upon nothing, as the food was winched in out of reach. Nelson nearly jumped back, amazed and almost terrified from being in such close proximity of an amazing animal. It fell back down and began circling back. Water splashed again, slapping against Nelson's sweatshirt. Forster grabbed a scoop of chum and splashed it onto the meat for additional scent.

"Well, that was a dick move," Nelson said. "Why did you not let him have it?" Forster pointed at the shark as she moved back to the control.

"See what it's doing?" she asked. Nelson watched the dorsal fin moving outward, as if the shark had given up. "When I lower it again, he'll circle back. I need it to come up a little closer to the gunwale. Hopefully, the rope will hold on long enough for me to drug it." She lowered the beef down, then adjusted the crane slightly to help gain the shark's attention. The circling back from the dorsal fin proved the plan was working. She raised it up again about a foot above the water. "Come over here." Nelson walked over, and she handed him the control. "When I tell you to, hit this control. That'll raise it again."

"You're gonna make him miss again?" Nelson asked.

"No, but it'll cause him to come up further," Forster said. "I'll let you know when." She quickly grabbed the pole and stood by the portside rail. She looked down at the water below the bait. Except for the red tint from the dripping blood, it was almost crystal clear. Seeing the white emerge would be no problem. The fin disappeared as the shark dipped down. She watched between the monitor and the water.

Finally, there was the brief glimpse of its pectoral fin moving upward across the screen as it passed over the camera. She looked down. Beneath the clear water was the unmistakable grey shape.

"Now!" she said to Nelson. He pressed the button on the control pad. The winch reeled in the beef until it was level with the edge. Forster reached back with the pole, ready to plunge the tranquilizer into its jaw line.

Just as the great white's nose broke the surface, another shape came into view. All Forster could initially make out was a large red body and a black marble shaped eye before the water exploded.

****

Isurus Palinuridae strategically watched the white as it made its pass toward the boat. By not moving its tail, it allowed itself to sink in order to provide itself more momentum later.

The white, oblivious to the predator below watching it, dipped down as it moved back toward the beef. Its eyes locked onto the target, just in time to see it lifting once again above the water. It swung its tail to gain speed to catch it before it was out of reach.

At that same moment, the hybrid seized the opportunity. It slashed its tail against the water behind it, propelling the six-thousand pound killing machine upward at a fifty-degree angle. Eyes rolled back, as did its antennae, and the jaws opened to their maximum potential.

Only when the jaws sunk into its hide around the left pectoral fin did the great white sense the intruder. The beasts collided, with momentum driving both of them upward.

Forster yelled in terror while falling on her back, witnessing the great white lifted out of the ocean by the mysterious red shark. Both titans cleared the surface, sending a huge splash washing onto the *Neptune* like a tidal wave. In one terrified jump, Nelson found himself backed all the way to the starboard side, while watching the two creatures angle back down. The white's head smacked against the side of the boat, denting the railing, while the hybrid's tail slashed the crane. Sparks flickered and joints groaned as the mechanism was forced into a different position. The *Neptune* rocked viciously from the hit. In the same moment, another massive splash encompassed the boat as the two hit the water.

The white squirmed within the hybrid's grasp. Its blood filtered into the mouth that held it, enticing the hybrid further to finish the kill. It opened its jaws slightly and bit down again, creating several more dagger-like wounds. It moved rapidly in a tight circle, pushing the shark along. Swinging its tail harder, it gathered more speed and straightened its course.

Like an underwater wrestler, it rammed the great white into the side of the *Neptune*, denting the hull.

The impact rocked the vessel hard to starboard, nearly flipping it over entirely. Nelson and Forster fell to the deck and found themselves pulled to the side. The water came up to the gunwale and trickled down the inner side. The boat righted itself into position, rocking back and forth until it stabilized. It drifted in the direction of the anchor cable, causing it to slacken in large coils.

The hybrid shook the stunned white like a rag doll. Though they were nearly equal in size, the hybrid contained greater overall mass, and easily maintained the power to physically maneuver its prey. Finally, the pectoral fin tore away completely, leaving a gaping hole in the shark's left side. In a single gulp, it swallowed the appendage.

The great white, free of its grasp, quickly drifted several feet away. Its brain did not yet register the injury. Its only concern now was survival against a dangerous predator.

The hybrid moved in for another bite. The white swatted its tail, just in time to avoid the jaws. The hybrid missed, and turned to follow its prey. The white simultaneously turned to the left, hooking at a path that led to its enemy's hide. It extended its jaws and bit down just behind the red dorsal fin.

Teeth cracked and splintered against the rigid shell. White shards sprang from its mouth like shrapnel, and slowly spiraled to the ocean bottom. Having instantly lost several teeth, the white was only holding the target with its gums. Hardly a moment later, nerves in its mouth lit up after one of the protruding spines along the hybrid's back pierced its gums.

The white let go, and with no other alternative, decided to flee. It barely initiated its run when the hybrid turned itself toward it, and extended its jaws. Teeth sliced into the flesh where the caudal fin connected to the tail. The white, now bleeding from its side and tail, swung its entire body to-and-fro. The attempt to free itself proved ineffective.

The hybrid swallowed tiny bits of flesh that tore from the wound, while continuing to hold on as the white wore itself out. It slowly moved itself along, just enough to get a small flow of water through its gills. A shadow overtook the two fish as they started passing underneath the *Neptune*. The white continued tossing itself, eventually becoming entailed within the loops of cord.

Finally, the hybrid yanked its head back in a powerful motion. The entire caudal fin tore away, leaving a bleeding stump at the end of the white's tail. Now shaped like a bulky eel, the bleeding shark started to sink as it was unable to swim. Its body rolled like a log as it descended, furthering its entanglement within the cord.

Nelson helped Forster to her feet. "What the hell was that thing?" She shook her head, equally astounded and terrified.

"I don't know! It just came up...I've never seen anything like it!" She looked at the monitor connected to the camera feed. The screen was cracked, and the water had shorted the circuits. She then hurried into the wheelhouse and switched on the nearest computer. She clicked a button, flipping through camera images until she found something from the feed on the bow hull. She saw the white sinking, and the mysterious red shark moving in toward it. She noticed the anchor cord wrapping itself around the white's body as it rolled.

"Oh, shit!" she said.

The Hybrid sped forward, ramming the white downward. It bit down on the dorsal fin. The cord quickly went taut, squeezing the white's belly.

The *Neptune*'s bow dipped down and swung slightly to starboard like a fishing pole with a prized catch.

Forster and Nelson both stumbled again, this time rolling forward. Forster lost her footing and fell, cracking her forehead against the helm. Blood quickly trickled down her face.

"Oh, Jesus!" Nelson called out, hurrying to her side. He grabbed a dry handkerchief from his pocket and pressed it to the gash on her head. He looked up through the windshield. His body tensed again with fear when he saw water spilling over the bow rail.

The cord snapped. The *Neptune* lurched backward, tilting to stern and back. After it steadied, he brought himself to his feet. He lifted Forster off the floor. She was nearly unconscious. He moved several items off the table and laid her across it on her back. He rolled a towel and positioned it behind her head for support. She started to mumble gibberish.

"Shhh! Just relax, Julie. You'll be okay!" he said.

He quickly turned to the helm. Luckily, the engine was still on. He located the throttle and began moving the boat. His initial course of action was to alert an EMS squad by radio, but glowing orange lights on the control board gave him concern. The boat had likely suffered major damage during the assault. He turned the *Neptune* toward home and throttled at full speed.

With the island in distant sight, he grabbed the radio speaker.

"This is Chief Joseph Nelson of the Pariso Marino Police Department. Have an ambulance squad ready at the dock at Felt's Paradise!"

Below, the hybrid ripped away chunks of flesh from the dead great white. In a powerful motion, it tore the dorsal fin completely off and swallowed it, tracking device and all. Its body became camouflaged in the bloody water, as the red cloud engulfed the ocean around it.

CHAPTER
14

Blurry, contorted images flashed rapidly in her mind. She repeatedly saw ocean blue stretching out for miles. At that point, everything seemed peaceful. Then there was grey. At that point, the serenity steadily began to fade, and a shaky feeling of madness started to cast over like a storm cloud. She saw the image of the great white, and then a massive blur of blue. Only this time, it wasn't peaceful. It was explosive and chaotic. Then there was the red image of the mysterious leviathan. Teeth bared, it leapt from the water. The peaceful feeling was gone, and now everything seemed like an earthquake. The entire boat jolted, and seemed as if it would go under. The last thing she remembered was falling to the floor.

Adrenaline blasted through her veins.

"Shark!" Forster yelled. She sat up abruptly, nearly knocking the assisting RN to the floor in the process. The doctor hurried into the room.

"Whoa, whoa! Julie, you're alright! You're in a hospital!" he said. The nurse also quickly hurried to the bed to calm Forster down. Forster hyperventilated for a moment before realizing she was not on the *Neptune*. Her breathing quickly steadied, and she laid back in the bed. She looked at the doctor, a bearded man in his forties. He was about to administer a sedative, but held back after she started improving on her own. "Hi, Julie. I'm Doctor Ebraheim. How are you feeling?"

"How did I get here?" Forster asked.

"The police chief brought you to the harbor, and an ambulance brought you here an hour ago," he explained. "You've been in and out since you arrived."

"I don't remember," Forster said. She felt the bandage on her forehead. The pain set in, like a bad migraine. She winced and gritted her teeth.

"You suffered a good blow to the head when you fell," the doctor said. "You've got a couple of stitches, and a mild concussion. Luckily, it wasn't worse. I would suggest taking it easy for a while." Forster looked down at herself. She was dressed in a hospital gown, which was basically a thin sheet with hardly any weight to it. She immediately hated the bare feeling of not having any clothes on. The doctor understood what she was thinking. "I'm sorry, we had some aides get you out of the scuba gear you were wearing. They were constricting you too tightly."

"No, I understand," Forster said. It didn't make her hate being there any less. "Am I free to go, or..."

"This isn't a jail," the doctor joked. "I would advise resting for a few more minutes. Your clothes are here. The chief was kind enough to bring them from the boat."

"The Chief.... Joe!" Suddenly she worried that he was injured in the incident. "Where is he?" she asked.

"He's in the lounge," the doctor said. "He actually arrived a couple of minutes ago. There's word going on about the water being unsafe. I'm not sure what it's about, exactly."

Forster knew, however. A flood of images rushed through her mind, each of them clearer than those from her recent chaotic dream. She remembered the huge splash, and the glimpse of the mysterious red creature lifting the white from the water was burnt into her brain. There was a sense of dread that something so violent and powerful could exist. The shock of what unfolded right in front of her face still had her heart racing. There was also the curiosity of what that creature was. She only saw it for a moment, and she wasn't sure how accurate her memory was. The questions that lined up in her mind worsened the headache.

The doctor pulled a prescription pad from his coat pocket and scribbled on it.

"Here's a prescription for 800 mgs of Ibuprofen," he said. She took it from him and he turned to leave. "If you feel worse, feel free to come back."

"Thank you," she said. The doctor left and the nurse removed the IV lines. Once she had the room to herself, Forster got dressed into her clothes and steadily made her way down to the checkout counter. Once she checked out, she headed for the lobby. It didn't take long for her to find Chief Nelson. He stood at the far wall in the lobby, dressed in his police uniform. He had his cell phone to his ear, and had his free hand cupping his other ear to block out chatter from within the room. Forster waited for him to finish his conversation, which seemed an unpleasant one judging by his tone. After a few moments, he ended the call, then saw her standing there.

"Oh hey!" he said. "I was about to head up to your room."

"Oh, hell no," she said. "Not in that hospital gown." He smiled at her joke, and struggled to shake the image from his mind, though it wasn't a disagreeable one.

"How are you feeling?" he asked. Forster put her hand on her forehead.

"Hurts like a bitch," she said. "But I'll live." She looked toward the front door, which led to the parking lot. She remembered she didn't have her car. "Would you be so kind to take me back to work? My car's there."

"I'd be happy to," Nelson said. "I think you should take the rest of the day, at least. Perhaps it's a good time for you to plan that trip."

"Yeah, I think so. Nevertheless, I need to leave instructions for the aides," Forster said. She held up her prescription pad. "Just let me get this filled, first."

The trip from the hospital to the aquarium was a short, direct one. Forster had already taken one of her pills and prayed it would kick in soon. The pain throbbed in her forehead, and a little bit in her temple. Because of the pain, she hadn't spoken much throughout most of the fifteen-minute trip outside of minor small talk. But now, she could use anything to get the pain off her mind. She recalled Nelson's seemingly unpleasant phone conversation in the lobby.

"So, everything alright in your world?" she asked. Nelson glanced at her, unsure what she meant. "You seemed 'ecstatic' when I found you. Problems with the ol' lady?" It was a rhetorical joke; she knew he wasn't married.

"No, that would've been less a pain in the ass," Nelson said. "That was the Mayor. He's up my ass right now, because after you were taken by the ambulance, I tried to get an order out to ground all vessels." Forster's mind went back to the shark, and the damage it seemed to cause effortlessly.

"I'm guessing he didn't take well to that idea," she said.

"Nope." He shook his head. "I'm still stunned. I've never seen anything like that. You're a scientist; what the hell was that thing?" It was the inevitable question that she knew was coming.

"Honestly, I have no idea," she said. "Also, I didn't get a good enough look at it. All I saw was a red thing that was shaped like a shark, but it doesn't fit the description of any species I'm aware of."

"Something that big, you'd think it'd be well known," Nelson said. "Whatever it is, I'm not comfortable with fishermen going that far out. It's a mean bastard."

They arrived at the resort. Nelson parked near Forster's car, and they both stepped out.

"Thanks, Chief," she said. "I'm just gonna run upstairs and leave my instructions, then I'll be out of here."

"Good deal," he said. Forster went inside and took the elevator. She went into the care exhibit, where the sick dolphins were still being looked after. She spoke with the aide on duty and wrote down instructions for the next couple of days.

She fumbled in her locker, looking for her car keys.

"What the..." she mumbled after failing to locate them. Then she remembered, "Oh, they're in the boat."

She took the elevator back down. Upon exiting the double doors, she walked past the Great White Exhibit, which was still blocked off by tents and signs. The *Neptune* was at the dock. She could see the crumpling in the port side, and the missing portions of guardrail along the bow. The crane was usually folded down when not in use, however, it was stuck in a curved position. A gear was likely jammed from the hit it took. At the moment, Forster didn't care. She wanted nothing else but to go home and surrender herself to the couch and the television. She couldn't even remember the last time she was able to do that in peace. She located her keys, which had fallen onto the floor. She snatched them up and started back out the entrance.

On deck, she noticed the monitors, which had both fallen during the attack. The camera monitor's screen was cracked, while the tracking monitor appeared to be okay. Looking at the cracked camera monitor, a wave of curiosity filled her brain. She dipped back into the wheelhouse and took a seat at the table, switching on one of the other monitors. The camera feed was recorded into all the computers. The computer came on, and she brought up the camera files. A bar on the bottom left corner of the screen allowed her to select a specific date and time to narrow down the search.

She set the time to their approximate arrival on scene. The feed was from the portside mid-section. She fast forwarded through several minutes of nothing but blue ocean. Then, a quick view of the great white's tail swept over the screen. It was from its first attempt to snatch the bait. She waited a couple of minutes, until she saw it return for its second pass. It was a slightly clearer view. She could see its white underbelly, and the edge of its jaw.

Then, in the blink of an eye, the mysterious red creature burst into frame. The motion was so fast, that when she freeze framed it, the screen caught nothing but blue. She reversed the frames slowly until she recaptured the image. She could see its head, shaped basically like that of a shark. Its nose was pointed, and there was a clear upper and lower jaw. In the frame, she could barely see the connecting point for its pectoral fin.

Then there were the abnormalities; firstly, the red coloring. No shark of that size was known to have a red pigment. What was more mysterious, however, were mysterious appendages that appeared to be attached to its snout. The image on the frame was slightly blurry, so she adjusted to the next frame. The creature was just coming into view from the lower right corner.

"What the hell?" she mumbled to herself, astonished at what she was looking at. The protruding objects resembled antennae, like that on a crustacean. The fascination acted like a natural painkiller, numbing her headache almost completely. She switched the feed to the stern camera, which pointed almost directly downward. After fast-forwarding through some blank footage, she finally got a view of the white and its attacker. She froze the frame once again. This time, she had a wider shot of the mysterious creature.

It only grew more mysterious the more she looked at it. She noticed the bizarre texture of its exterior, which contained multiple pointed spines. In addition, it appeared very rigid, though it was difficult to tell through the image. Its body seemed to be jointed to provide movement.

What am I looking at?

"What the hell is that?" A voice spoke from behind her. Forster nearly jumped in her seat. She turned and saw Felt looking over her shoulder, staring intently at the screen. Suddenly, her headache returned with a vengeance.

"I don't know," she said, trying not to wince in pain.

"Is that what attacked the boat?" he asked. Forster was about to answer, when he nearly shouted another question. "And it killed the white?!"

Is it a special day for stupid questions?

"Yes," she said. She clicked *play* and Felt watched in astonishment as the creature ripped into the white. There was no doubt in Forster's mind that he was upset about losing his prized shark.

"Oh, God," he said. She couldn't tell if it was spoken out of fascination or distress. Finally, he looked away from the screen and noticed her bandage. "Oh..!" it was as if he had forgotten she had been to the hospital. "I'm glad to see you're feeling better."

I feel like shit. Her fascination was completely replaced by her desire to leave. With a few clicks of the mouse, she saved the frame image and emailed it to herself. She then reached into the pocket for the doctor's note.

"Actually, the doctor wants me to stay in for a few days," she said. She placed the paper down on the table. Felt stared at it, as if in defeat. "I already left instructions to the aides on how to care for the dolphins," Forster quickly said. She stood up, wanting to leave before Felt could express any displeasure.

"Okay..." his voice trailed off. With a doctor's note, he knew he couldn't stop her. However, he was still desperate for answers. "What about that shark...thing?"

"I'll look into it," she said.

"Could we go out and find it again?" he suddenly asked. The headache worsened. She walked out onto the deck.

"What do you mean?" she asked. She instantly regretted asking. Felt followed her outside.

"Oh, come on," he said. "Clearly you're curious about it! You've never seen anything like that, have you?" Forster didn't answer as she climbed down to the dock. She did desire to study the tapes more, but more than that she wanted peace and quiet. And more painkillers. Felt didn't stop. "Listen, you're the scientist. Perhaps we could..."

"I *was* a scientist," Forster said. She could almost taste the bitterness of the words, "...and barely that. I'm an animal doctor now."

"But clearly you're interested in this thing," Felt persisted. "You saved those images. What were you planning on doing with them?" Forster stopped walking. The pain throbbed harder with each word Felt spoke.

"I know a biologist in Maine," she said. "I studied under him. I was gonna send him these images and consult with him. He has the resources to deal with this kind of thing." *As long as he doesn't disown me like everyone else.* Felt stood quiet for a moment, while staring at the empty Great White Exhibit. Forster knew exactly what he was thinking, and why he was interested in her course of action.

"You know...we could..."

"Oh, no!" she nearly shouted. "That thing almost killed me, whatever it is. I'm not going to try and catch it." She turned and started walking away, followed by her boss.

Chief Nelson stood by his vehicle with his phone once again to his ear. After he had dropped off Forster, he received a call from one of his officers, relaying new information to him that prompted him to phone the Mayor's office again. It was the same agenda; to ground all watercraft. And once again, it was the same uphill battle. However, the new evidence convinced the Mayor to allow him a forty-eight-hour period. The local community would be in an uproar, but Nelson didn't care.

"*Like I said, Chief, that's all I can grant you,*" the Mayor said. "*If you don't find anything during that time, then people can go back out.*" Nelson wasn't sure if it would be adequate enough time, but he knew it was all he was going to get.

"I'll do my best, sir," he said. His eyes went out towards the dock. He saw Forster walking from the dock, followed by Felt, who appeared to be pestering her with questions. Nelson could read Forster's body language. Her face was pained, and the rapid way she walked indicated stress. Most importantly, he noticed the unconscious tightening of her hands. "Gotta go!" he said and hung up on the Mayor. He walked past the pool over to them.

"I'm telling you, Julie," Felt said. "Think of all we could learn from it!"

"You mean, all we can *earn* from it," she said. He never cared for the science. He just wanted another tooth monster to mesmerize people.

"Well..." he shrugged his shoulders, "How do you think I sign your checks? Understand, that white was our biggest attraction, and now it's gone. What do you expect me to tell everyone?"

"First, that it wasn't our biggest attraction," she told him. They had only recently put it on display. "Second, tell everyone the truth; that somebody broke in and released it. Not hard."

"Don't you think we could go out again and..."

"Nobody's going out, anywhere," Nelson chimed in. Felt straightened his posture once he saw the chief, as if to exude some degree of authority.

"Excuse me, Chief, but I didn't ask your opinion..."

"It's not a matter of opinion," Nelson said. "It's the law right now. All boats are grounded for the time being." Felt tensed briefly.

"Wha—you can't do that!"

"I sure can," Nelson said. "I cleared it with the Mayor just now."

"That's horseshit," Felt said, not holding back. "I know why you're doing this. You're in love with my employee here, and you're trying to show how much you care." Nelson's blood pressure went up, but he kept in control.

"Mr. Felt, unless you're blind, you saw the damage that thing did to your vessel. Also, there's a bigger issue at hand."

"What happened?" Forster asked.

"I just got word that parts of a wreckage were found adrift. The boat, what was left of it, belonged to a Bob Willis. There's another person missing, along with his fishing boat. Old Hal, you know him?" Forster nodded, and realized what Nelson suspected.

"Oh, God," she said. "You think it might have..."

"After what that thing did to us, it adds up," Nelson said. He exhaled sharply. "Needless to say, I have a lot of work ahead of me. I'm gonna try and get a consultant on the case. In the meantime, Julie, are you gonna have a problem getting home?" She grinned, as the question pertained to both her injury and her annoying boss.

"I'll be fine," she said. "Thanks for the ride."

"No problem," Nelson said. She started for her car. Nelson deliberately waited, seeing that Felt didn't follow her. The two shared a minute of unpleasant eye contact with each other. After which, Nelson turned and left.

Felt stood by himself, staring at the empty pool. With more reservations being cancelled after the incident, he saw the future of the resort being equally empty.

CHAPTER
15

Evening cast a twilight shadow over the island community at the usual time of *8:30*. For the first time in months, Forster didn't even notice the daylight slip away, nor the usual quietness of the community as people settled in for the night.

Dressed in loose athletic shorts and a tank top, Julie Forster laid on her living room couch. She sipped on a soda while a movie played on the television. It was such a normal pleasure, easily taken for granted. Yet, it was the first time in what seemed like forever that she enjoyed it. With her phone turned off, and some Excedrin to numb the pain in her head, this was the most relaxed she had been in a long time. Leaning back against the arm of the couch, she felt herself beginning to drift off.

A knock on the door snapped her back into reality. She stood up, wondering who it could be at this hour. Forster opened the front door. There stood Felt.

"Hi," he immediately said. His eyes opened wide, and he suddenly turned red before turning to look away, pretending to be casual. Forster looked down at herself, realizing her outfit barely covered her goods.

"Oh, damn it," she said, embarrassed. She put a hand over her cleavage and stepped back into the house. "Uh... give me a sec," she said. She went into her bedroom and dug for a shirt to put over her tank top. Felt peeked into the living room.

"Mind if I come in?" he called.

"Sure," she called back. Felt stepped into the living room and closed the door behind him. Forster came out of her bedroom, now wearing a zipped up light jacket. Felt could tell she was less than pleased to see him.

"Sorry, I tried calling, but it kept going straight to voicemail," he said.

"You think you'd take a hint from that," she said.

"Well, uh, you know...we're on an island and signals are sometimes bad around here..." he said. "I just stopped by to check and make sure you were doing alright. I was told you had a nasty bang on the head there, and..."

I can't take this bullshit any longer.

"What do you want, Will?" she interrupted him. Felt grinned uncomfortably.

"I know you're on medical," he said. "But I really want to run a thought by you. It's about that thing on the camera, whatever it is. Have you sent the images to that professor, yet?"

"No," Forster said. *Oh damn, why didn't I lie and say Yes?* "Luckily, I called first, and I guess he's out of town for a while. I'm gonna wait until he's supposed to get back, so the message isn't buried under a hundred other emails."

"Oh, good," Felt said, as if relieved. He then saw Forster staring at him questioningly. "Oh...well, I think there is a unique opportunity here before us. I was hoping you would be willing to track down that creature, and bring it to the resort."

Once again, that headache was returning. Forster hissed a sigh of annoyance.

"You've got to be kidding me, Will," she said. "Listen, we don't have the resources."

"We have the pool!" Felt said. Forster shook her head.

"We know nothing about this thing. We don't know how much to feed it; or what to feed it. It's most definitely dangerous!"

"Clearly it eats everything a normal shark does," Felt said. "Listen, hear me out. If we manage to find this thing and contain it, we'll truly have something that no other zoo or aquarium has. It'll be something new! I'm telling you, people will FLOCK to see this thing if we manage to capture it." His hands waved with every word, and his face was very animated.

"Oh, jeez," she said. "There's no way I'm going after that thing. First of all, the *Neptune* is damaged..."

"I already have people repairing it," Felt said.

"It won't be done for a few days, I can guarantee you that," Forster said. Felt bit his lip as he pondered ideas.

"Well...you could take the *Fairbanks*."

"The MAINTENANCE BOAT?!" Felt jumped in place. Forster was surprised that she actually shouted at him. She held up her hands, as if questioning him further. She shook her head again, "You know what?" She dropped her hands. "It doesn't matter anyway. There's a maritime ban in effect, remember? If I go out there, I'm risking being arrested. I've been through that already, and I already pushed my luck far enough yesterday. Hell, no."

"You know as well as I do that they don't patrol the waters that often," Felt said. "If it makes you feel better, I'll have people on lookout. They'll let me know where the police are, and if they're out on the water."

Forster was growing tired of the conversation. In fact, she was fed up with Felt's very presence. It seemed she couldn't even enjoy a simple relaxing night without her employer intervening.

"Will..." she spoke slowly, maintaining her composure, "...I know you're my boss, but please...give it a rest."

It was as if her words had the opposite effect. Felt became more energetic, holding his hands out in front of him as if illustrating his ideas.

"Tell you what...you do this for me and you'll get a huge raise!" he said, with his arms spread as if about to give a big hug. "I'll hire more help around the aquarium, including another doctor, and I'll get you another assistant! Also, you want more time off, you'll get it." These offers did more to agitate Forster than anything. If nothing else, most of these intended enticements were things she felt he should've been providing. On top of everything else, there was the realization that her employer was blatantly willing to break the law.

The offer of time off nearly made her snap, considering he was currently interrupting her medical leave with an unwelcome visit. Her silence communicated to Felt that his offers weren't working. He realized by offering these bribes, he sounded like a low-level gangster, or a snobby politician. He sighed and brushed a hand over his face.

"Listen…this'll benefit both of us. It'll renew interest in the resort like that!" He snapped his fingers. "The best part for you; you'll be credited with the discovery of a new species! Think of it, you found it, you discovered it!"

Forster cupped her hands over her face. She couldn't take anymore.

"Will…Mr. Felt…please, go home," she said. She spoke each word softly. Felt sighed again, this time defeated. He started toward the door. He opened it, stopped, and looked back at her.

"If you catch the thing, you can study it all you want," he said. "After all, it'd be your discovery. I seem to recall that's why you became a scientist. Just sayin'." He stepped out, shutting the door behind him.

Relieved at his departure, Forster collapsed back onto the couch. After fumbling around the cushions for the TV remote, she turned the volume back up. The program she was previously watching had ended during Felt's visit, which added to her frustration. Having no interest in the following film, she flipped through a few channels. With no movies of interest, she switched to the *Discovery Channel.*

She watched a program on underwater caves. It initiated with explaining caves in reefs and near kelp forests. With much of her education in geology, she couldn't help but nitpick the film's accuracy. It displayed two divers preparing to enter a limestone cave off the coast of Alaska, and the narration described a deep dive as any depth below fifty meters.

"It's forty. How do they get that wrong?" she said to herself. She continued to watch and nitpick, until she eventually grew bored. She was about to switch the TV off when suddenly the show went to commercial break. The first commercial was an advertisement for another show, due to air the next day. It showed dark, deep trenches, and mysterious looking creatures. It was a program about life in the deepest reaches of the ocean.

To anyone else, it would have been nothing other than simply an interesting show. To Forster, it was another dreaded reminder of the life she pursued, and ultimately ruined.

Felt's use of the word 'discovery' rang through her mind repeatedly. It was exactly what she wanted to do with her career: to explore and discover new species and geology. When she lost her position with the BRIZO program, she knew she lost any hope of achieving those dreams. To make it worse, they weren't just her dreams, but her father's as well.

The mental barriers came down, and she allowed herself to ponder the possibility of capturing the strange creature. She intended it to be a fantasy; just another nice escape from her daily misery, but it quickly escalated from that. Now, she wondered if it could become a reality. It would be a nightmarish mission, and she knew she would want to wait until the *Neptune* was repaired. The results, however, would be worthwhile if it was successful.

A rush of optimism swept over her. Forster suddenly believed there was yet the possibility she could make a contribution to the world of science; an opportunity she previously feared she would never see again. With this opportunity came the incessant need to take another look at the footage. She went into her office and turned on her computer.

She uploaded the images and video from her email account, and first looked at the stills. Once again, she examined the strange features; the strange antennae, rigid exterior and segmentation, the red color, and the numerous spiny formations on its body. They weren't like that of barnacles, as they more closely resembled the features of an exoskeleton from a crustacean.

She wondered if there had been any other sightings. She browsed the internet, and typed the description of the creature in the GOOGLE search bar. Nothing of relevance came up. She then typed in *strange sightings near Florida Keys and East Coast.* Even after adjusting the search engine for most recent articles, it appeared nobody had reported sighting this particular creature. However, other articles caught her attention. She read of the mysterious disappearances of private fishing vessels north of the Florida Keys within the past few weeks. A dreadful chill crept down her spine. She considered the odds that these vessels disappeared around the approximate arrival of this creature, which had displayed destructive capabilities. It was an odd coincidence indeed.

She returned to the uploads. She switched on the video feed and watched as the creature tore into the great white. Analyzing the encounter, she tried to think of a method of capture. If it really had a rigid exoskeleton, penetrating the hide with a tranquilizer would be impossible. It would have to be inserted in the mouth. Such a task would be considered daunting for any normal large shark, but this was even worse. Already, Forster ruled out the idea of using a shark cage.

She continued watching, seeing the Great White become entangled in the anchor cable. Then the hybrid came down and chomped on it. It was then she noticed something, other than the obvious carnage. The hybrid had bitten off the dorsal fin and continued feeding. She instantly remembered the White's tracking device, which was pinned to the dorsal fin.

She stood to her feet, "Oh my God, we can track it!" It seemed to solve another problem she was dreading: finding the creature again. It was unknown if it staked a claim on the waters near the island, or it happened to be passing through, and finding it in the open ocean could be like finding a needle in a haystack. However, another problem quickly arose in place. Forster would have to act quickly, as she knew the tracking device, if still functional, would not be in its system for too long.

She took her seat again and leaned back. Staring at the ceiling, she pondered the situation. *Wait until the Neptune's fixed, and go out more prepared, and just hope that you can find it again...or go out tomorrow in the Fairbanks and be able to track it quickly. Sounds great, as long as the thing doesn't sink me.*

She felt the need for a stiff drink. She helped herself to one in the kitchen, all the while thinking about the situation. There was the realization that if she was caught, she could get in far worse trouble. She downed the freshly mixed margarita.

Well...no pain no gain, she thought. She grabbed her iPhone and selected Felt from the contact list. As she expected, he answered on the first ring.

"Felt," she said. There was a brief pause, as she absorbed the awareness of what she was getting herself into. "I'm going to need a lot of supplies by morning. You've got a long night ahead of you. Now grab a pen…"

CHAPTER
16

Freshly released from the hospital, Marco sank into the backseat of a taxi cab. A fractured collarbone left his right arm in a sling, and his bruised ribs felt as if they were compressing on his lungs.

"Take me to Felt's Paradise, please," he told the driver. "And give the bill to the owner." Even talking caused him to ache. Luckily, the doctor instructed him to stay home and rest for a few days. First, he would need to pick up his car, and inform Felt of the situation.

The trip brought them to a stretch of road over a hill. That hill gave a clear view of the ocean, and the east port. The morning sunrise cast a beautiful golden glow over the water. The harbor was full of boats, an unusual sight for this time of day. Word of the chief's order on fishing spread like wildfire, and that fire grew hotter with the anger of the fishing community. As beautiful as it was, it was odd to see the ocean free of watercraft.

Except there was one. Leaving the harbor was a large tugboat, with another large vessel in tow. Marco leaned in toward the window, recognizing the *Neptune*. The portside damage was visible even from his viewpoint.

"Holy..." he said. He thought immediately of Forster, wondering what could've happened. "What in the hell?" The driver glanced to the boats and chuckled.

"Oh? You didn't hear?"

"Hear about what?"

"That fish-doctor lady, who works at the aquarium, went out to do some sort of work on that big boat. Not sure what the story is, but the police chief went to help her. Ha, Stud." The driver chuckled again. "He claims that some big shark attacked the boat and put that lady in the hospital."

"Dr. Forster? What happened to her?" Marco asked.

"Word is she got a little banged up..."

"But she's alright?" Marco asked. The driver chuckled again.

"What, you in love with her or something? I think you've got serious competition, bud!" He glanced back at Marco, then stopped his giggling. Even with the sling and visible bruises, Marco still looked plenty intimidating. Especially when staring with considerable irritation. The driver cleared his throat. "Uh, yeah, I think she's fine. Word would've spread pretty quick if it was anything more serious. Like with Old Hal and Bob Whisker, you hear about that?" Marco nodded. "Don't know what to say, except there's a lot of strange stuff going on. And something busted that science boat, but not a shark. They probably just pissed off a whale, or something. Same for Hal and Bob." He made the sign of the cross. "A lot of fishermen have said they've seen a lot of them lately. More than usual, and acting aggressive. Like there's a devil in the water. But hell, I've been out there, and seen everything there is. No shark could do that much damage to a boat like that. Either way, no residents are allowed out on the water. No fishing, skiing, boating, nothing."

The road curved, and the harbor disappeared from view. Marco was now feeling a new pain, this time in his stomach. Rarely did he feel the physical manifestation of anxiety, but the sight of the *Neptune* was immediately haunting. With the bizarre turn of events, such as watching the news reports of Old Hal going missing, to finding the dead whale, to the damaged *Neptune*, and the Chief's report, however extraordinary, only one thing was certain; something was definitely wrong.

****

"Come on, let's hurry it up," Forster said to Felt, who helped load up supplies onto the *Fairbanks*. After being up nearly all night, he was still wearing the same business clothes as the previous day. He had discarded the jacket, and his tie was loosened to the point where it was hanging around his neck. His white shirt was ragged and covered in filth from dragging the dead juvenile blue shark for bait. His fingers and palms were taped up with Band-Aids after attempting to drag the shark without gloves.

Getting the shark overnight was not an easy task. He had to contact a fisherman from the mainland and pay nearly triple to have the fish delivered by dawn. In addition, he had to get more tranquilizer supplies and a large fishing hook.

The sun had just broken over the horizon, which increased the urgency for Forster to get out on the water before people started coming out. The morning staff would soon be arriving, and the visitors would be up and moving shortly. She switched on the tracking monitor. The blip appeared, nearly two miles to the northeast.

"God only knows how much time I have left," she said. "I've got to get out there. I'll organize the rest of this when I get there."

"What, are you afraid he'll crap the tag out or something?" Felt asked.

"No. Assuming his digestive system functions like a normal shark, he'll regurgitate it," she said. "That's how they get rid of non-digestible items. He ate a fair amount yesterday, so he wouldn't spew it immediately without losing the actual sustenance. But now, he's had time to digest, and who knows how fast he can do that."

Felt looked down at the blue shark laying on the deck, which had been 'operated' on by Forster. Needles protruded from its head and back like a porcupine. During the last hour, Forster had carefully installed syringes loaded with tranquilizer into the body of the fish, pointing outward, and secured them in place with careful use of sewing and taping. It almost resembled something he would see in a horror film.

"Is this a common practice? Or…" he asked.

"Nope, completely improvised," Forster said. "If the guy bites down on this shark, hopefully one of the needles can get the soft skin in his mouth. It should take effect immediately. Hopefully, in the same bite, he'll get caught on the hook, because there's no way I'm getting into the water to strap a towing harness on that thing. If he does, I can tow him right in." Hearing herself speak, the realism of the situation was setting in. The plan would have to work perfectly in order to work at all. And the sense of danger suddenly seemed real. She forced the thoughts from her mind, focusing on the grand prize: discovery.

There wasn't any more time to waste. Felt watched from deck while Forster drove the boat out into the bay. He checked his watch. A quarter to *7:00*. Luckily, she would be out of sight by the time staff started arriving. Of course, they would likely see her come back in. However, if she succeeded in catching the creature, he figured people would be too fixated on the new discovery than Forster being out during the boat grounding.

Felt backed away from the dock after watching the *Fairbanks* become smaller with distance. He turned around, intending to go to his vehicle. He stopped, surprised to see Marco standing before him. He watched past Felt, as the boat disappeared into the distance. His eyes then went to his boss.

"What's going on here?" he asked. Felt quickly tried thinking of something to say. "I saw it was Julie on that thing. You guys do realize there's an order out for all boats to be grounded?"

"Yes, but Marco..." Felt went to put a hand on his shoulder, but stopped when he noticed the injury. His mind scrambled, unsure whether to tell the truth or come up with a makeshift lie.

"Why is she going out? Is it something to do with what happened to the *Neptune*?" Marco said. Felt gulped. "Yeah, I saw it. Chief Nelson apparently reported that he saw something out in the water. Everyone thinks he's full of it, but now I'm starting to think different. What's out there, and why is Julie heading out there in a maintenance boat?"

Felt could feel beads of sweat starting to form. All there was to say was the truth. Hopefully, a promise of extra money would be enough to keep Marco quiet.

****

Chief Nelson nearly slammed his phone to his desk, finishing a phone call from the Mayor's office. Local residents had been calling in nonstop to both the Mayor and police station, making their displeasure vastly known. Thus, the Mayor demanded to know if Nelson had made any progress on his investigation. He dreaded giving the answer.

After leaving Felt's Paradise, he had spent the rest of the day trying to get in contact with various universities for a consultant. First it was the University of Miami, who declined to send someone out. Though they were polite, he could tell that they thought he was a lunatic. The representative at the University of Florida was more straightforward, telling him that the creature he described could not possibly exist. The senior ichthyologist from South Caroline Marine Institute simply laughed in his face.

A long, tiresome phone conversation lagged between Nelson and the Mayor. The Chief endured prolonged criticisms of his lack of progress, and the insistent demand to allow people back onto the water. Nelson stood his ground, informing the Mayor he needed more time. More ranting followed before Nelson was told he needed to arrive at a press conference. It was a sudden thing that the office arranged for the public. Nelson suspected it was a way to put him on the spot, and hopefully back down from the pressure and allow everyone back onto the water. It was due to begin within the next half hour.

Finally, the conversation came to a close, but not soon enough. Nelson's blood pressure was on the rise. After putting his phone down on his desk, he sat in his seat, taking advantage of the few minutes of peace and quiet before going to deal with the public.

The desk phone rang. Nelson glared at it with disgust, as if the phone was deliberately interrupting his relaxation. He picked it up.

"Nelson here," he answered.

"*Yeah, Chief, we got somebody up front wanting to speak with you,*" the front desk officer said.

"Is the guy willing to have somebody else help him? I've got to get ready to leave shortly," Nelson said.

"*He says it's urgent,*" the officer said. Nelson held the phone away from his face as he groaned.

"Alright, I'll be up there," he said and hung up. He looked at his watch, doing an approximate drive time to Town Hall. Without notes, he was just going to have to wing the press meeting. He put it out of his mind and went to the front check-in. It was a separate entry from intake, where visitors could come in and express a concern. He located the desk officer. "Okay, what's going on?"

The officer pointed at a tall, muscular individual seated in the lobby, with his arm in a sling. Nelson quickly recognized him.

"Marco!" he said. His voice was a combination of surprise and joy. He was happy to see him out of the hospital in relatively good condition. Nelson's enthusiasm faded when he saw Marco's subdued expression. "You okay, bud? What can I do for you?" Marco stared at him, feeling slightly conflicted. He knew he would be getting his friend in trouble. However, the feeling of her out in the water alone, looking for the strange whatever-it-was, made him feel sick inside.

"It's about Julie," he said. Nelson suddenly grew anxious.

"What's the matter? Is she in trouble?" Marco took a breath, and finally began to tell everything he knew.

CHAPTER
17

The *Fairbanks* drifted with the current after Forster brought it to a stop. Keeping track of the monitor, she had followed the creature toward a kelp forest located directly off the point of the East Peninsula. She kept enough distance in order to not draw it in too quickly. She still needed to get the bait into the water.

The blue shark dangled over the water by its tail, attached by a small crane at the stern. It was a simple hook design, intended for lifting and lowering metallic parts. She preferred the crane on the *Neptune*, but it worked for her needs. The shark had a line tied to its tail, which was strung up to the cleats at the transom. The plan was to create a chum trail, draw the creature in, then drop the bait from the crane and drag it along the water. If all went well, the creature would bite it and be pierced within the mouth by the syringes and the hook. Then she'd be able to tow it to the pen. She wished she had more help and resources, which would allow her to come up with a more elaborate plan. She forced herself not to think of that and focused on the situation at hand.

It didn't take long for the chum trail to start reaching far out. Forster could see the red line extending from the boat. The day had blessed her with good, clear weather, and great visibility. She could only hope the rest of the mission would be so bright.

****

Nelson sped his police vehicle down to the docks, where the harbor patrol boats were located. With the intense speed in which he drove, along with the flashing lights, pedestrians and passing drivers grew concerned that a major crime was in progress. It was that level of intensity that Nelson was feeling at the moment.

His tires kicked up gravel as he pulled to a stop. He exited the truck, leaving it parked crooked in a space, and rushed to the small police outpost near the docks. Inside were two officers, one assigned there to issue keys, another there to visit. Nelson recognized the officer as Charles Beck, a new recruit fresh off his training period. Beck looked at him, appearing guilty as if he was caught socializing on the job.

"Get me a key," Nelson spoke to the desk officer. The officer didn't waste any time, and quickly pulled a key from the locked cabinet. Nelson took it and turned to Beck. "Good thing you're here. You're coming with me." He went around the desk to a small locked room. He opened it, revealing a small armory for the boats. He grabbed a Mossberg shotgun and gave it to Beck.

"What's going on, sir?" he asked while checking the chamber.

"We're going to get someone," Nelson said, grabbing a Carbine Rifle and inserting a magazine loaded with 5.56mm rounds.

"A suspect?"

"No," Nelson grabbed another shotgun and started out the door, "just someone doing something really stupid." The two of them boarded the police vessel. Nelson ignored the routine inspection required prior to taking a boat out, only taking time to make sure it had a tow line. He started the engine and steered the vessel out. As soon as he cleared the harbor, he throttled to top speed and steered toward the north. He felt along his belt for his handcuffs. The feel of the metal rings gave him a bitter trepidation. The young officer stood at the starboard railing, feeling the wind rushing through his hair.

"Sir, may I ask what the concern is?" he asked. Nelson almost didn't want to say anything, believing he would just sound foolish, but the officer deserved to know.

"We've got something big out there..." he started to explain.

****

Forster threw another scoopful of chum out. So far, only a few small sharks came to nip at the trail. She studied the monitor again. The blip seemed to hardly move at all. It was a red flag for her, as it was unnatural activity even for a normal shark. While she knew this creature wasn't any normal shark, she was able to see its gill slits in the video footage, and found it likely that it needed to continuously move to stay alive. The blip had remained in the same general location for the half hour she had been chumming.

She dropped the scoop and went to the monitor, punching a few notes in the keyboard. A reader came up, which gave information regarding the subject such as depth, speed, and exact location. Depth read *0 Feet,* and speed listed *0 MPH.* With the signal being within view, Forster quickly grabbed a pair of binoculars and scanned the water. A red creature on a clear sunny day should be easy to spot along the surface. However, she saw nothing but blue.

"Shit," she said to herself. It was a delicate situation. She needed to know for sure if the creature was actually there. She stepped to the helm, then hesitated for a moment while considering the danger of drawing close to it.

Then again, this whole thing is already risky to begin with. She throttled the boat slowly, while keeping an eye on the screen. As before, the blip remained in place. As she drew near, she looked for any sign of the creature. Nothing. The water seemed empty, which it almost was anyway because of the toxic effects from the pollution dumping.

A bubbly stream of frothy white directly ahead caught her attention. She adjusted the boat's direction and stopped alongside it. She stepped out onto the deck and looked down to examine the strange substance. It was a stringy stream of foam, roughly ten feet long, with tiny bits of meaty residue caught within it. After a minute of studying it, Forster saw something yellow and rigid under a layer of foam. She grabbed a pole and jabbed it into the substance, clearing it away. The yellow tracking tag floated in clear water for only a few seconds before the froth closed in on it again. Forster was too late. The creature had already regurgitated the non-digestible device.

"Goddamnit!" she cursed, and threw the pole down hard on the deck. It bounced up and splintered before settling down. After it did, she kicked it again, sending it crashing into the hydraulic lift. Forster allowed herself to cool down, and not let her temper get the better of her. She took a breath and began to think rationally. She thought of starting again with the chumming, and hope the creature was still nearby. It was the least she could do at that point. However, thinking of this was just a reminder of how difficult it would likely be to find it again; especially after considering the fact that the tag had likely been regurgitated for at least a half hour. The feeling of defeat sank in. The high she had experienced while tracking the creature came crashing down, and now she felt she was back at her normal low point.

The sounds of a screeching siren in the distance drew her attention to the south. The sight of red and blue flashers drawing nearer to her boat brought the realization that her low point just got lower.

Nelson shook his head in disappointment when he saw Forster standing on the deck. The young officer stood at the stern, keeping watch for the creature which Nelson had described to him. It was hard to believe such a thing was real, but as long as he was in the Chief's presence, Beck was going to treat it as if it was.

"You want me to board the boat, Chief?" he asked.

"No, not yet," Nelson said. "I'll do the talking." He pulled the boat next to the *Fairbanks*, splashing away the froth. A feeling of anxiety coursed through Forster, and it swiftly worsened after locking eyes with the Chief. She thought the looks of irritation a few nights ago at the bar were bad. After seeing him now, she found herself wholly wishing for that look again, as this one was much worse. Without words, she already knew what he was thinking.

Then came the words.

"What in God's name are you doing out here?!" he questioned. It took all of his strength to not yell. Forster knew he wouldn't like any answer she had. She quickly tried to think of which explanation to give; scientific discovery, pressure from Felt, or trying to live up to the hopes her late father had.

"Chief, listen," she said. "I…"

"No, *you* listen!" Nelson said. "I ordered all island residents to remain off the water for a reason." He reached across and grabbed the side of the *Fairbanks*. Lifting one leg over the side, he carefully crossed over. Standing on deck of the *Fairbanks*, he brushed some dust from his pants before returning his attention to Forster. "Jesus Christ, Julie. I figured I would have to chase after a few boaters. Maybe a fisherman or two, but I never thought *you'd* be the one I'd be trying to keep off the water." He then looked around, examining Forster's setup. He noticed the shark, with the hook and syringes. "*THIS*…is your brilliant plan? What the hell, Julie! Are you *trying* to get yourself killed? What about the time off you were going to take?"

Nelson's anger further dug in the realization that Forster made a poor, selfish decision. Like antibodies to a virus, her mind dug through the rationalizations. She believed she was right to be out.

"Tell me, Chief," she said. "What were you planning to do about this thing? You wanted a consultant, but you never asked me."

"Give me a break! Have you looked in a mirror lately? You're exhausted, plus you were just in the hospital!"

"Let me guess," Forster said. "Whoever you contacted, denied you a consultant." Nelson felt foolish for taking the bait, which locked him into an argument that he didn't have time for. He felt his phone buzzing in his pocket. It was the third time in the past ten minutes, and he knew it was the Mayor wanting to know why he wasn't at the press conference.

"That's beside the point," he said, growing more irritated with each vibration. Forster crossed her arms.

"What was your plan then? Just sit around and hope for this thing to go away?"

"The first thing for me to do is ensure safety! To do that, I have to enforce laws, such as the one you're currently violating," he said. Realizing she wasn't getting the better of him, Forster uncrossed her arms. The confidence she briefly felt had quickly slipped away. There was a long moment of silence. Forster tried thinking of a way out of her predicament, only to come up short.

"Chief, I just…"

"Stop talking," Nelson barked. He turned, briefly looking into the water, then turned toward her again. "I'm so pissed right now Julie, that you put me in this situation." He took a breath, then pointed at her and moved his hand in a slight circular motion. "Turn around, put your hands behind your back."

Those words nearly triggered a physical response from her, as if she was punched in the gut. Forster's mind felt as if it was moving a hundred miles an hour. She wanted so badly to plead her case, but knew it would do no good. Anything from here would just make the situation worse.

Forster turned, and locked her arms behind her back. She felt the cold metal from the cuffs compress her wrists, and for the second time in her life, she listened to the Miranda rights. After Nelson was done, he guided her to the hydraulic table.

"So, you want me to drive this boat in, or are we gonna have to tow it?"

"Keys are in the ignition," she said. She spoke softly, as if each word carried her shame. Nelson helped her take a seat on the lift and then walked back to the side. Beck waited on the police vessel. A rookie on the force, he was slightly disappointed he didn't get to put on the cuffs, as he had yet to make an arrest.

"You okay with driving that thing back?" Nelson asked.

"Not a problem, sir," Beck responded.

"When you get there, take a patrol car and pick us up at the resort," Nelson said. Beck gave a casual, two finger salute and moved to the helm. Nelson examined the console for the maintenance boat, which was a slightly different design from what he was used to. Both officers throttled forward and created a bit of distance between the boats. They turned toward land and traveled parallel for the time being.

Forster sat silently, watching the water swirl from the distortion. The peaceful blue did little to soothe her sickened feeling. Looking at her set up, while feeling the sensation of metal on her wrists, she thought of how her pride had gotten the better of her. Luckily, this would likely only result in a few nights in jail. Certainly, no prison time. However, she felt even more like a failure. She had just one opportunity to make a name for herself, and live up to her dreams, and yet she failed. Knowing that was worse than any jail sentence.

Then, there it was. Out of the corner of her eye, the red shape came into view. It was a few feet under the surface, with its dorsal fin just shy of grazing the surface. But it was unmistakable. It trailed behind the police vessel, gathering speed and drawing close. Her eyes went to Officer Beck, who drove the boat unsuspectingly.

"Chief?" Forster said. Just as she spoke, the creature dipped down from view. Nelson glanced back at her, saying nothing, and returned his attention to the path ahead. Forster stood up from the table and carefully watched the water. Though there was no sight of it, she could feel its presence. "Chief?"

"Not now," Nelson said. Forster felt her pulse throbbing in her temple. Not being able to see the creature only worsened the anxiety. She looked behind the *Fairbanks*, then around the starboard side, trying to see if the creature had directed its pursuit toward them instead. But there was nothing, so it seemed.

She looked back to the police vessel. She screamed.

"LOOK OUT!"

The hybrid soared through the water at a slight upward angle. Its head, red and armored, connected with the stern.

Beck had just heard the scream when the boat kicked up. It was a similar sensation to what he felt when his car was rear ended on his way to college years back. Only, this was fifty times worse. The boat moved into a tailspin, as if he was driving on ice. The bow chipped the side of the *Fairbanks*, sending a tremor coursing through the entire boat. After a complete turn, the resistance from the water brought the spin to a stop.

Nelson slowed the *Fairbanks* and turned toward the patrol boat. Forster stood at the side, looking for the creature to reappear.

"It's here," she said.

"Nick? You all right, kid?" Nelson shouted to the officer. Beck tried throttling the boat again. It moved, but swerved heavily to port.

"Shit," Beck cursed to himself. He looked to the Chief, who approached on the *Fairbanks*. "I think one of the propellers is broken!" The *Fairbanks* pulled up alongside.

"Toss me a shotgun, and move on over," Nelson said. Beck already had one of the guns in hand. He tossed it to Nelson, who caught it by the barrel and quickly positioned it against his shoulder. Beck grabbed the other shotgun, then began to reach for the *Fairbanks*. Nelson scanned the water with his weapon, looking for the devil-red leviathan to emerge. And it did, only much more swiftly than even Nelson had anticipated.

A huge splash preceded the creature as it darted between the boats. It hit both vessels at once, separating them from each other like bowling pins. Water crashed against the *Fairbank*'s hull as it rotated. Nelson removed his finger from the trigger, and clung to the side as the boat rocked violently. Beck fell backwards onto the deck of the police boat, but not before losing his shotgun to the thrashing waves.

"Get me out of these cuffs," Forster said to Nelson, who managed to steady himself. He looked at her, then looked back to the water. The fin emerged. He aimed the shotgun and followed the path of the shark. It passed around the other side of the police vessel, rendering Nelson unable to shoot it.

"Beck! Shoot the damn thing!" he yelled out. The officer rolled to his hands and feet and crawled to the console, which was where the rifle was located. He snatched it up and positioned himself to his feet. He shouldered the weapon and put the shark in the sights. There was a brief moment of disbelief as he laid eyes on the creature, which was a few feet larger than his own boat.

"Shoot it!" he heard Nelson yell. Beck squeezed the trigger, firing off seven rounds in rapid semi-auto succession. Each bullet found their mark, only to crush against the shell. The shark dipped below the surface once again. The thrashing waves slowly calmed themselves. Beck stood, ready and waiting for it to reemerge, while completely unaware that he inflicted no damage.

On the *Fairbanks,* Forster marched over to Nelson, "Dammit, Chief, get these cuffs off, and I can drive the damn boat!" Nelson almost ignored her, but finally realized he needed the extra pair of hands. He placed the shotgun down and quickly uncuffed Forster.

"This is why I wanted the waters clear!" he said. The cuffs fell from her wrists. Nelson snatched the shotgun back up and yelled to Beck. "Grab the wheel and take us over to him!" Without hesitation, Forster did as ordered. She turned the *Fairbanks* to starboard.

The hybrid had finished toying with the two inedible organisms. It continued its rapid descent, until the water around it had turned completely dark. The creature stopped, then swiftly angled back toward the surface. With each swipe of its tail, it increased its speed. Like a surface to air rocket, it closed the distance between the dark depths and bright surface in a mere few seconds, coming up directly underneath Beck's boat.

The middle portion of the patrol boat lifted, as the stern and bow were still touching the water. Both ends of the halves were separated, as the hybrid emerged from between them. Airborne, it opened its eyes to view the world above the one it lived within. It saw the two fleshy lifeforms onboard the other vessel, fueling its desire to ravage further. It fell back into the water, spewing bits of hull from the sides of its mouth. Bits of debris peppered the area. Forster dropped to her knees as fragments of metal pounded the console.

The impact flung Beck into the water, skipping him like a stone until he settled several feet from the two halves of his boat. The stern and bow both tilted upward before filling with water and sinking beneath the waves. Accidentally swallowing a mouthful of salt water, he began to gag, spitting some of it up in the process. Though disoriented, he could see the maintenance boat and frantically paddled towards it.

Forster closed the distance, coming to a full stop as the bow had just begun to pass him. The momentum brought the stern close to Beck, who paddled toward it. Nelson reached down, nearly touching the water to grab the rookie's hand.

"Come on, you're almost there!" he shouted. Beck reached, and luckily managed to secure a grasp on the first try. Nelson gritted his teeth as he struggled to pull the slightly overweight officer over the side. Beck groaned as his stomach pressed against the gunwale, while his feet dangled over the water.

The hybrid had searched around the wreckage, looking for the edible inhabitant that had occupied it. Multiple moving bits of machinery sent all sorts of distorted messages to its Ampullae of Lorenzini. Finally, it sensed a familiar rhythm: a rapid heartbeat. It swam around the patrol boat's submerged stern and spotted the target near the other vessel. It immediately moved in for the kill, though realizing the target had been hauled out of the water. This didn't stop the creature from achieving its goal.

It burst from the water. Its head smashed through the gunwale in a flurry of airborne debris. The impact threw both Nelson and Beck to the deck. Nelson ended up against the portside wall, while Beck landed directly on his back, hitting the back of his head. The boat leaned heavily to starboard, as the shark weighed down on the side. Forster yelled in fright. Never had she even heard of such an aggressive shark. Even more amazing, it didn't slide back into the water despite the boat leaning heavily to starboard. It seemed to 'cling' to the side.

Nelson scrambled to his feet and snatched the shotgun from the deck. He leaned against the port, looking into the face of the enormous, demonic head that nearly took up the entire deck. He shouldered the firearm and aimed right between the eyes. He felt the kick of each discharge. Buckshot splattered against the creature's head. With his ears ringing, he looked in utter shock. Other than a few minor scratches on the top of its head, the firearm inflicted no damage. The boat leaned further, causing him to lean back to maintain his balance. He fired off another round, right at the creature's snout. The fragments bounced off and scattered in random directions; one of which entered Nelson's left shoulder.

The fragment cut deep, causing Nelson to yell out. Beck, still on the deck, tried scooting away. With the boat sloping to starboard, gravity started pulling him ever closer to the huge snapping jaws. He turned to his stomach and clawed against the deck. He felt the bottom of his feet press against the solid nose. Then there was the sensation of flesh being ripped apart, as teeth punctured his left leg on both sides. One tooth ripped through the calf muscle, while a tooth on the lower jaw broke through the tibia. Beck yelled out in the worst pain he had ever felt. Seeing the officer about to be pulled over the edge, Nelson grabbed Beck's outstretched hand.

Forster watched in horror as the bloodshed unfolded in front of her. The boat was on the verge of capsizing. She pulled herself to the helm, intending to try and throttle away, but she quickly realized she couldn't do that without losing Beck. The situation seemed hopeless. Then she saw the pole with tranquilizer inside the vial. Her brain barely processed the new idea that transpired. There was no time.

She threw herself down to the deck and grabbed the pole. After pulling herself to her feet, she jumped toward the monster. Like a Spartan with a lance, she rammed the rod between the jaws, plunging it into the soft gums. The shark opened its jaws in a brisk motion, releasing Beck and going after her. Its snout struck Forster in the chest, throwing her to her back before the jaws could snatch her.

Immediately, the hybrid felt a sensation it hadn't experienced prior. It felt slow, and its vision suddenly seemed shadowy. With a wiggle of its body, it slipped back down into the water, confused in its drowsy state.

The boat leveled out, and Nelson quickly rushed to Beck's side. Blood gushed from his nearly severed leg. The flesh was ravaged, and he could even see the splintered white of the bone through the blood and meat. Nelson tore off his police shirt and wrapped it tightly against the wound. He looked to Forster.

"GUN IT!" he said. She put the boat on full throttle and pointed the bow toward land. Nelson tightened the shirt around Beck's leg. "You'll be alright, kid!"

"The guys at the bar are never gonna believe this!" Beck said in a pained voice.

At least he's got a sense of humor about it.

The hybrid felt the distortion from the propellers. The target was moving away at great speed. Despite the bizarre disorientation it was experiencing, its aggressive tendencies took over once again. It could not allow the prey to escape. It moved after it, slashing its tail against the water. It required much effort, but the hybrid pushed on.

Nelson saw the fin behind them, "Holy shit! He's not giving up!" Forster glanced behind them, seeing the fin for herself. She could tell it was slowing due to the tranquilizer, but it must not have had a large enough dose. Another idea formed in her mind. She knew exactly how to subdue it for good. She dug her phone from her pocket and made a call. She drove the boat with the phone lifted to her ear. Each ring seemed to take forever.

"Pick up! Pick up! Pick up!"

****

Felt sat in his office, eyeballing a bottle of whiskey after going over bills and ticket sales. He reached for the whiskey, needing something to sooth his nerves. Then, he noticed his phone buzzing on the desk, and Forster's name on the screen. He suddenly grew excited. He snatched it up.

"Hey!" he said in a delighted voice. "Tell me the good news!"

"Will! Open the pen doors right now!" Her voice was loud and intense, which he mistook for excitement.

"Oh my god!" he said. "You mean, you really caught the--"

"Jesus Christ, Felt!" Now there was no mistaking the tone. *"Do it now! Open the damn gate! Now!"*

Felt stumbled as he jumped out of his seat. He ran through the lobby of the building to the elevator. He stepped in with a group of people, only to see several floors lit up before it would reach the 1st floor. He reached out, preventing the doors from sliding shut, and dashed from the elevator. He darted for the stairwell and descended rapidly down the steps. Out of shape, he felt himself quickly running out of breath. By the time he got to the 1st floor, he was soaked in sweat. He ran out the front doors and pushed through crowds of visitors.

"Excuse me! Pardon me!" he called out in a vain attempt to seem polite. He reached the pens and dipped behind the tents blocking the Great White Exhibit. He pulled his card and ran it through the swipe at the console. The doors beeped loudly as they began to open. He looked to the blue ocean, seeing the *Fairbanks* rapidly approaching in the distance.

****

"Keep pressure there," Nelson directed Beck, before snatching up the shotgun. He stood at the transom and pointed toward the beast. He fired three more shots, before the weapon finally ran empty. He tossed it down and drew his Sig Saur from the hip, rapidly firing off .40 caliber rounds at the hybrid. He could see the individual splashes caused by each round as they zipped toward the target. It did not slow its pursuit. With one last pull of the trigger, the slide locked back. "Fuck!"

"Chief!" Forster yelled back to him. "The bait! Remove the hook from the blue shark! Then, on my signal, take the rope off it!" Nelson didn't waste any time asking questions. He holstered the gun and grabbed the fish. He twisted the hook until he was finally able to remove it, cutting up his fingers on the denticles in the process.

"How am I taking the line off?"

"You have a knife, don't ya?" Forster called back. Nelson dug into his pocket and grabbed a pocket blade. Forster glanced back, seeing him about to cut the rope. "Hold on! Not yet!"

"When, then?!" Nelson said. He looked to the bow, realizing they were closing in on the exhibit. "Uh, Julie…what the hell are you doing?!" She ignored him, watching her path carefully. She aimed the nose of the boat right for the open doors. Three hundred feet. Two hundred feet. One hundred feet. Fifty feet. Twenty.

She brought it to a full stop, allowing the momentum to bring the boat the rest of the way inside the pen.

"Now!" she yelled to Nelson. With a single cut of the rope, the blue shark dropped into the water below. Forster looked to the control console, seeing Felt standing there, amazed at what was happening. She glanced back to the entrance. The creature entered. For a moment, it seemed to continue coming straight at them. Then, finally it dipped for the bait. She looked to Felt while turning the boat. "Close the gate!" she yelled. Felt hit the button, and the high-pitched beeping screeched, and the yellow lights flashed again. The *Fairbanks* skidded off the edge of the pen as Forster manipulated a sharp turn, then gunned it for the closing entrance. She cleared the doors, and they gradually slammed home.

The hybrid shredded the dead blue shark, unwittingly injecting itself with more of the tranquilizer. After consuming the meal, it turned to continue pursuing its target, only to slam against a wall of reinforced steel. It turned and tried a different path, only to find another dead end.

Before it could analyze the situation, it suddenly felt a drop in blood pressure, followed by loss of energy. It struggled to swim, only to succumb to the added dose of tranquilizer.

Forster directed the boat to the nearby port. She grabbed her phone and quickly called the number for one of the techs. They answered.

"Get the underwater drone and the air pump, STAT!" she ordered. She looked to Nelson, intending to embrace to celebrate the miraculous task they pulled off. But that joy disappeared when she saw him on the radio, yelling for an ambulance. Blood had completely covered the deck. Beck rested on his back, barely conscious. She dropped the phone and went to aid Nelson, keeping pressure on the wound.

Nelson looked at her with fiery eyes. "Proud of yourself now?!" he bellowed. She didn't answer.

Meanwhile, Felt jumped up and down at the Exhibit console with a joy that he hadn't felt in years. A crowd began to form, equally confused by the drastic event taking place at the boat, the commotion that had just occurred in the pen, and the resort owner's ecstatic celebration.

CHAPTER
18

With walls made of a mixture of granite and sea pebbles, the lower observation room had the smell of sea salt. A huge fiberglass model of a great white shark hung from the ceiling, while other smaller models of other species were lined along the walls. The center of the room was lined with dozens of chairs, intended for visitors to witness underwater feeding demonstrations. Orange cones and yellow caution tape were set up along the entrances to the large room, preventing any unauthorized personnel inside.

At the front of the room, Forster stared through the massive plate of glass which separated her from the pen. Inside, the creature rested motionless on the floor of the pen. It lay several yards away, its head pointed off to the side. Forster could just see its mouth well enough to see that it was open. She knelt down to operate a flat controller unit that was hooked up to a laptop. The screen showed nothing but a bright blue, with yellow streaks of light. It resembled a cloudless sky, but it was the water's surface, with the feed coming from the underwater drone. She could see the maintenance workers lowering the pump into the water, and the camera moved swiftly as they lifted the drone to hook it up to the end of the pump. There was no audio on the monitor, so Forster had to keep in contact via radio.

"Let's go, guys, we don't want to lose it," she said. As one of the men was manipulating the drone, the camera briefly panned to one of the other workers. He was clearly mocking her with a disdained look on his face while talking. "Knock off the horseplay, Harris." Luckily for Forster, she could see the amused reactions from the other workers. Finally, the screen was directed toward the water, which overtook the image after the drone was lowered inside.

Forster carefully manipulated the drone toward the downed creature. The added weight from the pump made the controls more sensitive. If she moved it down even the slightest bit, the drone started to take a nose dive. The workers lowered it as the drone descended, helping to alleviate the weight on the mechanism. To do this, they had to lower it slowly. This created a pull on the hose which made turning the drone left or right nearly impossible.

Forster alternated looking at the screen and looking through the glass, which made it easier to gauge the distance down to the shark. It finally came into view on camera. Its nose was pointing at the drone, and after sinking a bit lower, she could see that the jaw was slack.

"Oh, thank God," she said. This made it easier to apply the pump. With it attached to the drone, there was no other way than to simply drive it between the jaws. She watched the mouth grow larger on screen, until it 'consumed' the electronic image. Then there was nothing but black. Looking through the glass again, she could see the unconscious creature's head wiggling slightly as the drone worked the pump inside. She grabbed her radio.

"Alright guys, switch the pump on. Let's see if this works," she said.

"*You got it,*" the supervisor responded. A flow of bubbles filled the screen, clouding the dark background. Looking through the glass, Forster strained to see if the airflow was moving through the gill line. The fluctuation in the water near the gills suggested that the operation was successful.

"Alright, guys, thanks for your help," she spoke into the radio, and clipped it to her belt. She stood up and turned to walk out, only to nearly bump into Felt. "Oh, jeez!" she exclaimed.

"Sorry," he said, returning his gaze to the creature. His demeanor was improved vastly compared to what it had been during the past several weeks. He looked like a child in a toy store while looking at the pen's new inhabitant. "It's so beautiful!" he said. Forster thought he sounded like a generic mad scientist.

"You wouldn't think so if it was coming after you," she said.

"I guess I'll never have to find out," Felt said, without skipping a beat. Forster wondered if Felt even noticed the damage to the *Fairbanks,* or even realized a police officer's life was in jeopardy.

Since docking, she was overwhelmed by a heavy sense of shame. Her mind dwelled on the reality that if she had not gone out, the officer would not be in the emergency room. A remark from Nelson indicated that the man was recently married, which further dug in the guilt complex. She wanted to call Nelson and ask for any updates, but she doubted he had any interest in talking to her. She returned her attention to the creature, which provided the perfect distraction. The pump continued pumping oxygen into its mouth.

"I just hope we aren't too late," she said.

"So, you're going to just leave the drone in its mouth?" Felt asked. Both eyebrows raised on Forster's head.

"Um, yes," she said. "That was the only way I was willing to get the pump down to it. No way in hell am I letting anyone down there in that tank, under any circumstances."

"Oh, but isn't it tranquilized?" Felt asked.

More stupid questions. Forster resisted the urge to tell him to stick to business and let her deal with the animal care.

"Eh, doesn't matter," Felt said before Forster could answer. "I just can't wait to open this exhibit again! When will it wake up?" Forster looked at him, puzzled.

"You want to open it already?"

"Of course!" Felt said. His voice filled the room. "Julie, we have something the world has never seen before. People will go nuts over seeing this thing! I'm telling you, this place will go from zero-to-a-hundred in no time. And like I said before, you'll get to be credited with this discovery. Scientists will be consulting *you*!" Somehow, hearing it this time didn't give Forster the same glorious feeling as before. She shook her head.

"Sir, there's no way you can open this exhibit already," she said. Felt's expression turned to disgust, like a five-year-old who got served broccoli for dinner.

"Why not?"

"First of all, we need to learn more about the thing," Forster said. "We need to know more about its nutritional needs, how its metabolism works, if it'll be in need of any particular medication." Felt shrugged.

"I just figured it eats the same stuff any normal shark eats," he said.

"Yeah, but it's bigger, heavier, and has a different body structure," Forster said. "All that can play into its metabolism, meaning we likely will have to feed it a lot more than the white. Besides…" she looked back to the shark, "it took enough tranquilizer to put down something twice its size."

"Is that bad?"

"It's not good," she said. "Either we overdosed it, or it means this thing could be very difficult to contain. On that note, we don't know how it's gonna handle being in captivity. Either it'll get pissed and start attacking the walls, or stressed, and when fish get overly stressed, they can die. And is that what you want; to open this exhibit, and have this thing die in front of everyone?" Felt stood quiet, which provided an answer in itself. "That's what I thought. Probably wouldn't be the headline you wanted."

"I suppose not," Felt said.

"I'd be fine with that!" a voice echoed from the entrance. Chief Nelson stepped into the room, followed by a protesting maintenance worker.

"Sir! Officer! You can't come down here," the worker said. Nelson ignored him and approached Felt and Forster. His shirt was wrinkled and unbuttoned. Dried blood crusted around the tear in his right shoulder where the ricochet hit him. Felt immediately groaned, looking at the ceiling for a brief moment.

"Don't you get sick of coming here and interrupting my business?" he said. Forster cringed at the remark, knowing Nelson's state of mind. She stepped toward him.

"Chief, how's he doing? Is he alright?" she asked, referencing Officer Beck. She prayed in her mind for a positive response. Out of good human nature, she wanted the young officer to pull through okay. Just as much, she was desperate to know she didn't get someone killed by going after the creature. Nelson ignored her and went right to Felt.

"Don't get smart with me," he told him.

"Hey, I'm the owner of this property! You don't get to come here and speak to me like that! In fact, you shouldn't be here at all!" Instead of backing down, Nelson rapidly approached, standing nose to nose with Felt. It wasn't the response he expected, especially not from an officer on duty, particularly the chief. It was almost as if he insulted somebody in a bar. A brief but tense moment passed, and Felt slowly took a step back.

"You want to talk about things one shouldn't do?" Nelson said. "How 'bout making this young lady go out there ALONE to catch this thing, after you were damn well sure of what it was capable of!" He pointed to the shark. Felt gulped.

"Well it was her id--…" he paused, re-thinking his retort. Forster's jaw dropped slightly in grim astonishment, realizing Felt was about to throw her under the bus. "I…I…Well, I didn't *make* her…"

"You certainly manipulated her," Nelson said. Felt crossed his arms, in a pathetic attempt to look tough.

"Now, you can't just come here making wild accusations!" he said. "What exactly are you here for, anyway?" Nelson looked to the shark, quickly noticing the air pump.

"You're keeping it alive?"

"Uh, yeah," Felt said. *Duh*. Nelson shook his head, which Felt interpreted as disapproval. "Let me guess; you have an issue with that."

"You're wasting your time," Nelson said. "When I leave here, I'll be contacting the Coast Guard and have them properly expose of this thing." Felt scoffed.

"That'll be a cold day in hell," Felt said. Nelson turned toward him again, looking as if he was going to square up for the second time. "This thing is on my property, which makes it my property. You have no jurisdiction regarding this shark." Forster watched the anger develop on the Chief's face.

"This thing is responsible for God knows how many deaths," he growled. "It nearly killed my officer, it wrecked our patrol boat, killed Old Hal Mendes and Ben Shreiner." Felt put his hands up.

"Whoa, wait, wait, wait!" he said. "How do you know this thing killed them? Are you even sure if they're dead?"

"Pieces of wreckage were found floating near the Rivera Trench," Nelson said. "It's a spot where those guys were found dumping illegal traps."

"Isn't that a little outside your jurisdiction, Chief?" Felt said, further trying to challenge Nelson. Forster whispered to him to stop, but Felt didn't hear…or rather he chose not to listen.

"Listen pal, under certain circumstances, we can go as far out as we please," Nelson said. "Bits of wreckage were found, mostly from Ben's boat, although certain debris we believe was from Hal's boat. However, from everyone I've spoken to, Ben doesn't drink whiskey, and there were a couple of floating bottles near the wreckage. We brought up the traps, and discovered that they were smashed in, like something tore them apart. Name one thing that could do all of that that lives around here."

Felt shrugged, nonchalantly, "Sorry, Chief, it sounds more like speculation to me. I'll ask again, do you have any evidence directly linking this thing to anyone's disappearance?" Even Forster struggled to hide the disgust within her expression. Felt sounded like a defense attorney, fighting to keep the defendant from getting life in prison on a technicality. She noticed Nelson's slight quivers. He was awfully tempted to knock Felt to the floor. Felt knew just as well as everyone that the creature contained in the pen was undoubtedly a man-eater, but it didn't matter as long as bundles of cash was at stake.

"Chief," Forster said. Nelson didn't answer. "Chief…Joe?" Finally, Nelson turned his gaze toward her. It was the first honest use of his first name by Forster. "How's Nick?" Nelson took a breath, slowly soothing his temper.

"He's probably going to lose the leg," he said in a somber tone. "It's early yet, we can't say for sure. He's stable, though." Forster felt a mixed bag of emotions. She was happy that the officer pulled through and didn't lose too much blood, but on the other hand the guilt factor was at an all time high.

"Oh, God," she said. A flood of questions came to mind: donations, charities to the wife, anything she could do to assist in his rehabilitation, etc. She barely got the first syllable out for the first question when Felt started speaking again.

"Listen, Chief, I'm sorry about your officer. I really am." If nothing else, he at least sounded sincere. "But think logically for a second. Do you really think Wildlife Control or the Coast Guard will want to put this animal down; a rare, new species, already in captivity? Come on, you know as well as I do that they won't dare touch this thing." Nelson stood silent. At least this time, Felt spoke the truth. Still, Nelson wasn't satisfied. He thought of the ease in which it ravaged the boats, while simultaneously studying the walls of the pen.

"They won't kill it," he said, "but they'll definitely want to remove it from here."

"I beg your pardon?"

"You seriously think you'll be able to contain this thing here?" Nelson said. "If this thing gets pissed off, it'll bust through these walls like nothing."

"These walls are meant to contain whales," Felt said. "I think they can handle a crustacean fish, thing..."

"You wouldn't think that after seeing what I saw!" Nelson raised his voice again. "That damn thing went through the patrol boat like a blow torch through butter. Hell, most whales couldn't do that."

"This thing probably killed a whale," Forster chimed in. Both men looked to her.

"What are you talking about?" Felt asked. Forster looked to Nelson.

"The whale hit by the speedboat that I towed the other day...there was a larger gaping wound. We thought it was from the speedboat, but I found it odd even at the time because the injury didn't quite add up to what we thought happened. The whale was torn up, as if something had ripped chunks out of it."

"Jesus, it killed something that big?" Nelson exclaimed.

"Whose side are you on?" Felt said to Forster, turning his frustration toward her. "You're not implying that we can't contain this thing, are you?" It was the kind of question that demanded a specific answer, and Forster could read between the lines.

"I'm just saying, in order to keep it under control, we'll probably have to give it a continuous dosage of sedation," she said.

"Oh, nonsense," he said. "That's what people want! To see the thing at full force when we feed it." Nelson couldn't take any more of the closed-mindedness. It was as if Felt refused to look at anything other than dollar signs. It was clear that he had no concern for the lives of his staff, as demonstrated by having Marco feed the great white, and allowing Forster to ship out alone to hunt the predator. These continued actions by Felt furthered Nelson's anger.

"Listen, schmuck," he said, "you're putting people's lives at risk by even having this thing here! You've already nearly gotten two of your people killed, and one of my officers..."

Felt squared up again, however being sure to keep a step back. "You want to come in here unwelcome and call me names? How about we see how the Mayor takes to this after I pay him a personal visit?"

"Go ahead, pal," Nelson said. "I'm sure he'll be delighted to know how you illegally sent somebody out onto the water and caused the destruction of government property."

"He'd probably thank me," Felt said. At this point, he was simply looking for an edge in the argument. "At least *my* boat and *my* employee made it back in one piece!" He regretted the words even as they came out, but there was no time to retract them. Nelson's face lit up like a man possessed. Felt couldn't even flinch before the Chief lunged forward with both hands outstretched. He grabbed fistfuls of Felt's suit. They were deep grabs that ripped a couple of chest hairs from their pores. Felt yelped as he felt himself lifted off his feet and slammed against the thick glass.

Forster put her hands over her mouth. She wasn't sure if it was pure strength or adrenaline, but Nelson had lifted the hefty businessman completely off his feet and managed to keep him suspended. The commotion drew the attention of a couple of maintenance men and one security guard, who came rushing into the room. All three looked puzzled, surprised to see the normally mild-mannered Chief Nelson suddenly so enraged.

Her heart pounded in her chest, unsure of what he'd do next. With the cold glass pressed against his back, Felt stuttered, unable to say anything coherent because of the overwhelming anxiety. Forster stepped forward.

"Chief...put him down," she said. Nelson ignored her. "Chief!" This time she raised her voice, "let him go! Now!"

The water in the pen suddenly erupted in a fury of spirals, as if a tornado had touched down on it. All eyes went to the glass. Nelson jumped back impulsively, dropping Felt who landed on his feet and moved away. Bubbles twirled about, and the water swished, as the reawakened creature tore through the exhibit in a circular motion. Sluggish and uncoordinated, the creature continuously hit the walls as it raced about. A sense of self preservation struck everyone in the viewing room, including Felt. Even he worried of what would happen if the creature struck the bulletproof glass.

Forster whipped her gaze toward the entrance, where the light switches were located. Nearby, one of the maintenance men pressed his back to the wall.

"Hit the switches!" she yelled to him. He looked at her, puzzled for a moment before the instruction set in. He hit both switches in a single swipe. The room went black, except for the blue luminosity coming from the glass. The creature raced in a few wild circles, before slowing. What little strength it had, it spent. Its antennae stretched out, as if searching for something. They brushed against the glass. Forster felt a nervous chill run down her back as the beast seemed to be staring directly into the room.

It angled down, stretching the antennae toward the floor. It allowed itself to sink down in a circular motion, gaining some distance from the glass. It settled on the floor, opening and closing its mouth in large motions. Everyone in the room gradually moved toward the glass for a better look.

"What's it doing?" Felt asked. "Is it dry-heaving?"

"No," Forster said. Her voice contained amazement. "I think it's pumping water over its gills."

"Don't they have to swim for that?" one of the maintenance men said.

"Some sharks can get water over their gills while resting, like nurse sharks. This guy must have the ability to…" she stopped speaking, and stepped toward the glass as she witnessed the creature's next action. Its body rocked back and forth, as something emerged from underneath it. Large, thin appendages unfolded from its underbelly, and extended until their tips were pressed against the bottom of the tank. Like the legs on a spider, the six digits lifted the creature a few feet upward. Then it walked, however slowly, along the bottom.

"What…the…fuck…" the security guard said.

"Julie, what the hell is this thing?" Felt said. The anxiety and adrenaline from the recent encounter was overtaken and nearly forgotten from this bizarre event. Forster didn't answer right away, as she was taken aback by the new development.

"I…I don't know," she said.

"God, that's how it clung to the boat," Nelson said. Forster looked at him for clarification. "Remember, when it broke through the side. The boat leaned over, but it didn't slip back down into the water." The realization set in.

"It has these legs to move around during periods of rest," she said, "but it also uses them to cling on to an enemy or larger prey. And it's a scavenger!" She looked back to Nelson. "You said Hal had traps that were busted? This thing…I think it lived somewhere deep. After Wan Industry dumped in the water, that killed off a lot of its prey. It traveled along the deep, found Hal's traps, then found its way toward our island. Killed the whale, which got away…and that explains the claw marks…and the whale got hit by the boat. Then the thing stuck around, after finding a new abundance of food." She cupped her hand over her mouth again. "Oh God, and Old Hal is definitely…"

"We don't know that for sure," Felt said again. Nelson shook his head, feeling himself growing irritated again. He already risked his career by assaulting Felt, there was no use in digging a deeper hole for himself. He started walking out of the room. "Hey Chief!" Felt yelled after him, exactly what Nelson hoped wouldn't happen. He turned and answered with a silent stare. "So, what do you plan to do?" The question was surprisingly straightforward.

"If I hear that this thing injures anyone else, I'll come put a shotgun in its mouth myself," he said. "Otherwise, do what you want." He turned and left. Forster thought of walking out with him. She grew increasingly worried about Nelson. It was clear that he, like her, was getting very stressed from the recent events.

"Damn, this thing is freaking amazing," Felt said. He rubbed his chest where Nelson had grabbed him. Normally, he'd press charges, but it was clear he won the day when he got the Chief to lay off on his intentions for the specimen. That was all he needed, as long as Nelson didn't interfere further. Having an undiscovered species in his exhibit gave him an uplifting buzz. "Doc, it's all yours. Study as much as you wish. We'll be famous." Forster faked a smile. The accomplishment didn't feel as good as she thought it would.

"Thank you, sir," she said.

"You think you'll be able to figure out where it came from?" he asked.

"That would require me to do some traveling," Forster said. "To see if there are any more."

"Well, we'll have the *Neptune* back shortly," Felt said. "As long as you manage to care for this thing, and keep it under control, you can do as much research as you please. Our new sales will certainly fund it. The tax write-off won't hurt, either."

"Maybe take your travels to Mako's Center!" one of the maintenance workers said, followed by laughter. Forster looked at him, confused. The laughter stopped. "You remember? That hoax that went out a few years back? Everyone said a huge crab-squid monster attacked the island, and some Rick Napper, or however you say his name, went on record exposing the government for..." he altered his voice to sound spooky, "creating the monster as a weapon for military purposes." He chuckled again.

"Didn't he eventually recant the story, admitting it was fake?" the security guard asked.

"Yeah," the worker said. "Kind of a shame. Imagine if that really happened."

I can only imagine... Forster thought. She recalled the news reports, and how it swept the media, followed by the uproar when Rick Napier admitted the whole thing was made up. But there was something else about that story that itched in her mind, but she couldn't quite recall it. Something that reminded her of something else. She ached to get to a computer and read about it, wanting to know of the loose end to the story she couldn't figure out.

"So, what's your plan for this thing?" Felt interrupted her thoughts.

"Oh!" she said and looked at the creature. "Let me dump some scraps down here and see what it does." There was still plenty of food in stock which had been intended for the great white. She quickly exited, hoping the day would pass quickly.

CHAPTER
19

It was early in the afternoon when the Police Department announced the waters were safe to re-enter, though they never specified why nobody could be out to begin with. There was only the vague explanation that a shark had attacked the resort's research vessel. However, there was no press on the great white's escape. Scott and Ben found this somewhat surprising, but probably figured the owner didn't want the bad press. And they were fine with it, because it also meant that they had left no clue of their involvement.

As soon as the waters were reopened, Ben and Scott were immediately out on the water. For hours they drifted, while Scott made a chum trail, hoping to attract the white which they had illegally released. So far, all they found were stray tuna and a few baby dog sharks.

Scott scraped up the last of the chum from the empty container and dumped it over the stern of the *Twist Off*. Tired, bored, and frustrated he moved the empty container to the side of the deck before taking a seat. He turned to face the portside, looking inland, as the evening sun started sinking below the mainland skyline. Streams of horizontal light made it nearly blinding to look to the west, which forced him to squint as he chummed. Meanwhile, Ben stayed in the wheelhouse, ignoring the various complaints from his first mate. Wearing sunglasses to dim the sunlight, he continuously glanced to the fish finder, waiting for that large blip to appear. However, the screen showed nothing but a few tiny dots, like grains of salt, which represented tiny fish. He looked away often from the screen towards a pump-action shotgun leaning against the back wall of the cabin. Each glance to the weapon helped spark the glorious image of him putting a shell through the head of that shark and putting a hook on it before towing it away. It would be a great story to tell at the bars, assuming word didn't get out that it was Felt's shark. The fantasy helped him keep up the drive to hunt it. Scott, however, was growing more anxious by the hour. Looking at the reflection in the rearview mirror, Ben saw Scott sitting. He turned and stuck his head out the back window.

"Dude!" he said. "We don't have time for sitting! You see that sun over there?" He pointed to the horizon, as Scott looked and shielded his eyes.

"Yeah, I do!" the young, muscular fisherman replied. "I've been baking in it all damn day!"

"Yeah? Then you should know we have limited daylight left! I already see you've emptied the one tub of chum, now open the other one," Ben said.

"When are we heading back?"

"After we catch the bastard," Ben said. "Since we had to miss a day, we are already running late on schedule." Scott thought for a second, *What schedule? You never called the butcher to set this up.* He stood back up, and sluggishly dragged the full container of chum to the stern. After getting it to its spot, he straightened his stance and looked to the captain.

"You know…it's probably gone," he said. Ben could sense his drive had completely dissipated.

"I doubt it went too far," Ben reassured him. "It's probably looking for food. I heard they smell blood from miles out…or something, at least I think so…but either way, if he smells this from that far away it would take him a while to get here." Scott stared at him, deciding whether or not to inform his boss of what little sense he just made. Ben seemed already aware of this, and felt a desire to end the conversation. "Whatever, just quit complaining and get back to work," he said, and simply disappeared back into the wheelhouse, though he left the window open. Scott returned to his duties. He opened the tub, accidentally dumping a splash of red goo onto the deck. Guts splattered over his boots and pant legs.

"Great," he said, and proceeded to chum. As he did, his mind continued to wander, focusing on the deed they had committed the other night. For the past twenty-four hours it haunted him; not because of the impact to the resort or its employees, but something else he feared happened as a result. The news of Old Hal's disappearance, as well as Bob Whisker, spread quickly. Though Hal was not a favorite even among the fishing community, it still came as a shock when police identified the wreckage of his boat. Scott felt sick, and the constant, agonizing smell from the guts didn't help. He looked back to the wheelhouse, seeing Ben through the open window.

"I don't know man," he said. "Are we gonna head in after it gets dark?"

"You're still complaining!" Ben interrupted him.

"No, I'm *asking*," Scott said. "Because of what happened the other night, you know?" Ben sighed and stepped out onto the deck.

"Scott, I already told you, the shark didn't kill Hal," he said.

"You really think so? It just seems odd that the same night that we let it out, he disappeared," Scott said.

"It sucks that those guys are gone, but I'm done crying about it," Ben said. Scott thought he sounded surprisingly sincere, despite knowing what he was about to say next, "Right now, we have more important things to deal with." *Like make a buck.*

"I don't know, man," Scott said. A wave of realization hit Ben.

"Oh, I get what it is!" he said. "You're just anxious! You think that the shark sank Hal and Bob's boats, and will get us too if we stay out too late!" He started laughing, destroying the sincerity he exhibited before. Scott felt suddenly embarrassed.

"No! I, uh…" he stuttered. "It's just that…"

"Listen, kid," Ben said. "Sharks can't sink boats. It's not like the movies! Now, get a grip on yourself. We're gonna catch the bastard and make a bunch of money off him."

"Did you ever get a quote?" Scott asked, while turning around to resume chumming. Ben remained quiet for a moment.

"Sure did," he lied. "Five grand, the guy said."

"Five grand?" Scott asked. Ben nodded, while taking small indiscreet steps back to the wheelhouse, in hopes of sneaking out of the conversation.

"Uh, great white meat is a rare delicacy, and sells for lots of money. Hell, the guy will probably make three times what he'll pay us. Heh, chump! Oh well, but that's the word. So, uh, keep at it." He dipped back into the wheelhouse. Scott could feel the boat moving forward, meaning Ben likely wanted to try a different spot. The boat turned to the west, allowing the wheelhouse to cast a shadow over the deck, much to Scott's relief. He worked the chum, focusing on the five grand. Though he sensed the deception in Ben's voice, he chose to believe he was being truthful in order to justify the strain on his back.

"Oh shit," Ben's voice poured through the window. Scott stopped and peeked around the structure. Straining through the direct view of sunlight, he could just see the outline of an approaching boat.

"What's wrong? Who is that? A police boat?" he said, making himself nervous in the process.

"I don't think so," Ben said. "Probably just some fishermen. Stop chumming for a sec. I don't want anyone to know what we're up to. They might want a cut of the dough." For what seemed like the hundredth time, Scott dropped the scoop and took a seat. He looked around for something inconspicuous to do, so he grabbed a tangled net balled up in the corner and started working out the knots. The other boat's engine rumbled as it approached. Scott worked on the net, waiting for the boat to pass by.

"Hey, Ben!" a voice called out. "What are you doing out this late?" Scott could barely hear Ben curse under his breath before stopping the boat. The other boat stopped as well. Scott looked at the twenty-five-foot vessel, seeing one of Ben's drinking buddies at the helm. Morgan Purvis was a heavyset man, but managed to carry it well. Wearing a sweater and jeans, he stepped from the wheel to his starboard side. Ben greeted him with a wave.

"Nothing, really," he said. "By that I mean, almost literally nothing. That's all we've caught."

Tell me about it, Scott thought. Morgan scratched his goatee, seemingly sniffing the air.

"Yeah, we netted a few along the south side, but nothing significant," he said. His attention seemed drawn elsewhere even as he spoke. "Who knows, maybe we'll have to apply for welfare." He started eyeballing their boat, almost as if he was suspicious. He looked at the water behind them. Ben noticed this.

"Everything alright?" he asked, hoping he didn't sound nervous. Morgan didn't answer and kept looking at the water to the east. He tucked back toward his helm and grabbed some binoculars, then stepped back to the rail. Looking at the water, he saw the splashes of small sharks as they nipped at the chum trail. With the sun to his back, the red watery line in the water had a clear contrast against the surrounding water. He lowered the binoculars then stood up on his toes, trying to see into the *Twist Off's* deck. He could barely see the open container, with bits of blood spilt over the edges.

"Wait a sec…" he said. He suddenly burst into laughter. Maintaining his straight face, Ben tightened his fists out of view as his way of physically expressing his irritation. Morgan looked down toward an open hatch in his deck.

"Hey, Phil! Get up here!" A skinny man, dressed in exercise pants and a white t-shirt, climbed onto deck.

"What's up?" he asked.

"Remember that the Police Chief reported seeing a shark?" Morgan said. Phil nodded, and chuckled. Morgan pointed to Ben and Scott. "These guys are trying to hunt it! See the chum?" Both men erupted with laughter.

"No, not really…" Ben stuttered. Scott turned and winced, mentally begging Ben not to speak further, as he was not a good liar. "We're just out here to…"

"Well, you're not trawling," Morgan said. Ben gave up. If anything, he was relieved. So far, they didn't appear to be aware of the Great White's release. "One thing you are doing, is wasting your time. No shark would hang around here, there's no food. And even if you caught it, what would you do with it?" Ben suddenly found himself on the spot, after lying to Scott. All he could think of was to go with that same lie.

"I know a guy who'll butcher it on the mainland," he said. "He's willing to pay big bucks for a nice sized Great White." Morgan stared at him for a moment, as if reading his thoughts. Ben grew nervous, though he dared not to show it.

"Ha!" Morgan laughed again. Now Ben felt frustrated.

"What's so funny this time?" he said. Morgan wiped some spit from his face.

"It's illegal to fish for Great Whites in these parts," Morgan said. "There's no market around here that'll take it, not even its fins!" Scott perked up after hearing this. Though Ben didn't look at him, he could feel his first mate's eyes burrowing into his temple. The anger he sensed was real.

Scott wanted to confront Ben right away, but restrained himself. Doing so was hard. He had no problem committing such a felony as long as it meant a good payday. As Ben had deceived Hal by telling him they'd release the shark as revenge for the supposed tampering of his traps, Ben had deceived Scott, even if accidentally. Morgan could sense the unspoken tension that had awoken, though he was unaware of its meaning. However, the amusement had turned to awkwardness, and he suddenly wanted to leave. Phil felt the same way, as he disappeared back into the lower deck.

"Well, I suppose we'll be heading in," Morgan said. "Good luck on your endeavors. You know…you can still catch some blue shark if they're around." The attempt to offer encouragement only resulted in more silent awkwardness. Morgan stepped back to the helm. *He won't be drinking with me today.* "Good night!" He throttled the boat past them. Scott watched the boat move by, following the long trail of chum they had created.

Ben stepped back into the wheelhouse, as if it somehow hid him from Scott. It wasn't long before the portside door opened, and the first mate stepped in. His eyes looked demonic, and every facial muscle was tense. For the first time, Ben worried that Scott would physically harm him.

Then, strangely, Scott's angered look changed. Ben saw his eyes turn down toward the fish finder. Slowly, Ben looked to see what drew his attention.

There it was, the large green speck indicating that something big was underneath. The creature it represented, which they believed to be their great white, passed underneath. It seemed to approach Morgan and Phil's vessel. As it did, the image ascended. Not only did it ascend, but it did so with great speed, like a space shuttle burning thrusters. It touched the top of the screen. The echo of devastation, like a train collision, filled their eardrums. Both men raced out onto the deck, beholding the horror of Morgan's vessel. The stern was caved in completely, allowing water to rapidly seep in. The stern, or what remained of it, had almost completely submerged, and the bow tilted up.

Scott and Ben stared at the scene in stunned silence. The boat turned in the water like a top, completely in place. Water lifted like large mountains over the submerged stern, while small but vicious tidal waves formed as the hull from the bow swept along the surface. It was as if something had a hold of the boat from underneath. As it turned, the stern sunk down lower. The water that filled the compartments had added too much weight, in addition to the stress it was currently enduring. Metal groaned as bits of the vessel began to pull apart.

Morgan climbed out of the cabin, holding on to the door. His feet nearly slipped out from under him, and he nearly tumbled down into the thrashing waves. Ben turned and hurried into the wheelhouse and turned the wheel. The *Twist Off* moved in a circular motion until it had completely turned around. For once, Ben was doing the decent thing as he moved the boat closer to the devastation to help his friend. By the time they had turned, Morgan's boat had come to a stop, with the starboard side facing their bow. Cracks had formed in the hull along the side, and the vessel leaned heavily to port. They didn't see Morgan.

"Morgan! Phil! Get out on deck!" Scott yelled to them. There was no answer. The waves settled, leaving a dreary silence that was more unsettling than the active devastation. Then the silence was broken. A spine-chilling scream filled the air. Ben stopped the approach and felt his jaw quiver as he saw his friend emerge from behind the boat, waist up from the water. Both arms were stretched out, as if trying to cling to the air for safety. Blood poured from his mouth as he was dragged along the surface, his torso bending backward from the force. A huge shadow traveled underneath him, taking him wherever it went, leaving a trail of blood. Morgan yelled out until his lungs ran out of air. The shape hooked around and went back to the boat, continuing to drag the captain. Then, in a swift motion, it dove. Morgan disappeared under the waves, and another eerie silence replaced the chaos.

Ben slowed his boat, gradually taking it around the side of the half-submerged wreckage. He worked his way around the bow, keeping a distance of twenty feet. Scott stood in the center of the deck. Fright caused his teeth to chatter as if he was standing outside in twenty-degree temperature. Their boat came around to the portside, which was almost completely submerged by water. There was nothing but calm water and wreckage. Ben looked hopelessly at the water, which seemed so deceptively peaceful.

A splash erupted, sending a huge wave at the windshield. Ben jumped back, then laid eyes on the water that slid down the glass. It was red with Morgan's blood.

"Oh my God!" Scott screamed. Ben opened the door and leaned outside, seeing his first mate backing away in terror. On the deck was one of Morgan's arms, severed just above the elbow, before being thrown by the splash.

Self preservation took over. Ben jumped back inside and put the boat on full throttle. Scott turned and looked down at the water, dry heaving after witnessing the sickening gore. The engine hummed as the *Twist Off* gained speed, leaving the sinking vessel behind.

"Come on, come on, not too far," Ben said to himself to try and relax his nerves as he watched the island grow steadily larger. He wasn't even going to find a port; he was going to dock anywhere he possibly could as long as he could set foot on dry land.

A glowing light caught his eye. The fish finder was still on, and Ben couldn't help but notice the large green blob was still on the screen. Directly underneath them. Ascending rapidly.

As Scott looked into the water, he was only able to see the enormous shadow for a brief moment. The next thing he saw was a mad flurry of debris as the starboard quarter seemed to explode. Fiberglass and wood shot in every direction, and the boat flipped to port and rolled like a log. Scott felt himself thrown into the water, several yards away. He sank several feet down. His body was momentarily paralyzed from the stunning impact. His eyes were open, and he found himself staring at the *Twist Off*. It was completely capsized, with the wheelhouse pointing downward.

The door was busted off, and bits of wreckage surrounded it like an asteroid field. He saw Ben emerge. His teeth were clenched, and it was clear he was in immediate need of air. He struggled frantically toward the surface. Then the shape emerged.

Motionless in the water, Scott beheld the immense creature. Red in color, shaped like a shark, but with a jointed body and a rigid exterior. Strange appendages protruded from its snout, and spiny formations were formed all over its body. He witnessed Ben shriek under the water before the jaws snatched him up. Teeth punctured his torso, forcing Ben's entire body into its mouth. His arms and legs dangled from the jaws, waving incessantly as Ben still fought for dear life. The creature shook him viciously from side to side. A cloud of blood burst from the chomp, and suddenly the limbs were torn from the body. They floated away, each leaving a trail of blood.

Scott felt his strength return to him, and he swam to the surface. He took a gasp of air and turned toward the island. It was when he started to swim that he realized he had no more energy left, despite the adrenaline pumping through his veins. It was as if his body shut down.

Bobbing in the water nearby, he saw the detached wheelhouse door floating several feet away. He used what strength he had left and made his way to it and climbed on top of the flat piece of wood. He laid face down on it, keeping a hold on the edges. He watched the fin emerge and course the water in a circle. It was as if it was searching. He kept still, hoping he would remain undetected.

The red fin made several passes. Each minute seemed to last forever, and it appeared that the strange creature would not give up. Suddenly, it stopped. After a few seconds, the creature turned away, and darted for the wreckage that was Morgan's boat.

Phil had moved the last of the cargo out of the way as water filled the storage compartment. The impact had thrown him to the side, nearly knocking him unconscious. When his senses returned to him, he was almost completely underwater, leaning against the wall. The compartment was flooding, and the hatch was blocked by large crates. As the water filled the remaining space, he raced to move everything out of the way to get to safety. By the time he was able to open the hatch, the entire compartment was completely submerged.

Despite the confusion of what was happening, there was still the sense of relief once he escaped the watery tomb. That relief only lasted for a moment. Up to his chest in water, clinging to the railing, he saw the fin cutting through the water toward him. Then the creature's snout lifted over the surface, and the mouth opened, revealing white jagged teeth over two inches long. The jaws encompassed him, and he felt each tooth puncture his body. The jaws tightened their grip, driving each tooth deeper. Internal organs were punctured. Phil let out a pained scream until the teeth pierced his lungs, deflating any air he had. Blood burst from his mouth, and he was dragged underwater. The creature released its grasp, only to make a new bite and drive him deeper into its throat.

Scott closed his eyes as the screams finally ceased. He clung to the door, listening to the distant thrashing in the water as the creature searched the wreckage for other prey. Soon, exhaustion consumed him, and he slipped into unconsciousness as the current carried him towards shore.

CHAPTER
20

The final streaks of sunlight stretched over the resort as the clocks struck *9:00.* The rides ceased activity, the concession stands started storing away merchandise and food for the night, and the doors to the aquarium were locked shut. The late-night visitors had mostly vacated from the park and aquarium to the resort, most of them to their hotel rooms. Others gathered at the late-night bars, where overpriced drinks were constantly being served.

Nine-year-old Eric Neman texted away on his iPhone, staring at the tents blocking the Great White Exhibit. He didn't pay much attention to his dad, who sat on a bench nearby, taking slow breaths. The fried chicken strips he ate over an hour ago were not sitting well. His wife sat next to him, continuously asking him how he was feeling, which only agitated his condition.

"Just...hang on," he said. He held a hand up toward her, signaling for her to wait. He kept his eyes shut and focused on the cooling night air. The wife simply mouthed "okay" and scooched away from him.

While his dad struggled to keep his dinner, Eric kept trying to peek past the tents and other barriers that blocked any view into the pen. Since they had arrived yesterday, he anxiously waited to see the great white, only to be disappointed by the announcement that the exhibit was temporarily closed. His parents took the liberty of asking employees when it would reopen, only to receive vague responses that didn't really answer much. It was as if they knew but weren't allowed to give any information. Every time they passed by, Eric looked for a way to sneak around and get a peek, but never found a good opportunity. A lover of all things sharks, he was immensely disappointed, to the point where it impacted his enjoyment of the rest of the resort.

Just a peek at the big fish was all he wanted.

The dad coughed a few times, followed by a pained moan. The wife scooted back next to him, instinctively putting her hand on his shoulder.

"Honey, do you think you can make it back to the hotel?" He simply shook his head but stood up anyway as if to attempt. She stood up alongside him. "Just relax, take one breath at a time." Her words seemed to have the opposite effect. He took a breath, but as if he was bracing for something. His eyes opened wide, and his expression alerted her to the situation. "Oh shit," the wife said. She looked around frantically, hoping to find a trash can. Surprisingly, there didn't appear to be one in the immediate area.

What kind of place doesn't have garbage cans around? She rushed to the front doors to the aquarium and peered through the glass. There were restrooms just a little way away, but the entrance was locked. Looking inside, she saw a security officer walking across the lobby. She tapped on the glass, gently enough not to scratch it. He looked toward her, recognized her fervent mannerisms, and quickly met her. He opened the door a crack.

"Is everything alright, ma'am?" he asked.

"I know you guys are closed, but can you please let my husband use the restroom? He isn't feeling well, and trust me, he won't make it to the hotel." The security guard looked to the husband, and immediately saw that he was on the verge of vomiting. The policy was 'no unauthorized persons in the aquarium after hours', but his natural compassion took over.

"Yeah, come on in," he said, immediately hoping the guy would not lose it on the freshly cleaned floors. He held the door open wide for them.

"Oh, thank you," the wife said. She quickly turned toward her husband, who didn't hesitate to enter. As soon as he was past the doors, he was running to the men's room. The wife entered after him and turned toward Eric. "Come on, hon! I want you to wait in here." Eric dragged his feet along, as if still expressing his disappointment about the shark, and entered. The security guard shut the door behind them and followed the wife toward the restroom.

"Does he need medical assistance?" he asked her.

"No," she said. "Just a bad dinner. I'll check on him if that's alright?"

"Yeah," the guard said. He remembered he still needed to lock the back entrance. He thought of putting it off, but didn't want to risk people strolling in through the unlocked doors. It always resulted in a hassle getting them to leave. "Just stay with him, and I'll be back shortly. I just need to take care of a couple of things real quick," he said.

"Okay, thank you," the wife said. The security guard walked off, disappearing into another hallway. The wife looked at Eric as she walked toward the bathroom. "Just wait in here, hon." She disappeared behind the door, leaving Eric waiting alone in the lobby.

He could hear his father's retches even from where he stood. Getting his mind off the matter, he strolled around the lobby while eyeballing many of the displays. He looked at the center glass tank, shaped like a large tunnel that traveled from the floor to the ceiling. Inside, fish of many different shapes and sizes swam about. With the lobby lights turned off, their colors didn't stand out as much. While he thought they were cool, they weren't what he was hoping to see. He walked past it to the nearby wall. He noticed a stairwell door with a sign posted nearby: *Great White Exhibit*, with an arrow pointing downward toward the basement level. A piece of paper was taped to the center of the door, reading *CLOSED* in bold letters.

The seeds of temptation were planted. Eric figured his dad would be stuck in the bathroom for a while, and the security guard seemed like he was busy. All he wanted was a peek at the shark.

He twisted the handle. It was unlocked, and it opened into a dark stairway. Eric looked down, seeing a few lights and nobody in sight. He carefully made his way down until he reached the basement. It immediately led to a tunnel, illuminated by neon lights, intended to represent creatures from the ocean's deep. Knowing he only had limited time, he made his way through, stopping just long enough to make sure he wouldn't be caught. Arrows with a shark illustrated on the stem confirmed he was going the right way.

The tunnel led him into a large room. The only light in the room came from the huge plate of glass on the wall, which looked out into the pen. He shuddered with excitement, coupled with the uneasy feeling in his stomach for trespassing. However, the thrill he was experiencing felt worth it, and even more so after he peered into the glass. There was just enough light coming in from over the pen to illuminate the basic shape of the shark. He could see it nearly in the center, off to the side. Oddly, it seemed just to sit at the bottom.

Eric felt nervous. From the books he had read, he learned that sharks needed to constantly swim in order to stay alive. Here the shark was seemingly motionless. Is it dead? Is that why the park is closed? He didn't hesitate to tap on the glass, hoping to get its attention.

It worked. The shape lifted off the floor, curious to the sound that had echoed through its entrapment. It moved in a slow, swerving line toward the source. Eric pulled his iPhone out, intending to snap a couple of pictures before exiting. The creature turned and swam across the glass. Its huge body was barely in full view of the glass that was only a few feet longer. As it passed, Eric felt something was odd about it. It was dark, almost a silhouette, but he though he saw something odd protruding from the head. He looked at the wall, just outside the glass. There was a panel, barely ajar. He opened it completely and used his phone to shine lights on several breaker switches. He looked at the listing, finding one for overhead pen lights.

Oh man, they'll kill me for this, he thought. He justified it in his mind, thinking he'd only have the lights on for a moment before turning them right off. He tapped on the glass again, drawing the creature near. He waited until the shape was up to the glass, then he flipped the switch. The lights came on and he quickly snapped several photos, before stopping and looking at the creature. It was no great white.

The hybrid saw the potential meal, and moved in, only to be stopped by a strange invisible barrier. The glass shook, and a small crack started to form where the nose had struck. Eric jumped back. His heart pounded in his chest, and his body shook with fright. Only for a moment was he mesmerized by the shark's red color, rigid exoskeleton, antennae, and other bizarre features. Then that fascination turned to fear when he realized the huge shark intended to eat him, and could easily break through the glass. The shark grew frustrated and began to swim around in a crazed frenzy. Eric hit the switch, turning off the pen lights, and ran for the tunnel.

He had just reached the stairwell when Security raced down. Flashlights shined upon him, held by two guards, one of which was the one from the lobby.

"Hey! What are you doing down here?" Eric didn't answer, and looked back. The radio blared.

"*It's moving rapidly, but I think it's slowing down. I don't know how many times it hit the glass. You guys at the viewing center?*"

"Yeah, it's some kid," one guard replied on his radio.

"I'm sorry," Eric babbled.

"Come on," the guard said, motioning for him to go upstairs. Eric followed them. As he did, he pulled his phone out, and brought up his *Facebook* account. Making a new post, he uploaded the photos, along with the text: *New shark at Felt's Paradise.*

With a click of the button, the post was complete.

CHAPTER
21

Forster barely noticed the living room light switch off after it timed out. Laying along her couch, her eyes were fixed on the laptop screen while she read through various articles from three years ago. She read reports on the supposed creature attack that took place, in which multiple people were killed. The body count rose with each report, until it grew to be several dozen deaths, including those of law enforcement officers. Depictions of the creature indicated that it was squid-like, but with characteristics and features of a crustacean, notably a crab. Speculation grew that it was a new species, while others argued that it could have been a mutation of sorts. But soon, officials announced in many different press conferences that such a creature did not exist, and that the creature was simply a Colossal Squid of magnificent proportions.

Then there were several exclusive interviews with a man named Rick Napier. He went around speaking of the events in great detail. In one, he named a Dr. Isaac Wallack, who created the creature as a weapon for the government.

Forster grew more curious with each article. She had heard of it back when it took place, but didn't think much of it after it was announced to be fake. She came across many articles regarding that issue as well. Following the statements from the government officials, reports indicated that the damage reported by locals, and Rick Napier, were highly exaggerated. The 'sunken boats' were never recovered, though it was reported that the creature did attack with its whips when it surfaced. The articles reporting on the hoax reported that the video footage that had been released was altered via computer, to create a false story based on a real tragedy. After a while, the reports stopped, save for Napier, who for months made various appearances via online news forums explaining the existence of the Behemoth, and how it was created.

This led Forster to look up the video footage. Opening up a new window, she first found the original leaked footage of the attack. The video began with a warning, explaining that it contained graphic language and footage. The image was shaky, likely taken from an iPhone. As soon as she hit *play*, the volume burst with panicked screams as people raced up the beach. There was a quick view of an enormous wave, uncovering the bulk of something enormous. The video panned down to the sand as the recorder shifted his position to avoid a flood of fleeing swimmers. As the camera lifted toward the water, the monster had completely breached the surface. Forster paused the video to look at it, entertaining the idea that it was not a hoax.

She noticed that it contained the basic bodily form of a giant squid, but with a rigid exoskeleton. Multiple whips protruded from its body, not from the head like normal squids, but from the side in a similar manner as legs on a spider.

Or a crab. She watched as it slaughtered several individuals, one after another. Some it devoured, others it just killed. While it was very much an animal, it also seemed like a machine, made solely for killing. She saw the two large front arms, thicker than the tentacles, and armored like the rest of its body. Each arm contained pincers, much like those of a crab.

Forster stopped the video, sickened from the bloodshed. She eyeballed the still image of the 'fake' monster. If this was fake, it required a lot of imagination. It was a perfect blend of two specific species. Much like the creature contained in the exhibit. Had she not encountered the mysterious beast, she would be among the many people suspecting this video to be a fraud. However, she began to speculate; what if this thing was real?

On the screen was a side bar with a list of suggested videos, one of which was a segment from an exclusive interview with Rick Napier. She immediately clicked on it. The page opened up and the video was ready for viewing. The camera was focused on him as he sat across a square table. He was unshaven, and seemed tired, possibly stressed. She had never met him, but Forster thought he had several concerns on his mind. If he really believed this creature was made by the government, it made sense. She clicked *play*.

"*No, it is not a freak of nature, nor a miracle of nature,*" he said, presumably answering a question asked before the cutoff point. "*It was an abomination; scientifically engineered from different organisms to create an ultimate weapon for the government.*" It was odd hearing him speak. On the one hand, he certainly sounded crazy, but on the other hand, something about what he said resonated with Forster. The camera switched angles as Napier and the interviewer spoke.

"*Why did the scientist kidnap you? You said before, you were just a fisherman. You didn't even have your doctorate at that time. What was so special about you that this Dr. Wallack and his hired mercenaries had to single you out?*" Napier took a brief sigh. Forster believed he was either tired of rehashing the same answers over-and-over, or possibly hating to relive the memory.

"*Most of the fishermen here don't operate with the largest vessels,*" he said. "*Me, at the time I had a fifty-foot trawler. Dr. Wallack was funding this operation out of his own pocket, as a way of redeeming himself for it getting loose; or showing he was capable of remaining in control of it. But he only had enough funds to buy the mercs. He had no other sufficient supplies, so he located me and took me hostage, along with Chief Bondy, my fiancé, daughter, and her boyfriend. He used them as hostages to goad me into using my boat to aid their cause.*"

"*And you eventually found it, correct?*" the interviewer said.

"*Yes,*" Napier answered. "*They subdued it with tranquilizer.*"

"*And what happened after that?*"

"*I managed to help Bondy and Lisa get off the boat. They went on a motorized raft and made their way to the Coast Guard Cutter, Ryback, which was nearby. In the meantime, I was still on the Catcher. We hit a rock, and were trying to weld a patch, when the thing woke up.*"

"*Wasn't it tranquilized? How long were you there?*"

"*Not long,*" Napier said. "*It was estimated to be able to last for twelve hours. I don't know if it was an increased metabolism, or if the creature was just too big for the dose, but the tranquilizer wore off quick.*" Forster's interest rose at this revelation. It sounded familiar: eerily familiar. If the story was fake, then it was just another odd coincidence. She resumed the video, and Napier started speaking again. *"The damn thing started tearing the boat apart, and killed everybody, including Wallack."*

"That left you as the sole survivor?"

"My daughter and the kid she was seeing as well," Napier corrected him. *"The U.S.S. Ryback arrived just in time and killed it. They saved our lives."* The interviewer sat back, removed his glasses for a moment, while staring at Napier questioningly. Forster suspected he had to deal with these looks often.

"What do you have to say about the Coast Guard formally announcing that they've never encountered a creature as you've described?" he asked, while chewing on the arm of his glasses. Napier looked visibly tired, in a way that he knew he was fighting an uphill battle. It was not the first time he had heard this news, but it must've been new enough to where it weighed heavily on him. It seemed like he was the only one willing to tell the truth.

"Of course not," he said. *"The government wants to keep this quiet. Everyone in the military has been given strict instructions to remain quiet."*

"Your fiancé hasn't said anything," the interviewer said. Napier knew he was being baited.

"I can't speak for her. Her twenty-year tenure is nearing its end, and it was hard-earned. I don't want to get her in any trouble."

"She's with the military?"

"I can't speak further on that," Napier said. *"Hence, I won't even mention her name."*

"And what about that police chief?"

"He's under similar pressure. Though he runs a small force, it's still a government job, and guess who's ordering him to not say anything."

"As it stands, researchers claim that the creature was none other than a regular giant squid, or colossal squid. Its size is considered a marvel, and it's been baffling oceanographers and marine biologists, but it has been confirmed that it was not a hybrid creature."

"Oh, give me a break," Napier was growing restless. It was clear that there was no reaching this interviewer, who either bought into the reports, or was bought by someone else to press Napier. Forster could easily see that Napier was considering walking out, but he remained seated, possibly hoping to reach out to the viewers. *"And you probably believe the footage is computer enhanced."* The interviewer shrugged. *"By the way, it was never 'confirmed'. They just reported it, but provided no fu...evidence."* He paused to keep himself from cursing. *"And who are these researchers who supposedly verified this? We've seen them on TV, but we know nothing about them. Who do you think they work for?"* The interviewer didn't answer. He returned his glasses to his face and looked at his notes.

"You still suspect there's more of these government hybrids out there?" Even just listening to him was annoying for Forster, how condescending the interviewer was.

"*I suspect something's going on,*" Napier said. "*Or at least there was. There was the disappearance of that sailing yacht, the K. McCartney, just a couple days later. Maybe twelve miles from our island.*"

"*I believed it was determined that it was lost in the storm,*" the interviewer contradicted him again.

"*Oh, yeah?*" Napier said. "*Seems odd, considering their last transmission indicated that they had reached a clearing. And should we just assume that the heavy military activity in that area was just a coincidence?*" The interviewer tilted his head and fumbled with his glasses again, as if trying to think of something to say. Napier continued, "*There were many reports of Navy choppers sweeping that area, not patrolling, but in a formation indicative of pursuit. They were chasing something.*"

"*You trust unverified reports? Fishermen, sailors, supposedly seeing something in the distance?*"

"*I am a fisherman,*" Napier said. "*At this point, I trust them more than the feds.*" The video came to a close. Forster found herself staring at the inactive screen, while she pondered everything she just heard. She didn't expect to hear him speak about the *K. McCartney.* As it turned out, she wasn't the only one who connected the dots between the disappearance and the strange events leading up to now.

Suddenly, she felt really stupid, as if believing a conspiracy theory. She slapped herself in the face, mimicking punishment.

Oh, come on! she thought to herself. *It's not even real. The guy himself admitted that he made it up. Just some asshole trying to get fifteen minutes of fame.* She forced these thoughts through, hoping to convince herself to let go of the subject. Perhaps the creature really was just a freak of nature. Everything evolves after all, right? Still, she couldn't help but notice the odd similarities between the creature at work and the 'fictional creature' on the video.

In an attempt to convince herself it wasn't real, and free her mind of the subject, she clicked on the video which showed Napier making a press release admitting the story was fake. He stood at a small podium, while many journalists sat in multiple rows of chairs. Dressed formally in a suit and tie, Napier struggled not to flinch from the onslaught of camera flashes. Already, Forster noticed something odd. *All these reporters for this? Even his exclusive interviews didn't get that much viewership.* It was another bit of trivia she learned in her hours of researching. Immediately, she was speculating. Were these reporters all genuinely curious? Or did someone possibly put them there to make sure this particular story was spread? Hell, the way most people heard of the story was of how Napier was ripped apart in the media for his remarks.

Damn it, I'm doing it again.

Napier looked even more tired than before. It was like he hadn't slept in weeks. His tie was barely tied, and his suit looked rugged. If she had clicked on this video without knowing the pretext, she would've assumed he was on drugs.

"*Thank you for being here today,*" he began. "*I'd like to extend my most humble apologies to the people I've hurt, most especially those whose tragedy I have exploited. As you probably already know, I've come here to admit to you all*

130

that there was no sea monster. My reasons for fabricating this story are my own, but I will say they were selfish, and I am deeply sorry. None of what I said was true, and falsely based on a real tragedy that I should have never acted on. I would also like to extend my humble apologies to the United States Coast Guard, who I'm aware has been under scrutiny since the story came out." That was the only part that Forster felt was genuine. Everything else it seemed was based on a script. "*You guys are great, and I thank you for your service to our country. To everyone else, I understand this caused a lot of confusion. For years now, we've been living in troubling times, and trust for our government has been shaky at best. I'm sorry to have exploited that, and for possibly adding to the tension. Now, as I close, I just want to reiterate; there was no hybrid experimentation that I'm aware of. The creature did not and does not exist. I admit to you all that this story is absolutely false.*" He looked up from his notes. Forster heard the sound of the notepad hitting the podium, as if he was barely containing a rage within him. "*That's all I have for you. Thank you.*" Reporters stood from their seats in unison, extending microphones out toward Napier. Questions from all over the room blended together in a chaotic mixture of noise from the audience. Napier, however, had no intention of being there any longer than he had to. Walking with a couple of other men in suits, he moved toward an exit and disappeared into a hallway. The video concluded.

As before, Forster found herself starting to analyze what she saw, only to wince from a splitting headache. With everything on her mind, she almost forgot she had suffered a concussion. She turned off the laptop and took her prescribed Ibuprofen. She looked at the time: *11:45.*

"Oh shit," she said. She had completely lost track of the time. She forced herself to forget about the videos and entered her bedroom. Hopefully, her busy mind would settle down and allow her to sleep.

CHAPTER
22

It didn't. Forster dipped in and out of consciousness for hours. Even when she was asleep, her dreams were fixated on the footage or the shark. To make matters worse, only an hour or so before she was due to wake up did she finally fall into a deep sleep. Waking up was a nightmare.

Stumbling from the bedroom to the kitchen, Forster felt like she had downed four martinis in rapid succession. As she often did before getting to work, she stepped into the living room and switched to the local news network. She rarely paid attention to it, but the background noise often helped with the waking up process. The talking heads began speaking about the usual topics, from politics to current local events. Hardly listening, Forster downed some more Ibuprofen for her headache, along with a small protein shake. Still feeling as if she had risen from the grave, she made her way to the shower and undressed. Leaving her clothes in an unorganized pile, she turned on the hot water, which came out as ice cold. The icy shock helped a little bit to wake her up, but not nearly enough. She smothered her hair in shampoo, hearing the news anchor voices.

"...*More on that at 6:30. Meanwhile, Felt's Paradise is drawing much attention for a possible new discovery. Dan?*" Another voice took over.

"*Thanks, Marie. I'm standing here outside the aquarium, near the former Great White Exhibit.*" Suddenly, Forster was wide awake. She snatched up a towel and wrapped it around herself as she dashed to the living room. Ignoring the shampoo dripping from her soaked hair, she watched the television, seeing her workplace on a live feed.

"What the hell..."

"*...Mr. Felt has explained to us that there was no way this thing was responsible for the sinkings, that it was captured before the tragedy took place. He'll be speaking further with us, so in the meantime, we'll be waiting here. Marie, back to you.*" The feed switched back to the news station.

"*As of right now, Ben Whitaker, Morgan Vohagan, and Phillip Mile are still missing. Scott Willis is still in the hospital. Police have not yet given any details on his condition.*"

Forster stood, baffled. She had missed part of the broadcast, but it was clear that Felt had announced the discovery of the new shark. She checked her phone, but there were no messages or missed calls. Whatever was happening, nobody had bothered to notify her. She hurried back into the bedroom and lined her work clothes on the bed. A drip of shampoo fell from her scalp and splattered onto her freshly clean shirt.

"Lovely," she said. She stepped back into the shower to rinse, then hurried into her clothes and out the door.

****

By the time she arrived, there were a dozen news vans in the parking lot. Some were local, while others were ferried from Georgia. She slowly drove through the crowded lot, until she found her way to the employee parking. Even there, a couple of news vehicles had parked. She got out, and immediately flagged a passing maintenance worker. The man stopped as she ran to him.

"Hey, what is all this? What's going on?" she asked.

"You know that shark you guys caught? Some kid got photos of it, and now they've made their way to the internet." Forster looked up with a pained expression.

"Oh, shit," she said.

"Oh, it gets better," the worker said. "Some guy's claiming it killed some of his friends."

"Who? What guy?"

"Some fisherman. I don't know if he saw the images, but he's saying he was out on his fishing boat, and the thing sunk it. So, Felt invited all these reporters here for damage control."

"That explains how everyone got here so quick," she said. "When did this happen, the attack?"

"Last night, I think," the worker said. "Cops found him washed ashore, so something happened. But then again, who knows. Maybe he's trying to invoke a lawsuit from this place."

"Last night? That's impossible," Forster said, more to herself than to the worker. "It was here. There's no way it could've..."

"Hey! There she is!" a voice called out. A flood of reporters burst from the aquarium doors and rushed toward Forster. Microphones were extended toward her, followed by a bombardment of questions.

"Doctor, you made this discovery? How did you manage to bring this creature in?"

"Dr. Forster, where did this species come from?"

"Is it the largest species of shark?"

"Are you worried about environmentalists protesting its capture?"

"Do you believe this shark is a man-eater, Doctor?"

"What is the name of this species?"

"Doctor?

"Doctor?

"Doctor? Doctor? Doctor? Doctor? Doctor?"

It was like a feeding frenzy, and she was the meal. She shouted out random answers, mainly "I don't know," as she struggled to fend off the reporters. Standing on her tip toes, she could see Felt in the back of the crowd.

"Excuse me," she said, and started making her way through the reporters. The first few were accommodating, but further into the crowd, other reporters stood in her way, trying to get their chance at asking a question. "Excuse me, I need to get through." Further in, she had to forcefully shove people aside, until finally she reached Felt.

"Hey Julie," he said. "I was going to…"

"What's going on here?!" she yelled. Felt looked at her, flabbergasted that she was angry.

"I thought this is what you wanted," he said. He pointed toward the reporters. "Look, they're all interested in talking to you! You wanted to be a household name in science…"

"I told you to wait…" she trailed off as she looked to the water. She realized the barriers had been removed, with a sign stating that the exhibit was available for viewership. She looked to the aquarium. A lazily built sign hung over the entrance.

Come and view the Lobster Shark; an incredible new species, found only here at Felt's Paradise. She turned back toward Felt.

"You opened the exhibit?"

"It's my business, Julie," he said. "I can do whatever I want. Don't forget, you work for me. Listen…" he took her by the shoulder and led her inside. The reporters started following them in. He held out a hand to stop them, while faking a nice business smile. "Please, wait out here for just a moment, everybody. We'll be right with you, I promise." He shut the door behind them, which latched shut. Luckily, the business hours had not yet begun, so he wouldn't have to worry about visitors.

"Okay, listen, I'm sorry I didn't keep you in the loop, but this thing happened suddenly. Pictures of the fish were leaked online and, holy crap, they spread like wildfire. Word of this thing was already out. I just had to take control of the situation," he said. Forster rested her fists on her hips.

"Did you take them down to the viewing area?"

"Yeah, but only for a sec. We need to replace the glass," he said.

"Replace the glass?"

"Yeah…apparently this thing tried attacking somebody through the panel…" his words slowed, as if he didn't want to admit them. However, Forster's eyes were almost hypnotic as she cynically stared at him. He heaved a sigh, "…and, when I took the reporters down there, it moved in like the devil. The glass is barely holding together."

"You shut the steel barriers, right?" Forster said.

"Of course," Felt said. "We just have to replace the glass." By the way he spoke, it was like there wasn't a problem in the world. This only upset Forster more.

"I told you, it's possible we can stress the thing out," she said. "It could be very dangerous having it here, but I agreed to do it as long as I had complete say on how to handle it. I told you that taking people down there might get it worked up. Why do you have me here if you're not going to listen to me?"

"Hey," Felt raised his voice slightly. "The business comes first. You want a paycheck, I need this place to run in order to get you that. Besides, it's working!"

"What do you mean?"

"Just this morning, we've already had twelve new reservations!" He threw his fists out, in a victorious fashion. "People want to see this thing. There'll be more coming in! Some are even last minute for this week! And we already got calls from some universities. Literally, this morning! These places are offering big bucks to let their researchers come over and examine this thing!"

"I thought that was supposed to be my job," Forster said. Felt stood silent for a moment, remembering what he promised her when she agreed to capture the creature.

"Oh, well, you're still credited with the discovery. I mean that's the main thing you wanted." Forster slowly exhaled, feeling as if she was venting steam. Not only was Felt belittling her, he didn't even realize it. Felt looked to the glass doors and saw the reporters growing impatient. For him, it was timely. "Oh, well, we need to appease our crowd. Let's go."

"Wait," she said. Felt stopped and looked at her again. "What's this about somebody claiming this thing attacked them?"

"Just some guy who saw the pictures and figures he can cook up a story for a juicy lawsuit. Luckily, as I told these nice people here, the story doesn't add up. You captured the thing early in the day, this guy claims he was attacked last night. Obviously, it couldn't have been our shark. So, I took the advantage, since we already had these people here, to announce that we have a new exhibit. That's why I need you to come here with me." That uneasy feeling crept its way back down Forster's spine. Something wasn't adding up. The photos spread, but so quickly that this fisherman could concoct a story out of a real sinking? According to the news, two boats apparently did go down. At the very least, it was an odd coincidence.

"Okay, thanks," she said. "I'll let you get to it. I, uh, have a couple of things to take care of." Every fiber in her being was desperate to research the matter. The first thing would be to call Nelson, who likely had to interrogate the fisherman. And him! She desired to speak with the fisherman and hear his description of what happened. She felt like a conspiracy theorist, but the sick feeling would not go away.

"Oh, I guess I should've explained further," Felt said. "When I said 'we need to appease our crowd', I really meant you and me." Forster glared at him.

"I'm not a public relations person..."

"Just answer some questions about the fish, as best you can," he said. "Then allow them to observe you doing what you do to care for it. We need to show people we have this thing under control."

"But I'm still figuring much of that out," Forster said. Felt leaned in.

"Then do the best you can to BS it," he said. He looked again to the crowd and waved at them to signal he was coming back out. Returning his eyes to Forster he said, "Now come on," and led the way to the door.

The next several hours were long and tedious. In addition to learning about the creature and its needs and tendencies, she had to do it while answering what seemed like hundreds of questions from the reporters. Many of these questions were the same, just worded in a different way so each journalist could differentiate their article. After answering questions, Forster led them on a tour of the aquarium, taking a special tour of the recovery area for the dolphins. It was a stalling move, as Forster thought of ways to demonstrate how she would handle the shark. Clearly, the reporters weren't interested in this, but it at least provided her with a dialogue to explain how they had the supplies to handle a variety of species.

Finally, she led them to the docks. The reporters gathered around the deck on both sides of the exhibit, looking down into the pen. The creature's red color was impossible to miss in the clear filtered water. Looking down, without a glass barrier, was a genuine thrill for many of the journalists. While they snapped their photos, Forster climbed on to the hydraulic lift. Wearing a lab coat, she discreetly pulled out a syringe and injected a mild sedative into the large slab of beef. She made a point to make sure she wasn't noticed, otherwise it would become apparent that the creature was not safe to be contained. Lifting the beef was difficult. It was over twice the size of the slabs that they fed the white.

Thank god I'm still in shape. With both boats out of service, she had no crane to lift the bait, and the workers seemed to be busy. She used her legs to lift, and finally she picked the heavy meat off the hydraulic table. To the best of her ability, she tossed it into the water, being careful not to lose her own balance. The bait splashed into the water, and bits of coagulated blood oozed from the splits in the meat. The creature detected it instantly and swung its body around. In a single swoop, it snatched the meat. The water thrashed as it twisted and turned, bumping into the walls. The reporters all exclaimed as the creature tore it apart. For them, it was entertaining. For Forster, it was haunting. Most sharks would either swallow it whole, or break it down into enough pieces to swallow individually. This creature tore at its food in a crazed frenzy, like its sole purpose was to kill rather than feed. The more she observed it, the less like an ordinary animal it seemed.

The desire to know more grew in her like a mad hunger. As the reporters were fixated on the pen, she took the moment to pull out her phone. She made a call to Nelson, hoping he'd have some insight for her. The line rang several times before going to voicemail. She hung up and grew increasingly worried. Usually he answered. Her mind instantly pondered the possibilities. Was it something to do with the sinkings? Was there more to the story? Would he believe her if she told him she suspected this shark's existence is related to the Mako's Center incident?

Then she remembered their last encounter. The guilt she was trying to steer her mind from had instantly returned. She then wondered if Nelson was avoiding her calls. Either way, she now wanted to know the injured officer's condition.

It was just as well that Nelson didn't answer. The reporters started turning their attention toward her again. Forster resumed the tedious task of answering questions and making demonstrations.

Finally, after several hours, the reporters and journalists had their fill. She waited for them to clear out before she left. After a second failed call, she had officially decided to visit the Chief. She did her normal activities, such as tending to the other creatures, until finally all the vans were gone. She kept a casual appearance while walking to the lot, making sure she wasn't seen by Felt. She successfully arrived at her vehicle and left for the police station.

CHAPTER
23

In life, there came unexpected moments that could turn one's world upside down in the blink of an eye. It could begin with a normal routine day, which would go as smooth as usual. Then out of the blue, something happened that changes everything. A typical store manager woke up one morning, got dressed, filled his coffee mug, and left for work. Two miles from his store, an elderly man crossed the street, unable to hear the approaching truck. Five seconds later he was killed on impact. Though he was not directly at fault, the manager's world was forever changed.

A game show host was in the middle of filming a session of *Know-it-Alls*, a ripoff of *Jeopardy*. It had started out to be a good day. The host had achieved a high paying job, for a program that was slowly gaining in popularity, and he was on the road to achieving celebrity status. Then his life turned upside down as federal agents marched into the studio, aided by local police, seeking the host for questioning. They informed him that his brother had committed a shooting, which resulted in numerous deaths, including that of a police officer, and they wanted to speak to him for questioning.

Colonel Richard Salkil had four such moments in his life. The first occurred when he was thirteen, watching television one night with his father. A normal evening turned into tragedy when his father clutched his chest and died right in front of him of a heart attack. The second was in 2004, when he returned home from an operation in Iraq, and learned that his nineteen-year-old son had been arrested for multiple breaking-and-entering charges, leading to prison time. The third time, twenty-nine months ago, Salkil arrived home only to discover divorce papers on the kitchen table, and his then-wife's belongings all gone.

Then there was the forth unexpected moment. Only months away from retiring after nearly thirty years of service, Colonel Salkil just hoped to milk his remaining time in the U.S. Army. He was stationed stateside, working in an office on a base. The phone conference was almost like a managers' phone meeting for a retail chain. Meetings such as this were usually in person, but on this occasion, it was done to have several high-ranking military officials on a secure line. Just listening to a political general, who had never seen combat nor led any real battalions, flap his gums at him and whoever else was listening about national security. But it was simple, and he was glad it wasn't in-person, because it allowed him to silently mock the General as he spoke. If that was all he had to deal with for the next four months, after many years of combat on so many different levels, he was happy to take it.

During this phone conference, the office door opened. Salkil looked to the communications officer who entered, angrily gazing at him for both the improper entry and the inconvenient time. The officer, however, wasted no time getting to the point. He placed several papers on the desk, and the Colonel sorted through them while somewhat listening to the General. What he saw were leaked photographs that had reached the internet within the last fourteen hours. Suddenly, he didn't hear a word the General was saying; it was no longer important. Not bothering to announce his departure from the conference, he slammed the phone down.

"Where is it?" he asked the officer.

"A small island, about forty miles from the coast of Georgia," the officer said. "Pariso Marino. There's an aquarium there. Owner's name is William Felt." Salkil sorted through the papers, looking at each photograph. There was no mistaking the creature, and it was too exact of a match to be a coincidental hoax. After all, nobody knew of the hybrid; at least, not until forty-eight hours ago. The last three papers were local reports of missing seamen, and other vessels surrounding the area, the latest having come in since last night.

"Have we confirmed that these are results of *IP-15?*"

"Negative, sir, but it's likely," the officer said. Beneath his formal composure, he was troubled. Being one of the few made aware of the project's existence, he understood the gravity of the situation. "Do you have any suggestions on how to handle the situation?"

"I'm working that out now, Sergeant," Salkil said. He grabbed a phone, linking him directly to Senator Deborah Avery from South Carolina, the one who helped sign the authorization for the Warren Project, and had put him in charge of destroying all evidence after the disaster took place. The call was picked up immediately.

"*I was wondering when you were going to call,*" the Senator said. Her voice was stern and unpleasant, and there was no doubt she was directing her attitude specifically at the Colonel. And so it began, another moment when Colonel Salkil, a proven veteran and commander who had seen it all, was about to be lectured by a Harvard Graduate, who never held a firearm, much less served in an infantry, about how to properly run a military unit. To his understanding, she never even held a private sector job in her life. Put through school by a millionaire family who made their fortune in the energy industry, she seemingly went straight to organizing a campaign for the SC senate. Though he was not a native of that state, Salkil found it odd that she seemed to breeze her way through the primaries until ultimately winning the general election. Something about it seemed odd, and after factoring in her family's history, one couldn't help but make assumptions that something occurred behind the scenes. Nevertheless, she was a senator, her first job of any sort. That spoiled attitude, which Salkil and others like him loathed, only grew worse. The Colonel exhaled quietly.

"Yes, ma'am," he said. "I was just notified of the leaked images. I know the location of the island where it is located."

"*This is an embarrassment,*" Avery cut him off. "*You had everything you asked for; equipment worth millions of dollars; and multiple lives were lost during your attempt. And look; a simple aquarium doctor was able to subdue it. I guess I should've hired her to capture the thing three years ago.*" As soon as she started ranting, the Colonel held the phone away from his ear, just close enough to hear the faint echo of her rambling voice. Over his many years, he had been reprimanded from superiors at every level. It was part of the job, so he accepted it. But now, he was catering to who he viewed as a whiny, spoiled brat. He especially refused to listen to any scolding regarding the lives lost, as she and the other senators, who were almost equally ignorant, did not allow him to provide sufficient information about the target, in an attempt to keep it as secret as possible. As the ranting came to a close, he returned the phone to his ear.

"Ma'am, I'm getting straight to work on creating a clean-up operation," he said. "It's very important that we move fast on this. The time is…" he checked his watch, "*11:15*. I want authorization to take a unit for an extermination."

"*Extermination? The thing is already contained. And so far, there doesn't seem to be anything linking it to the Warren Project.*"

"Wait, hang on a sec," Salkil said, allowing a sternness to come over his voice. "Are you implying that we should just leave it over there? In a civilian aquarium?"

"*Didn't you hear me, Colonel?*" Avery's voice grew more intense. "*Three years ago, we were able to cap a lid on this thing. Nobody believes the disaster at Mako's Center actually took place, nor do they suspect we were creating biological weapons that went amok. Better yet, the whole thing has been practically forgotten. Now, so far, nobody is making the connection. All the reports indicate that they believe it's a new species. If we start moving troops and agents into that area, we're risking exposure in the matter again.*" Salkil couldn't believe what he was hearing. He never had respect for Senator Avery, and he always held the personal opinion that she didn't have two brain cells to rub together. After hearing her demanded course of action, he wondered if it was literally the case. All she cared about were the interests of the Federal Government and the special interests they catered to. In other words: herself.

"Senator, it is not a safe situation. If that thing gets loose, we're risking many more people getting killed. That hybrid is more than capable of breaking out of an enclosure."

"*If that happens, it will be chalked up as a simple containment incident. After all, they captured a new species without knowing anything about it. I already have teams working on statements if people start getting suspicious. But for now, the less we do the better.*"

For Salkil, that answer was unacceptable. Being near the end of his tenure, he couldn't voice that thought. His blood sizzled to the point where his face turned red. Three years ago, he pursued the hybrid. Many Navy lives were lost. To top it off, he found himself with no choice but to rain hellfire missile on a civilian yacht in order to 'kill' the creature. It was perhaps the worst moment of his career, and as he had recently discovered, it was for nothing. Now, all that the Senator wanted to do was sit and wait, hoping nobody would link the hybrid's discovery with the tragic incidents years prior. Incidents, which if ever came to light, would be attached to the Colonel's name. 'Hoping' wasn't good enough for Salkil.

"Roger that," he said. "You know where to reach me," he remarked. The Senator hung up without making her farewell. Salkil was grateful, as it spared him from having to listen to another sentence from the moron. He looked at the phone before putting it in his pocket. He took a seat and looked down at one of the lower cabinets of his desk. He dug a key from his shirt pocket and started to lean down toward the cabinet. About halfway to it, Salkil then looked up, noticing the Sergeant still in the room. "Thank you, Sergeant, you are dismissed." The Sergeant took the hint and left, shutting the door behind him. The Colonel unlocked the small door, pulling out a phone. It was an old phone, basically an old fashioned 90's flip phone. However, it contained only a couple of specific numbers. He selected the one he desired and sent the call.

"Thank you for calling REUBEN'S. Which location would you like to book your trip?"

"Would you recommend Niagara Falls, or Devil's Tower?" Salkil responded. There was a slight pause before the line went on hold. After a few more seconds passed, another voice answered the line.

"Colonel Salkil?"

"Lieutenant Hendricks," Salkil greeted the former Navy Lieutenant, who he had personally visited on many hospital visits since their last operation. "It's been a while."

"Yes, sir, it has," Hendricks said. "What do I owe the pleasure?"

"Well, I figured you'd be interested in something," Salkil said. "I got some photos here of an old friend I believe you're a bit familiar with."

"I don't follow."

"Let's just say, this guy took you for a bite." Salkil hoped the remark wasn't too inappropriate. He could imagine the former Lieutenant placing his remaining hand over the healed stub where his left arm used to be. He knew, however, that Hendricks was bitter about it. After all, it ended his career in the U.S. Navy, and made opening ketchup bottles a real pain.

"It's still alive?"

"Yes. How many men do you have?"

"I'll get everybody," Hendricks said. *"Any advice on equipment?"*

"That'll be the tricky part, but it's essential," Salkil said. "We're going to need choppers if you have them. It's kind of a ways, so we're going to need a sea worthy vessel that'll carry them. You know of the *Pyramid*?"

"Yes?"

"You think you can commandeer it?"

"Damn right I can."

"Good. I'll handle the legalities of it. Now listen, here's what we'll need...."

CHAPTER 24

Another phone call to Nelson resulted in no answer as Forster drove to the station, heightening a concern. Once she arrived, she had spoken to an officer at the front desk, who informed her that he was on police business. When Forster asked what the call was, the officer refused to tell her. Matters such as this were need-to-know only. This only made Forster more intent on speaking to the Chief, and she opted to wait.

The wait proved long. Whatever Nelson was handling, it was no small matter. Another thing that caught her attention was the massive influx of calls that she overheard coming in. Forster was by no means aware of exactly how busy the island police were on an average day, but judging by the demeanor of the officers that passed in and out, as well as the desk officers and dispatchers, something was going on that monopolized their time. A police officer came in and entered the electronically locked door, which latched shut behind him. Forster watched through the glass window as he spoke to one of the desk officers, who looked puzzled at whatever he was telling her. After he was done speaking to her, another call rang in. The call-taker took it, and quickly turned to the officer and called his attention. He gave a nod and quickly started moving out the door, passing by Forster. A transmission blared over his radio.

"We have another one by Cove Pedro."

"Ten-four, I'm on my way over. Dispatch, please update the EPA."

"Ten-four, Chief."

Forster tried to appear as if she didn't overhear, not that it would matter. The officers were occupied. Forster waited a few more minutes and finally stood up from the chair. She stepped to the window.

"I see you're busy," she said. "I'll speak to him another time." The officer replied only with a small nod, enough to inform Forster that her lie was believed. Forster returned to her vehicle, and quickly assessed her phone. She knew Cove Pedro was on the south side of the island but wasn't familiar with the exact location.

Well, if I see flashing lights, I'll know I'm in the right spot. She started the car and quickly steered out of the lot.

****

Red and blue flickered in the distance ahead as Forster drove along a dirt road. This section of the island almost looked like an old country town in the Midwest, except the area was crowded with tropical trees instead of oak. Dust kicked up behind her car, and dirt crushed under her tires. She was extra grateful for her phone, as she would have been otherwise lost in these series of back roads.

The police vehicle was parked where another road dead ended with the street she was on. There was nobody inside it, but no barriers closing off the road. Forster slowly turned and followed a narrow path until the trees started clearing up. Sunlight illuminated the cove, which was a narrow inlet of ocean water. At its widest point, where it opened out into the ocean, it was barely a hundred feet. The end of it came to a near perfectly shaped point, like that of a dagger increased exponentially in size. The road ended at this point. A dirty beach lined the thin shore on both sides of the point, not a particularly popular place for people to swim, especially with a much more luxurious beach a few miles east. At the dead end, Forster looked ahead. Another police vehicle had parked along the beach, having dipped into the water level to get there. The flashers were switched off, and three cops stood beside it. Chief Nelson, unmistakable in her eyes, stood in the middle. He seemed to speak into his radio, while he and the other two officers stared out into the ocean.

Forster drew a breath as she followed their gazes. Looking into the body of water, she saw three patrol boats forming a perimeter. Several black bodies, almost as big as the boats, floated between them. She switched off the ignition and started walking along the shore. With a closer look, she recognized the floating bodies. As her view changed, she recognized there were more which were blocked by the boats.

"Oh my..." she cupped her mouth. An entire pod of dead killer whales floated before her eyes. Though many meters out, they were unmistakable to her. The sight was horrific, possibly the worst thing she had ever seen. It looked as if a massacre had taken place. The mammals bobbed in the current, which led them closer to shore. She scanned the water, trying to get a count of the bodies, when her gaze swept back over the cops. They were looking at her, and she could see from their expressions that they were wondering why she was there. Chief Nelson started making his way over to her. Forster raised her hand to wave, but the gruesome sight caused her to shiver.

"Hi, Chief..."

"What are you doing here, Julie?" Nelson asked. Judging by both his look and tone, he was exhausted and not in the mood for nonsense. His uniform shirt was worn and dirty. The pants below the knees looked damp, as if they had been drying in the sun after stepping into the water. In addition to that, she suspected he was still displeased with her for going out after the shark.

"Chief...I'm sorry, I didn't know about this..." she stuttered. "I needed to talk to you about something. You didn't answer your phone."

"That should've told you something right there," he said. "If you have an emergency, you have to call 9-1-1, and they'll..."

"It's not that kind of emergency," she said. "It's about that shark..." Nelson stared at her, waiting for the clarification. "I'm worried it might not be the only one." Nelson's demeanor suddenly changed. It was a bizarre display of emotion. On the one hand, he looked increasingly worried, but there was a side of him that seemed relieved. Forster immediately knew why. "You think so too, don't you?"

"You obviously know of the sinkings," he said. "I don't believe in coincidences like that. And this..." he looked over his shoulder at the floating graveyard. "Nothing out there can do this."

"I don't think so either. Are there bite marks on them?"

Nelson nodded, "All of them. Each of them has been gutted. Chunks just ripped straight out of the bellies. Flippers and tails ripped off. It's horrible. By the way…" he pulled out a clear plastic bag from his coat pocket. Inside of it was a long, yellow tag, meaning a researcher had been keeping track of the pod, or at least one of its members. "We already got in touch with whoever was tracking this pod. They'll be sending someone out to investigate the matter."

"Anyone else missing?" Forster asked. Usually, Nelson's first reaction would be to inform someone asking these questions that policing is his job. However, this was a unique situation, and Nelson realized her insight was valuable.

"Three fishermen, which you obviously heard in the news. We dredged the water but found nothing but debris. This morning, some guy was playing with his dog, playing fetch in the water. The dog went after the ball, never came out." He took a breath, feeling overwhelmed. "So, that's why you're here? To tell me you think there's another one of those things out there?" Forster answered with a quiet nod.

"There's something else," Forster said. She paused, concerned that she was going to sound foolish. However, with Nelson clearly not in the most patient of moods, she got straight to the point. "I have a suspicion where these things came from." Nelson perked his head.

"Really?"

"I think they're, uh…they might be…" she stuttered, fearing she'd sound crazy. "Oh, fuck it! Did you hear of the thing that took place in the Mako's Ridges Island chain a few years back?" Nelson looked at her, wondering if she was being serious, then chuckled.

"Wait… you mean the story of the hybrid monster that attacked the shore?" he said. Suddenly, it seemed like he wasn't taking her seriously anymore. "Julie, that was made up. The guy admitted it!"

"Joe, hear me out," Forster said. "It was said that the thing was like a perfect hybrid. It was like a squid with crab elements to it. It was designed for Naval warfare, but it got loose, and because of the results, the government swept in and created a huge cover-up."

"So, what?" Nelson said. "You think that your shark is a government weapon? Designed to kill anything it encounters…" somehow, hearing his own words made it seem more plausible. He thought of how it ravaged the police boat, and strategically attacked them, as it had done the Great White a day prior. Still, the idea of a genetic hybrid organism seemed too much to be true. "But that one guy, whatever his name was, admitted it was fake."

"Did he, or did someone get to him?" Forster said. Unfortunately, Nelson understood government tactics well enough to know that a simple fisherman was likely an easy target for manipulation. Whether they paid him off or threatened him, it didn't sound too fictitious.

"I mean, I guess that's possible. But come on, a government hybrid monster?"

"Were you working here when the *K. McCartney disappeared?*" Forster asked.

"Well yeah, but we just heard it went down in that storm…wait…you're not telling me that you think…"

"What about Navy Choppers? Did anyone report seeing them around that time?" Usually, Nelson would have to think hard to remember. However, he recalled a fisherman making a big fuss about seeing an explosion when he trawled a few miles out. He claimed there was a military ship in that area, and that the Navy was heavily active. The fisherman was a drunk, so he never took the story seriously, and it was out of his jurisdiction, so he couldn't legally look into it.

"So, let's just say you're right," he said, without answering her question. "What would we do about it? Call the Coast Guard? I might need to do that anyway…"

"First we need to make sure we're right," Forster said. "That guy who reported the claim regarding the hybrid. His name is Rick Napier. I need to get in contact with him, but I can't find any information." Nelson shrugged his shoulders.

"Can't really help you there," he said. "Even if I did, I'm obliged to keep any personal info confidential."

"Okay, how well do you know law enforcement officials in other island communities?" Forster asked. Nelson looked at her with questioning eyes.

"I know a couple of them, but it's not like we hang out and play poker on the weekends or…"

"There's one that Napier mentioned…uh, the name began with a *B*." Forster thought for a moment. "It was a short name. Brundy? No, uhh…"

"Bondy?" Nelson asked.

"Yes!" Forster said, nearly jumping in place. "That's him! You know him?"

"Not well, but we've met," Nelson said. "When I was in Miami, we partnered up for a bunch of training exercises that was mandated for everyone in the area. Because he was an island cop, they put him in with us. Nice guy, we actually went out for a few drinks. Haven't spoken to him in years though. Are you telling me he was attacked by this squid-crab thing?" Forster bit her lip.

"According to Napier's interview," she said. Nelson shook his head, still highly skeptical.

"I don't know, Julie," he said. "This is thin, like really thin."

"If it's real, he might at least help us get in touch with Rick Napier. We'll see what he says. That's all I need. Joe, listen… if this thing is real, and not some natural result of evolution, who knows what'll happen."

"CHIEF!" One of the officers interrupted, running towards them. "Dispatch needs you on the radio." Nelson turned up the volume, after turning it down to speak with Forster.

"This is Nelson, go ahead."

"*Chief, I wanted to let you know directly. We have a report of two water-skiers missing.*" Nelson's eyes went to Forster, who looked equally alarmed.

"Where?"

"*On the east side of the island, near a residential area. Nobody knows exactly, but the caller insisted that the jetski was hit by something underneath.*"

"I'm on my way," he said. "Try to get an exact address." He depressed the transmitter and looked at Julie. Her concern was increasing by the moment, and he knew that she believed even further in her suspicions. He clicked the transmitter again. "Dispatch stand by for a *TX*." A "TX" was code for incoming phone call. He walked back to his car, dialing the dispatch number on his phone. The dispatcher answered. "Hey, it's the Chief. Look up the number for the Police Chief in Mako's Center, will ya?"

Forster walked beside him. Hopefully, Chief Bondy would be willing to get them in contact with Rick Napier and allow them to get to the bottom of the situation.

CHAPTER
25

Dr. Rick Napier stood out in front of his house, looking out into Razortooth Cove where he had now lived for many years. The ocean, clear and crystal blue, seemed to stare back at him. It was deceptively peaceful with its 'gaze', though he knew that beneath the flat sea was a contained fury. Much of that fury was usually nature taking its own course. However, the worst of it was the manipulation by man, and three years ago, Napier found out that the ocean world which he loved so much had been tampered with in the worst way. It was a time he wanted to put behind him. However, it always resurfaced in his life, and again with a phone call from a close friend.

"I don't see how I'll be any help for these people," Napier said into the phone. He heard Steve Bondy, exasperated, on the other end of the line. It was a touchy subject for the both of them, and it went way beyond the incident they had to suffer through.

"Rick, please just talk to this lady. She just wants to ask a few questions. You owe it to me," Bondy said.

"Oh, we're not doing this again," Napier said. "You know exactly why I did it."

"I understand that," Bondy said. *"But look what it did for you in the end."* It was the same remark that Napier had been hearing for over two years now. That remark was something that brought him to consider relocation so many times, and each time the thought became more enticing. Mako's Center, an island community that once adored him, now seethed each day he resided there. For Napier, it felt unfair, but he accepted it as the way of the world. He didn't bother asking Bondy again why he never stepped forward; the answer was obvious and was possibly more severe than what Napier had faced. Stress had caused his black hair to turn shades of salt and pepper, and his face was slightly more grizzled, due to the increase of nicks during shaving. The stress he once faced on a daily basis, hardly having an income, bills skyrocketing out of control, boat falling apart, and a kid to put through school; all of these paled compared to what he was feeling now. Now, it was the simple but unrelenting nightmare of guilt and fear, like none he ever experienced. Napier looked at the notepad. He had reluctantly jotted down a phone number, above it was written the name Dr. Julie Forster.

"So...this person just wants to ask me questions?"

"Something like that," Bondy said. *"Just call. That's the most I can say."*

"You're such a great help," Napier joked.

"That'll probably be my epitaph," Bondy said. *"Have fun. We'll talk again soon."*

"See ya, Chief," Napier said and hung up the phone. He looked at the written number again, feeling a bit bitter that Bondy didn't give him much detail.

All he knew was that somebody had questions about his 'story'. It was clear that Bondy didn't trust his phone, after what he had suffered through after the incident; government officials investigating his office, interrogating him and his deputies, threatening his job and pension. Bondy then found his phones tapped, and people suspiciously watching him for months. To this day, whenever the topic came up, he was as vague as possible.

Napier dialed the number and waited for someone to answer.

****

Forster snatched the phone up as it started to ring, "Hello, this is Doctor Forster."

"*Yes, this is Dr. Rick Napier. I'm told that you had some questions for me.*"

"Thank you for getting in touch with me, Dr. Napier," Forster said. "I'm here at Pariso Marino, where I work at Felt's Paradise."

"*Nice place,*" Napier instantly remarked. Obviously, being in the world of marine science, he was well aware of the controversy with Felt's association with Wan Industries.

"Trust me, this place is seeing more problems beyond the dumping of toxic waste," she said.

"*Dr. Forster, why do you want to speak with me?*" Napier said. Forster detected a blend of reluctance and annoyance in his voice, despite his attempt to sound polite. It was beyond clear that he had no desire to be talking with her. She figured he already knew she was going to bring up the incident. She understood his reservations about the subject, as he was scrutinized publicly and throughout the internet since.

"Unfortunately, there's no clear answer to that question," she said. "Something strange has been going on around our island, and I suspect that you might know why."

"*What strange occurrences?*"

She said, "Gosh, how do I answer this? I found something lurking in the water up here, and it makes me suspect that your 'story' isn't so much a story. I would like to know what happened three years ago, Dr. Napier."

"*Just look it up online,*" Napier said. All of a sudden, he didn't sound irritated, rather nervous instead. He spoke as if he suspected somebody was listening. "*It didn't happen, plain and simple. I'm not answering any questions on the subject. I've done enough of that.*" Forster felt like he would hang up at any moment, which increased her urgency.

"Dr. Napier!" She increased her volume. "People have been disappearing around here, and I think it's linked to the creature we captured."

****

Napier stood puzzled. This individual, whom he had never met nor heard of, had his attention. It brought a sick feeling to his stomach, which was nearly strong enough to make him abandon the conversation. However, he needed to clarify what she was indicating.

"What creature?"

"*I recommend you look up Felt's Paradise online, particularly for pictures, if you haven't already,*" Forster said. "*You'll see what I'm talking about.*"

"And what would I see?"

"*A shark.*"

"Yeah? The ocean's full of them."

"*Really? Have you seen them with exoskeletons strong enough to deflect high powered rifle rounds? Or how 'bout ones that sprout legs and crawl along the ocean floor?*" Napier prayed that it was a cruel joke. Memories flashed before his eyes. A massive bulk, with tentacles tearing at his boat; pincers ravaging the mercenaries; the mandibles snapping with hunger. For three years, *Architeuthis Brachyura* haunted him, even after its death. However, this was no crab/squid hybrid; it was something else, but the properties added up. There was no doubt that Dr. Wallack had developed other hybrids, and he had already suspected that *Architeuthis Brachyura* was not the only specimen that escaped. His silence spoke volumes for Forster, who knew she had his attention. "*I'll add this; this shark lives up to the Hollywood stereotype. It's not like anything I've ever seen. It attacks anything it sees. It sank a police boat almost effortlessly, and we think this thing has killed other people too.*"

"You captured it?"

"*Yes, but I don't think it's the only one,*" Forster said. "*I need to know anything you have to share about the hybrid.*" Napier didn't answer. During the silence, he searched for a way out of the conversation.

"It's probably best we don't discuss anything further," he said. Like Bondy, he had every reason to believe his calls were being monitored, and the last thing he wanted were federal agents arriving at his doorstep. "I'm sorry, there is nothing I'm able to tell you. I have to go now. I wish you the best of luck in…"

"*Dr. Napier, I'm not buying that you made up the story!*" Forster's tone grew intense. If it was a hoax, she was playing the act very well. "*As I said, I've contained the creature, but I don't know how long we'll be able to house it. Sedation only has a limited effect, and honestly, I think it's more than capable of breaking out. More to the point, I think there's at least one other. I'm not sure what we're dealing with here, but I need to know any characteristics from the other hybrid, in case there are similarities.*"

Napier felt like he was caught in a whirlwind. There was a moral conflict storming within him. He wanted so much not to be involved with the situation. Simultaneously, he instantly felt an obligation to help. However, the fear was like a hurricane traveling across open water. With each mile, it grew larger and more powerful.

"Destroy it," the words came out almost in a croak. His voice grew shaky, and it even made Forster nervous. Though it wasn't an admittance, it confirmed what she hoped wasn't true. The attack was real, and there was a world of monsters that she wouldn't have dreamed of even in her worst nightmares. Napier hissed a breath, wiping sweat from his brow. "You hear me? Do not let it survive. And another thing…don't tell anyone. Destroy it, and just shut up about it. Let it sink to the bottom of the ocean."

"*Napier...I need your help,*" Forster said. "*There are things I need to know. Why don't you come out here and have a look...*"

"NO!" It came out as a shout. "I already told you what you need to know. Alright? Don't ask me anything else. Okay? Good luck, and take care."

****

Forster attempted to plead her case once more when Napier ended the phone call abruptly. She stood alongside her car, parked atop one of the tall hills for the best reception. The hill looked out to the bay, which opened out to the vast body of ocean water.

Forster stared out at the endless blue. As Napier was doing at that same moment, though she wouldn't know it, she thought of how deceivingly peaceful the water seemed, and it made her wonder what coursed beneath the waves.

Sadness swept over her. Not only did her venture to capture the beast result in severe injury and near-death of a police officer, it turned out it was for nothing. She had believed she had discovered something, which was the basis of her dedication to science. But all she truly discovered was the dark side of science, the bastardization of life, by people who were arrogant enough to think they could control it.

CHAPTER
26

"Easy, easy..." Jessica Majewski called from the cockpit atop the superstructure of the fifty-foot fishing trawler *Ocean Creed*. Wearing a sleeveless vest with a tank top underneath and jeans, with blonde hair bunched into a ball cap, she looked as if she was ready to attend a sporting event rather than fish. Her first mate, a man of thirty named Kenneth Sterling, carefully stood at the stern ramp. Up to his ankles in water, he had the line secured to the second of two dead killer whales.

"Got it, Captain," he said. After the line was secured, he stepped off the ramp and onto the deck, adjusting the winch so the line was tight.

"Yeah, Kenneth! Listen to your mother," Carlos Hurd called out. Kenneth looked over to port, where another trawler of equal size was also in the process of putting a line on one of the dead orcas. A large hunky man, like his first mate Cuervo, Hurd enjoyed picking on Kenneth for working under Majewski, who held out a middle finger for the jab at her age.

"You should've listened to yours when she told you to try the appetite suppressant," Kenneth bantered back. Hurd mocked a pained face and then laughed. Kenneth was usually slow when it came to the comeback remarks, which made everyone enjoy picking on him even more. The foursome always worked together, often contracting for boat towing and other maritime services when the Coast Guard or other companies weren't available. Though Kenneth, the youngest of the group, had a brotherly love for Cuervo and Hurd, he was pleased to be partnered with Majewski's boat. Though she was almost forty-five in age, she did not look it. Despite always working around fish and grit, she maintained very good skin hygiene, which resulted in her looking at least ten years younger. Being a physically active person helped the image, and it provided Kenneth something nice to look at during the workday, though he dared not to admit it.

"We're ready to go," he said to Majewski. He looked at the floating animals, their lifeless bodies stiff in the water. His eyes were locked on the red fleshy wounds along the belly of one, exposing external organs. The sight of the other orca was worse, as its entire face had been turned into a huge fleshy mess. The only thing to identify the head was the slack jaw, which exposed another oddity. Many of the teeth were chipped or simply broken. Though he was no scientist, being a seaman, he had seen plenty of killer whales, and even had the pleasure of seeing a couple feed. Usually, their teeth were in good condition, whereas these dead ones looked as if they had been trying to bite down on solid granite before they died.

Looking at the graveyard was disturbing in itself. Looking at the numerous floating bodies, and the various wounds each orca suffered, he wondered what happened. It was as if these orcas had engaged in some medieval war. He wondered if they got into fighting amongst themselves, although such behavior was unheard of. Then again, he was no expert.

"*We're ready to go...Mom!*" Hurd called out, messing with both Kenneth and Majewski.

"Alright, it's getting old, asshole," Majewski said. Hurd laughed again.

"I guess so! Kinda like..."

"Don't even go there, Tubby," she said, pointing a finger at him. Though her tone sounded threatening, everyone knew she was bantering back. Very few people could get away with remarks about her age, and the same went for Hurd with his weight. She looked to the stern of his vessel, seeing that they had three orcas hooked up behind them. "Jesus, guys! Take it easy. You'll rip out the cleats!"

"Hey, it's not a short trip for this scientist guy, and we've got more of these guys to pick up. We're paid by the job, and unfortunately fuel costs aren't included in the price." There was a *thanks to you* vibe in his voice, as Majewski was the one who negotiated the job with Dr. Kane, the biologist tracking the pod.

"With the added strain on the engine, you're using up that fuel either way," she said.

"Hey!" Cuervo said. Majewski noticed the shit-eating grin on his face, knowing he was up to no good. "If we deliver more whales, that means we get more shares, right?!" An obnoxious smile filled Hurd's face and he nodded while looking at Majewski.

"Nice try, boys," she said. "Doesn't work that way."

"Awe...Moooom!" the two jerks exclaimed. Majewski shook her head.

"Hopeless," she said. "Anyhow, we have two other trips to make after this, so let's go, we're burning daylight."

"We'll be behind you shortly," Hurd said. Majewski gave a thumbs up and started throttling the *Ocean Creed.* The two thirty-foot orcas trailed the boat. Kenneth stood at the stern, again looking at the injuries. Tiny bits of flesh broke away as the water washed over the bodies, which would likely interfere with the biologist's intended autopsy.

"Why are we the ones doing this, and not the Coast Guard?" he asked his Captain. Majewski looked down at him from the structure.

"You're complaining?" she said.

"No, not at all," he said. "I just thought its weird that they're not doing this. Don't they normally dispose of deceased wildlife?"

"Usually, and I think the doc tried to get in touch with them," Majewski said. "But to my understanding, he couldn't get in touch with them for some reason. Who cares anyway? He's paying us top dollar."

"Yeah, I know," Kenneth said. He took another look at the orcas and finally decided to put the questions out of his mind. It was more fun to think of what to do with the upcoming paycheck. He took a seat and enjoyed another luxury that most people don't get to enjoy on the job; he reached into a cooler and cracked open a beer.

"Toss me one," Majewski said. Kenneth was way ahead of her. By the time she turned around, he already had it airborne. She snatched it and turned back to the wheel. Kenneth switched on the portable television. It was over an hour's trip to the port, and then back to repeat at least twice more. It would likely be dark by the time they finished.

****

Their prediction proved true, as the sun dipped beneath the horizon as the *Ocean Creed* made its way back to Pariso Marino for the final haul. Kenneth yawned uncontrollably, as the seemingly endless hours of waiting made him drowsy. Spotlights illuminated the path before the vessel, and Majewski kept her eyes on the horizon. Traveling in the dark was always more difficult, even with a GPS. It didn't help that the day was long and slow. Jobs like this that required long hauls brought along long periods of quiet travel. After a while, even the television didn't help much to alleviate the boredom. Like Kenneth, she found herself struggling to stay awake.

The much needed second wind came to her after she spotted lights on the horizon. Each one was small, but unmistakable. They were property lights from houses that lined the west shore. She adjusted their route slightly as they neared the island. She traveled a half mile off the shore, eventually seeing the southwest port. It served as a landmark, meaning the orcas' position was roughly a half mile southeast. After moving past it, she noticed another set of lights in the distance, this time further out in the water. Boat lights, for sure. The vessel was still in the water. As she drew her boat nearer, Majewski knew it was Hurd and Cuervo. The question in mind was 'why are they anchored?' She pulled up alongside them, seeing both men on deck. They huddled around the winch, looking over at her nervously as the *Ocean Creed* slowly crept up.

"Oh, hey, boss," Hurd said, sporting a nervous smile. Majewski shined a flashlight to their deck, instantly seeing the smoke rising from the winch.

"What did you do?!" she said. Hurd tried hard to think of an excuse. Majewski already knew the answer, confirming it by panning the light to their stern, where five orcas floated behind the boat, three of which were hooked to a single line. They tried hooking more in at a time using a single winch, and the weight proved too much. "You've got to be fricking kidding me," she said.

"Oh, this?" Hurd said. "Uh, it's nothing, I'm sure!"

"Don't even utter another word," Majewski said. "Just...ugh!" She put a palm to her forehead. "You guys realize what this does to your share..." both fishermen looked forlorn, as if they didn't think she'd actually penalize them. But as she instructed, they didn't utter a word. Majewski could barely contain her anger. "Goddamn, you two...just...how many orcas are left?" Hurd and Cuervo both cringed. "How many?!"

"Maybe one..." Cuervo said, just above a whisper.

"Oh my... you two are so..." Majewski stopped herself. "Just wait here." She throttled the boat, splashing water onto the upper hull as the *Ocean Creed* nearly soared away. She eased on the throttle, realizing she was on the verge of putting a strain on the engine by accelerating too quickly.

After moving around a small rocky peninsula, she scanned the water with the spotlight to look for the remaining carcass. Each jerk of the spotlight was fast and violent, representing her frustration to her employees. Kenneth noticed the fury in his captain as she pounded the water with the light.

"I see it over there," he said, pointing to the starboard quarter. Having been distracted, Majewski had driven past it. She geared the boat in reverse and turned to back it to the carcass. Kenneth got onto the ramp as they approached it. "Alright, that's good," he said. Getting his arms and legs wet, he got the line around the fluke.

"You done yet?" Majewski asked.

Don't be pissed at me. Kenneth tightened the final knot on the noose and secured the line.

"Yep," he said, and stepped off the ramp. He barely had both feet planted on the deck when Majewski started moving the boat back. The frustration radiated from the cockpit. Kenneth initially thought it was best not to say anything, but as they moved back around the rocky peninsula, he found the awkward silence unbearable. "So...how much is it going to cost to fix the winch?"

"To fix it; I have no fucking idea," she said. "If it needs to be completely replaced...thousands!"

"Oh!" Kenneth had no understanding of mechanics, nor the economics of them. "So, that really is going to come out of their share, I guess."

"You're damn right," Majewski said. The boat cleared the peninsula and she turned northward toward Hurd and Cuervo's location. "You hear that, you idiots?" she called into the night. Her shout was followed by a gasp, which instantly drew Kenneth's attention.

"What?" he asked. Majewski's expression was an answer in itself. Her face was completely covered in shock. Kenneth climbed his way to the cockpit and realized what she was looking at. The waters ahead were illuminated by the *Ocean Creed's* spotlights, and Kenneth saw the thrashing waters. It was as if a storm surge had swept through. Spreading out from a common point of origin were hundreds of pieces of what was the *Warhammer*. The bow pointed directly upward, like a tent in the water, broken away midway through the bow deck. Kenneth recognized parts of the port and stern quarters as they drifted in opposite directions. Everything else was just a jumbled mess. Majewski throttled the boat to the wreckage as she and Kenneth called out for Hurd and Cuervo.

There was no sign of them. Kenneth couldn't help but realize that the carcasses had disappeared as well. The waters had calmed down to normal at this point.

"What in the hell?" he said. He climbed down to the deck to use the lower level spotlight. His captain snatched up the radio.

"This is the trawler *Ocean Creed*. Mayday, mayday! Anyone listening, we have a wreckage at..." her eyes went to the west, and what she saw put her to silence. What she saw would be the last for her eyes, and the sounds of Kenneth's terrified scream would be the last for her ears.

A mountain of water took up their entire view. Like a massive tsunami, it swept over the vessel, as it had the one before them. As the water swept over the boat and its occupants, a solid impact struck the portside. While capsizing, the

Ocean Creed split in two, sending both Kenneth and Majewski into the thrashing waves.

Kenneth felt himself being tossed around under the waves. Finally, he opened his eyes, while struggling to hold his air. All he could see initially through the stinging water was darkness. Then there was a beam of light from the spotlights, rotating like a bowling ball in the water. He saw half of the vessel as it broke apart into many smaller pieces.

Then there was something else. Something submarine shaped among the wreckage. He could not recognize it, as the churning waters bashed him like a rag doll. He did not see Majewski anywhere, and for a moment, he lost track of the shape.

The waters started to calm, and with the help of his life vest, he made his way to the surface. He drew in a breath as his face hit the cool night air.

He had only begun to collect his thoughts when another swell emerged. He looked to the sound of churning water, just in time to see the immense shape break the surface. And in his final moment, the boat's spotlight rotated in his direction. All he saw was a world of red, which opened up into a cave like mouth. Jagged white shapes lined the mouth. That mouth closed around him, and in the same instant, Kenneth felt his last sensation...as his body was sliced in two by one of the huge shapes.

CHAPTER
27

For the past twenty-four hours, Rick Napier tried to live his normal life, struggling to not even think of anything that would remind him of his recent phone conversation. Sadly, he had to rely solely on hobbies for that to happen. Unemployment left him a very bored, and somewhat bitter individual. Previously living the life of a poor fisherman, he had a brief window in life where things were going well after the incident. He found new love, got married, wrote a dissertation which achieved his doctorate, and found himself with a job teaching Oceanography at the University of Florida.

When the 'truth' came out about the hybrid and the Warren Project, the University was quick to let him go, claiming they didn't want the bad press that he brought. For a while, he resumed fishing, but even the people in his residential island of Mako's Center seemed bitter towards him. None of the markets wanted to do business with him. He resorted to sending out applications to several colleges and universities, even high schools, but he didn't hear back from any.

Luckily, he wasn't lonely. His wife, Lisa Napier, formerly known as Lisa Thompson, had recently retired from her twenty-year commitment to the United States Coast Guard. To be retired at age forty was no small thing, and she cherished it. However, after a few months, she needed something to do as well, so she started teaching flying lessons. It was a nice additional income to her retirement.

Lisa had spent the entire morning teaching at the airfield, leaving Rick home alone. He had gone to the gym, keeping his body in fairly decent shape. After that, he'd usually spend his mornings reading and enjoying the view of Razortooth Cove. Ever since he came to the island, the view never grew old to him. It was a great thing to wake up to every morning.

However, starting yesterday, the view of the water made his stomach hurt. The phone call, which he tried so hard not to think of, haunted his mind. He constantly told himself it was just a joke, that it wasn't real. He thought of Colonel Salkil, whom he had words with on more than one occasion. If any other hybrids escaped, no way would that guy let any of them roam the waters freely. The one positive thing Napier could say about Salkil, he was determined to see the project shut down. Unfortunately, he also was in charge of keeping it covered up, and he was not afraid to use any means to achieve that objective.

It was the main reason Napier reminded himself to stay out of it. *Don't even read about it on the news*, he would tell himself. However, it was the common mistake that many people succumbed to; the effort to avoid something is sometimes what brings you to it. For Napier, his attempts not to think of the hybrid and the phone call only put it right at the front of his mindset. There he was, sitting on the front porch while looking out into the Cove. His eyes would turn to the book, only to scan over the text without actually taking anything in. He found himself reading the same line of text over and over again, until finally he slapped the book down on the table. He stared out to the water and felt as if it was staring back.

Finally, he was inside. *"Look up Felt's Paradise,"* he remembered. He snatched up a laptop and typed the name of the resort in the search bar, specifically looking for images. In no time, he saw the creature that Dr. Forster had described. By now, there were hundreds of photos from the journalists that had arrived there to conduct their articles on the mysterious find. For the next hour, Napier studied the stills of the creature. Like what he encountered three years ago, it was a perfect hybrid. A pure fifty-fifty gene split. In his mind, Napier cursed the people involved with the Warren Project, once again disgusted at the abominations they had created. He only could imagine what other ghastly creatures they stirred up in that lab; worse, what they were possibly planning on doing in the future.

Next, he clicked on a video one cameraman took when they went into the viewing room. Napier jumped in his seat as the hybrid came at the glass, determined to kill those on the other side. Being well versed in the world of Marine Science, he knew the typical behaviors of sea life, especially sharks. This thing he watched did not act like a hungry creature, rather it seemed like it wanted to kill anything that came near it.

The footage eventually led him to Dr. Julie Forster, who appeared to be tasked with leading the journalists. He couldn't help but notice how flustered she was in the various interviews and tour. If Napier had to guess, he would assume she was slapped with the assignment unexpectedly, with no preparation. For the assault of questions about the creature, she had no choice but to give the same answer; "I'm looking into it." It was clear to Napier that she didn't know anything about it, and what she did suspect, she wanted to keep from the media.

"Smart kid," he said out loud.

The front door opened. In came his wife, Lisa. A blonde haired, athletically built woman of forty, she always carried herself with the confidence she did when she was a Coast Guard Lieutenant. However, when Rick looked over to her, he noticed a sense of urgency the instant she let herself in.

"Hey!" she said. "Have you been watching the news?!"

"Huh? No, what..." Lisa grabbed the remote and switched on the television. The black powered off screen ignited to a newscast. The camera view was an overhead view from a chopper, looking down onto an oil rig. Flames roared from the northeast corner like a savage beast on a rampage, multiplying itself with every inch it gained. A tornado of black lifted from the fiery disaster, twisting into an ugly funnel as it ascended into the clouds. What was originally a bright and sunny day, was now darkened by the black fumes. Napier stood next to his wife, his eyes glued to the screen. As the camera panned out a bit further, he could see the various vessels surrounding the enormous rig. Some were moving in closer to provide an effort to control the fire, while others seemed to be assisting in getting workers off of the platform. As the news captured the event, the news anchors spoke over the audio, speaking with somebody on location who was likely on that chopper.

"...for everything down there. As you can see, the Coast Guard is deploying every possible resource to control this fire. Experts are currently underway to see if there is a spill, as we said before, we're uncertain if there's a leak."

"Martin, I know you're high in the air, but are you able to see any people still on the platform? We know that the Coast Guard has been active in getting everyone to safety..."

"It's hard to see any of the major details because of the smoke. This huge cloud of smoke, as you can see, seems to change direction with the wind. It's been a struggle for our pilot to avoid it while maintaining this viewpoint."

"Thanks Martin. For anyone just tuning in, you're looking at a breaking news story. Around Eleven O'clock this morning, an explosion occurred at the Whitaker Drilling Rig, located roughly twenty miles off of Florida. Details are sketchy at this point. It is unclear whether or not this was an act of terrorism, if it is, we'll keep you informed. Right now, experts are currently working to find out if there's a spill. Currently, the priority is getting everybody to safety, and preventing further damage to make it safe for an investigation to take place and control any further disaster."

The news switched their feed to the U.S. President making a press statement, explaining how all resources will be provided to provide assistance and relief. After a few minutes of the speech, the Florida Governor spoke, saying much of the same thing. Rick and Lisa stood silent as they listened to each word. Finally, the feed returned to the burning rig, and the news anchors continued talking in the background, starting with a male voice.

"You just heard the President and Governor, and I'd say it's obvious they're taking the matter very seriously. They're actively looking for the cause, particularly to find out whether terrorism was involved. Uh...I don't really know how they can possibly..."

"Oh, hang on Derrick," the female voice interrupted. *There was a moment of pause, as she was getting information on the spot.* *"We have a call coming in...we're told that this individual witnessed the explosion. Here's the caller, identifying himself as Jonas. Jonas, are you there?"*

"Yeah I'm here."

"Jonas, can you describe what you saw?"

"Yeah, I was actually on the rig when it happened. I was on the other side of the platform, heading that way when I just saw this big ball of flame just inflate like a balloon in front of me."

"Oh my goodness, do you have any idea what caused it?"

"I don't know for sure, but I'll say this; it looked like a controlled explosion to me. I know for a fact that there was nothing on that part of the rig that could set off a spontaneous explosion like that."

The exchange continued, and the camera remained fixed on the disaster, which was unfolding live. Lisa continued watching the broadcast, almost resenting the fact that she retired. While she no longer considered herself an adrenaline junkie, she still had that overwhelming desire to help people in dire situations. And if this was truly terrorism, she would love to hunt down anyone responsible, as the Coast Guard would be involved in doing in this scenario.

"Can you believe it?" she said to Rick. There was no response.

Looking to her right, she realized her husband wasn't standing next to her anymore. Turning around toward the kitchen, she saw him seated at the table at his laptop again. He was typing away awfully quick.

Seriously? Is this boring you? She walked over to him.

"What are you doing?" she asked. He didn't answer. She peeked at the screen, reading what he had typed in the search bar. *Incidents at Pariso Marino.* Results came up immediately, with the most recent one having been uploaded from that morning. The title: *Tragedy Strikes as Rogue Wave sinks fishing Trawlers.*

The article opened with a large photo from shore, capturing the image of the tide washing in large pieces of wreckage. Another photo showed police on scene, while trucks arrived to help clean up the wreckage. Lisa stood over Rick's shoulder as they read the narrative, which described the boats and the occupants believed to have been boarded at the time of the disaster.

Napier studied other images and articles about the incident. Local reports included interviews with residents who lived along the shore near where the incident occurred. One individual stated that he heard the crash, and when he came outside, he saw water surging up onto the beach. Another individual, who claimed he was at a nearby harbor, stated that he saw no such tidal wave where he was at.

"A rogue wave would have swept the entire side of the island," Rick said to himself. "Why just this spot?"

Lisa started to get worried about him, finding it odd that he was more interested in this seemingly random event than the one occurring on screen. More specifically, she found it bizarre the newscast seemed to trigger the thought of looking up this information.

It wasn't just now that Rick had been acting mildly strange. She knew somebody had spoken with him, asking about the hybrid attack from years back, however he was vague about the conversation. He had briefly mentioned it to her, and he seemed to blow it off as nothing serious. But his demeanor was off. She could feel him tossing and turning in the bed, unable to sleep. And here he was now, looking incredibly uneasy.

Finally, she put a hand on his shoulder.

"Does this have anything to do with that phone call yesterday?" she asked. He paused a moment and looked up at her. There was a brief silent moment of eye contact, during which Rick remembered the number one rule: no secrets. That rule trumped everything else. He had been vague about the phone call, hoping to spare Lisa from the possibilities they'd feared about for years. Despite his best intentions, he couldn't keep the truth from her.

"You remember how we suspected the government lost another hybrid?" he said. Lisa removed her hand. She looked concerned, but in a different way from when she was watching the news.

"Yes?" she said, in a way that was both an answer and a question.

"That person who called me, she said they've captured this…" Rick clicked on a different window, revealing the crustacean shark. Taking control of the mouse, Lisa looked at the various images and read some of the information of how the creature had been captured.

"Oh my God," she said.

"The biologist who works at that resort...I thought she was pulling my leg at first...but she's worried. There have been more disappearances around there, and most recently..." he clicked back to the most recent sinking, "...this one, which happened overnight."

"But, you said they captured the shark," Lisa said. She was still getting over the sight of the creature. In her mind, she tried to justify its existence by figuring it was a miracle of nature, or possibly just an undiscovered species. Those thoughts were just dreams, as her conscience knew the truth.

"It's been three years," Rick interrupted her. "Either two of these things escaped, only to suddenly come back, both at once, here at this island. Or...there's the other explanation." He stopped speaking, not wanting to voice his suspicion. She stopped and remembered. It was a particular moment on the boat, *The Catcher,* when Dr. Wallack had delightfully described the characteristics in his creations. One particular characteristic had been designed to help cut down the steep costs of generating the hybrids.

"Oh, God," she stepped back and watched the television, while the footage of the burning refinery continued. "So, what about this?" She looked back to Rick, while pointing at the screen. "You saw this, and instantly you knew something was up at that island. I know it's the first time you've read about that sinking. You had a suspicion, and you proved it right. So, something's on your mind. Are you thinking there's a relation between these two occurrences?" As she spoke, it seemed she didn't believe it. Or, at least she didn't want to. Rick leaned up against the kitchen wall, gathering his thoughts.

"They're not going to want the public to have knowledge of the thing's existence," he said.

"Yeah, but people have already seen this thing, and the pictures are already on the internet," Lisa said. "What could they do to cover it up at this point?" Rick tilted his head toward the disaster on the television. She looked at it and back at him, eyes open wide. "Oh, come on now...you don't seriously believe the government did that..."

"Lisa, look at what's going on," Rick said. "A bomb explosion, right when this 'amazing discovery' happened. That's an awfully big coincidence. The only way for them to contain knowledge of this thing is to create bigger, more sensational news. I mean, look at this," he pointed to the television. "They've got the attention of the entire country fixated on this. Plus, they're using the magic word, *terrorism.* Right now, nobody's gonna care about the government taking away some shark from a facility. I'm telling you, something's in play right now."

"All for a shark?" Lisa said.

"It's not just a shark," Rick said. "It's a killing machine, connected to a project that got God-knows-how-many-people killed. And now, these people who caught it are in danger, and I doubt they realize what's coming." Lisa looked at him, now feeling slightly suspicious. She could sense when Rick was up to something, only this time it worried her.

"Honey," she calmed her voice, "there's nothing you can do about it, alright?" He looked at her. He didn't have to say anything; she knew he was thinking of going over there. Here he was, Rick-do-the-right-thing-Napier. It was a quality that made her fall in love with him. This time, however, she gained a hatred for it. She shook her head, feeling the tears welling behind her eyes. "Oh no," she said. "We made a deal. You're not going over there. You remember what happened before…"

"I know, Lisa. But I can't stand aside and let this happen…" Lisa turned and marched upstairs. Rick stayed behind, dropping his hand which he had reached out, intending to be comforting. He heard the bedroom door slam shut.

Lisa leaned back against the bedroom door, with her eyes squeezed shut. It was like a demon from their past had returned to haunt them. All she wanted was to be past it all; to simply enjoy her marriage, retirement, and pursue new hobbies. To live a typical life, was that too much to ask?

She moved to the bed and laid on her side, while the flood of memories zipped through her mind like a montage.

There was the beginning, when she first came to Mako's Ridges to investigate the mysterious sinking of a fishing vessel near Mako's Edge. Mako's Edge was an island in the chain, notorious for the countless rocky structures that filled the surrounding water. It was like a miniature mountain range, with the tips of each mountain breaking the surface, and becoming a potential hazard for any boat that came near. It was easy to assume that was what happened to the fishing boat. What seemed like a simple assignment turned into a nightmare. She and her subordinates stayed out past dark, trying to find the wreckage. Only, they found something else.

All she saw was a fury of tentacles and a cloud of blood that belonged to her fellow diver. Reporting to her superiors, everyone suspected she was crazy. How could they not? Who would believe that a giant creature, a squid with pincers like a crab, would exist? Though she knew what she saw, she couldn't convince everybody.

Another day passed, and she was on leave, a suspension of sorts with a likely court marshal in her future. That's when she reconnected with Rick Napier, her high school sweetheart. Up until then, his name was one she despised after leaving her for another girl, who became his wife. Ironically, with everything that was happening, he was the one ray of light.

Then the beast appeared, in a horrific turn of events that would leave many lives shattered. She witnessed many boats ravaged, and many more lives lost as the hybrid attacked anything in sight. Rifles proved useless against its thick shell, as the police force found out, at the cost of several of their own lives.

Things only got worse that night. Lisa and Rick, along with his daughter and two others, found themselves taken hostage by a small group of mercenaries personally hired by Dr. Wallack. Forced to help them capture the hybrid, Rick successfully managed to help her escape and make contact with the Coast Guard Cutter, *Ryback*. Lisa had boarded the rescue chopper, making it back as the hybrid was ravaging Rick's boat. By the skin of her teeth, she rescued her future husband, and the *Ryback* made minced meat of the hybrid with the use of the 70mm gun.

It seemed the nightmare had ended, but it seemed another chapter had just begun. Military officials arrived at the island, led by an Army Colonel, whose name they'd never forgotten; Salkil. At first, it seemed to be a relief effort. Men in black suits arrived at the house, often accompanied by Salkil, wishing to speak with everyone in the family, including Rick's daughter. The police department had its files ransacked, and any physical evidence of the hybrid's existence was soon swept away. Boats had dredged the area where it had been killed, retrieving all fragments of its body. The newly discovered cave, which had secretly been the location of the first Warren Project laboratory, was demolished to prevent any further discovery to the fact that the creature was building a nest in there. News media quickly released the 'facts' that reports of a hybrid creature were a result of mass hysteria, and that the creature that came ashore was simply an enormous colossal squid. The video released online was 'determined' to be computer fabricated.

Rick couldn't stand for it. He never considered himself much of a rebel, but he couldn't live with standing by and watching this tragedy be swept under the rug to protect a few political careers. He knew the truth needed to be heard. Despite threats from the mysterious men in black, Rick went to news outlets, intending to tell the country the truth. Initially, he had no problem getting his voice out. However, soon the news was distorting his words. He found himself misquoted, and the video interviews were clearly edited in a way that made him look like a conspiracy theorist.

During this time, he found himself being followed. Walking down the street, he'd notice people watching him. What scared him the most was that they were not coy about it; they clearly wanted him to know he was being watched. Eventually, another man in black visited, offering them a massive sum of two million dollars. For Rick, it would require him to 'admit' to the news market that he fabricated the story, and to deny the existence of a hybrid. Rick refused.

He turned to private news organizations, such as radio talk shows. They ran with the story, and it began to pick up steam. This lasted for months, during which Rick was awarded a doctorate degree after writing a dissertation.

It was midnight, when suddenly Rick and Lisa woke up to a loud knocking at the front door. They were engaged and living together at this point. They barely made it down the stairs when they were ambushed by men in black, holding pistols with silencers to their heads. Though they didn't specifically identify themselves, it was clear they were from the government. On his knees on his living room floor, they tossed down photographs of his daughter, who had left for college in Miami. She was unaware she was being tracked, but the threat was obvious. The leader informed Napier that the deal still stood: take the money and withdraw. Rick knew the plan. The government was well aware it would look suspicious if the man exposing them suddenly turned up dead. They would rather bribe him to retract his story. However, Rick realized the ugly truth. If he declined, they would rather risk the controversy than allow him to continue exposing them.

The threat to his daughter broke him. Rick Napier took the deal. Within days, the name of Rick Napier had become the subject of ridicule. He found himself heckled on news outlets and the internet and fired from his newly obtained job at the University of Florida. Even worse, residents from Mako's Center, especially those who suffered from the attack, despised him. Looking at his newfound wealth, they looked at him as the one man who benefited from the incident. Even Chief Bondy seemed to harbor resentment toward him.

Still wanting to do something positive, he began the initial stages of starting a benefit with the money. He didn't get far before he gained another warning from an official, stating by starting a benefit for the victims, he was drawing attention to the matter. The only way to honor the deal was to keep the money for himself and his family. What could he do but honor the deal? Rick Napier had conceded defeat. The best way for him to do that was to pretend, in his mind, that nothing ever happened.

Laying on the bed, Lisa gazed at the ceiling, cursing the world for the injustices she felt were forced upon her new family. To her, the money meant nothing. All it brought was misery and disdain from everyone she and Rick knew.

The door opened. Though her eyes remained fixated on the charcoal colored ceiling, through her peripheral vision she could see Rick walk up along the side of the bed. He sat down on the edge, looking down at her.

"Was that our first argument?" he asked. Even with the mental anguish Lisa was feeling, she couldn't contain a small smile.

"You forget when you spilled coffee on my blues," she said. She sat up and looked at him while his face creased with a mischievous grin.

"I don't know what you're talking about," he lied.

"Oh, please, you were like a clumsy two-year-old," she said. "Then you went and lied about it."

"I never was a good liar," Rick said. "And that's why I have to tell you the truth right now." Lisa sighed and stood up. She didn't need to say anything, as Rick already knew how she felt. "Listen, you don't need to go. But I have to go over there."

"And do what?" she said.

"I need to see the thing," Rick said. "And, I need to find out if there's another one out there. If there is, I need to destroy it before it kills anyone else, and it needs to be done before any 'officials' show up." He held up air quotes. "All I ask, is you get me over there. That chopper of yours can make the trip, can't it?"

Lisa turned around to face him, with her hands placed firmly on her hips. The terrified, upset woman who ran upstairs was gone, and the tough stern Coast Guard Lieutenant was suddenly standing in her place.

"You think I'm letting you go there by yourself, while I stand on the sidelines and just hope you'll be okay?" She spoke as much to herself as to her husband. She knew the likely truth and couldn't hide from it. Rick felt conflicted. On the one hand, having her help and support was beneficial. On the other hand, he dreaded the idea of putting her in harm's way. He could stomach the thought of hunting and putting himself in danger, but for Lisa it was a totally different story. She knew he thought this. "It doesn't work that way. If you think there's another hybrid loose over there, then we need to do something about it. Together. And don't preach to me the risks; I know them. We've been through it." Rick gazed into her eyes, grateful to have such a strong and loving woman in his life.

"How long do you think the trip will be?"

"Probably a couple hours' flight," she said. "Bring a book." Rick opened a closet, dragging out a suitcase from the side. He tossed it onto the bed and opened it up.

CHAPTER
28

"For Christ sake, John, I've got two fishing boats down, with three local fishermen still unaccounted for, a missing jet skier, and we're still picking up scraps from these trawlers, and no sign of the people that were on them. On top of that, we've got a guy who claims he's seen the damn thing, and still, you're not letting me restrict access to the water." Nelson's voice seemed to bounce off the walls of the Mayor's closed office, drawing attention from those outside the door. Footsteps thumped the floor in the hall, as people gathered to make sure the argument did not get out of hand.

Mayor John Calvin remained seated while the Chief stood in front of his desk. His tie was loosened around his collar, and the top two buttons of his shirt were left undone, almost symbolic of the rough week the island had gone through.

"I get it, Joe," he said. "But our community cannot afford another grounding. We've taken an economic impact over this past year. We're getting a record number of residents going on welfare. Restricting everyone from the water will just make the matter worse."

"Oh, but letting them get munched is perfectly fine," Chief Nelson barked.

"You have yet to provide evidence that these accidents are the results of shark attacks," the Mayor said. He emphasized the word "accident," which irritated Nelson. It seemed as if the Mayor didn't want to acknowledge the bizarre chain of events plaguing the island.

"We had a fisherman report a sighting, recently," Nelson said. "And what else could've sunk those boats? Coral reef?"

"That first one sounds like a boating accident," Mayor Calvin said. "Those two boats could have easily collided. And we already know a rogue wave took out the trawlers."

"Oh, give me a break," Nelson said. "A rogue wave would've swept the whole side of the island! Not just a beachfront property."

"You're not seriously gonna tell me you think a shark wrecked those trawlers," Calvin said.

"I don't know, it didn't have much of a problem busting through my patrol boat," Nelson said.

"A twenty-foot boat," Calvin said, shaking his head with doubt. "And that shark is in captivity. Besides, I find it highly unlikely it sank two fifty-foot trawlers in a matter of seconds. I'm sorry, Chief, but it doesn't seem like you have any evidence."

"But the fisherman reported that he saw the thing," Nelson said. *Do you not fucking listen?*

"Okay, where is he?" Mayor Calvin asked. "I know he made this claim to the news station, but has he said anything since?" Nelson sighed heavily and looked away, putting his hands in his pockets. "Am I supposed to guess, or…"

"We can't find him," Nelson said. "We don't know if he left the island, or what happened, but nobody knows where he's at." Mayor Calvin leaned back in his chair, staring at Nelson. Nelson saw the look on his face. It was enough to express Calvin's thoughts. There was no point for the Mayor to speak, though he did.

"Sorry, Joe, but I'm not giving you permission to place restrictions on the water. There's too much going on right now. We've got fishermen trying to put food on the table, and on top of that, we've got an influx of tourists coming to Felt's Paradise. We're getting ferries coming in, with a bunch of visitors who expect to go swimming and boating. We can't afford to close the beaches, and…what's that look you're giving me?" Nelson gazed down at him like a prosecutor facing down a defendant in a courtroom.

"No reason," he said, and turned around. There was no point in talking to Calvin further. It suddenly became apparent that he had words with William Felt, who "somehow" convinced him to keep the waters open. For a man claiming to be running low on funds, Felt seemed to have deep pockets. Unfortunately, he couldn't prove it. Without the Mayor's support, and the Coast Guard preoccupied with the events down south, Chief Nelson found himself on his own in dealing with the situation. Unless he obtained proof that more of these sharks inhabited the waters.

There was only one person he knew who could help.

****

The hospital lobby was just filling up as Forster walked through the door. Flowers in hand, she wanted to express her apologies for creating the scenario that gave Officer Beck his devastating injury. Unable to get Officer Beck's room number because of HIPAA laws, she had to use her own intellect on determining where he was. With the knowledge that he lost his leg and underwent surgery, he was most likely in Intensive Care.

With only a few minutes before she had to arrive at work, figuring out the maze of the hospital became very frustrating very quickly. Finally, she found a staff member and told a lie, stating that she was his sister. Luckily it worked, and the staff member pointed out the location. Upon entering the unit, she suddenly felt foolish for arriving. Standing outside one of the hospital rooms was a young, petite lady, whose face was red with tears. When her eyes turned toward her, Forster realized she had been recognized by Beck's wife. Forster recognized the rage that was suddenly swelling within the wife and knew it was best to leave. Placing the flowers on the nurse's desk, she turned to leave. Just as her hand clutched the door handle, she felt a hand on her shoulder, turning her back around.

"Why are you here, huh?" Mrs. Beck said. "You found your fish, and nearly cost my husband his life. What, you think you're sorry or something?"

165

"I am," Forster said, trying to pull away. "I really am so sorry. I just want…" A solid fist to the left side of her face made the room spin around her. For a small petite woman, she could hit hard. Forster staggered back, pressing a hand to her face while naturally holding her other arm up defensively. Her blurred vision refocused just as her attacker came at her with another swing. Forster leaned back, letting it miss, while two nurses rushed in-between them. The room flooded with employees and visitors, drawn in by the sudden commotion. It took both nurses to hold the wife back, while a third got on the phone to call security. Finally, Mrs. Beck ceased her effort to rush Forster.

"Go back and play with your fish," she said. Forster said nothing. As she turned to leave, she noticed the sour expressions on everyone gathering in the room. Forster was always well known on the island and was even more so after the incident leading to the hybrid's capture. As her notoriety increased, so did the disdain that the island population had for her.

She hurried out the door, trying not to listen to the shouts coming from all around her. Even as she walked into the hallway, she mentally shielded herself from the bombardment of insults and foul language that blasted her. Her walk turned into a run, and with each step, the bruise on her face throbbed worse.

The lights seemed brighter, and the sound of water filled her ears. Then there was a voice that spoke louder over all the insults.

"Julie. Julie. Hey, Julie…"

****

"Julie? Hey, Julie?"

Forster lifted her head off of the desk table, suddenly taking in the scenery that was the marine hospital. Water splashed as the dolphins, having improved from their sickly conditions, swam about their pools with greater enthusiasm. Forster then looked to her left, seeing Marcus standing over her.

"Oh gosh, Marcus," she said. Her jaw ached as she spoke. She put her hand to her bruise. Her dream had perfectly captured the real life encounter she experienced that morning. The only element it didn't include was the exhaustion she was feeling, both physically and emotionally. Even with the burst of joy she was feeling, her body struggled to fight the fatigue as she stood up to give him a friendly hug.

"My gosh, how are you doing?" she asked him. Marcus hugged her back with his remaining arm, as his other was still in a sling.

"I'm good. I'm doing really good," he said. He looked at the dolphins swimming in the pens. "Looks like they're feeling good as well." He then noticed the bruise on her face. "Jeez, what happened there?"

"Oh, it's nothing," Forster said, slightly embarrassed. She worried that he suspected she got into another brawl with local residents. She stepped back after the hug, determined to change the subject. "So, what's going on? Are you coming back to work already?" Marcus smiled.

"No… I've decided that I'm done with this place," he said.

"Huh?" Forster instantly shrieked, immediately putting her hand to her mouth afterwards. It was not news she was expecting to hear. "You're leaving?"

"Yes, ma'am, I am," he said with a nod. "Going back to see my dad in Utah. I was able to land a job at the college back at home. Nothing special, just being a financial aid tech. But the best benefit is, since I'll be full-time, I can go back to school for free. I've been thinking about it, and especially after everything's that been going on around here, I'm going to do it." Forster forced a smile, while standing quiet for a moment.

"Wow, Marcus, that's...that's great," she said, trying to sound enthusiastic.

"I'm catching the ferry shortly, and tomorrow I'll catch a flight home. I'll be staying with my folks until I get situated." Marcus saw a window on the far side of the room, which gave a partial view of the Atlantic. He sighed. "I gotta say it's weird; I love seeing the ocean every day, and thought I'd be sad if I ever had to leave. But after what we've done to it, being associated with a guy whose partner soiled these waters, I find myself sad being around it now. I guess it's a good time for a change."

"So, I guess you're here to drop off your ID and gather belongings?"

"In part." He looked back at her. "I wanted to say thanks to you for what you did the other day." The haunting image of the Great White swimming toward him flashed in both their memories. "You saved my life. Thank you." Forster smiled. This time, it was much more authentic.

"Actually, it's I who hasn't thanked you," she said. Marcus gave her a puzzled look. "I know you were the one who got Nelson to go after me, when I went out there after the hybrid. I was an idiot going after that thing. I was just chasing old dreams. Point is, I'd probably be dead if those guys hadn't come after me. And they wouldn't have if it weren't for you."

"Just glad you're alright," he said. He looked at his watch, realizing he was short on time. "Crap, the ferry leaves in twenty minutes," he said. "I wish I wasn't rushing, but I have to leave." Forster gave a tearful smile, and they gave another hug.

"Good luck, alright," she said. "Take care of yourself. And do your homework!" Marcus laughed.

"I'll do that, doc," he said. He stepped away, grabbed his belongings from the locker, and started toward the door. He looked back to Forster one last time. "Hey...dreams don't have to die." Forster responded with a slight nod, and another smile. She waved farewell, and Marcus walked out the door for the last time.

The emotion she felt was a strange mix of happiness and depression. She was genuinely glad that Marcus was bettering himself, and was getting away from the misery that was ironically called Paradise. Then there was a slight feeling of jealousy, as she wished she could get away. She thought on his parting words and wanted to believe it was true. But how? Her criminal history had basically ruined her career. Finding a way out seemed impossible, and her dreams seemed dead in the water.

More than anything, she felt more alone than ever.

The next twenty minutes consisted of Forster trying to gather her focus by getting back to work. She personally administered the protein cubes to each dolphin. Luckily, this process was now going much more smoothly than a few days prior, as the dolphins were vastly improving in health. As Forster worked, she tried to tally all of her remaining tasks in her mind. She needed to inspect the aquarium tanks, apply medication to the waters and see to it that the fish were fed, check on the shark. Then there were reports she needed to write and get to Felt, and she needed to make orders for supplies. Most importantly, she would need to be able to release the dolphins soon. Even the task of simply going over everything still left to do made her increasingly overwhelmed. She was doing the jobs for three people minimum. Though Felt had promised to hire more assistants, so far there were no job postings that she was aware of.

She administered the last of the cubes to the final dolphin and climbed out of the pool. She grabbed a towel and started drying off her waist and legs and started toward the changing room to get out of her wet shorts and shirt. She quickly changed into professional looking business pants, with a white button shirt. With the sudden influx of visitors, Felt decided he didn't want employees having any casual attire, despite the hundred-degree heat. The past couple of days saw an influx of new customers, and suddenly there were over twice as many people at the resort. As she changed, she heard some chatter as people entered the medical room. She couldn't make out any words, but the tones sounded frantic.

Probably watching the news, she thought, as many people had gathered around the television screens all day monitoring the oil platform explosion. She stepped out of the changing room.

"Oh, wait! There she is, she's in here!" a janitor said, pointing at her. Two thoughts entered Forster's mind; *What does Felt want now?* And, *Holy crap, what time is it?* He stepped aside, and a security officer entered the room. He was breathing heavily as if he had tried out for the Olympics, and his eyes were wide open as if he had been frightened out of his mind.

"Ms. Forster! Please, we need you right away at the exhibit!" he said. She didn't waste time. She followed him out the door, and they both entered the nearest stairwell.

"What's the problem?" she said, carefully maneuvering over each stair.

"It's the shark!" the officer said. "It's gone NUTS!"

"Can you be a little more specific-- oh shit!" Forster exclaimed after nearly slipping on the edge of a step. She recovered and continued down.

"It's banging the walls, like it's mad!" the officer said. "I don't know why. It just started a few minutes ago!" As they approached the bend which led down to the first floor, a flood of screams echoed upward. Forster and the guard stopped, as dozens of people ran up the stairs from the basement level, crying in terror.

They clambered over each other, rushing up the stairs. A few people stumbled, and one completely lost his footing, hitting each step as he tumbled backward down the stairs. The officer froze, briefly unsure of what to do.

"Help them, I'll go to the exhibit," Forster said, making her way down the last few steps before bursting through the double doors to the main lobby. As she made her way to the main entrance, she immediately saw the huge gathering of people by the guardrail at the ledge of the pen. She couldn't see the pen itself through the blockade of moving bodies; however, she couldn't miss the huge spray of water shoot overhead, with a loud thud simultaneously echoing through the floor. Forster instantly grew nervous. Whatever was going on, the hybrid was hitting the wall hard enough for her to feel the floor vibrate.

She hurried outside and started making her way to the guardrail. Like a quarterback, she pushed her way through the huge gathering of visitors until she reached the pen. As she grasped the metal guardrail, a surge of water splashed up at her as the huge red shape lifted its head above the surface. Forster shrieked and jumped back just as it rammed its nose into the ledge where she had stood. Like shards of glass, chunks of cement shattered into pieces of various shapes and sizes. The hybrid dipped beneath the surface, leaving a large dusty crater in the cement ledge. In a jolting motion, it hooked toward the right of the pen. Like the crazed beast it was, it mindlessly rammed the steel wall. Water rippled both inside and outside the pen, and the adjacent deck shook intensely.

All the way to its far end, the deck was covered with panicking people. Several of them fell to their knees as the deck shook from the blow. Water swirled in the pen as the creature turned and rammed the opposite wall. It collided, spraying water into the air.

"Get back!" Forster yelled to the crowd. "Back away! Move!" It took several more shouts from her before the crowd started taking her direction. She rushed toward the entrance to the deck, where a large crowd stood baffled by the scene. As they stood, they blocked the way for the line of people trying to get off. "Move back!" she yelled at them and ran toward the deck. The crowd finally moved aside like a floodgate, leaving way for the wave of people who fled the deck. Forster stood to the side and urged everyone on as they dispersed toward the interior of the park. Her eyes turned upward toward the hydraulic lift. An individual stood up on the platform, watching the shark.

"What are you doing up there?! GET DOWN NOW!" Forster yelled at him. The man knelt down and grabbed a briefcase before hopping down. Forster noticed a VIP tag clipped to his white shirt as he passed by her. For the briefest of moments, her mind went from figuring out how to get the creature under control to wondering who he was.

Not important. Her eyes scanned the deck and the crowd, making sure everyone was at a safe distance from the pen. Security officers had gathered around, helping to keep the visitors at bay. Many people spectated in awe, while others hyperventilated in fright. Forster then noticed a frantic couple rushing toward one of the security officers. Through the disarray of chatter, she only caught two specific words: *help,* and *son.* It was at that moment a crying sound suddenly filled the air.

She turned and looked around the hydraulic lift. Toward the far end of the deck, a small four-year old boy had fallen to the deck after accidentally being separated from his parents amidst the chaos. He struggled to get to his feet, as he was held down by his shirt which had been caught in a nail. As all eyes went to him, the crowd erupted in unanimous panic.

Adjacent to the boy's location on the deck, the red shape emerged along the surface. Rather than mindlessly smash into the wall, it breached the surface, drawn to the cries of potential prey. It lifted its head clear of the surface, while swaying its tail to keep it up top. Forster watched in horror as the creature turned its head, gazing upon the boy. It snapped its jaws like a hungry canine and swayed its tail to bump it into the wall. It raised its head again, unable to reach the boy.

"Shit!" Forster didn't even allow herself to take a breath to prepare. She made a mad dash down the deck for the kid. As she was midway down, she shrieked and nearly came to an instinctive stop as she watched one of the creature's legs unfold and raise over the water. Like that of a massive insect, the leg crashed down onto the deck, splintering wood where it landed. The hybrid's head rose further from the water, and Forster immediately knew it was attempting to climb out of its entrapment.

She skidded past the embedded claw-like appendage, and quickly wrapped her arms around the little boy's waist. She yanked him up, tearing his shirt where it was pinned to the nail.

"I got you!" she comforted him. She turned around, seeing another leg rise over the side of the pen onto the deck. The creature's head was pointing straight up as it clung with its two front appendages. In a straining motion, it started heaving itself out of the water. Its head tilted down toward them, and those enormous jaws opened. With the boy in her arms, she jumped around the nearest leg, and ran toward the shore. The hybrid's head fell onto the deck, barely missing them. Determined to catch them, it quickly swayed its head to the right and snapped its jaws. Unable to compensate for the shift in its own weight, its two legs lost their "grip" on the deck. Wood splintered as the entire portion of decking gave way, and the creature fell backward into the water, buried beneath a tremendous splash.

Hugging the little boy tightly, Forster cleared the deck. She knelt to put him down, and he quickly ran to his parents, who tearfully embraced him. Security officers set up physical barriers to help keep the crowd back. The gathering split up as a white maintenance truck drove toward the event. In the bed was the carcass of a goliath grouper. They parked and left the engine running while they rushed out to unload the large dead fish. Forster looked back to the water, only able to see the water thrashing about. It almost appeared as though a whirlpool was forming while the beast rampaged. She then looked to the security guards, looking for the supervisor on duty. She spotted the white uniform shirt, which contrasted from the blue ones his subordinates wore. She signaled to him with her hand, and he approached.

"What's the action plan here?" he asked.

"Could you call the aides on the top floor and tell them to bring my sedation supplies," she said. The supervisor quickly got on his radio and switched the frequencies to call the aides. Forster started walking toward the truck. One of the maintenance men met her along the way.

"We got what you asked," he said. "You think it'll be enough?"

"We can only hope at this point," Forster said. "I'm gonna pump it full of tranquilizer, and then just hope that it'll eat it, *and then* hope we'll be able to keep the thing under control until it sets in. Unfortunately, there's a lot of hoping in this plan."

She wished she could inject it in the mouth with another hypodermic needle, which would cause an immediate effect, but knew it would be an impossible task. There was no way she could get anywhere near it. Even previously on the boat, she barely managed to successfully implant the needle without ending up in its jaws.

Forster turned around, hearing somebody shouting over the crowd to let them through. She hurried to meet the approaching person, believing one of the aides was bringing her the vials of tranquilizer. People made way, and suddenly William Felt emerged from the crowd. He took a moment to catch his breath and straighten his tie. Despite the urgency of the situation, he seemed calm and collected, much like the enthusiastic businessman he was when he first hired her. He had his normal color back to his face and didn't smell of sweat. The only thing resembling urgency was his confusion regarding the current situation.

"What's going on?" he said. Forster glared at him.

Are you serious? She swallowed hard, trying not to lose her temper with him. After all, as she constantly reminded herself, he is her boss...and the only person who would hire her. *Only to exploit my record; ignore my advice; break the law; deliberately risk lives of employees...and now visitors...*

Her reserve dissolved.

"I warned you about this!" she shouted at him. "I told you we might not be able to contain this thing, and..." she looked over to the bay as the roller coaster fell down its slope, creating the same loud vibration it always did. At that same moment, another splash erupted from the water as the hybrid broke into another frenzy. It was as if the ride was deliberately trying to make her point. "You see that? All the vibrations and echoes, the sight and sounds of the people as they gather at it. And having the lights on downstairs, where it can see the people through the glass..."

"What's your point?" Felt said, seemingly unfazed by her criticisms.

"I advise you to do something, you do the goddamn opposite!" Forster said. Suddenly, another person emerged from the crowd. This individual almost resembled a work-study, wearing khaki shorts, a white button shirt, and glasses. She noticed the VIP tag on him, and *PHD* in the text with his name, *Glenn Tucker*. He was not the same VIP as the other person she directed off of the hydraulic lift. "And who are these guys?" she said. Felt looked at the VIP, realizing who she was referring to, then glared at her. Forster realized the answer for herself. "The researchers from the universities," she said aloud to herself. "What the hell were they doing with the shark?"

"We were testing its reflexes, by sending mild electrical impulses into the water," the VIP spoke up. "We were just studying responsiveness to stimuli."

"Oh really?" Forster pointed to the pen. "There, you have your answer, genius." She looked back to Felt. "Will? What are you thinking, letting these guys do this in broad daylight, with everyone around?"

"People found it interesting," Felt said. "Besides, you've been sedating it with each meal. I thought it'd be fine."

"Are you seriously that dense?" she said. "I've told you this thing has a resistance to sedation, and yet again you ignore me, and look what's happening." She turned her head as the echo from another metallic crunch filled the air. It was coming from the steel doors, and the creaking of gears confirmed her fear. The beast had figured out that the barrier led to the open ocean.

The warning she received yesterday suddenly resonated in her mind: *Do not let it survive.* Words spoken by someone wise enough to know this creature was bred to kill. And if it succeeded in its escape, killing is what it would do.

"Oh no," she said. She pulled her phone from her pocket. Felt noticed her scrolling through the contact list.

"Who are you calling?"

"The Chief," she said. "I'm sorry, but we're gonna have to put this thing down."

"Excuse me?" Felt said, walking around to face her directly. His relaxed posture was gone, and he was now very tense. The VIP biologist rapidly approached as well.

"You can't be serious!"

"You bet I am!" Forster said. Both of them looked as if they would attempt to snatch her phone, leading her to instinctively step back.

"This thing is an evolutionary marvel!" Dr. Tucker said. "For Pete's sake, you captured it yourself! There's no way you're killing it."

"It's a monster!" Forster yelled at him. "It's no marvel, it's no miracle; it's a killing machine...made from..." she stopped herself. She remembered the other warning. *Don't tell anyone.* Expressing knowledge of how this creature existed would do nothing but make herself, and anyone she told, a target for the government.

Felt lifted a finger to her face. Not physically threatening, but making a point. "Listen, Julie, this is MY park, and I own everything here! You want to leave, go ahead. Go back to being unemployable, like you were when I found you. That's exactly what'll happen if you dial that number."

The consequences flashed in her mind's eye. No doubt doing this would cost her any future she had. Not only with her past history, but with the new knowledge that she tried to destroy a "new species." The world of science wasn't aware of the true reality of the hybrid, and because of that, destroying it would be considered sacrilegious. In addition to that, Felt would undoubtedly blacklist her for destroying his new attraction. It'd be difficult even to get a job at a coffee stand.

She took a breath, letting everything sink in. Her eyes went from her phone, to Felt. His tense look slowly started to retract, as he could sense the conflict within her. He knew what mark to hit. After all, that was the reason he specifically hired her. Someone with limited options was much easier to control. He felt certain she was back under his spell.

"Fuck yourself," Forster said, and sent the call. Felt's expression turned to one of surprise and anger, as did the marine biologist, who instinctively lashed out to snatch her phone. Forster predicted this action and sidestepped. Dr. Tucker's reach missed entirely. Forster pointed at him. "Don't even try it," she said, while silently praying for Nelson to answer the call. Finally, on the forth ring, he picked up.

"*Julie?*" he said. Felt could hear his voice. He stepped toward her and pointed a finger for the second time, this time prodding it into her shoulder.

"I swear, you tell him to come over here and I'll...FUCKING BITCH!" He cried out as his finger bent backward at the knuckle. He dropped to his knees, pulling his hand away after Forster released her grip on his busted finger.

"Julie, what the hell's going on?"

"Chief," she said, keeping the VIP at bay. He gave up his aggressive stance, and stood near Felt, who was still on his knees in pain. "We need your help! The shark...it's out of control! We need to kill it...bring..." Hundreds of screams filled the air, and the crowd suddenly broke apart as people fled in panic. Forster looked to the pen, seeing the creature emerging. Its lower jaw smashed down on the guardrail, flattening it completely onto the cement. Clawed legs dug into the pavement as it attempted to pull itself ashore. It was aware of the fresh meat above and was successfully heaving itself onto dry land. Even Felt stood up and backed away. Halfway over the ledge, the creature's second pair of legs started to get a grasp.

By now, Felt had taken off running. Right behind him was Dr. Tucker.

"I'm on my way!" Nelson said, able to hear the chaos unfold. Forster heard him, but didn't answer. He wouldn't get there in time. She thought for quick solutions.

She backed into the maintenance truck, abandoned by the workers who fled along with everyone else. The keys were left in it, and the engine was still running. An idea came to mind.

"Julie?" She heard Nelson's voice. There was no time for her to explain.

"I gotta go," she said, and hung up the phone. She climbed into the truck. She cut the wheel to face the creature. At this point, only its tail was still in the water. Its red snout was facing directly toward her. Its black, non-blinking eyes gazed at the world from each side of its head. Another pair of legs took hold on the dry cement, and the hybrid was almost completely on shore.

"Oh, this is stupid," Forster said to herself, and quickly fastened her seatbelt. She would need it. She floored the accelerator. The truck kicked into gear. Tires screeched as the truck went from zero to a hundred. Forster clenched her teeth together and leaned back heavily into the seat. In three seconds, the truck closed the distance. Its engine smashed head-on into the creature's snout.

The whole front of the truck instantly caved in, bringing the truck to an instant stop. The front wheels flung out of place, rolling away from the crash, while bits of metal peppered the cement. The airbag deployed right into Forster's face. As she faceplanted, shards of windshield glass rained into the truck's interior. Several pieces came down onto the top of her head, embedding into her scalp.

A huge splash washed over the wreckage as the creature fell back into the pen. Water sprayed through the broken windshield, washing over Forster's bloody face. Her eyes stung from her own blood and the saltwater. The world spun as she reached blindly for the door handle. Locating it, she attempted to open the door, but it was stuck. Briefly leaning to the right, she swung her body back, putting her left shoulder into the door. With a metal crunch, it swung open, barely hanging by its hinges. She stepped out, wiping her face with her sleeve. Unknown to Forster, streaks of red smothered the white sleeve, and red drips came down on her shoulders. Her head throbbed. Each step became more difficult than the last. Through her blurry vision, she could see the splashes in the pen while the hybrid began another mindless rampage. She knew it wouldn't be long before it would try to climb out again, and she was the closest prey.

Her vision was shaky, like watching a home video filmed by a toddler. First, she was looking directly ahead, then up toward the sunny sky, then finally down at the pavement. The pavement suddenly grew much nearer, as her legs gave out, leading to her collapse. She rolled herself to her back, looking at the peaceful sky, the sight of which contrasted sharply with the maniacal thrashing about within the pen. Her vision faded into darkness, and she slipped into unconsciousness.

CHAPTER
29

Like she was caught in a maelstrom, Forster was caught in a dream that was like a race through time. Faces she hadn't seen in years flashed in front of her, and their voices echoed through her blue, swirling surrounding.

"*You have potential like no other.*" Standing in the storm, she saw her father, as he was when he took her sailing for the first time as a teenager.

"Dad!" she yelled out to him. The image did not answer. He drifted away, and in rapid progression, she saw a mirage of faces, while hearing their voices echo in her ears.

"*I bet your dead daddy would be really proud of you, ratting out your friends.*"

"*Make new discoveries. That was the dream, right?*"

"*You are hereby expelled from BRIZO.*"

"*Do not let it survive. Let it sink to the ocean floor!*"

A light consumed the strange swirling storm of images. More voices echoed overhead, louder and more focused.

"*Looks like it missed the temporal artery.*"

"*Blood pressure's one-fifteen-over-eighty.*" The light grew brighter, and suddenly a flood of sensation electrified her senses, as two more voices simultaneously echoed over the dream world.

"*Dreams don't have to die.*"

"*She's waking up. Relax, keep calm...*"

"Just keep calm, you're in an ambulance," the paramedic said to Forster as she woke up. Her mind had instantly reset to the most recent memory, which was trying to get away from a shark-crustacean that was attempting to escape captivity. After several seconds, she calmed from the need to escape. She was seated up in the stretcher, and right away she felt the bandages around her head. As she felt them, she noticed the blood on her shirt. The paramedic leaned in front of her view.

"Hey, how are you feeling?"

"I'm alright," Forster answered.

"Can you tell me your name?"

"Dr. Julie Forster," she answered. *A doctor of what?* She despised her automatic inclusion of that detail.

"How many quarters are in a dollar?" the paramedic asked.

"Four," she said. As the paramedic started to ask another question, she raised her hand. "I'm alright!" She then remembered the blood on her shirt, "I am, aren't I?"

"You had cuts from glass in your scalp," the paramedic said. "We were able to remove them ourselves, as they didn't pose any threat to any major arteries.

However, I would recommend you get yourself checked at the hospital. We're aware you have had a recent concussion, and considering you were in a truck crash gives us greater concern."

"I was keeping the hybrid in the pen…" suddenly Forster's brain went back into high gear. "The hybrid! What's happened? Has it got out?" She grabbed the paramedic's coat.

"Whoa!" he said, easing her hands away. "It's alright, from what I understand, it's in the pen. They've got it under control." Forster leaned back, feeling partially relieved, though also confused. *Who sedated it?* She supposed one of the aides could have managed to do it, though everyone had fled the exhibit. The back doors of the ambulance were open, and she could hear the roller coaster rumbling in the distance. They were still at the park. She sat up more and swung herself over, touching her feet to the floor. The paramedic braced, worried she would stumble. "Hey, take it easy," he said. "You still lost some blood there, and you may have suffered another concussion."

"I'm fine," Forster said, and stood up. She took it slow as she walked out of the ambulance, taking each step carefully on the Aquarium parking lot. Though feeling woozy, she was able to keep her balance as she walked away. She noticed other ambulances in the area and paramedics and EMTs tending to people, most of whom suffered injuries from falling down during the chaos. In one of the ambulances, she could see a familiar face through the open doors; William Felt sat up on the stretcher, wincing in pain as the paramedics tended to his broken finger. Forster turned away, unable to hold back a slight smirk, though it faded at the thought of likely assault charges. A throbbing headache gradually started settling in, and everything seemed to be happening in slow motion. Looking toward the emergency vehicles, she noticed two police cars. She then remembered having called Chief Nelson, and immediately desired to see him.

"Hey! Julie!" a familiar voice called to her. She turned and saw Nelson approach. She sprinted and ran to him.

"Oh Joe, thank God," she said. He smiled.

"What's with this sudden trend of calling me by my first name?" he jokingly asked. His smile faded as he then saw the bandage on her head and blood on her white shirt. "Good lord, you sure you're alright?" She looked down at herself.

"Yeah, it looks worse than it is," she said. They both started walking toward the shark exhibit. Several maintenance crew members were at the scene, uprooting the remnants of the guardrail, while a towing vehicle loaded the totaled truck onto its ramp. Visitors casually walked around the physical barriers toward the aquarium and park. What was previously an anarchic setting had returned to being calm and casual. Watching the people, it almost was as if nothing had happened at all. She only saw one couple standing at the barricades, staring at the pen. She gazed past them all, into the pen. She knew that stillness in that water was only the calm before the storm. It was only a matter of time before the creature would attempt another escape.

"Any idea what the damage is?" she asked.

"According to your maintenance guys, the doors are still holding," he said. "I think it ruptured the replacement glass in the downstairs viewing area, which has been sealed. As far as I know, none of the walls have been breached, but you can definitely tell they took a pounding. The sides look like big sheets of crumpled paper that somebody tried to flatten out."

"I need your help," Forster said. "We have to kill it."

"I know, I know," he said, and sighed. She suddenly stepped in front of him, forcing him to step in its tracks.

"I don't think you understand," she said. "We need to destroy this thing, right now. This thing has endangered human life. You can get authorization."

"It's not going to happen," Nelson said. "My good ol' buddy, the Mayor, won't stand for it. I'm pretty sure he had a chat of sorts with Mr. Felt." Forster scraped her shoe against the pavement.

"My God, you should've seen it," she said. "I'm telling you, it's not a shark. It wasn't acting out of hunger. Hell, we've been feeding it. It tried crawling out, deliberately to attack the crowd." She looked back to the water. The calm water caused a question to re-emerge in her mind. "Who sedated the thing?"

"Actually, I was about to talk to you about that," Nelson said. He led her to the barriers, where that same couple was waiting. It was a man and woman, staring off into the water, deep in conversation with one another. The man heard their approach and turned around. Forster instantly recognized each feature on his face, from the unshaven five-day beard, to the black hair, that was gradually turning into salt-and-pepper.

"Oh, my..." Forster was overwhelmed with surprise. Rick Napier extended his hand, which she accepted.

"Good to meet you, Doctor Forster," he said. "This is my wife, Lisa." Forster and Lisa shook hands as well.

"That took guts, what you did there," Lisa said. Forster smiled.

"Thanks," she said, and looked back to Rick. "So, it was you who..."

"One of your aides brought the supplies," Rick answered. "The Chief got you to safety, while his officers and I got the fish into the pen. Luckily, the bastard took it." They started walking back to the barricades. A solemn vibe filled the air. "I had to see it for myself, to know it was real," he said, looking at the water. They could barely see out to the far end, where the creature had settled at the bottom. Its red hide was barely visible from where they stood. "It's real."

"I've never seen anything like it," Forster said.

"I have," Rick said. Everyone knew he was referring to the Mako's Center attack. He looked at the numerous people passing by. "Let's go somewhere a little more private, away from prying ears. We have a lot to talk about."

****

"Are you serious?" Forster said, nearly spilling coffee all over her own kitchen floor as she turned to look at Rick. Standing by the counter, Chief Nelson put his mug down, feeling disbelief at the revelation he just heard.

"Are you sure about that?" he asked. During the past hour, Rick and Lisa explained in great detail the events that occurred three years ago, leading up to his suspicions regarding the oil rig bombing. Rick sat on the sofa next to Lisa. His mouth felt dry from telling their very long story.

"I can't say for sure," he said. "I do know that if the government wanted to get rid of this thing, they would want the nation's focus on something else." Nelson was interested in everything up until this point. Now, he looked at Rick as though he were a conspiracy theorist.

"Listen, Doc, I know there's a lot of shady stuff that goes on, with Black Ops, and hush-hush-type of things." Nelson said. "But blowing up an oil platform? It just sounds far-fetched. Would they really go to such lengths?"

"They did last time," Rick said.

"I believe you, but here's the problem," Nelson said. "Where are the operatives? I mean, the explosion occurred early this morning. As you said, the eyes of the world are on it. Why haven't we seen anyone?" Rick Napier sat silent for a moment, taking in the Chief's point. It was a good point. Last time, military and government officials arrived almost right away after the news finally got out that the hybrid existed. So far, it had been nearly a whole day, and so far, there was nothing. With the creature currently in captivity, there was no truly quiet way of obtaining it without gaining some sort of attention. He looked to his wife.

"Lisa, you have a better understanding of this stuff than me," he said. "What do you think?"

"The Chief has a point," she said. "We'd be seeing people by now...especially you, Chief." Nelson perked up, intrigued by her point. "On our island, Chief Bondy was probably the first to be spoken to. Considering you helped bring this thing in, I'm shocked they haven't issued you a warning days ago." She looked back to her husband. "Rick, maybe we were wrong about the diversion." Rick thought about it. If they were wrong, the bombing was just a separate incident. It suddenly started to make sense. After all, there has been no media or speculation connecting the shark's existence to the Warren Project. With it in captivity, seen now by thousands, it would make sense that the government's best course of action would be to allow the public to assume the creature was just a miracle of nature, or a new species. The incident was sweeping itself under the rug.

"Unfortunately, it presents a problem unto itself," he said. "If they're not coming to destroy this thing, and with the Coast Guard occupied with the threat of potential terrorist attacks, then that means nobody's coming to destroy these things. You guys are obviously convinced there's at least one more, right?"

"Boats sinking, people disappearing, orcas turning up dead with huge bite marks...you tell me," Nelson said. "Listen, docs, here's the deal here. If you're right, then nobody's coming. That leaves me. I'm going to go out and kill this thing." Forster set the coffee pot down and walked around the counter table.

"You're what?"

"Listen," he said. "Unfortunately, I can't shut these beaches down. In fact, even more people are coming to see Felt's pet. Also, the fishermen are starting to venture out. Even today, my office has gotten calls over fishermen who haven't returned yet. This island is turning into a smorgasbord."

"Joe, you saw what the one did to your boat," Forster protested.

"Exactly, and that's exactly what'll happen if people keep going out into the water," Nelson argued back.

"Yeah, but how are you going to kill it?" Forster said. "Guns don't work. You shot it point blank, and it didn't even flinch!"

"And besides," Rick chimed in. "There's a question of numbers. I'm not convinced you'd be dealing with one shark." All eyes turned toward him.

"Excuse me? How many of these things did they lose?" Nelson said.

"Best case scenario, two," Napier said. "OR...just the one."

"I don't quite understand," Forster said.

"*Two* is the best-case scenario?" Nelson added. There was a nervous anticipation to his voice. Rick himself even looked uneasy, as if he didn't want to admit his suspicion.

"Last time, in pursuing the hybrid that attacked our island, we discovered a little bonus item," he said. "That maniac, Dr. Wallack, engineered these creatures to reproduce asexually. No mating, no nothing. Just, spawn new hybrids; a nice little way to make extra soldiers and save costs."

"You've got to be kidding me," Nelson said. Losing his appetite, he put his coffee back down.

"Are you sure?" Forster asked.

"When we found it, we discovered it was preparing a nest," Rick said. "If anything, it was pure luck it was destroyed before it could spawn." Silence struck the room, as Forster and Nelson realized the horrible possibilities of what could eventually happen if more creatures were out there.

"And the spawns," Forster softly spoke, "you think they are..."

"Capable of reproducing?" Rick said. "Oh, yes." Forster sank into the living room chair. A very real fear clouded her mind. The thought of an army of sharks, each of which would kill anything that would cross them, roaming the ocean. Each one armored with an impenetrable hide. The worst cases of invasive species would not hold a candle to what they would do. Not to mention the threat to humans, whether on the coast or traveling across the water.

"But wait, wouldn't the government be concerned about this?" Nelson asked.

"I'm not sure they know," Rick said. "Especially since nobody's seen anything until now. And the only confirmed sighting is the one in captivity." He looked out the window, getting a view of the ocean. Just like back home in Razortooth Cove, it was deceptively peaceful. "Now look," he said as he turned back to face everyone. "There have been no reports of sightings of these things outside of this island. There is a good chance that if the thing gave birth, this is the only litter so far. If we find them and destroy them, it can all end."

"Does that mean you're volunteering to help?" Nelson asked. Rick and Lisa shared a glance, as if checking with each other. They knew the risks; they'd faced them together before. They both looked back to the Chief.

"You bet," Rick said. To his own surprise, he did not feel reluctant at all. On the contrary, there was an odd sense of relief, along with a slight optimism. Perhaps it was the fact he was facing down his demon. Nelson was visibly gratified.

"I'm in too," Forster added. Nelson looked over at her. His appreciation turned to apprehension.

"Julie, that won't be necessary," he said.

"Yes, it is! And don't argue," she said, silencing any further protest. Rick and Lisa shared another quick glance, each thinking the same thing.

Something's going on there. A small smirk slipped through Rick's mental guard. It showed for only a moment, but it was enough for Forster and Nelson to see.

"What's so funny?" Forster asked.

"Nothing," Rick said, realizing to stray away from that topic. "Listen, there's another important aspect to this. If we manage to locate these things and kill them, it's extremely important for us to figure out which one is the original. If the mother is among the group, that'll be a good indicator that this was the only litter."

"Carbon date the teeth?" Forster asked.

Rick nodded. "That's right." Nelson began scratching his head. He felt himself starting to grow increasingly overwhelmed by the thought of multiple creatures.

"That's fine, but do we even have a plan to kill them? I doubt they'll let me stick a shotgun in their mouths, and we don't have anything to blow them up with."

"I think I have an idea on that," Rick said. "But our first priority is getting a boat capable of taking a pounding from these things."

"What about that boat from the aquarium?" Lisa asked Forster.

"The *Neptune*?" Forster asked. "It's out for repair."

"No, it's not," Nelson said. "Didn't you see it get returned today?"

"No...I've been so overworked, and nobody said anything." She grew flustered, as she hadn't told anyone she had been fired. In addition, the idea of going back to the aquarium didn't sit well, especially since Felt would not react very positively to her presence. "I mean, I suppose it would fare better than anything else on the island..."

"It took a few good hits last time," Nelson added. "The main damage was from when the anchor was ripped free. Other than that, it was a few dents, but no breaches."

"Then that wins the vote," Rick said. He noticed Forster looking uneasy. "You okay there, kid?"

"There's another problem," she said, just above a whisper. "I, uh," she paused again. "I don't...work there anymore." Knowing Nelson's constant concern for her, she braced for a bombardment of questions. *What? What happened? What did he make you do? Why did you quit?*

Instead, there was quiet. Nelson didn't even look surprised. Rick and Lisa didn't seem concerned regarding the lack of access to the *Neptune;* rather, he seemed to exhibit a confident appearance.

"I can take care of that," Rick said.

"How?" Forster asked. Rick chuckled, as did Nelson.

"Oh, come on," Rick said. "You should know, Felt's the kind of guy who loves to make an extra buck. I've got some spare change to throw at him." Forster felt her eyebrows rise with intrigue.

"Wait…you're gonna *buy* the *Neptune*?" Rick's smile grew bigger.

"You're damn right."

CHAPTER
30

The evening sun had cast a blinding stream of light onto the resort when they all arrived. Forster drove with the Napiers in her car, while Nelson arrived separately in his own vehicle. Forster had predicted that Felt would be working late, supervising the reconstruction to the exhibit while trying to get someone to manage care for the animals in the aquarium. Her prediction proved correct. Cement crews were already on site, trying to patch in the damage to the ledge while restoring a new, sturdier barrier. Felt's black suit appeared grey from the dusty residue from the cement truck.

Rick could see the uneasiness in the worker's faces as they worked along the ledge. Clearly, word had spread on what happened, though Felt had probably made up some story. His voice echoed through the air as he spoke with high energy. Forster could see the white splint and bandage on his right index finger. Rick noticed as she slowed her approach.

"Is there a problem?" he asked.

"Let's just say, it's best you do the talking," she said. After all, they were there to negotiate a purchase for the *Neptune,* and Rick was the money. Rick remembered her stating that she was no longer employed, and felt no need to ask anything further. Forster stayed back near the corner of the building, as Rick and Lisa crossed the pedestrian walkway to Felt. Nelson decided to stay behind with her, realizing he had nothing to contribute to the exchange. They watched the Napiers both step over the physical barriers. Felt saw them approach. Even from a distance, Forster could see that bright, fake business smile that Felt wore on his smug face. He and Napier started to engage in conversation, though Forster and Nelson couldn't quite overhear.

As they waited, Forster thought of the incident between herself and her former boss. She felt a slight wave of guilt for busting his finger; but only *slight.* After all, both he and the biologist were rushing at her. Nonetheless, she worried of what would possibly come from this. It was bad enough her career was at a lower point than ever. The one job that would take her, she had lost. Not that she liked working at Felt's Paradise; she hated it. However, it didn't dull the reality that now she was jobless, and finding a new career seemed impossible. She didn't know how to do anything else, and also, she had no other real interests. A possible battery charge would strain her future even more, on top of her previous criminal history. After a few minutes, she caught herself dwelling on this, not even paying attention to the exchange between Rick Napier and William Felt.

Nelson stood next to her, silent, and with his arms crossed. She figured the incident would come to his attention eventually. He might as well hear it from her. She exhaled nervously, which in itself gained Nelson's attention. He glanced over.

"You all right?" he asked, still standing with his arms crossed.

"Yeah," she lied, then realized she was stalling. "No, actually. I haven't told you why I'm not working here anymore. I'm assuming you haven't spoken to Felt." Nelson shrugged his shoulders.

"Eh, you should've broken more of his fingers," he said. Forster stood quietly, flabbergasted to the unexpected acknowledgement.

"Wait...you already knew?" she asked.

"Yeah, the prick tried to bring up charges. Luckily, there were a couple of honest people around that saw what really happened," he said. Forster exhaled again, only this time with relief. The reprieve she felt was so overwhelming, she felt as if she would float away. She even cracked a smile. Seeing that, in turn, made Nelson smile. "Even if nobody else spoke up, I wouldn't have done anything," he said. "After everything that bastard has done, with everyone's safety he has risked...basically I just told him to go to hell." They watched from afar as Rick, Lisa, and Felt walked over to the *Neptune*. They weren't sure what Rick was offering, but if seemed evident that Felt was intrigued.

"I guess, after we're done with this, I'll have to figure out what to do," she said.

"You and me both," Nelson said. Surprise returned to Forster's face, which he noticed. "I'm not staying here," he said. "This jerk will just keep exploiting more of the island, and knowing him, he'll surely get some other business partner to help him milk along. The Mayor's just going along with the whole thing. I've got nothing against rich people; in fact, many of them are good and beneficial. But these guys have destroyed the integrity of this place, and I'm tired of it. Besides...I'm certain I'll be let go anyway."

"What do you mean?" Forster asked.

"After we eliminate the other sharks, I'm gonna kill this one myself," he said. "That alone will get me fired. Hell, more than that; I'll probably find myself hunting for a new career." He stood quietly for the next several moments, waiting for the outcome of the exchange, not noticing the warm gaze from Forster. As she looked at him, she thought about how she didn't feel alone. Despite the worst misery she felt during the past several months, Nelson was always there. Somehow, she never acknowledged it until now. Perhaps it was because they were united against a common threat, of which the rest of the world was oblivious.

"Maybe we can open a bait and tackle shop," she joked. Nelson grinned.

"Or collaborate on a book. *How to Catch a Sea Beast,*" he said.

"I'd be down with that," she said. They shared another small laugh, before seeing Felt and Rick shaking hands. The deal had concluded successfully.

****

Rick kept the *Neptune* close to the shallows as he brought it to the East Harbor. Most of the fishermen who lived on the island's interior usually kept their vessels near the southeast and southwest docks. Luckily for Rick, this allowed him to park the thirty-eight-foot vessel with little concern for maneuvering around several fishing boats. By now, the sun had dipped further into the horizon, setting the stage for night. Lisa stood out on the deck, providing an extra set of eyes as he carefully pulled alongside the dock. She tied up the line and secured the boat.

They saw two sets of headlights in the distance. Both vehicles parked, and their drivers stepped out. Rick stepped out of the wheelhouse, while Forster and Nelson came up to the dock.

"What'd you think?" Forster asked.

"It's a hell of a nice boat," Rick said. He put his hand on the gunwale and walked along the starboard side, continuing to inspect it. "If it was damaged before, they did a nice job patching it up. This is a similar design as for the landing craft used for warfare, especially during World War Two."

"It's not invincible, though," Lisa said, serving as the skeptic of the group. "Those things can still sink this thing, especially if there are many of them."

"Unfortunately, we don't have a helicopter," Nelson said.

"It'll be durable enough for us to lure them into the trap," Rick said.

"What's the plan?" Forster asked. "Load up some bait with poison and feed it to them?"

"I've thought of that, but the problem is that it won't work fast enough for us to hightail it out of dodge," Rick said. "Even if there's only one other hybrid, it'll still be able to attack for a while until the poison shuts down its organs. By then, even with this boat, it could be too late." He climbed up onto the deck, and looked at the sunset, then checked his watch. "Is there a hardware store in town open this late?"

"Yes," Nelson said, curious what Rick was getting at.

"Good," he said. He looked to his wife. "You think steel mesh should work, right?"

"Absolutely," Lisa said.

"Wait a sec," Forster said. "Metal, bendable mesh…" she suddenly realized the plan. "Are you gonna bait the net, and hook it up to an electric current?"

"Awe, man," Rick said. "I had a whole one-liner planned." He chuckled to himself. He pointed to the crane. "We have a perfect system in place. We have a cable, which we can lower the bait, which will be wrapped with the mesh like tin-foil on a meatball sub. Only the sharks won't peel it off."

"And we'll hook an electric wire to the mesh," Forster clarified.

"Touch that wire to a battery, and zap!" Rick said, clapping his hands together for effect.

"That might work," Nelson said. "What kind of battery will we need?"

"Something big and fully charged," Lisa said. "A car battery won't be nearly enough."

"What about a high-powered generator?" Nelson said. "We have a high voltage one at the station. Being in an area frequently visited by hurricanes, it comes into use. It can deliver up to a hundred amps."

Napier nodded. "That'll be more than enough to stop its heart." He exhaled sharply. "Okay, then…I guess we have a plan." He looked at Lisa. "I suppose we'd better get the supplies." Nelson raised his hand, as if to make a protest.

"Oh, no," he said. "You already supplied the boat. The rest is on me," he said. "Do you guys have arrangements to stay anywhere?"

"We have a hotel set up," Lisa said.

"Obviously, you don't have a ride. I'll drive you there," Nelson said. "Then I'll pick up the things we still need. After that, we'll meet back up here tomorrow…say nine?" Everyone nodded in agreement.

"Sounds good," Rick said.

"Alright," Nelson said. "Everyone get some sleep. We're gonna need it."

CHAPTER
31

The light from Forster's phone illuminated her bedroom. For what seemed like the hundredth time, she checked the time, and laid back down. Unable to fall asleep, she stared at the ceiling. Each effort to zone out was fouled by unrelenting thoughts that her mind became fixated on.

There was the apprehension of what lay ahead. Ten years of college and specialty training; a lifetime of ambition; all for what? She constantly tried to be grateful her father wasn't around to witness her failure. It didn't do any good. A believer in Heaven, she often felt as if her father was always watching. If he was truly in that 'better place' people talked about, what did he think of her?

Then there was the financial worry. Though she had money saved from her employment at Felt's Paradise, it would only last her a year at most. She tried to think of other careers to pursue, but there was nothing else she knew. Besides, she knew Felt was on the ball to cause detriment to her record. As far as she knew, she was completely un-hirable.

Mostly, it was a fear that gradually set in during the evening. Seeing the hybrid climbing out of the pen, determined to slaughter its spectators, made her much more consciously aware of how aggressive it was. Knowing they were up against another one of these creatures made sleep impossible. She thought of the plan. Though she was confident it would work, there was still a high risk. She wanted to be a scientist and explorer, not a hunter. Very rarely did she experience a true fear of death. And this fear was all too real.

Relaxation became unachievable.

Couldn't be wider awake, she thought. Feeling as if hours had gone by, she checked her phone again. As she figured, it had only been minutes since she last checked. It was no use. She sat up and walked to the kitchen, opening the refrigerator. There wasn't much to drink, due to her never having time to go on a shopping trip. Now was she not only awake, she was frustrated.

"The hell with it," she said to herself. A nightcap sounded more appealing than ever. A quick remembrance of what happened the last time she visited a bar caused a slight delay. She briefly worried of a repeat, but decided it was worth the risk. Besides, she was no longer associated with Felt, and had broken his finger. The island residents would probably throw her a parade.

****

"~You heard about the Pirate boat!~"
"~That daring one, the sea did float!~"
"~She was the Alabama!~"

Sitting at the bar, Forster raised her glass, surrounded by the dozens of fishermen that filled the bar. Beer bottles reached for the ceiling as the crowd gathered in song. In the blink of an eye, Forster had gone from being one of the most hated people on the island to being a celebrity. To her amazement, her humorous premonition had become a reality. She was recognized by several patrons. But instead of acting hostile, they each offered to buy her a drink. Apparently, other staff at the resort had quit earlier in the day because of the same incident, and while bar hopping, they talked about how the marine biologist "broke that bastard's finger."

The tension had successfully subsided for now. In fact, Forster found herself having a good time. Between prison and job hunting, she couldn't remember the last celebration she had. Suds splattered onto the tile floor as the drunken crowd continued to sing. Forster downed her drink and sang along, swaying from side-to-side with each lyric. Buzzing with joy and booze, she lifted her beer mug and sang like a sailor in colonial times.

"She was the Alabama!" She concluded the song and downed the rest of her beer. As the bottom went up, she could hear the stool scoot next to her as somebody took a seat. She immediately assumed someone was offering to buy her another drink. She belched as she slammed the mug down on the counter. "Good, you're here," she said to the person. "I'm ready for more mead!"

"I think you've had enough." Recognizing the voice, Forster whipped her head around, seeing Chief Joe Nelson sitting beside her.

"Whoa! Chief, uh…Joe!" she said. "What are you doing here?"

"Same reason as you: couldn't sleep," he said.

"How did you know I couldn't…"

"Julie, I can read you like a speech," he interrupted her. She smiled.

"Well, okay maybe I had a case of nerves," she said. "But I will say, coming here really has helped to relieve the tension."

"Really?" Nelson said. "You're not drinking like someone who's tense. You look like someone who's celebrating." Forster thought about his words for a sec.

"Hmm, yeah," she said. "It feels appropriate enough. After all, we're going after something that could very well kill us tomorrow. So, to treating a night like it's your last ought to merit celebration."

"It's a fair point," Nelson said. He snapped his fingers at the bartender. "*Budweiser*, please," he said. Forster started chuckling. "What?"

"Is that how you celebrate? Plain *Budweiser*?" she said.

"Fine," he said, then looked back at the bartender. "Double-Scotch. Neat." The bartender poured the drink and served it in a fine glass. He took it and downed half of it. He shut his eyes for a minute, allowing the desired effect to take place. He looked to Forster and smirked. "Now that's the stuff."

Throughout the next hour, they celebrated the night in song with the crowd of fishermen. With the final lyric of each song, everyone raised their glass above their heads. Laughter filled the bar, and smiles could be seen in every direction.

Forster heard the legs of the nearest stool scoot against the floor as someone took the seat. She looked over, her smile disappearing when she saw the forty-year-old man staring at her. She recognized his face, as did Nelson. It was

Jeffrey, the man whom she had an encounter at the *Lionfish* bar. The Chief placed his hands on the bar table, ready to spring into action.

The bar went quiet, just as it had when Jeffrey confronted Forster days prior. Jeffrey said nothing. His eyes looked down at Forster's hands, which had begun to tighten into fists. Her demeanor wasn't aggressive, though she was growing increasingly nervous. Jeffrey suddenly laughed, exposing his missing tooth from their previous skirmish. Forster squinted, confused. Suddenly, everyone in the bar joined in with Jeffrey's laughter.

"What the..." Forster began to nervously smile. "What's going on?"

"I'm just screwing with you," Jeffrey said, and tapped her shoulder. "I wanted to apologize for the other night. I was an ass, to say the least." Forster was overwhelmed.

"Oh, gosh, it's really me who should be sorry! I knocked out your tooth, for heaven's sake!"

"Ah, don't worry about it," he said. "Dentist will be giving me a new one soon. The wife even picked out the one she liked the most." Forster smiled, then instantly wondered how he would pay for it, remembering he was doing poorly on money. "I got a new gig on a sword fishing trawler," Jeffrey said, as if reading her mind. He looked to the bartender. "Another round for these folks! On me this time!" The bartender refilled their drinks. They touched glasses and drank in unison. Songs rang through the building once again.

Nelson and Forster once again joined in with the melodies. When the fishermen raised their glasses to a toast, so did they. Forster noticed Jeffrey stand up and step aside. A fisherman with a long grey beard took his seat next to Forster.

"I overheard you talk about celebration," he said. "Are you celebrating getting away from that resort owner?" Forster gave a drunken laugh. She wiped her face with a napkin.

"That's a bonus," she said, struggling to sit up straight. "But uh, actually the Chief and I are doing something very important tomorrow." The crowd again grew quiet, and she realized they were listening in. It was no surprise, as Forster had become the star of the night.

"The way you talk, it sounds like it's something dangerous," the fisherman said. Forster's smile faded, as did Nelson's.

"Obviously, you guys know of the ships that have been going down lately," she said.

"Yes," the fisherman answered. "We've been drinking to them all week." The crowd answered with a unanimous "Aye." Forster turned around, seeing the cheerful faces turn solemn, as they thought to their lost friends. The reality of what she was chasing after came swarming back in her mind.

"That creature at the aquarium, we believe there's at least one other. Maybe more," she said. "The Chief and I are going out tomorrow to kill it. Otherwise, it'll continue killing. Us and some others. So, it seems appropriate to have a farewell drink."

"Sounds like you're going after your own Moby Dick," the fisherman said.

"I guess so," Forster said.

"Perhaps we can help," he said. "Many of us know how to catch a shark." Forster shook her head, though reluctantly. The offer of help was tempting.

"Unfortunately, no," she said. "We have the only boat that can stand a chance. Everything else, this thing, or things, can ravage with ease. We're grateful, but unfortunately you guys would just provide more targets."

The fisherman stood up. At first, it seemed like he had enough conversation. Then, she heard his voice assert a hum. She looked over at him. He stood tall, with his eyes closed. His head was tilted up slightly, as if about to speak in prayer. Then, in a remarkable, slow hymn, the words of song escaped his mouth.

"Of all the money that e'er I had...I spent it in good company...And all the harm I've ever done...Alas it was to none but me." He continued singing the Scottish melody, quickly joined by Jeffrey. Soon, another fisherman joined in, followed by another. Soon, the entire group of fishermen joined the singing.

"So fill to me the parting glass, and drink a health whate'er befall, and gently rise and softly call, good night and joy be to you all."

Like a church service, the hymn grew louder, and the emotion grew. Forster and Nelson locked eyes. Each was as moved as the other by the comforting effort by the crowd. Forster fought back a tear, and softly joined in. A group which she was formerly at odds with had now become her companions.

And as she sang, the fear slipped away.

CHAPTER
32

It was nine o'clock sharp when Rick and Lisa Napier, Chief Joe Nelson, and Julie Forster boarded the *Neptune*. For several minutes, they loaded all of their supplies on deck. Rick and Nelson tensed as they lowered the three heavy fuel barrels from the dock to the boat. Lisa and Forster teamed up with each other to load the tubs of chum and bait. Rick and Nelson then loaded the hundred-and-fifty-pound generator, placing it at the starboard side across from the crane control. Then it came time to wrap the bait in the metal mesh, as it would be easier to do on shore than on the boat. They carefully folded the metal netting tightly over the meaty carcasses so the predator would still be able to taste the flesh. Then they strung up a leather harness to each one with an individual clip to attach to the crane when necessary. After a half hour, everyone was already starting to sweat, and the day was only starting. They released the tie-off line, and Rick took the helm. Backing out of the small port, they were off.

As most of the incidents had taken place to the west, the team decided to launch their search there. With Forster's guidance, Rick steered the large vessel around to the north. After twenty minutes, they began to clear the east peninsula. Bringing the bow west, they moved across the northern coast. The sight of the resort came into view. Rick looked through the open window at the relaxing pool and spas that opened up to the visitors. He was quite impressed how far the artificial pools extended out into the bay. Though none of them were deeper than eight feet, they had reinforced glass flooring that helped the illusion that one was out in the open ocean. No wonder Felt was always on edge about finances. No way this special design was cheap to produce. As they moved between the peaks, he saw the private harbor, and the familiar shark exhibit, though it was barely visible from their perspective. A couple of maintenance vehicles were parked along the ledge, finishing up repair work.

Then a mechanical rumbling noise rattled throughout the air. The amusement park had started its many runs on the roller coaster. The car followed its path, reaching far out into the bay from the west peninsula. To provide the rush of speeding over water, only the beginning and concluding portions of the roller coaster were secured to the shore. The rest of the mechanism extended far out into the bay, locked down by steel supports that lodged into the seafloor. Further up the peninsula, prize games opened up on large docks, built in square formations. From high above, it looked like a watery checkerboard with people walking between the squares. Further inland, many of the standard rides began their typical operations.

Standing on deck, Forster looked at the design of Felt's Paradise, particularly the amusement games on the docks. She prayed that Felt's biologist contractors were keeping the captured hybrid under control. If it were to escape, it could easily tear those docks apart.

After several long minutes, they passed along the pointed tip of the west peninsula.

Forster downed two Excedrin to combat her headache. She knew she had stayed way later at the bar than she should have, but she didn't regret it. She looked out at the endless reaches of the ocean. The weather was perfect once again, with a sunny forecast for the rest of the day. Behind them, the island seemed to shrink as they moved further away. Standing at the bow, Nelson spoke on a radio. Today, he had opted out of his blues in favor of simple jeans and a grey long sleeve shirt. Just warm enough to deflect the ocean breeze, but thin enough to keep from roasting in the summer heat.

"That's a roger. We'll be monitoring all radio transmissions from here. That said, keep me informed of any reports that come in by phone."

"*Ten-four, Chief. Will do,*" Dispatch responded.

"Thanks. Over-and-out," Nelson said, and placed the radio down by his large duffle bag. They could hear the boat throttling down to a near stop. The engine still hummed as Rick stepped out of the wheelhouse.

"Is this the spot?" he asked.

"This is the approximate area," Forster said. "We found the whale drifting about half a click back. It had probably drifted for a while before the skiers came across it. We don't know where exactly the shark attacked it."

"Well, it's as good a place to start as anywhere," Rick said.

"Whatever you do, don't kill the engine," Forster said. "If things don't go as planned, we'll need to get out of here in a hurry."

"Sounds like good advice," Rick said. He went over to the chum bucket located near the crane on the portside. He pulled the lid off, took a moment to adjust to the smell of the 'delicious stew' and grabbed a metal scoop. Lisa stepped onto the deck. She had removed her denim jacket due to the heat, sporting a white tank top.

"I'll keep my eye on the monitors," she said. As before, the *Neptune* was still equipped with several underwater cameras which were still functional. Nelson stood up from his seat and snapped his fingers.

"Hang on, just a sec," he said. Rick froze, having yet to dip the scoop into the mixture, and Lisa stepped further out on deck. Nelson knelt down beside the large black duffle bag and started unzipping it. Rick stood up, curious to see the contents. Nelson pulled the sides apart and reached in with both hands. With one, he pulled out a high-powered rifle, and with the other he grabbed a large Remington Auto-loader. Rick's eyes went wide, and he cracked a true American smile. He peeked downward, seeing that there were several more weapons in the bag.

"Hot damn, Rambo," he said. Nelson shared a similar smile.

"Perks of the job," he said. "Get to play with the good toys whenever I feel like." He looked over to Lisa. "Mrs. Napier, you spent a career in the Coast Guard. I'm assuming you're competent in the use of these fabulous tools." He held the butt end of the weapon toward her. She accepted it and checked the specs like a true professional. The weapon was already breached, yet to be

191

loaded. Her handling of it answered his question. He looked to Rick. "How about you?" he asked, while handing him the rifle. Rick accepted it.

"I'm no expert marksman," he said, "but these guys will be hard to miss. Not sure how much good it'll do, though. You guys said yourselves that you couldn't penetrate the exoskeleton on the other one."

"Yeah, but I'd rather have these handy just in case," Nelson said. "Who knows, perhaps we could deal a lucky hit. Maybe hit it in the eye, or in the mouth."

"Aim for the joints," Forster said. They all looked toward her. "The connecting tissue there is softer than the rest of the shell. It's possible you could do some damage."

"Sounds logical," Rick said. He handed the rifle back to Nelson. "Keep that handy for me. I don't want to get tuna grease all over it." He returned to the bucket and filled the scoop with the red-and-brown mixture of tuna, blood, and oil. He tossed it over the side, and repeated. The minced meaty substance drifted off in a diagonal direction from the starboard quarter. Soon, bits of meat traveled away from the chum line, carried by the extra oil to send out extra scent.

****

In the marine hospital room of the aquarium, two aides stood outside the two pools as the dolphins chattered to them. All three dolphins, which had been terribly ill a week prior, were now bursting with energy. The aides had opened the window to allow more sunlight into the room, and the fresh air brought in the natural smell of the ocean. The two aides laughed with the happy mammals as they played tricks in the two pools.

The plan was to move the dolphins from their pools into the much larger pen, near the shark exhibit. To avoid rousing the shark with placing the dolphins near it, maintenance was scheduled to move the second pen further down the peninsula near to the gaming docks. Though the dolphins were doing much better, it was still advised by Forster before her departure that they be monitored for a few days in a larger space before being returned to the wild. It was as if the dolphins could sense they were finally going to be moved from the cramped space.

Both eyes turned toward the entrance as the door opened. The maintenance foreman walked in. Initially, they were happy to see him, as they thought he was here to deliver the good news that the pen was ready. Then they noticed the frustrated, disapproving expression on his face. Whatever it was, it wasn't directed toward them, but his feelings weighed heavily enough to drag him down.

"What's going on?" one of the aides asked. The foreman looked back through the entrance, waiting for someone to approach. He looked back to the aides.

"Felt's made a change in plans," he said.

"A change?" the other aide said. "Are we not moving the dolphins today?"

"We're moving them," the foreman said, "but not to the pen." The aides replied in a simultaneous "huh?" The foreman shook his head in frustration.

"Moving the pen and hooking it up to a whole new filtration system will take up more time and cost than what Mr. Felt is willing to put up. It seems the dolphins have improved enough in health that they can live back out in the wild. So..." he sighed and held up his hands, palms up, "...the boss has rented a boat to take the dolphins out."

"That's absurd," one of the aides said. "We don't know if they're ready yet."

"They look ready to me," Dr. Tucker said as he entered the room. Though he was acting, and speaking, on behalf of Mr. Felt's wishes, his body language indicated that he too was reluctant. But unfortunately, the new deal between Felt and the university was that Dr. Tucker was to assist in the care of the aquarium's assets until a new full-time caretaker was hired. "I know you two care very much for these dolphins, and you've put a lot of time and effort into getting them well. If you want, you can come with us as we take them out. We'll probably be ready to load them up within the next half hour." The aides realized that he, like the foreman, was simply a person put in an uncomfortable position. What he really wanted to say was, *"Felt is a cheap bastard, and just wants to reduce expenses he deems unnecessary."* Now that he had renewed revenue with the capture of the hybrid, he was no longer concerned with redeeming his image in the public's eye. The aides understood.

"We'll go," they both said.

****

The chum trail extended to a brownish-red line that traveled far out into the crystal-blue water. Rick scraped the bottom of the tub with the scoop, gathering the last of the chum. He dumped it over and watched it splash over the side. He stood up and poured water over his hands, then wiped them dry with a towel to scrub off the grease. He pulled a handkerchief from his pocket and patted his sweaty brow.

"You okay there, sport?" his wife said from the wheelhouse. "I can take over the next one."

"No, I'm good," he said. He stuffed the handkerchief back into his pocket and looked out to the water. The *Neptune* had been drifting south over the past hour. Rick noticed something in the distance, straight ahead of the bow. It appeared to be some sort of formation in the water. He glanced to his left to look at the island, confirming that the boat didn't get turned around. "Hey, Dr. Forster?"

"Yeah," Forster said. Rick pointed out to the strange formation.

"What is that?" he asked. Forster looked at the large structure, realizing what it was.

"Oh!" she said. "That's the atoll," she said. "We think it was once part of the island, but possibly broke away due to an earthquake. It's just a theory, but one thing's for sure: we don't want to go near it."

"Is the water around it too shallow?" Rick asked.

"Not only is it shallow," Forster said, "but the atoll is surrounded by rocks. Big, jagged rocks that come up from the shallow seabed. Most of them break the surface. Driving a boat through there would be like driving through an asteroid field." Rick started to chuckle. He couldn't help but find the odd coincidence amusing. Lisa stepped outside, after overhearing the conversation. She clearly found the information amusing as well.

"Well, that sounds a bit too familiar," she said.

"Yeah, I'll say," Rick said. Forster cracked an awkward smile, not fully understanding what was so funny. Her confusion was obvious to Rick. Realizing he needed to explain, he cleared his throat. "As you know, Mako's Ridge is an island chain. One of our islands is a place called Mako's Edge. It's a barren rock, not very suitable for many habitats, and completely surrounded by jagged rocks that stick up from the ocean floor. It's basically a much bigger version of your atoll. Needless to say, taking a boat through there is a nightmare."

"Yeah. That's where the hybrid was hiding out," Lisa said. Her smile faded away as the memory took over. "According to the mad doctor, the landscape resembled its original habitat. Because of that, the hybrid was attracted to the landscape. So, it set up camp, only coming out whenever it wanted to hunt."

A thought instantly lit up inside Rick's mind. His grin disappeared, and a serious expression took over.

"Hey Lisa, could you take us closer to that atoll?" he asked.

"I beg your pardon?" Lisa asked.

"Yeah, did you not hear me when I said it's not safe to go near there?" Forster added. The Chief stepped out of the wheelhouse, also feeling alerted to the new change in plan. All of a sudden, all of his crewmates, including his wife, were crowding up on him. He felt as if he had spoken blasphemy in the presence of a king.

"Whoa, relax," Rick said. "We'll stay clear of the rocks. I just want to get close enough to chum."

"Care to venture a reason?" Nelson said.

"I want to test a theory," Rick said. "The other one was attracted to that kind of landscape. I'm wondering if these hybrids are attracted to the same habitat." Forster thought about it.

"Alright, let's try it," she said. Lisa stepped back into the wheelhouse and throttled the boat forward. The engine hummed and water kicked up around the hull as they approached the atoll.

****

Thirty minutes went by, and the *Neptune* slowly cruised around the large atoll. Nelson took a turn driving the boat, allowing Lisa to enjoy the fresh air. By the crane, Forster took a turn at chumming while Rick looked at the bizarre formation. The center landmass was still far away, with a whole forest of rocks between it and the boat. He held binoculars to his eyes, while looking at the atoll. Though it was difficult to see because of the distance and obstructions in his view, he was able to notice the smooth shore.

"Funny," he said. "For a big rock, it almost appears that it has a beach."

"Not one I'd want to sunbathe on," Forster said, tossing another scoop of mixture into the water. Rick examined the generator. A large copper wire was coiled next to the five-foot unit, ready to be placed at the circuit. At the other end of the wire was a metal hook to route the electricity to the bait. He looked at the specs on the generator, confirming that it was capable of giving out up to sixty-thousand volts.

Damn, he thought. As long as the hybrid held on to the bait for long enough, the current would be plenty sufficient to stop its heart. He looked out to the chum trail, which extended far from the portside. To his surprise, nothing seemed to be touching it.

"Usually, we would at least be seeing some fish or small sharks coming to nip at the chum," he said.

"Things have been pretty bad since Wan started dumping her shit in our waters," Forster said. Her voice expressed the bitterness felt by the island residents, as well as her own personal disgust.

"Where exactly did it take place?" Rick said. Forster placed the greasy scoop down and pointed past the wheelhouse, to the north.

"A few miles that way," she said. "The EPA has been at work to clear it up, but it seems the damage is done. God only knows how long Felt has been turning a blind eye to it."

"Speaking of him," Rick said. He crossed his arms and leaned against one of the heavy fuel barrels. "I've got to ask; what does a resort owner need with a thirty-eight-foot Munson boat?" Forster smiled and wiped her hands clean.

"It was a ploy to make him look better in the public eye," she said. She stood up and stretched her legs. "Hoping to remedy the damage to his image, he decided to turn part of our aquarium into a makeshift animal hospital. So, he scraped up the funds to buy this boat, and sent me out to retrieve dolphins and other animals that were sick from toxic exposure." Her voice grew more frustrated with each sentence. "So, not only was I the general caretaker for the aquarium, but now I had to act as a veterinarian. My lovely contribution to my field of study."

She sighed and knelt back down to continue chumming. Rick remained quiet as he reached into the cooler for a water. He emptied half the bottle onto his face, which felt like it was blistering in the hot sun. He was now regretting his choice of wearing a long sleeve shirt. He wiped his eyes clear of the water and looked back at Forster.

"You sound disappointed," he said. She stopped and looked at him again.

"Listen, I love sea life, but I didn't become a marine biologist to become a caretaker," she said.

"Ah!" Rick exclaimed. "So, you're a scientist with big dreams." Forster wasn't sure whether it was a question or observation.

"Well, yes. I wanted to explore and discover things. You know? To *really* make a difference." Though she shrouded it, Rick could feel the emotion within her. It was something he had come to know well during his years of learning about marine science, especially on a teaching level.

"You're already doing it," he said. She scoffed.

"Yeah, sure," she said.

"Well, then you're completely missing the point of it all," he said. Her eyes shot at him, as if insulted. How dare he question her ambitions, or worse, the hopes her father had for her. "There's more to Marine Biology than discovery. Becoming a scientist in this field, it's about improving the world we live in. Yeah, discovering new stuff is important. But there's so much more. Having a new species of pufferfish named after you isn't as important as saving an endangered species or putting a stop to an invasive species. It's not about becoming famous, it's about bettering the ecosystem. It's about bettering humanity."

"I'm bettering humanity?" she said in an unconvinced tone.

"You caught the hybrid," Rick said. "It's not out there murdering people. So, you tell me."

Forster rested quietly in her kneeling position. She looked into the horizon, trying to take in what Rick Napier was explaining. She couldn't argue against his point. Still, it was difficult to let go of her life's dreams. With no interest of discussing it further, she went back to chumming. She submerged the scoop into the bucket, and lifted it out. A whole intact fish head, severed behind the gills, came up inside the scoop. Forster winced at the gruesome sight. The dead fish almost seemed to stare at her with its lifeless eyes.

"Go out there, and better humanity," she whispered sarcastically to it, before chucking the scoopful of chum over the side. The mixture landed in a murky splash, with the fish head floating in the middle. Forster looked at it, watching it bob a couple of times in the ripples.

A splash erupted around the fish head. Water thrashed about as Forster witnessed the piece of bait disappear around a set of jaws.

"Oh, shit!" She jumped back from the side. Rick and Lisa swiftly turned to look, alarmed by her reaction. Nelson burst from the wheelhouse entrance, with shotgun in hand. He rushed to the side, aiming the sights downward. Forster caught her breath and raised her hands up to put everyone at ease. "Relax! It's alright," she said. Nelson relaxed his grip, not seeing anything in the water, and turned his eyes toward her.

"What was that about?"

"It was a shark, alright," she said, while holding back a laugh. "But it was the wrong shark. Just a lemon." Nelson looked dumbfounded.

"Huh?"

"A lemon shark," she clarified. Rick's face turned red as he struggled not to burst with laughter. He moved to the side and looked down. Just a couple seconds later, he saw the lemon shark swimming about in the chum trail. Over seven feet in length, the yellow fish nipped at the chum trail. Considering this species was attracted to rocky sea bottoms, it came as no surprise it was in the area.

"These guys are usually night feeders. He must be really hungry to be going at this chum trail like this," he said. Getting an idea, he knelt down and grabbed the scoop, which Forster had dropped. He stirred it around in the bucket, managing to locate another decent size chunk of fish. "Come and get it." He tossed it out into the water.

The lemon shark had started traveling away down the chum path before it sensed the splash. Its dorsal fin cruised the surface as it turned back. Its head turned slightly from left to right while its senses worked to locate the meal. Its eyes picked up the sight of the small piece of fish floating just underneath the surface. It lurched forward, and in the blink of an eye, the meat had disappeared into its mouth. The shark hooked back violently, nearly splashing its audience with a stream of water from its tail. Everyone put a hand over their face while admiring the sight. Rick clapped his hands as if praising a job well done. They watched the shark turn back, continuing to move down the chum line in search of further sustenance.

Then, as fast as lightning, a shadow appeared beneath the waves. Then just as quickly, the sea around the shark erupted in a watery explosion. In a simultaneous reaction, all four of the crew jumped back to the port side. All eyes were wide, and all hearts raced with adrenaline at the sight of the red hybrid shark, flipping head over tail above the surface, with the lemon shark in its jaws.

The creature landed headfirst into the already thrashing sea. It swam in a tight circle, still holding its struggling prey. In a single, effortless motion, the jaws crunched down like a vice. The lemon shark's head and caudal fin fell clear of the jaws, spinning in a trail of blood towards the sea floor. The hybrid swallowed the body, then continued swimming in a slow, circular manner, interested in the large floating object.

Rick Napier moved to the bow, watching the twenty-four-foot red shark circle their boat. Its dorsal fin and the upper part of its tail barely grazed the surface. He inhaled deeply, slowly calming his nerves. His mind became fixated on two realizations. One: the opportunity to destroy the creature had arrived. Two: it had already clearly established an intent to ravage their vessel. This meant there was no room for error. Either they kill the beast, or the beast would kill them.

He looked back to the group. "It's here."

CHAPTER
33

The beast completed its first pass around the boat, continuing to go on for a second. Rick kept his eye on the fin, watching for any change in motion or behavior, while everyone got to work. Nelson opened a panel on the generator, exposing a lever that would start it. On the other side, he exposed the circuit, to which he would attach the copper wire to the bait. The wire was covered, but that did not prevent him from putting on his gloves. Forster wheeled the bait onto the deck on a dolly. She hit a lever on the crane's control panel and created a bit of slack in the cable. Rick turned around and helped her lift the carcass from the large container. The silver colored mesh was wrapped tightly around the large brown seal carcass, which was sopping wet from its storage. The gashes around its limbs appeared fresh as though it had died only minutes prior. Strung around the bait and mesh was the leather harness, designed to prevent a surge of electricity from surging through the crane.

After clipping its harness to the cable, she moved to the controls and manipulated the lever. The crane unfurled until it was fully extended. Towering fifteen feet above them, the winch went to work. She lifted the bait until it was high enough to lift over the gunwale. She stopped the lift, allowing Nelson to attach the wire to the mesh. After the wire was successfully secured, she slowly adjusted the crane out toward the water. As she did, she was careful to make sure there was enough slack in the wire.

"Hold it there," Rick said. Forster stopped the extension, allowing the bait to dangle two meters above the water. Rick gave a thumbs up to Nelson, who attached the wire to the circuit. He then pulled the lever, igniting the generator. It juddered as it kicked on, sending a vibration through the deck. Rick looked back out to the shark. Its pass narrowed to more of an oval shape rather than circular.

"Honey," he said toward Lisa. She stood at the helm, ready to throttle the boat out of the way. She switched her gaze between the events on deck and the video monitors. On each screen, she could see the beast's red spiny structure as it passed by.

"I see it," she said, realizing the beast was sizing them up. She put her hand on the throttle, ready to move at any time.

Forster felt her body begin to quiver. Anticipation and anxiety were taking its physical toll. In her mind, she cursed herself and her group for allowing themselves to get distracted. Otherwise, they would've detected the hybrid on the sonar as planned, and therefore would've had everything in place in time for its arrival.

Rick studied the meter on the generator. The little pointy hand inside was in the green, slowly bouncing toward the middle.

"How long should this thing take to be fully charged?" he asked the Chief.

"It'll be a few minutes," he said.

"That's what I was afraid of," he said. "We can't let that thing grab the bait yet. The meter has to be in the red. Otherwise, we won't deliver a high enough voltage." He then looked at the rocks. They were clear of them, but still a bit too close for comfort. If the hybrid hit the boat just right, it could point the bow right toward the rigid forest.

"Lisa, you think you could move us away VERY slowly?" he asked. "After all, we don't want to be served "on the rocks," am I right?" He smiled in a failed attempt to alleviate the tension.

Lisa eased on the throttle and cut the wheel to port, gradually turning the bow east until they were facing away from the atoll. The propellers rotated, pushing the *Neptune* away at a snail's pace.

The hybrid's pace quickened. Its tail slashed the water as it arched down for a dive. Rick rushed to the portside, desperately looking for its shape in the water.

"Shit, I don't see it!" he said. Forster checked along the starboard side. Nelson gripped his shotgun and also started looking out for the beast. There was no sign of it. Rick turned and dashed into the wheelhouse. Lisa was already looking at the three monitor screens. Each monitor displayed nothing but empty blue ocean. As he studied the feeds, he noticed words written in small black text on the upper left-hand corner of each screen, naming the camera angles. *Port Quarter, Starboard Quarter, Center Stern.*

"Dr. Forster, are there any more camera feeds?" Rick shouted through the open window. Forster rushed into the wheelhouse and joined them at the table. She snatched the mouse from Rick's hand.

"Click here," she said, moving the cursor to the right of the screen. A bar came into view and she clicked a button. A different feed came into view, reading *Starboard Bow.* Like the others, they saw nothing but ocean. Another click, and they saw the *Port Bow,* and *Forward Bow.* Nothing.

One last click brought to view the *Underbelly* feed, looking down directly underneath the boat. Their eyes had no time to process the sight. In one instant frame, there was blue ocean. Then, in the blink of an eye, out from the distance, the red shape darted inward until its snout filled the screen.

With colossal force, the thirty-eight-foot boat lifted several feet over the water as if picked up by a giant hand. All four occupants found themselves lifted off their feet, suspended in air. For the slightest, yet terrifying moment, none of them had control of anything. The boat smashed back down, creating a wall of water on each side. Everyone hit the floor hard. The monitors went black, and the hum of the engine ceased as it stalled.

Rick struggled to his feet. He quickly looked to Lisa, who had landed on her back. He scrambled to get to her.

"I'm fine," she said before he could ask. On the other side of the room, Forster pushed up to her feet. She had all her wits about her. She looked to Rick, who pointed at her head. She touched her scalp, feeling the blood oozing from the reopened cuts.

"You alright?" he asked.

"Yeah," she said. She hurried to the helm and tried to restart the engine. With each turn of the key, the gears groaned and went silent. "Shit."

"HEY! I could use a hand out here!" Nelson called out. Everyone hurried outside. The deck was covered with spilled equipment, which had scattered in every direction. At the far end, Nelson was laying on his back, pressed against the wall by the fuel barrels which had fallen on him, one of which had landed on his leg. Rick and Forster hurried over, and immediately rolled the heavy fuel barrels off of the Chief. They gritted teeth as they pushed each one back up the deck and stood them up correctly near the crane. Nelson gripped his right leg, grimacing hard as he struggled to stand. Rick placed a hand on each shoulder, ready to catch the Chief should his legs give out. His eyes looked past Nelson to the water. The dorsal fin emerged. A swell moved like a small mountain, paving the way for the creature's bulk as it cruised at them.

"Look out!" he yelled. The beast's snout hit the starboard corner of the bow. The hybrid lost no speed as it passed through, knocking the boat out of the way. The *Neptune* rotated in place like a merry-go-round while leaning heavily to port. Forster felt her balance spiral out of control. She reached out and kept from hitting her head as she fell against the port gunwale. She found herself leaning over the side, staring directly down into the splashing water.

The spin slowed to a stop. Rick pushed himself to his feet, while Nelson was still on his back in a daze. Rick hurried to the generator and peeked at the meter. It was millimeters away from the red.

The boat rocked back to starboard as it settled. The bait, dangling from the crane, swung toward the deck - right toward Forster. In a single stride, Rick rushed to her, pulling her away from the edge just as the metal mesh hit the metal gunwale. Sparks ripped through the air in a brief fiery display.

"Good God!" Forster yelled out. The bait swung back, leaving behind a smoking black mark on the boat. Rick didn't respond, and hurriedly began looking for the shark.

His gaze barely reached the water when the bow dipped suddenly, following the sound of a huge splash. The hybrid launched itself out of the water, bringing its chin down onto the square bow. The crunching sound of metal filled the air as the whole front of the boat crumpled. The creature clung on with its claw-like legs extended from under its belly. The bow pressed down into the waterline, creating a downward slope. Laying on his back, Nelson felt a heightened urgency as he felt himself sliding toward the snapping jaws. He reached out with both arms with a dual purpose: to keep from sliding down, and to locate his shotgun. And he saw it, several feet out of reach, propped against one of the standing fuel barrels. His hands found nothing but smooth metal flooring to grab. He kicked his heels at the snapping jaws in a last ditch attempt to fight it off. The hybrid pulled itself further onto the boat and reached down with hyperextended jaws. Three-inch teeth displayed, mere inches away from the Chief.

Lisa Napier burst from the wheelhouse, holding the shotgun given to her earlier. She pumped a shell into place, then placed the shark in her sights. Rick saw the barrel of the weapon lift just past him, and he quickly ducked.

"Don't move, Chief!" she yelled. Nelson pressed himself as flat to the floor as possible. She squeezed the trigger, creating a deafening burst. The first shot landed inside the creature's mouth. In a reflex, the creature lifted his head away from the Chief, tasting its own blood as it bled from the roof of its jaws. The painful shock was only momentary, and its interest quickly returned to the Chief. Lisa fired off several more shots, each of which skidded off the rigid shell of its head. The final trigger pull resulted in an empty click.

"Shit!" Lisa yelled. Once again, the creature was inches away from Nelson! He tried crawling away, but the gravity of the slope was too much. Lisa looked for more shells, but quickly realized the duffle bag was near the bow, directly underneath the hybrid's bulk.

Rick clung to the crane controls, all the while fumbling with them to keep the arm extended far from the boat in order to prevent the electrified bait from making contact. Everything started sliding down the slope, including the generator. Lisa rushed over to it. Hanging onto it with one hand, while gripping the side of the boat with the other, she struggled to keep it from slipping into the watery pool that was forming at the bow. Forster held on, keeping from falling toward the bow as well. Clinging to the gunwale, she watched hopelessly as Nelson neared the jaws.

Barely unable to reach its prey, the creature turned its head back and forth as it began to climb further. Its five-slit gills opened and shut like window shades, as its body was demanding water circulation.

She thought of the Great White when it had initiated its attack on Marcus and her intervention.

Gills...the most sensitive point. She looked down to the floor, seeing Nelson's dropped shotgun pressed against one of the still-standing fuel barrels. She pushed off the side and fell to her knees. She snatched up the shotgun, chambered a round, and fired a shot. Pellets rained into the open gill slits. In a lightning fast, twisting motion, the hybrid lurched upward and fell back into the ocean. The *Neptune* leveled out again. The water spread out over the deck, no higher than an inch. Nelson pulled himself up, and looked at Forster, thankful and impressed at the same time.

"Holy hot damn," he said.

"I grew up in Texas," she said, and tossed the weapon to him. He snatched it out of the air and aimed it toward the water. The beast had again disappeared from view. Rick looked to the meter. It was in the red.

"Finally," he said. His eyes searched for the dorsal fin.

"There!" Lisa pointed to the portside. The fin cut through the water, coming at them directly again. The positioning was perfect. Forster took to the crane controls. The wince whined as it slowly lowered the cable. The fin grew closer, and soon the cone shaped nose came into view. She stopped the bait inches from the surface.

"Chew on this, you son of a bitch," she said. Everyone braced with anticipation as the shark neared. With a wide swing of its tail, it propelled itself in a burst of speed. It passed directly under the electrified bait, ignoring it completely. Its nose connected with the mid-port section of the hull. The *Neptune* buckled to its right and skated several meters along the surface. The hybrid dove underneath the boat. The boat rocked back. The bait swung and smacked into the hull, sending out another flash of sparks.

"Christ!" Nelson yelled, having stumbled to the starboard side. "I thought this thing wanted food." Rick peeked over the side to observe the hull as best he could. The side was dented in like a soda can. Had it caved in any further, it would have breached.

"It does," Rick said. He spoke softly, as a realization came to mind. "Though it's a living thing, it's been engineered as a weapon. It's after living prey." Nelson suddenly looked sick.

"You mean to tell me our plan's not gonna work?" he inquired. A stiffening feeling came over all of them, which worsened as the hybrid circled in the distance. It moved around until it was lined up with the portside again. It was clearly readying for another assault. This time, it would certainly impale the reinforced steel. He looked at the crane. A new idea came. It wasn't one he was thrilled about, but it beat waiting for the shark to sink them.

"Yeah it will," he said. "We just forgot one other ingredient."

"What are you talking about?" Forster said. Rick didn't answer. He jumped onto the arm of the crane, holding on to any mechanical ledge he could grip. Everyone stepped in after him.

"Rick!" Lisa said.

"I'll be fine, honey," he said. He climbed further. "Julie! Raise the cable and lower the arm!" Forster looked to the controls, then at Lisa, as if expecting approval. "Now!" he shouted. The shark had begun its approach. There was no time. Forster grabbed the controls, and quickly winched the cable nearly all the way up, until the bait dangled over a foot from the head. She lowered the crane itself, arching it until the bait was nearly touching the water. Rick held his hand out. "Okay, stop there!"

He had climbed all the way to the head. He squeezed his knees together, balancing carefully on the arm. He looked to the fin. It was thirty yards away. Twenty. There was no time. He saw a sharp edge in one of the gears. He winced in anticipation, then slammed his palm into the pointed edge.

"Holy mother of ass!" he shouted in pain. He quickly held his arm out, centimeters away from the electrified mesh, and squeezed his fingers into his palm. Blood dripped into the water, just below the bait.

Signals flared in the hybrid's brain as the scent of fresh blood entered its nose. Its gaze angled up, and it saw the bulk of flesh just above the water. Near it, was one of the lifeforms. It slowed from its attack speed, ceasing the intended strike.

Rick gulped as the snout broke the water. The beast rose up directly at him. Jagged teeth reflected the bright sunlight, and the abyss of a mouth ascended toward him.

He rolled perfectly onto his back, balanced just right on the arm. The jaws closed around the bait. Teeth and gums clenched around the mesh.

The shark instantly convulsed into a massive seizure. Every muscle in its body tensed, including those in its jaws, causing it to unintentionally grip tighter. Smoke billowed from the mesh, coming out each side of the jaws. The intense spasm caused the crane arm to shake viciously. Rick blindly grabbed at the arm, desperately holding on.

Everyone on deck tensed at the horrific sight. The twenty-four-foot shark convulsed, unable to let go of the contraption. Its eyes were only half shut, as the muscles controlling the lids were frozen from the current.

Forster realized it had enough. She went to the generator and moved the lever back, stopping the current. The seizure stopped, and the hybrid dipped back into the water. Its jaws still clung to the mesh. After several seconds, the loosening in its muscles, combined with the force of gravity, helped it fall loose. It submerged entirely. Its body motionless, it rolled like a log as it sank.

"Holy shit," Nelson said in an exhausted breath. Tense and tired was how everyone was now feeling. Then, there was astonishment, then joy. The plan worked. The hybrid was dead.

"WOO!" Rick yelled. He smiled and looked to the group. Forster and Nelson started laughing victoriously. Lisa smiled as well, though taking the time to give Rick a scolding glare, obviously not thrilled by his stunt. He shook his head and laid back down on the arm of the crane. "Oh, I'm in trouble," he joked to himself.

CHAPTER
34

Screams of excitement filled the air as the skier bounced on a large swell of water. Trailing thirty feet behind a twenty-foot red speedboat, he clung to the ski handle. Water splashed against his skis, and cool wind brushed against his face. The boat zipped in tight sweeps, creating whole new swells for the skier to bounce off of. The skier met each challenge, bouncing clear off the surface in long bounds and landing perfectly.

The speedboat raced in a wide semicircle. Once the pass had completed, the driver straightened the course and zipped the boat and skier in a straight line at top speed. They laughed out loud as they cut in front of a large white vessel, passing within a few meters of the bow. As the water sprayed onto the deck, the speedboat was already far out of the way.

Steve, the driver of the yacht slammed his fist angrily against the dashboard. "Stupid sons of bitches!" he yelled out. Dr. Tucker climbed up to the superstructure, and watched the red speedboat perform more tight turns in the distance.

"Morons," he said. Steve nodded in agreement. As they cruised forward, Tucker kept his eye on the boat to make sure it wouldn't make a return pass. After watching them move further toward the island, he figured they wouldn't be any more trouble. He climbed back down to the main deck. The aides were knelt by the dolphins, sprinkling sea water on their smooth grey skin to keep them from drying in the hot sun. Laying on white stretchers, the dolphins whistled to each other. They wiggled their fins, as if waving to their human helpers.

They took the boat out for a few more minutes. Dr. Tucker gazed at the water, then looked back at the island. As the only reason he even came to Pariso Marino was to study the shark, he resented being placed on this assignment like a regular employee. However, the university agreed to Felt's demands, and therefore instructed him to act as the aquarium's temporary caretaker. Eager to get back to the exhibit to further observe the shark, he decided they had moved out far enough.

"Let's stop here," he called up to the driver. The aides looked up, holding concerned expressions on their faces.

"I thought we were gonna move them further out," she said. "There aren't many fish in this area, and they can't..."

"This'll do just fine," Tucker interrupted. The boat stopped and drifted in the calm water. The aides looked at him with disapproval, but unfortunately had to comply. One of them stepped down to the stern ledge and held the handles to the first stretcher. Tucker took the other side, and gently lowered the dolphin into the water. As its body touched the ocean, the dolphin wiggled with excitement. It flapped its tail and squirmed until it had splashed down. Having been stuck in a small pool for a week, the free space of the open ocean was truly paradise. It splashed in the water, looking back up to the aides. It clicked and whistled as they lowered the other dolphins into the water.

They circled the boat, performing various jumps as they exercised their muscles. They toyed with each other, twisting about in the water. The aides watched them, happy that they were well again, but also worried about their future. Dr. Tucker took a moment to acknowledge this.

"They'll be fine," he said. "The EPA's pretty much got the spill cleared up. At least, that's what I've heard." He looked back up to the superstructure. "Okay, Steve, let's head back."

"You got it," Steve called back. He throttled the boat slowly, keeping track of the dolphins so he wouldn't accidentally hit them. He turned the boat in a wide arc until the bow was pointed toward the island. From his view, the island almost resembled a large green and brown wall in the middle of the ocean. Between it and the boat was the speedboat guiding its skier, appearing like little bugs dancing on the water in the distance. They raced in tight circles, and the driver could just barely hear the motor and the enthusiastic yells, which never seemed to stop.

My voice would be dry as hell by now. Guiding his white vessel forward, he kept a careful eye on them in order to make sure they wouldn't attempt another foolish stunt. He hoped they would eventually move off either to the north or south, otherwise he would have to maneuver around. As he neared, it looked more likely that he would have to do so. The speedboat looped in an endless circle. Water sprayed into a mist from the skis angled up against the surface. Finally, the boater straightened the course to go in a straight line.

A burst of water sprayed upward around the skier. Steve yelled out "whoa!" as he watched the skis fly straight from his feet, while the man himself seemed to splash down. Steve burst into a fit of laughter. It felt as if karma had finally struck. He could hear the metallic vibrations of the ladder as Dr. Tucker hurried up to the superstructure.

"What's going on?" he asked. Steve pointed out to the speedboat, which had only just begun to circle back.

"Bastard could manage all these turns and loops, but going straight apparently was too much for him," Steve said. Realizing what he meant, Dr. Tucker allowed a small chuckle. Steve accelerated the boat, hoping to make it past them before they proceeded with the next stunt.

"Did he hit a swell?" Tucker asked.

"Probably one from their own boat," Steve said. The speedboat slowed near the floating skis, and they watched the driver stand up to look for his friend. The air filled with the echoes of his calls. Suddenly, both Steve and Tucker did away with their grins. The same thought went through their minds; *How is it taking so long to find him?*

Steve altered their course slightly, figuring they were obligated to help.

The calls were replaced by a horrid scream. From the distance, they watched the driver take his seat. The engine roared, and he suddenly started soaring away to the south. Water sprayed in large spouts from the twin propellers.

"The...fuck?" Tucker mumbled in confusion. "Where does he think he's going...HOLY SHIT!"

The jets of water were miniscule compared to the wall of water that burst around the speedboat. Through the misty barrier, they watched the red boat twist in midair and crash down.

"Holy...what the hell..." Steve couldn't manage to get a full sentence out.

"What happened?" one of the aides called out. They stood along the starboard guardrail, seeing the aftermath of the accident. The speedboat appeared to have broken in two pieces. The bow floated along the hull for a few seconds until enough water had seeped into the open segment, which weighed that side down. In seconds, the tip was facing upward at a ninety-degree angle. The remainder of the boat was completely capsized, surrounded by foaming water.

"Good God, get us over there," Tucker said to Steve, ignoring the girls. Steve cut the wheel and accelerated to top speed. Tucker snatched up the radio, placing the frequency at nine.

"This is the vessel *Raymond Young* calling PMPD Dispatch. We have an emergency out here, please acknowledge."

****

The *Neptune's* engine started up on the first turn of the key. Forster allowed it to run for several seconds, listening for any irregularities. To everyone's surprise, it was working just fine.

"Well, we'll have no problem getting back," she said. Lisa sat along the deck with Rick, tightly applying a bandage to his hand.

"Ow!" Rick dramatically called out.

"Oh, don't be such a baby," she said. She tore the tape away. Rick looked at the bandage, wrapped so tightly around his palm and thumb that it almost resembled a sprained wrist. He attempted to make a fist, but had limited motion. "Yeah, it's that way on purpose," Lisa said. "You're going to need stitches, baby."

"Hey, I baked a friggin' shark," Rick said with a grin, which quickly turned into a wince after trying too hard to move his thumb. Lisa shook her head disapprovingly at her husband's attempt at humor. Forster stepped around them to the back of the wheelhouse. She sorted through all of the supplies that had scattered all over the floor.

"Ah, here it is," she said, and grabbed a large red buoy. She took it outside and switched on the transmitter. She unraveled a line, not much thicker than a rope, and hooked it up to a small weight. "Should go deep enough," she said to herself and tossed it overboard. The weight and line quickly descended, and the buoy danced in the water.

"Alright," Rick said. "Now that the location is marked, we can return and locate the body, and hopefully we can get a tooth sample."

"In the meantime, lunch is on me today," Nelson said.

"Well in that case," Forster said, while stepping toward the helm, "let's start heading back!" Just as she put her hand on the wheel, a blaring crackle boomed from Nelson's radio.

"Dispatch to Chief, come in please?" He snatched it off of his belt.

"Nelson here," he answered.

"Hey, we just had someone report a speedboat accident, maybe half a click off West Peak." Nelson looked to Rick, who shared the same concerned expression.

"Alright, we're not far from there. We'll check it out." He started to place the radio back on his belt when he raised it back to his face. "Dispatch? Did they mention what caused it?"

"Negative, but he mentioned that it just happened and that there's a lot of damage."

"I'm on it," he said. "Rick, I know we're on your boat now, but do you mind if we…"

"Let's go," Rick answered. Forster nodded through the window, and accelerated the boat, turning it toward the north. Nelson grabbed a pair of binoculars and started to scan the distant horizon. After sweeping over the water a few times, he finally saw a small white speck in the distance. Definitely a boat. Judging by its distance from land, it was most likely the one who called it in.

"Let's head that way," he called over to Forster.

****

The ripples had just about disappeared as the *Raymond Young* pulled up near the wreck. The broken bow had drifted further from the main body, and both pieces had submerged to being barely above the waterline. Dr. Tucker scanned the area, not seeing the driver anywhere. He cupped his hands around his mouth.

"Hello?" he called out.

"Should we check where the skier went down?" Steve asked. Dr. Tucker suddenly felt a nauseous chill creep over him. He quickly became overwhelmed and unsure of what to do. He looked to the general area where the skier fell.

"It was just over there, and I don't see anything," he said, pointing to the skis, which floated only two hundred feet away from the stern. He looked to the surrounding water.

A ripple in the distance caught his eye. He looked ahead, several meters off the port bow. The ripple turned into chaotic splashing as the driver broke the surface. He slapped the water wildly in sheer panic.

"There he is!" Tucker said. He cupped his hands to his mouth again. "Hang on! We'll be right there…" his voice trailed off as he watched the water around him gradually turn red. Focusing on the driver himself, Tucker felt himself turn pale. The man was splashing the water with one arm, while the other had been completely torn from the socket. Tucker found himself completely caught off guard by the situation. He stuttered, unable to form words while falling into a state of panic himself. Steve managed to keep his composure and throttled the boat through the wreckage. He glanced back down toward the aides.

"Girls, get ready to grab him!" he said. He looked up at Tucker, who appeared pale and sluggish. "Don't you even think of passing out on me. Now, get down there and help him. There's first aid supplies in the lower cabin."

Tucker inhaled a deep breath and forced himself to his senses. Control returned to him, and he hurried down the ladder.

The boat cruised clear of the wreckage, coming near to the struggling boater. The water around him was almost entirely red, resembling a murky bullseye. He was only a few yards from the port bow, when Steve noticed another shade of red in the water. Only, it was several yards off, and appeared to be several feet under the surface. It had shape to it, like a missile aimed right at the driver. And like a missile, it shot forward with incredible speed. The driver lifted from the surface, first by the huge swell, and then higher, inside the jaws of a huge red shark. Over twenty feet in length, the beast breached the water with its prey impaled in its teeth.

The aides shrieked in horror as shock and terror struck at once. A wave hooked over the side, throwing bloody water onto the deck. The creature wagged its head while munching its jaws. Teeth shredded the man's chest, stomach, and back. The pressure crunched bone, softening the prey. The beast expanded its jaws and swam forward, bringing its newly minced prey into the back of its throat, where he was swallowed.

Steve could see the creature moving over to the north, keeping between them and the island. He cut the wheel to the south and thrust into full throttle. The vessel turned in a crescent shaped path, and the engine roared as it kicked into top gear.

Dr. Tucker stood by the port railing, looking back behind their racing vessel. He could see the fin cutting across the water. After a few seconds, he quickly realized it was moving parallel with them. He felt numb, replaying in his mind what he had just witnessed. There was no mistake; it was just like the creature at the aquarium. And he remembered the sheer ferocity, how it had attempted to come ashore to kill anything it could.

"Oh my God," he said.

****

"What the hell's going on?" Rick said. He stood next to Nelson, both watching the white vessel grow nearer. But it wasn't just their approach, it was cruising in their direction at top speed.

"I have no idea," Nelson said. "Julie, we may want to slow it down." The engines slowed, but the vessel still seemed to approach rapidly. Each feature came in to more definite view. Nelson waved his arms to signal the driver.

****

Steve shook his head at the man in the silver Munson boat. *No way am I stopping, man.* In plain clothes, he had no way of knowing that man was the chief of police. The adrenaline was coursing through his veins so rapidly, he didn't even realize the battered condition of the boat.

He swung his gaze to the water trail. The fin was cutting the water, several yards from the port quarter. It moved in a path parallel to theirs, but the distance was gradually decreasing. No doubt it was chasing them.

His conscience managed to pry a message into his racing mind. *The shark could kill these guys too.* With a hand still on the helm, he stood to his feet. He waved back to the man on the Munson boat.

"GET OUT OF THE WATER! SHARK! SHARK!"

In the moment after he took his eyes off the shark, it had altered its trajectory. Having closed the distance enough, it pointed its snout toward the stern. Just as it had done to the speedboat minutes prior, it swung its tail for a burst of speed. Its speed tripled, turning the shark into a six-thousand-pound projectile. In less than a second, its nose lifted above the waterline, smashing against the port quarter.

The shaking of the vessel brought Steve to his knees. As if pounded by a massive fist, the *Raymond Young* rocked heavily to starboard. Tucker and the aides fell to the deck as the boat went into a tailspin like a truck on an icy highway. Bits of steel and fiberglass peppered the water like a white hailstorm.

"Oh God, Rick, there's another one!" Lisa said. The victorious feeling each of them had previously felt had quickly sunk into their stomachs. Now, it was a renewed sense of urgency, with a heightened dread, for their worst fear was realized.

"This means the original gave birth at some point. No way did they lose more than two of these things," Rick said.

"Let's worry about that later," Nelson said. The *Raymond Young* had stopped its spin, seemingly dead in the water. The engine had quit, and they could see the operator working on the ignition. The hull was breached at the point of impact, but mostly above the waterline.

Forster looked to the crowd on the deck. She suddenly recognized the blue and grey uniforms from the two females. They were the aides she worked with at the aquarium. The other was Dr. Tucker, the jerk whom she nearly had a physical confrontation with a day prior. Despite what she thought of him, she didn't want to see him torn to bits by the hybrid. And especially not the aides, whom she had worked alongside for months.

"They can't take another hit," she called out. "I'll pull alongside them to pick them up!"

"No!" Rick yelled back. "We can't handle the extra weight, and plus, we're in critical condition ourselves." He switched on the generator and moved to the crane controls. Nearby was a tub, filled halfway to the top with chum. He didn't bother with the scoop; he grabbed the bucket and tilted it over the side. Minced tuna splashed into the water, forming a brownish red blob beneath the crane. He looked back to the fin.

The shark had lined up to finish off the vessel, until the smell of blood filled its nose. It had sensed the presence of the *Neptune* but was not immediately interested as it was focused on the *Raymond Young*. But the smell of blood and flesh created new interest, and it dipped down for a dive. Under the water, it moved in a u-shape upward toward the source of the smell.

Rick lowered the arm of the crane, positioning the bait in the same position as before. Just as he did, the hybrid's head rose from the water. Its jaws were opened wide, taking in the chum. The sight of the enormous head, equal to the size of a locomotive, caused Rick to jump back. The jaws clamped shut around the bloody water but took in no real sustenance. Its eyelid peeled back, exposing the black eye. For the briefest of moments, it gazed upon the four people on the vessel. The sight of them and the taste of blood boosted its craving to kill. After splashing back down, the creature allowed itself to sink several meters. Rick dared to look over the side. Through the murky water, he could barely see the pointed nose of the creature aiming right up at them.

"Oh, shit," he said. He grabbed the controls and quickly adjusted the arm of the crane, tilting it up at a higher angle. With the press of a lever, the cable quickly descended. With the added height of the crane, the bait now dangled only inches from the gunwale.

The water splashed, and the creature emerged, teeth bared. Its underbelly crashed overtop of the side, crumpling metal. The mesh bumped against its chin, sending a staggering zap through its body. The hybrid heaved its body in a huge rolling motion, completely surprised by the unexpected shock. The quivering sensation in its muscles was completely alien to it, and the creature spasmed as it sank. Several seconds passed, and it regained control. With a wave of its tail, it moved to gain distance again. For the first time ever, it was hesitant to launch another attack.

"Come on, you son of a bitch!" Steve yelled at the ignition. He twisted the key for what seemed like the thousandth time. With a roar, the engine came to life. The propellers did their jobs, and immediately they were off toward shore.

"At least they're out of harm's way," Nelson said. Forster took to the controls, leading the boat further to the south, intending to keep the creature's interest on them. The fin emerged several meters off the starboard side. It moved at a similar pace with the *Neptune*, keeping a nearly identical speed. Lisa looked at the meter.

"About halfway there," she said. "You think it'll go for it again?" Rick answered with a nervous smile.

"Well, we're facing a similar problem as before," he said. "It just wants live bait."

"Oh no you're not," Lisa said, realizing what Rick was hinting at. "You're not pulling that stunt again."

"I have no choice, hon!" He readjusted the crane until it was extended far outward, at a low enough slant in which he could climb and attract the creature. He put his hands on the metal surface, before looking back at his wife. As before, she was worried about him. They stared at each other, silently expressing their love.

I'll be fine. She could hear the thoughts as if spoken out loud. Rick turned back to the crane and placed his right knee on the ledge.

"Is the shark still over to starboard?" he asked. Lisa turned and looked. The fin was moving at a path nearly parallel to theirs.

"Yes," she answered. Rick knew his opportunity to get in position was now. He placed another hand forward and started crawling outward, ready to be the bait to lure the creature in. His eyes looked down beneath him, seeing the red within the water. But it wasn't chum or blood. His eyes opened wide, and he pushed himself backward. "Holy shit!"

He rolled backward onto the deck, falling down straight on his shoulders. At the same time, another splash consumed the deck, and the armored head of a twenty-four-foot shark emerged. Its jaws clamped down around the arm of the crane where Rick Napier had just been. Teeth snapped against the huge metal appendage, but the shark did not ease off on the bite pressure. Still biting down, it hung by the crane. It waved its tail and shook its body. Sparks flickered from the gears, and the mechanisms groaned. The footing whined heavily. Screws popped from their places, each one resonating like gunshots.

Forster rushed out on deck just as the crane broke free. The wire snapped from the generator, whipping past her face as it followed the shark into the ocean. She reactively put a hand over her cheek, surprised by how narrowly it missed her. Rick pulled himself to his feet and stepped to the forward bow. Off in the distance, the two fins slowly crossed paths. Everyone joined him, sharing the shock of the moment.

"Am I stating the obvious by pointing out that there's two of them?" Nelson said. The boat rocked hard again, following the sound of a heavy metallic thud. Everyone grabbed anything they could to keep on their feet. Forster and Rick both moved to the starboard side. There it was, another dorsal fin emerging after passing underneath the *Neptune*. He briefly looked to the bow, where the two other sharks were still beginning their circular path.

"Apparently not," Rick answered. The three sharks circled the boat. He felt the optimism he had fade away. It was as if the hybrids were deliberately taunting them.

CHAPTER
35

"I need you to send out an alert. Tell every boat to come in. And close the beaches! Nobody is to be out on the water." Nelson's voice shook as he barked orders through the radio to Dispatch. He watched the three sharks circling the boat, each of them sizing them up. Each shark, after every pass, seemed to tighten the circle like a noose. "Dispatch, you copy?"

"*Ten-four.*"

"After that, make a call to the Coast Guard, National Guard, hell, the friggin Israeli Army if you have to. Tell them they'll need explosives to kill these things." He lowered his radio and waited for a response.

"*We'll get on it,*" the dispatcher said. He could detect the confusion in her voice. He clipped the radio back to his belt.

"You better," he said aloud. He turned toward Lisa, who was knelt by the duffle bag. She had just finished loading his rifle. Holding it by the barrel, she extended it to him. He accepted it and she started loading the other weapons. Forster and Rick stood on opposite sides of the deck, keeping track of the fins. "Can we make it to shore?" Nelson asked them.

"Not with three of them on our tail," Forster said. "We need a decoy."

"Unfortunately, we *are* the decoy," Rick said.

"Very inspiring," Nelson said. "Guys, we can't just sit here."

"No, we can't," Forster said. The quickening pace of the sharks added to the pressure. "Hold on to something!" She rushed into the wheelhouse. Lisa and Rick looked at one another, then quickly did so. Nelson stood at the bow, rifle pointed out as if he was in a trench in World War One. Two fins crossed again at the bow, while the third was passing behind the stern. Then, in unison, they all disappeared under the surface.

"They went under!" Nelson said. Forster gunned the accelerator. As if kicked from behind, the *Neptune* raced forward in a sudden burst, lifting the bow up slightly. In nearly that same instant, one of the hybrids charged across, just missing the rear of the boat. Forster cut the wheel hard to port, swerving the large boat. It bounced in the sea like a car cruising on an uneven road.

Just then, another hybrid came into view, charging in from the port bow for an angular attack. As the boat turned, it passed alongside it, grazing the hull with its shell. The engines groaned as the Neptune raced at top speed, beginning to aim toward the island.

Then another red shape appeared dead ahead, between them and the distant shore. Forster couldn't cut the wheel in time. The timing and angle was perfect. The shark's nose crushed into the starboard bow, sending the front of the boat into a nosedive. The stern briefly rose above the water, propellers still racing in circular spins. Forster fell to her knees while everyone on deck clung for dear life. The boat leveled out and rocked forward and back. The hybrid moved again to gain distance.

A surging sound immediately worried the Chief. Nelson quickly peeked over the starboard side and looked down. The worst fear was realized. The hull was breached beneath the waterline. His eyes met those of Rick and Lisa, and his troubled gaze answered their unspoken question.

"Shit," Rick said. The sharks commenced circling the boat again. Rick watched the fins passing by each other. There was something oddly patient about their behavior. "I think they're waiting for us to sink," he said out loud to himself.

Red lights flashed along the controls, informing Forster of the breach. Even without them, she knew from seeing the body language from everyone on deck. She looked toward the island. Even without the sharks chasing them, the boat would sink before reaching the shore. And sinking here was certain death.

She then looked toward the atoll. There was no time to think or plan. With each passing second leading them closer to certain doom, she followed her instinct. She pushed the throttle, and the boat raced forward again. She turned the wheel, facing the bow toward the field of rocks. The sharks still circled the boat, even as it moved, as if they were trying to keep their prey cornered. Water cracked against the crumpled front of the bow, allowing water to seep onto the deck. Nelson and Rick realized the boat was moving and looked forward to see where they were going. The boat had swerved away from the island and was racing toward the blockade of jagged rocks between them and the atoll. They looked at Forster questioningly.

"Is this a good idea?" Nelson said, momentarily succumbing to his anxiety. Rick almost did the same, but hearing Nelson speak first put it in perspective.

"No, but we don't have a choice," he said. "Either we smash against the rocks, or sink like the *Titanic*, take your pick." Nelson quickly understood and regained his composure. Lisa stood at the starboard side, pointing a shotgun out into the water. Nelson handed Rick a rifle.

"We're gonna have to go to work," he said. Rick accepted it. He was no Army Ranger, but he knew how to shoot. He took position a few feet from his wife, while Nelson centered himself at the port. Hair brushed in the quickening wind as the *Neptune* gained pace. Everyone kept their breathing under control as the rocks seemed to grow in size. Even Forster was surprised. Some of the rocks towered over the boat, and they hadn't even entered the forest of natural obstructions.

The sharks ceased to circle the boat and accelerated their pace to keep up with the *Neptune*. Two traveled along the right, and one on the left, each of them trailing behind, but gaining distance. For a few moments they moved parallel, as if simply tracking their prey. But they soon angled their positions toward the boat.

Nelson squeezed off the first shot at the incoming shark. Lisa squeezed the trigger. Rick tensed from the deafening gunfire, being not as conditioned to it as the other two. Despite this, he placed the head of the nearest shark in his sights and squeezed the trigger. Tiny explosions of water sprayed where the projectiles cut through the surface, where they missed the target entirely or were stopped in place by the rigid shell.

Forster took air in through her nose and exhaled through her mouth. In thirty feet, they would be entering the field. Fifteen feet, five…the *Neptune* passed narrowly between two towering rock formations. The enormous sight and extremely close proximity caused everyone on deck to instinctively duck. Forster clenched her teeth, keeping the boat racing at full speed. They cleared the two rocks, only to have a huge round formation dead ahead. She cut the wheel, and the *Neptune* swung to the right. The hull scraped against the edge of the rock as they cruised past it.

"Jeez all mighty!" Nelson exclaimed.

The sharks pursued them into the rocks. Their organized formation broke, and they zigzagged around the formations, still trying to keep up with the vessel. They hooked around each rock they passed. After each dodge, the sharks would redirect their focus on the *Neptune*, only to adjust their trajectory again to avoid smashing into another formation.

Forster didn't bother looking for the sharks. Driving the boat took every ounce of focus. Another jagged formation was dead ahead. She turned the wheel to port. The bow turned, putting them on a collision course with another rock. She continued to turn until she was heading directly perpendicular to the path she wanted. She carefully maneuvered around the second rock, turning back to starboard, while grazing another, smaller formation. Metal screeched as they passed over an underwater rock, which rubbed viciously against the hull.

One of the hybrids grazed another rock before straightening out its path. It was no longer just hungry, with an insatiable desire to kill, but it was now frustrated. Its resolve was fueled, and it raced forward with an enormous burst of speed, aiming straight toward the starboard quarter.

The boat moved ever so slightly to the side, and the shark adjusted its charging approach as such. In doing so, it found itself smashing directly into a tower formation of rocks. A mixture of gravel and water burst into the air, accompanied by huge fragments of grey rocks. The hybrid sunk to the murky shallow, completely stunned by the crash. The other two hybrids continued their pursuit, leaving their comrade behind.

Another of the hybrids attempted a run at the boat. A boulder lay in its path. Moving at a burst of forty miles per hour, the hybrid hooked to the left to avoid it. Doing so, it smashed straight into another rock. It spun like a log rolling downhill, disoriented from the unexpected impact.

The murky, greenish-black mixture of soil that was the beach approached. Nelson's eyes went big upon the realization they were moving at it at full speed.

"Slow it down, Julie! Slow it down!" he said. Forster waited, until finally the slab of muck came into more definite view. She stopped the accelerator and allowed the forward momentum to do the rest of the work. The boat brushed against a small sandbank during its approach, causing the boat to hook slightly to the left, though it still moved toward the beach.

The boat rocked upward as it beached along the shore. The stern, still in water, swung slightly to port before it settled, bringing the starboard side in view of the ocean. And with that view came the sight of the third approaching hybrid.

On his knees, Rick was barely able to look over the edge of the boat. The shape of its shell was visible under the water, though clouded by the muck that had stirred up. Its approach slowed as its belly scraped against the bottom. It came to a brief stop, and its legs unfolded from under it. Its back lifted slightly above the waterline, including the top of its head. The black eyes seemed to look right at Napier, who stared the beast in the face.

Nelson rushed beside him and pointed his rifle at the hybrid. Rick held his hand out to stop him.

"It's useless," he said. "I have an idea. Hurry!" He pushed off the side and moved to the fuel barrels. Nelson kept his eye on the approaching beast as he joined him.

"And that plan is?"

"Help me move this!" Rick said. He wrapped his arms around the huge barrel. Nelson did the same, and with all their strength they scooted the heavy drum to the side. "Lisa, I need the chum bucket!" Lisa turned and searched for it, quickly locating it where the crane used to be. She brought it over to Rick. He snatched it from her hands, peeled off the lid, and dumped it all over the barrel. Bits of minced fish guts and oil splattered all over the container, raining down the sides like little brown waterfalls.

"What the hell are you doing?" Nelson said.

"Giving it something to taste!" Rick said, tossing the bucket away. "Dr. Forster, do we have a flare gun somewhere in there?"

Forster immediately started sorting through the spilled supplies inside the wheelhouse, looking for a silver container that contained the flare gun.

The hybrid was now up to the boat. Its legs, bent to the sides like insect appendages, straightened underneath it to give extra height. The front leg lifted and dug into the side of the boat, clinging to the ledge of an indentation formed by a ramming impact. Its weight tilted the boat to the side, causing everyone to gasp. Its head angled upward, and its jaws snapped.

Rick unscrewed the top cap and stuffed his handkerchief into the opening to prevent an overflow. He knelt down and grabbed the barrel by the bottom. The Chief did the same. They took turns leaning the drum in separate directions to get their fingers underneath, as their grips would slip off the now oily sides. Heavy metal pinched into their digits, causing teeth to clench and faces to tighten.

"Lift!" Rick yelled in a pained voice. He and Nelson grimaced and their legs shook. Lisa joined in from the side, helping to lift the heavy fuel drum. Every muscle quivered as they lifted it over the gunwale. On the other side, the creature's bottom jaw leaned against the boat as it secured another leg. Its mouth opened in preparation of dragging the boat down and devouring the occupants. The opportunity was now. They threw the barrel into the open jaws. The bottom slammed into the back of its throat, triggering a choking gag reflex. The hybrid lurched back. The substance was unfamiliar; it was solid and unliving, yet the taste of blood kept it from regurgitating it completely. It splashed back down and backed away, waving its head side to side to loosen the heavy object from its throat. Gasoline leaked through the soaked handkerchief, mixing into the surrounding water.

Forster found the silver container and smashed the lock with a hammer from the tool box. She peeled it open and immediately snatched the gun and a fresh flare. She was already out the door when she loaded the device. Everyone stepped out of her way as she leaned over the side and pointed it toward the frothing water. The flare burst with the sound of a muffled drumbeat, and it smacked into the water inches in front of the creature's head. The floating gas ignited, instantly spreading into the creature's mouth. The hybrid felt the searing heat inside it, the last sensation it would ever feel. The handkerchief ignited into flame, triggering a chain reaction to the jam-packed fuel inside the drum. Heat and intense pressure skyrocketed at once. Everyone on deck ducked just as the drum exploded within its throat, bursting its entire head. Fragments of shell rained from the air, and the softer tissue connecting its joints ruptured from the internal pressure.

Forster was the first to look again. The hybrid's headless body had collapsed into the water. Fire blazed in the surrounding water and on some of the nearby rocks where burning gas had been flung from the blast. It was almost exact to her envisioned appearance of Hell.

There was no time to catch their breath. The two other hybrids rapidly approached. They extended their legs to walk on the shallow bottom.

"Oh shit," Rick said. Nelson and Lisa looked as well.

"Let's get off the boat!" Nelson yelled. Everyone turned and hurried to the other side, ready to climb over. Forster stayed behind, watching the sharks.

"Wait," she said. One of the beasts snatched up the limp tail of its dead sibling in its jaws and started pulling it backward into the deeper water. The other joined in, and the two snapped at each other briefly for control of the meal. While making a show of force, the first one continued to tug back on the fresh meal, while the other bit on the ruptured shell to peel the exoskeleton away. Within several seconds, they were submerged completely.

CHAPTER
36

Wrapped in darkness, Rick's hands fumbled against the wall until finally locating the light switch. He flicked the small toggle with his finger, and a small overhead light brought the cargo hold into view. It was a surprisingly small space for a boat of this model. It wasn't even deep enough for Rick to stand up straight. His lower back ached as he hunched down. With the boat being relatively new, there wasn't much in the cramped space. The hatch above flipped open, and Julie Forster started to climb down with him.

Rick found the thin sheets of aluminum patches. They were in various sizes. He sorted through them to determine the proper fit for the breach. As he did, Forster grabbed some gas containers and checked the gauges. She located the welding torch. She knelt silently at it, looking worrisome.

"You ever weld a patch?" she asked. Rick understood that it was a question, and simultaneously a confession that she didn't know how.

"I've never had to do it," he said. "But I know how. It shouldn't be as hard since I won't be diving." He looked at a sheet of metal. It was roughly three-by-four feet. "This'll have to do." Forster waited for him to move up the hatch before following. Once he was up, she passed up the torch and containers, then climbed up into the wheelhouse. Nelson was there at the helm, operating the boat's radio.

"Coast Guard, this is *Pariso Marino* Police Chief Joseph Nelson, come in please." By the sound of his voice, it was another of many attempts. His other hand tapped impatiently at the console. No response came through. "I repeat: Mayday, mayday, we are stranded on the atoll located west of the island. We need immediate evac." The only answer was silence.

Rick and Forster carried the supplies on deck. Lisa sat up on top of the structure, cross-legged, serving as a look-out for the hybrids. Nelson followed them outside, snatching his police radio from his belt.

"Nelson to Dispatch," he said.

"*Go ahead, Chief.*"

"Any luck on getting assistance?"

"*Negative. Nobody's responding.*"

"Christ!" Nelson said through gritted teeth. He pressed the transmitter and disguised his frustration. "Alright, try Air Rescue. Tell them we need a chopper unit. NO BOATS! We've run aground at the atoll."

"*The atoll? Chief, we can send someone over.*"

"No!" Nelson said. "Anyone who comes by boat will not make it past these things. Just contact Air Rescue and keep me informed. Over and out." He put his radio away, before allowing himself to tense for a brief moment. He cursed himself for not pressing the Mayor to allow a chopper unit for the department years prior. If only he'd caved, they'd be out of this mess.

Rick climbed down a ladder on the starboard side. Halfway down, Forster passed the sheet down to him. He grabbed it by the bottom and finished the small descent. When his feet hit the shore, he was up to his waist in water. He examined the indentation on the hull where it was breached. The aluminum had split into four pieces like flower petals, each bending inward instead of out. Luckily, it made it easier for him to patch over it, as otherwise he would have to remove the fragments. All of which was time consuming. With the canisters already strapped to him, he put on his goggles to begin his work. Before igniting the torch, he tried positioning the sheet over the breach. As he pressed it to the area, it slipped from his gloved hand and fell into the water.

"Damn it!" he cursed. He secured the torch before reaching down to pick it up. He looked back up, seeing Lisa climbing down. She splashed alongside him. "What are you doing? It's not safe down here!" he said. She slipped her hands into a pair of utility gloves.

"Forster's looking out for the sharks," Lisa said. "You need somebody to hold this in place." She slipped a pair of goggles on, then took the sheet from him and pressed it against the breach. Rick knew there was no point in arguing. He ignited the torch and applied the flame to the nearest edge. Both their faces tightened from the combination of heat, sparks, and brightness. The aluminum from both the hull and the sheet melted and blended together. Rick slowly worked the flame down the side. At once, he and Lisa shared a quick glance, and with that, a smile.

"I can't say I thought we'd ever be in this situation again," she said.

"No, I suppose not," Rick replied. But they were, and this time of their own free will. But neither of them regretted it.

Forster kept her eyes on the splashing water. The water splashed along the rocks while small swells rolled toward shore with the tide. Her eyes played tricks on her occasionally. Fragments of shell from the exploded hybrid drifted about, occasionally being tossed by the small waves. Each time she saw one lift in the water, her brain sent a shock through her body, believing it to be a dorsal fin. One of the antennae washed up on shore several yards away. Five feet in length, it became embedded in the sand, soon to be buried as the tide washed over it. She wished it was already buried. The sight of it was a reminder of the horror that awaited them. Those remaining two hybrids would soon be done feeding on their sibling and would then return to kill more.

Several minutes passed, and Lisa climbed back up. Enough of the sheet had been fused to the hull, so she didn't have to hold it any longer. She saw Forster's solemn expression as she gazed out to the water.

"You gonna be alright, there?" Lisa asked her.

"Yeah," Forster said. "I'm just thinking."

"About the hybrids?"

"Yeah. They're all the same size, which must mean that the original gave birth a while ago. I just hope we can somehow kill these things and determine that the original is among them. If its not, then there's a strong chance it may have birthed other litters."

"Let's worry about getting out of here first," Lisa said. "Go on, I'll keep an eye out. Take a break. Otherwise, you'll stress yourself to death." Forster made a halfhearted chuckle.

"I feel that's all I've done since I first came here," she said. She started to climb down from atop the wheelhouse. She paused a moment to look at Lisa. "Hey, uh...thanks." Lisa smiled back. *You're welcome.*

Chief Nelson had climbed down to the shore and walked inland. There wasn't much to explore. The atoll was basically a small lump of rock and muck. There was a small little foothill to climb, shaped like a tiny mountain. He secured himself on little ridges and lifted himself up. Because it wasn't steep, it was an easy climb. The foothill only elevated to about sixteen feet, and in moments he was standing on top. He looked to the surrounding water, desperate for the sight of a Coast Guard cutter, or a helicopter. But there was nothing but ocean and rock.

Ready to climb back down, he turned. There stood Forster, who had climbed up behind him.

"Jeez!" he said in surprise. He never even heard her climbing the rock. He caught his breath. "Damn, girl, you're like a friggin' shinobi, or whatever those ninjas are called."

"Good to know, maybe that'll be my new occupation if we survive this mess," she said.

"Oh, we will," he said. Unfortunately, he could fake the smile to help express the forced optimism. He kept looking down at the lump of rock they were washed up on. Forster did the same, and then recognized what the Chief was thinking.

"We can't stay here," she voiced the thought.

"No...we can't," Nelson said. "We have nowhere to run if they come at us." A distant splash drew their eyes to the north. It was small and appeared to take place between two rocks. It wasn't a splash from the tide. Something briefly floated along the surface. Its color was a combination of white and red, and had a crescent shape. Its weight pulled it back under the surface.

They were looking at the severed caudal fin from the deceased hybrid. The splash was likely caused by one of the living monsters tossing it away after picking out the meat. It was another reminder that the clock was ticking.

"Shit," Nelson said. "We REALLY can't stay here." They both climbed down to the shore and hurried over to Rick. He was biting his lip while focusing hard on welding the patch in place. Nelson approached him, keeping a safe distance from the sparks. "Hey, Doctor Napier, I hate to rush you, but how long do you think it'll be?"

"Not long," Rick said. He stopped and made eye contact. "Why? Are they coming?"

"Not yet, but they won't be long," Forster said.

"We saw them to the north," Nelson said. "They're tearing through the dead one like crazy. When they do, we have nowhere to run. This isn't a big rock." Rick exhaled hard and looked at the boat, then at the water.

"Then we're gonna have to make a run for it," he said. He looked down at the sandbank which they were beached upon. "We can back out, but we're gonna have to shovel out some of this to free up the bow." Nelson looked to Forster.

"You didn't happen to have shovels on this thing by any chance?"

"On a boat?" she answered. "No, but we can break stuff down to use as scoops. The sand is fairly loose enough to scoop away."

"Whatever you're going to do, I suggest you do it fast," Rick said, while replacing his goggles. He ignited the torch and applied the flame to the sheet. Forster and Nelson quickly climbed up to the deck to sort through the supplies.

CHAPTER
37

Standing atop the foothill center of the atoll, Forster placed a hand over her eyes as a visor against the sun. She kept her gaze focused north, where she had witnessed the splash previously take place. There had been another splash, in which a large chunk of shell had been tossed from the sea. From time to time, there would be occasional thrashing in the water as they shredded the dead hybrid. Forster wondered if the two surviving hybrids were possibly fighting with each other for control of the meal.

Down at the shore, Rick and Nelson were waist deep in water, on opposite sides of the *Neptune*. Mountains of sand erected around them as they scooped sand out from beneath the hull in order to free it up. Water flooded further up the beach around the bow in the newly formed trenches. Both men, bathed in seawater and sweat, dug relentlessly at the sand. Each of them had a portion of a piece of the table top, which they had taken apart inside the wheelhouse to use as makeshift shovels. They focused on the deeper part of the sandbank, though they dug out some sand from around the front. Rick pried the end of the tabletop into the sand beneath and kicked his heel against it to help dig away some muck. He wiped the sweat from his eyes with his hand. Wet with seawater, it didn't help much.

"Chief, let's give it a try," he said.

"Alright," Nelson answered, and stepped back.

"Lisa? Go ahead whenever you're ready!" Rick called to his wife. The engine ignited in a roar, and Lisa placed the reverse throttle. The engine groaned louder, as if the boat was feeling the struggle as it tried to move from the sandbank. The stern swung slowly to port. The bow was loosened from the sand, but still embedded just enough. "Okay, stop," Rick said, holding out his hand. "Keep the engine running, we're almost there." He hurried around to the other side to help Nelson with digging out the sand.

Forster overheard the conversation from atop the rock, and decided it was best to get on the boat. Once the boat was loose, they would want to move immediately. She turned and slid her foot down the side of the rock, keeping herself propped up with her hands.

The sound of thrashing water quickly brought her attention back to the water. Two huge pieces of shell floated apart from each other, settling along the swells. Body fragments, no doubt. Immediately following the splash, two other shapes took form. Two cone-shaped shadows under the water swam in aimless direction, moving about the rocks. One then turned and zipped into the distance, quickly disappearing from view. The second one wandered for a couple moments, then it too moved out of view.

Their time was up. Forster descended down the side of the rock, nearly slipping off one of the tiny ledges. Her feet planted on the soft mushy sand and she dashed to the boat where Rick and Nelson dug.

"They're done with the dead one," she said. Both men looked at her, alarmed.

"Shit," Nelson said. "Alright, get onboard." He stepped out of the way, and Forster immediately started climbing to the deck. Nelson followed her. He stepped onboard, dripping wet, and looked down to Rick. He was shoveling out a few more scoops, knowing the boat needed to be as loose as possible. "Doc! We have no time!" Lisa poked her head out from the wheelhouse.

"Rick, come on!" she yelled. Napier tossed the improvised shovel away and climbed the nearby ladder, hoping they had dug it out enough. Forster took Lisa's place at the helm, being more familiar with the controls. She reversed the propellers, and the boat began to tug back. The stern slowly began to sway again, and Forster cut the wheel to the right. As the stern swung to the other side, the hull grinded against the remaining sand, crunching it up. The muck broke apart, filling into the trenches that Rick and Nelson had dug. The boat came loose in a sudden jolt, nearly causing Forster to fall backward into the seat.

"Finally," she said out loud. She carefully backed the boat away until she gained enough space to turn it around. After switching back to forward gear, she slowly drove the boat out through the field of rocks. She kept it slow and steady, which oddly added to the tension. They felt like sitting ducks at this speed, but they could not risk smashing into any rocks with the now fragile hull. She would not gun the accelerator until they were clear.

Everyone on deck was silent, each looking out into the water for any sign of their pursuers. A naïve hope grew inside each one of them. Perhaps the beasts had gorged themselves enough on the dead hybrid, and were no longer interested in chasing them? However, each of them knew that was not the case. These beasts would kill even when not hungry. They are weapons without aim.

They moved through the hazardous zone, carefully moving around each obstacle. The open ocean was up ahead, growing vaster with their approach. Beyond the blanket of water was the island. So far, there was no sign of the creatures.

"Where the hell are they?" Lisa finally asked.

"Around," Rick said. Just because they didn't see them didn't mean they weren't there. He was certain they were being tracked. He glanced over the side to check on the patch. It was in place and secure. Not bad for a first attempt.

They approached the outer perimeter of the rocky barrier. Hearts began to flutter. Everyone felt on edge, and eager to feel the sensation of the *Neptune* gunning to full throttle toward the island. Forster felt the worst of it. She turned the wheel to zigzag around formations. Finally, they had arrived at the edge. She drove the boat between the two towering rocks, which seemed to be the gateway in and out of the shallow field of barricades. As the bow cleared the opening, Forster throttled to maximum speed. The twin propellers sprayed water as they quickly shifted to maximum gear.

The sensation of racing wind was a welcome one for everyone on deck. A light ray of enthusiasm started to glow within the group.

"Finally," Nelson said to himself. He stood near the crumpled forward ramp on the bow and watched the details of the distant shore come into view. Once on the safety of land, they could form a whole new plan to go after the hybrids. Also, he would have to pay a visit to Felt's Paradise.

Rick leaned against the port side, feeling a bit more relaxed. He gazed out into the ocean, watching the rippling water as they raced by. He followed the waves as they stretched further out. The swell broke, as if stopped by a reversing force. Rick watched as new swells formed in the distance, pushed apart by the oncoming bulk of the red hybrid. He gasped a breath and whipped around toward Forster.

"Hard to port!" he yelled out. It was too late. The hybrid smashed into the starboard quarter. The boat juddered, and the engine moaned. Caught in surprise, Lisa and Nelson fell to their knees, while Rick managed to hold himself up. He saw the creature swim around the bow. He looked for any sign of the other.

The sound of smashing metal filled the air, and the boat jolted forward. Nelson yelled as he rolled forward from his kneeling position. Rick, still grabbing onto the side, saw the second hybrid pass under them. In the wheelhouse, Forster tried maneuvering the boat. The engine was still running, though there was the sound of rattling metal, like nails being shaken in a tin can. The boat did not move. She tried throttling back. Nothing. She hurried outside the rear door and looked into the water. Both twin propellers had been broken off completely. They were dead in the water. She re-entered the wheelhouse to pass to the main deck and warn the others.

The first hybrid descended several meters and circled about until it had lined up perfectly with the side of the boat. It pointed upward and launched itself to the surface. Momentum increased with each sway of its tail, and soon it broke the surface. Rick, Lisa, and Nelson saw the body emerge with a spray of water merely feet away from the port. The creature elevated several meters into the air before gravity pulled it down, right overtop of the wheelhouse.

Its stomach crashed down on the roof, causing it to crumple inward like a soda can. The glass windows exploded, sending fragments in every direction. The sides of the doorway crunched inward as the roof was squeezed downward. Forster fell to the floor, narrowly avoiding being hit on the head by the ceiling caving it.

The shark's head was leaning heavily off the boat after it crashed down. It tried unfolding its legs to attempt a hold on the boat. Unable to find anything to grab onto fast enough, its weight worked against it, and the shark slid into the water in a nosedive. Nelson sprang to his feet and hurried to the crunched doorway.

"Julie, are you alright?" he yelled.

"I'm fine," she called back. She tried to stand up, but the roof was smashed so far down that standing up straight was impossible. "They broke the propellers away. We can't go anywhere."

Nelson examined the entryway. It was completely closed in, with no space for anyone to slip in or out.

"We've got incoming!" Lisa warned. The boat shuddered from a hit to the port bow. Behind the sound of smashing metal was the sound of water. Lisa and

Rick both hurried to the side to check and confirmed what they already knew. "Shit," Lisa said as she watched the water seep into the newly formed rupture. Rick looked around the deck, frantically trying to come up with a new plan. There had to be something he hadn't thought of.

One of the hybrids rammed the starboard quarter, putting the *Neptune* into another violent tremor. A new breach was formed, and now water was seeping into the boat from both sides. Nelson clung to the bent-up doorway to stay on his feet. Desperation, fear, and anger flooded his senses, and he looked to the heavens with furious eyes.

"GOD! JUST GIVE US A FUCKING BREAK, WON'T YOU!" He slammed his fist onto the roof, which was now slumped downward like a ramp. After a quick breath, he regained enough of his sanity to focus. He tried pushing apart the sides, but to no avail. Forster checked the other door, but it was jammed shut. She was trapped inside. Nelson cursed as he struggled.

The engine's droning sound deepened, and soon transformed into a slow whirring sound. It came to an abrupt stop and died. Lisa looked at the waterline, which was now inches from the edge. They were sinking fast.

A new whirring sound took over. At first, she thought the engine hadn't fully died, not that it would do them any good. But then, she realized it was distant, and coming from above. She looked to the sky, turning every which way to locate the source of the hum. There it was, from the northwest. Like a pair of black dragonflies in the distance, two helicopters were racing toward them. They were high up, and distant enough for her not to fully be able to recognize their specifications. But one thing was for sure, they were military choppers.

"I think He heard you," she said to Nelson.

****

"*We've got two bogies circling the boat,*" one of the pilots spoke through the mic.

"*The boat appears to be taking on water,*" another pilot said. "*We do have a visual on the targets. Colonel, it's your call.*"

The choppers held position, nearly one hundred meters above the water. Colonel Salkil was dressed in all black tactical gear, as was the entire contract crew among him. He looked down at the silver vessel, and the helpless souls aboard. The bow slanted slightly downward, taking on water faster than the stern. The waterline crept up over the gunwale and was just beginning to spill onto the deck. A minute, two at most, they would be submerged, and fully exposed to the predators that waited for them.

The creatures circled the boat very closely. Their fins didn't graze the surface, but they were close enough for their shadowy appearance to be seen from above. Tactically, it was a perfect advantage. Unleash a payload of missiles, and the nightmare would be done for good.

The images of the yacht *K McCartney,* flashed within the Colonel's memory. He remembered his most notorious moment in his career, of which very few knew about. A time when he sacrificed innocent lives in a fruitless attempt to protect others. It was one of the few moments that kept him awake at night, and the worst part was that it was for nothing. Now he found himself in the same predicament.

"*Sir, we have a clear shot! We can take them out right now!*" another voice said through the comm. Salkil took a breath, needing to make a swift judgement. He stood between the two pilots. One had flipped a switch, arming the launchers. The boat and the surrounding water were locked on. The pilot had his gloved hand on the control stick, finger on the trigger.

"Hendricks," Salkil spoke into the comm. "My unit will take the lead and draw the creatures away with the 50. Cal. When we do, descend and pick up the passengers. We'll regroup at the *Pyramid*."

"*Sir?*" Hendricks' tone was both surprised and confused.

"That's the plan," Salkil ordered. "Do it!"

"*Aye, aye,*" Hendricks answered. Salkil could practically hear the unspoken thoughts going through the Commander's mind. *Saving these people would undoubtedly let them on to the plan. Perhaps the Colonel was growing soft in his old age.* Maybe he was.

****

"They're coming," Rick said as one of the choppers swooped down. He hurried to the doorway and began helping Nelson to try and pry apart the crumpled section of the wheelhouse. Meanwhile, Lisa couldn't help but watch the choppers. Her fist instinctual reaction was pure joy at the sight of rescue. However, something was off. She couldn't help but notice the type of choppers. Bell UH-1N Twin Hueys. Certainly not something the Coast Guard would deploy. Then there were the specifications. Black? Not a color used on these models by the Armed Forces, and another oddity was the armament. Each Huey was armed with 70 mm rocket pods. For a seaside rescue?

"What the hell's going on here?" she said to herself. The feeling of water rushing up to her ankles refocused her priorities. Sure, the situation seemed strange, but figuring that out could wait. The first chopper lowered itself until it was thirty feet above the water. Its nose pointed directly at the *Neptune*. Out of the starboard side, a gunner extended the 7.62 mm M240 lightweight machine gun toward the water. Multiple rounds peppered the water as the gunner opened fire on the visible shapes of the beasts.

Bullets cut through the water only to smash against the rigid exoskeletons. As planned, they drew the attention of the creatures. The shapes turned toward the helicopter. The vertical gusts of wind from the rotating blades pounded the water beneath, causing further vibrations that gained interest from the approaching hybrids. The Huey banked left, leading the creatures away.

Water poured over the sides as the *Neptune* gradually slipped beneath the waves. Rick grabbed a piece of metal which had broken from the crane's footing when it was torn away. He shoved it into the small open space that was once the doorway and leaned to the side to pry the sides apart. There were no results other than the sound of scratching metal. Rick pressed harder. He felt motion, briefly fueling his determination until he realized it was the metal bar itself bending.

"Damn it," he cursed, throwing the bar to the deck. It splashed down in water that was now up to their shins. The climbing water level was like a counter for a time bomb, and there was no way to defuse it.

They felt a huge gust of wind as the second Huey descended upon the boat. Even from inside the wheelhouse, Forster could feel the air surging in from the powerful blade rotations. Like a huge hummingbird, it hovered merely feet away from the now submerged gunwale. Water was now freefalling over the sides, and the deck was filling up rapidly. The Huey lined itself up parallel to the boat, and the side bay door opened. A man in black tactical gear waved them on over.

"We don't have all day," he called out to them. Nelson turned and grabbed both Rick and Lisa by the shoulders.

"Go! Get on the chopper, I'll be right behind you!" he shouted over the heavy whirring.

"But Chief, what about..." Rick started to protest.

"Just go!" Nelson said. There was no time to argue. Rick and Lisa turned and moved toward the chopper. The gunner reached out, first taking Lisa by the hand and helping her board. Rick was quick to follow. Dripping wet, they moved into the compartment and took a seat, across from another 'soldier' dressed in black. Both noticed something immediately peculiar about him; the artificial right arm stood right out. Of course, neither were going to mention it. Their attention and worries were quickly refocused to their friends. The gunner looked over to Nelson.

"Come on, pal! You're wasting time!" he yelled out. Nelson ignored him, and proceeded to climb overtop of the wheelhouse, the only part of the *Neptune* currently above water.

"There's someone trapped in there!" Lisa said. The gunner shrugged nonchalantly.

"Like I said, he's wasting time," he said. Both Lisa and Rick looked at him with disgust. Behind that disgust was a sense of hopelessness. All they could do was watch. The one-armed man said nothing as he waited for Nelson to make a move.

The hybrids followed the vibrations along the surface, as countless sixty-caliber rounds crunched against their solid foreheads. The target was above the water, its black exterior easy to see against the bright sunlight. It remained out of reach, matching their speed with its retreat.

Another vibration ignited sensory nerves within their lateral line. Water distortion coming from the target which they had abandoned. One of the hybrids slowed its pace, while the other one continued its pursuit. The first hybrid slowed to a near stop. It determined that this prey was no longer worth pursuing, and it turned to investigate the other. With a wave of its tail, it rushed back toward the *Neptune*.

The gunner aboard the second Huey saw the fin graze the water as the shark turned away.

"Oh, shit," he said, and placed his microphone in front of his lips. "Raven 2, you have a bogie headed your way. We're unable to intercept."

"Copy that, Raven One," the pilot said. "Hey boss, we've got company!" The one-armed man stuck his head out the other side of the chopper. He looked past the tail rotors. The shape was under the surface, forming small swells as it raced toward them.

"Climb!" he shouted and shut the door. The pilot pulled up on the stick, and the Huey quickly ascended. The hybrid lifted its head, snapping its jaws at the landing bar. The nose scratched the bottom of the chopper before splashing down. "Son-of-a-bitch," the one-armed man said. He looked to Rick and Lisa. "Sorry kids, we can't wait."

"You've got to," Rick said.

"They're almost under," he said. "We barely avoided being taken down ourselves. Sorry, but there's no choice."

"Damn it, Joe! Just get on the chopper!" Forster suppressed tears as she yelled through the window. She could hear the Chief stomping about above. Water was now rushing in through the broken doorway. The waterline was up to the windows, also bringing in further flooding. The water was now up to her chest.

"What's with the sudden obsession with my first name?" he called back. Forster shook her head.

"It's not funny!" she called back. "There's no chance for me to get out. You just need to…"

"I suggest you move as far to the front as possible!" he interrupted her. "Get away from the stern door."

"What are you talking abo—" she realized mid-sentence that the question was stupid and pointless. There was no time. She waded through the water. "Okay." Several loud bursts nearly numbed her eardrums, joined by the metallic clanging at the door handle. There was the sound of busting latches as his bullets pierced the door handle. Next came loud banging sounds as he tried to kick the door in while hanging from the roof. The door opened inward a few inches. Forster saw the opportunity and splashed through the water. She yanked the door open the rest of the way and stepped out. Nelson reached down from the roof. They locked hands and he pulled her upward. Her feet touched the solid dry surface.

Only it wasn't dry for long. With the added weight of the water, the *Neptune* sank increasingly faster. Water already draped over the roof, already covering the tops of their feet. They felt the downward pull as they were riding the boat into the abyss. With the water up to their legs, they waved at the chopper.

"Hey Boss, it looks like they got out," one of the pilots said. The one-armed man turned to look. As he looked out the window, he was joined by Rick and Lisa who rushed beside him to look. The *Neptune* was completely submerged, only visible by its silhouette under the surface. On top of it, Nelson and Forster sank into the water, now up to their knees in water. The man sighed heavily, feeling the eyes of his passengers burning into his temple. More importantly, he remembered the Colonel's instructions.

"Take 'er down," he said. The pilots looked to each other, both reluctant to descend and make themselves vulnerable for another attack. But they had orders. They drove the chopper down, touching the landing gears to the water.

Nelson and Forster squinted to see through the onslaught of wind that bombarded their eyes. The side bay door opened up, and the gunner reached out to both of them. Nelson grabbed Forster by the waist and lifted her up to the door, allowing the gunner to pull her inside. As soon as she set foot, she turned around to help pull him in.

She saw the red dorsal fin, and a huge set of jaws racing toward the Chief.

"JOE!" she cried out. Nelson saw the expression on her face, and dived for the landing rail, wrapping his arms around it. The chopper ascended and the shark raised its head. Its teeth passed by Nelson's dangling feet like small machetes.

"Ah! Damn it!" Nelson screamed out as he felt the slicing sensation of a tooth against his calf muscle. It ripped in a horizontal motion before he was pulled free, just before the jaws could close shut. Dangling dozens of meters above the surface, he squeezed his arms as tightly as possible, ignoring the piercing pain in his leg.

Rick and the gunner both reached down, grabbing him by the wrists. Nelson slowly eased his grip to allow them to pull him up. For a moment, he was completely at their mercy.

"Don't…you fucking…drop me!" he called out as he felt himself dangling from their grasps. They pulled him inside and shut the door. The feeling of dry, solid metal underneath him couldn't have felt more welcoming. Nelson caught his breath, as Forster embraced him with a sudden and emotional hug.

Lisa sank down into the seat, struggling to calm her nerves as well. Her mind returned to the black uniforms and the unconventional specifications to the choppers. She looked at the one-armed man. No way would active duty military be operating with such an injury, at least not at this type of job.

The one-armed man noticed her staring at him. His glare clearly indicated that he didn't appreciate it. He tapped his metal arm.

"You know, my mother taught me that it's not polite to stare," he remarked.

"Who are you people?" Lisa asked. The man tilted his head.

"We're the ones you should be saying 'thank you' to," he said.

"Thank you," she said. "Now, who the hell are you people?"

"Lisa," Rick stepped in.

"Rick, they're not military!" She raised her voice. Rick paused, recalling the events three years ago, when they were snatched by contract mercenaries to pursue the first hybrid. He looked at the man. At that moment, a voice blared over the radio.

"*Raven Two. Have you acquired the passengers?*"

The man touched his mic, looking bitterly at the passengers, "Safe and sound. You want me to make them hot cocoa?"

"*Knock it off,*" the voice said. "*We lost track of the bogies. Go ahead and regroup at the Pyramid.*"

"Copy that," he said, and took a seat. Rick kneeled on the floor, helping the gunner apply a bandage to Nelson's leg. Lisa and the man seemed to have a staring contest as they sat opposite each other.

"What's the *Pyramid*?" she asked.

CHAPTER
38

"Bravo-Two-Nine, we are on approach," the pilot spoke into the microphone.

"Roger, you'll need to stand by a moment. We're finishing up refueling for Raven One."

"Copy. Standing by." The forward momentum ceased and the chopper came to a stop, seemingly bouncing in the wind as it held position. Lisa and Rick pressed their right temples to the starboard window, looking down at the *Pyramid.*

"Holy shit," Rick said. They were looking down at a naval ship, roughly two-hundred-and-thirty feet in length. Its beam appeared to be slightly under forty feet. A Melara 76mm gun was mounted on the bow deck. On each side of the mast were Rheinmetall MLG machine guns. In the large structure in the center of the ship were compartments meant for containing French Exocet anti-ship missiles. "You guys brought a friggin' battleship?" Rick asked.

"Not quite a battleship," Lisa said. She looked to the lettering above the port bow waterline. The words were written in Arabic. "This isn't our Navy. It's a Baynunah-class corvette. Used by the United Arab Emirates Navy."

"Wait…" Nelson said, straightening himself up in the seat. He looked to the one-armed man. "You brought a foreign Navy ship here?" The man didn't answer.

"It's decommissioned, isn't it?" Lisa said. The man looked to her, then back at the window. It was as close to a *Yes* as she would get. Nelson shook his head.

"How the hell would they get a…"

"They planned a scheme through the black market," Rick interrupted. After his experiences, he had a basic understanding of how conspiracies worked. "Odds are, they got the armaments through an underground supplier. And somehow, they were able to acquire the funds to get the Corvette."

The conversation stopped as the chopper began to dip. It angled downward slightly and moved toward the aft helicopter deck. Forster stood up from her seat next to Nelson and looked out the window. The blades on the other Huey were starting to rotate, and a man in black was walking away from the bay door. The helicopter lifted off the deck and moved away, making clear the space for the approaching aircraft.

The landing was swift and smooth. The whishing sound from the blades took on a whistling sound as they slowed. The landing bars touched the deck, and the engine quieted down to a slight rattle. The pilots stayed in their seats to make checks while the one-armed man opened the door.

"Okay, kids, you may step out," he said. Lisa was the first to touch her feet to the deck. Several men in black and grey tactical outfits walked onto deck, gathering with the man who had stepped off Raven One. Corvettes were smaller warships, and she wondered how they managed to get it into U.S. territory, especially with the heightened alert following the oil rig explosion. Rick and Forster helped Nelson off of the chopper as the one-armed man stepped ahead.

"I'm fine," the Chief said, removing his arms from the shoulders of his friends. There was bitterness in his voice, though not directed at Julie. His weapon and radio had been confiscated by the mercenaries. *They think I'm planning to hijack this ship?* He balanced mainly on his right leg and took a step with his other. The nerves lit up like a holiday festival, and he yelped. Forster hurried back to him, and he reluctantly allowed her to take on some of his weight. "Okay, maybe not," he said.

Rick noticed the man from the other chopper. He wore a black ball cap matching the tactical outfit. He turned around and locked eyes with Napier. Memories flashed, and he suddenly felt as if his blood pressure was boiling, as Rick was face-to-face with Colonel Salkil.

"Mr. Napier," the Colonel said, also surprised at the meeting. "Fancy seeing you here!"

"You!" Rick snarled. He started marching toward the Colonel, each step resulting in a clang against the metal deck. The one-armed man turned and rammed his remaining fist into Rick's gut. Rick doubled over and fell to his knees, holding his stomach. Lisa rushed over to him. "I'm all right," he said, still catching his breath.

"Be nice, Hendricks," Salkil said to the one-armed mercenary. Hendricks shook his hand at the wrist, then backed away. Salkil stepped up to Rick and Lisa. As she helped him to his feet, Salkil noticed the wedding rings on both of their left hands. "I suppose congratulations is in order."

"Go to hell," Rick said.

"Not a nice way to say thank you," Salkil said. "Especially not to someone who made you a millionaire. Did it buy you a fancy wedding?"

"We went to the courthouse," Rick remarked. Forster listened to the conversation, noticing that the Colonel and the Napiers knew each other.

"What is this?" she asked.

"It's him," Rick said as he walked away from the Colonel. Lisa stayed behind.

"The Colonel who helped cover up the first incident," she clarified.

"So, it's true," Forster said. She raised her voice to speak directly to Salkil. "All of this...the hybrids...this is your doing?!"

"Not in the slightest," Salkil said. "I'm the one trying to stop these things."

"And cover it up," Forster retorted. Salkil stared at her silently for a moment, visibly irritated. He had rescued these people from their sinking vessel, putting his elaborate plan at risk. Plus, there was the added exposure, as he was officially nowhere near Pariso Marino. Yet, these people hardly seemed grateful.

"Call it what you want," he said, "but if I wanted a complete cover-up, it would've been much simpler to fry your asses along with the sharks. We could've done that, but I decided not to. And now, we've got to find them all over again." He walked past Rick, deliberately bumping him in the shoulder as a show of dominance. Salkil walked to Forster, and squared up with her. "And begging your pardon," he spoke loud enough for everyone to hear, "but I've been the only one concerned with killing these things. I'm disobeying orders right now. I was instructed NOT to do anything. The government wanted to chalk up the arrival of the creature as a new species. They of course didn't know it could replicate, but I took the time to read Wallack's notes before they were burned. I addressed the problem, but they didn't want to hear it. Unfortunately, I did too good of a job back at Mako's Center, with the help of Mr. Napier, of course." Rick took a step forward, but stopped himself. Salkil glanced back at him. Rick knew he was no match; Salkil didn't get to his position by pushing pencils. He grinned and began walking around the group like a college professor giving a lecture.

"Since everyone believes what happened was a hoax, they didn't think anyone would make the connection," he continued. "But I know the truth. I know what'll happen if these things continue to live. So, I took it upon myself to eliminate the problem."

"So, you hired mercenaries," Lisa said.

"Don't worry, it's a dedicated group," Salkil said. He pointed to the one-armed mercenary. "This is Lieutenant Hendricks. He was a distinguished member of the United States Navy. He lost an arm in our pursuit of the hybrid three years ago, thus his military career. But the blood of a soldier runs deep. He wasn't ready to quit, so he formed a little business, for lack of a better word." He slowly waved his hand to the crowd of mercenaries. "With a little help from me, of course. The point is, this mission's personal for him and me."

"So, if you're operating outside the government...how exactly do you plan on keeping this one quiet?" Forster asked. Salkil's grin disappeared. He started walking off, intending not to answer. Rick stepped behind him, raising his voice.

"It was one of your men who caused the explosion at the oil rig, wasn't it?!" Salkil didn't need to answer. A couple of widening gazes from the mercenaries confirmed his suspicion. Salkil stopped, paused, then turned again to face Napier. There was no point in denying it.

"You seriously think that when the eyes of the world are on something, that something else isn't taking place behind the scenes? The Ebola Virus craze? Every national tragedy? Sometimes it's real, sometimes it's not, but there's one common link. It's all a smokescreen."

Nelson perked his head. *Holy shit, the bastard was right.* He felt foolish for thinking Rick Napier to be a conspiracy theorist a day prior. Being a cop for several years, seeing what happens in the shadows, in both government and the private sector, he thought he understood it all. But this was bigger than anything he could have imagined.

"You son of a bitch," he said. "You may have killed God-knows-how many..."

"Nobody died in that," Salkil said, exasperated. "We at least took those measures. I'm not a monster, nor am I the mad scientist who created these things. I'm the one risking his retirement, and worse, to see these things gone."

Lisa gazed again at the ship they were on. Though small and decommissioned, it was a warship, and that raised more questions. Something about the Colonel's story wasn't adding up.

"Even with everyone fixated on the crisis down south, how exactly did you expect to sneak something this big in and out, unseen?"

"I have it under control," Salkil said.

"Do you?" Lisa questioned. "You do realize the Navy has probably detected the presence of this thing, right?"

"Yes...I do," Salkil retorted. He checked his watch. "On that note, we are pressed for time." He turned and walked into the hangar, disappearing through an open doorway. Rick helped Forster guide Nelson inside.

"Is the infirmary operational?" he asked one of the mercenaries.

"There's some supplies left over," he said. They started heading in. Rick looked back. Lisa stood on the landing pad, hair blowing in the wind. She gazed at the water, the chopper, and at the ship.

"You coming?" Rick asked. Lisa followed them inside.

"Something's not right," she said.

"Yeah, I know," Rick said. "Not much we can do about it right now." As they moved through a hallway, the ship began to move. The twin diesel engines rumbled, and the water jet propulsors gave speed to the warship. Rick looked at Forster and Nelson. "He wants to keep this under wraps? How the hell is he going to do this with a friggin' ship this size?"

"Hell, everyone on the island had to have seen it," Forster said. She thought for a moment. "Could that be part of the play, somehow?"

"You're asking if he wanted the ship to be seen?" Nelson asked.

"I mean, it's got to be possible," Forster said. "The explosion at the rig, the hunt for terrorism...a foreign vessel entering U.S. waters. I don't think this ship is just being used as a weapon to kill the hybrids; it's part of the cover-up."

"Yesterday, I would've brushed it off as just a conspiracy theory," Nelson said. "But today...agh!" A surge of pain swept through his leg, which caused Forster and Rick to quicken the pace to the infirmary. Lisa took the lead, having an idea where it would be located. Hopefully they would locate some painkillers. No mercenaries escorted them. At first, they found this odd, but given the limited hands to man the ship, everyone was probably busy with their tasks.

"Only, this is purely the Colonel's cover-up," Rick said. "He's playing everybody."

They made their way past the empty crew galley, which led to another corridor. Lisa couldn't read any of the Arabic labels on the walls, which forced her to guestimate the position of the infirmary. She led them down the corridor and stopped when she came to a large set of double doors.

"This might be it," she said. By now, Nelson's teeth were tightly clenched. The pain in his leg had increased drastically. Lisa tugged on the metal doors, which opened with a hiss. Cold air turned to steam as it entered the warm hallway. Lisa looked inside and cupped her mouth.

"Oh, Jesus," she said. Rick moved from Nelson and rushed to his wife in a protective manner.

"What? What is it?" he said.

"No, I'm okay," she said. Rick looked inside, and nearly jumped in place upon seeing the cold dead corpse seemingly staring at him from the metal table. "It's the morgue," Lisa said.

"Yeah, no shit," Rick said. As he turned away to leave, he noticed something within the dark of the room. "Hang on a sec." *Why is there a body in the morgue of a decommissioned ship?* He switched the light on. The illumination of the interior revealed multiple corpses, resulting in a reactionary gasp from the couple. Forster helped Nelson over to peek inside.

"Oh shit!" After the initial shock came the noticing of strange details. Every one of the dead bodies were Middle Eastern males. Each of them was dressed in guerilla-style tactical gear. Automatic weapons and handguns were stacked in the corner of the room. Rick counted at least a dozen of the bodies.

"What the hell? Are these ISIS guys? What is this?" Rick said.

"I think we just found another link in the conspiracy," Nelson said. Lisa stepped toward the munitions. The first thing she noticed was that none of the weapons contained magazines. The mercenaries likely stored them elsewhere. But the presence of the guns, as well as the gear on the bodies, made it clear to Lisa that the plan was to somehow frame this deceased group. She put it down and exited the room, being sure to switch off the light and close the door.

"The infirmary should be nearby," she said. Forster chuckled nervously.

"Are we not gonna talk about this?" she said. "There are dead bodies in there!"

"Shhh!" Lisa said, and looked down the hallway for any mercenaries. "I don't think they want us to know about this." She went down the hallway, passing a stairway. Rick stopped and pointed.

"Could it be here?"

"I think that leads to the pilothouse," Lisa said, and kept walking. She found another door and opened it. "Oh finally!" she held the door open, allowing Forster and Nelson to enter the infirmary. They helped Nelson sit up on a table and began to check his leg. The bandage was blood soaked.

"This'll need stitches," Rick said.

"I'll do it," Forster said.

"I'll see if there's any disinfectant," Lisa said. She went through some of the cabinets, many of which were empty. She opened a doorway that led into a storage room. "Ah-ha!" she said.

Rick and Forster found some rubber gloves and removed the bandage from Nelson's leg. The gash was about three inches across his calf and bleeding rapidly. Forster laid out a needle and tied up a thread. She began to stitch while Rick handed her gauze to help wipe away the blood. Each prick aggravated the pain, but Nelson held still. Forster closed the wound up. Blood seeped through the stitches, but at a much slower rate than before. She would wait until Lisa found some disinfectant before wrapping it in fresh bandages. She kept some gauze pressed to it.

"Hopefully she'll find some painkillers," she said.

"I'll be fine," Nelson said. Forster looked him in the eyes and smiled. There were many things she wanted to say, but all she could manage was, "Thank you."

"For what?"

"Oh please! For saving my life! You almost got killed!" Forster said. Nelson grinned casually, attempting to shrug off the heroic act. He tried to come up with a witty one-liner, but only stuttered.

"Well, uh, heh…you know…" he felt as if he was about to blush. The truth was, he couldn't live with himself if she died on his watch. He didn't know how to say it.

In the storage room, Lisa located painkillers and vials of disinfectant. She hurried back into the infirmary.

"Alright, I found the goods," she said. Her eyes went to her husband, who was staring out into the hallway. He was looking out toward the stairwell. She recognized the intent in his eyes. "Rick…don't!"

"You all stay here," he said, and proceeded out the door.

"Rick, leave it alone!" Lisa called after him.

"No!" he said. "We need to know what's going on. I'll be fine." He disappeared out the door. Lisa started after him, then stopped, uncertain whether to stay and help with the medical care or go after her husband.

"Just go," Forster said. "I can manage." Lisa placed the items on the table and rushed into the hallway. She heard Rick stepping up the stairway on his way to the bridge.

CHAPTER
39

"We've marked their location," Salkil spoke into the radio. He stood near the captain's chair, watching through the large glass window pane at the front of the bridge. The bow of the ship was pointing directly toward the atoll. A mercenary stood at the radar screen, giving a thumbs up to Salkil after confirming the readings. Two green dots blipped on the screen. More than likely, they were the hybrids. The area was close to the last confirmed location. Above the atoll, the two helicopters passed by, dropping bait into the water just outside the barrier of rocks.

"*We're delivering the package,*" Hendricks' voice replied through the comm.

"We see it," Salkil said. "Raven Two? You gonna get to it today?"

"*Doing it now, Colonel,*" Raven Two's pilot said. The radar tech turned toward the Colonel.

"Sir, I'm picking up two Air Force BARCAP jets on our screen," he said. On the other side of the room, a mercenary standing at the communications unit removed one of his headphones.

"Colonel," he said. "The Air Force is attempting to make communication."

"Give no response," Salkil said. "We'll be out of this shortly. Let's keep our eye on the prize." The mercenary replaced his headphones, monitoring the communications.

"They're warning us that the *USS Donovan* is en route," he called out. Salkil nodded his head. The *Donovan* was a Naval Destroyer which was patrolling the northeast coast. The mercenary spoke again. "There'll be another ship that'll intercept us first."

"The *USS Carnahan*," Salkil said. Just as he expected.

****

"Listen, Rick, can't we just wait?" Lisa tried not to be too loud as she followed Rick through the narrow hallway.

"No," he said. He stopped briefly to face her. "Something's going down. I need to know if we need to get off this ship." He continued walking until he reached the end of the small hallway.

They stepped through an open doorway into a room full of brightly lit electronics. The room was large enough to fit over a dozen people. In the center was a stationary captain's chair which was linked to what appeared to be its own computer screen. Standing next to it was the Colonel. Only five other mercenaries were on the bridge with him, one at the helm, another at the navigation device, and others at the comm unit and radar. A couple of them glanced at the Napiers, but seemed to have no interest in them. Rick was slightly surprised. He almost expected to have guns drawn on him, but then again what kind of a threat was he? He was only a loose end to them; a hinderance brought on by their leader, whom they couldn't object to. Rick stepped beside Salkil. The Colonel could sense his presence, but kept his eyes fixed on the choppers.

"So how exactly did you get this ship into U.S. Territory?" Salkil looked at him, then turned his eyes back to the window pane. The choppers passed by each other in the distance, like two vultures circling a carcass.

"I have resources," he said. "A bit of manipulating and diverting here and there. Though I'm Army, I have connections within the Navy and Coast Guard."

"But they're closing in on this ship, aren't they?" Rick said, more of a statement than a question.

"A littoral combat ship is on approach," Salkil said.

"You're cutting it awfully close, aren't ya?" Lisa said. Salkil didn't answer, which in a way was an answer in itself. He did seem worried, but not about the Navy. He stood silent and kept watching the operation. Rick was losing his patience.

"It was nice of you to have one of your guys lead us to the infirmary," he sarcastically remarked.

"We have limited manpower," Salkil said, uninterested.

"Yeah, too bad. We found it though. Had to check a couple of places first. One of which was the morgue." Salkil turned and looked at him. Still standing at the door, Lisa could see the eyes of every mercenary turn toward Rick. Each expression was serious. Rick kept his eyes on the Colonel. "Yeah, we saw the bodies." Salkil's concerned look quickly dissipated. He figured they would discover the truth one way or another. He continued watching the choppers.

"Who are they?" Rick asked.

"Nobody the world can do without," Salkil said.

"Terrorists?" Lisa asked. She hoped that was the truth. Salkil nodded. He walked toward the radar tech.

"Keep me informed of any updates. I'll have my radio on," he said. He turned and looked at Napier. "Why don't we get some fresh air?"

Salkil, Rick, and Lisa stepped topside. The upper deck gave an astonishing view of the bow deck. Rick gazed at the large Melara 76mm gun stationed at the bow. The barrel pointed toward the atoll.

"You guys have munitions for the armaments on this thing?" he asked.

"For some of them. Enough to get the job done," Salkil said. "Dr. Napier, if I may ask, why are you here?"

"Well, let's see, your men picked us up in a chopper and..."

"I urge you not to continue being a wise-ass," Salkil interrupted. It was a threat, and Rick knew it. "Shouldn't you be at home, enjoying your life free of a mortgage, or debt?"

"Or friends," Rick added, staring out into the water. He briefly thought about the resentment he felt from everyone he knew. People had lost loved ones, buried friends and family, and looked to him to make the truth known. Not only did he fail, he became rich off of the lie. He didn't get much of a choice in the matter, but it didn't matter. "Dr. Forster called me. She captured the hybrid and connected it to the incident in Mako's Center. I guess she didn't believe the cover-up."

"And you felt sorry enough to help her. How sweet," Salkil said. "I'm actually impressed. You guys actually went out to try to kill the hybrids."

"Hey man," Rick said, "we killed two of those things. How many have you killed?" Salkil ignored the question. Rick stared at him incessantly. "There's another thing; what are you going to do about the one in Felt's Paradise?" The Colonel looked at him silently, then turned his eyes toward the Melara. Rick followed his gaze, then backed away from the edge of the deck. "You're not serious?! You're not actually going to use that on a public area!"

"I'll see to it that everyone is evacuated," Salkil said. A few warning shots would likely do the trick. "You need to understand; these things CANNOT exist. And unfortunately, the world can't know they exist. The scrutiny you went through, I've been through it a hundred times fold. There are other people, other countries out there...BAD ONES...that if they knew these things could be created, they would not hesitate to create them. You want evidence? Look at history; the Nazi experiments, for example. Read about the U.S.S.R., at the breeding experiments Stalin was funding to create super-soldiers. Look at the world today! You think nobody will try to create hybrids of their own once they realize it's possible?" Rick didn't answer. Despite his natural resentment toward Salkil, he allowed the words to sink in. It put him in a difficult spot, morally. There did seem to be some truth to what the Colonel was saying. After all, it didn't take long for other countries to develop the atomic bomb after its initial use. On the other hand, covering up the matter seemed like allowing a free pass for officials who were responsible for a project that resulted in the deaths of many.

Rick closed his eyes and felt the cooling sensation of the light breeze that swept over. He looked to the helicopters and focused his mind on the one thing he and Salkil agreed on; the creatures needed to be destroyed.

"If you're trying to bring them up that way, forget it," he said. "You need live bait."

"He's right," Lisa said. "If you have Zodiacs on this boat, you'll have to send them out. Otherwise, those things won't likely come up. They've already fed."

Their sudden change in attitude caught Salkil by surprise. For a moment, he wondered if they were playing him, but then understood that they were serious. His memory flashed to the encounter three years ago, when three Zodiacs went up against the original escaped hybrid. It was a disaster.

"Out of the question," he said. "I can't have any of my men out there. You know firsthand what'll happen."

"Well, that's on you then," Rick said. "The reality is, these things prefer live targets. It's up to you, but as you've stated, time's running out." Salkil instinctively checked his watch. He watched the Hueys drop more bait into the water. He grabbed his radio and clicked the transmitter.

"This is Salkil. Any change in the creatures' positions?"

"*Negative,*" the mercenary responded.

"Damn it," Salkil said under his breath. He stood and thought for a moment, then lifted his radio back to his lips. "Raven One, do you have a harness on board?"

"*We do, sir,*" Hendricks' voice came through.

"Good. Have it prepped and ready to go. I'll meet you on the landing pad in five." He turned and walked into the entryway. Rick and Lisa looked at each other, equally confused, and followed him in.

"Care to tell us what the plan is, Colonel?" Rick said.

"You said it yourself. Live bait," Salkil said. "We don't have time to mess around." He entered the bridge. "Get me a wetsuit and some thermal gear STAT." The mercenaries looked at him with uncertainty, but swiftly went to action. There was no time for hesitation.

CHAPTER
40

"How's it feeling now?" Forster asked Nelson. He limped beside her, using a metal crutch found in the storage room.

"Same as when you asked five seconds ago...I'm fine," he jested. His leg throbbed like hell, and the pulsing sensation felt intensified because of the tight bandages. But with the assistance of the crutch, he was able to put some weight on the leg and walk on his own. They walked down the hallway, feeling the breeze from the open hangar doors.

The breeze grew stronger, as if a strong wind was surging down the hall. Sounds of running feet reverberated through the corridor. Forster and Nelson looked behind as two mercenaries ran down the hallway toward them. They thought of Rick and Lisa heading up to the bridge to confront Salkil. *Oh shit, we're in trouble, aren't we?* Forster thought. Nelson felt something similar. They put their backs to the wall, in surrender in case they were to be detained by the two armed men.

The mercenaries rushed past them, taking a turn at the end of the corridor. The inflow of wind grew stronger. Forster and Nelson looked to each other and decided to follow. Nelson ignored the pain as he followed Forster. They took a turn which led them to the hangar doors. Bright sunshine and cool ocean air washed over them like a wave. Looking outside the hangar, they saw the Huey resting on the landing pad. The engine still rumbled and the rotors were still spinning, creating a strong downdraft that rebounded from the deck and swept across the ship.

Standing near the open bay doors was Colonel Salkil. He was dressed in a red jumpsuit, wearing thermal gear underneath. In his hand he held an automatic weapon, freshly loaded, and pointed downward. He slipped on a helmet and tapped on a microphone that protruded toward his mouth. Standing near him were Rick and Lisa. Both held a hand over their eyes to protect against the sting of the downdraft.

"What, are they friends now?" Nelson asked.

"Something's going on," Forster said. They approached.

Colonel Salkil handed his weapon to Hendricks, who stood aboard the chopper. The nearby gunner handed Salkil a harness and helped him strap it on.

"Like I said, keep your eyes on that sonar monitor," he said to one of the mercenaries. "Don't even blink. Listen to these guys, they have an idea of how these things operate." He pointed a finger to Rick and Lisa. The last clip of the harness snapped shut. The gunner climbed back in place at the 50. cal. Hendricks was shaking his head. Salkil looked at him, ignoring the objecting expressions. "Be ready to climb in a hurry. We won't just be getting away from the sharks." He looked to the other Huey, maintaining position just outside the rocky barrier.

With the click of a switch, its weapons would be armed and ready to fire. That switch would be flicked the moment he entered the water. Hendricks stuffed a cigar in his mouth, then accepted a lighter from the gunner.

"Sir, permission to speak freely…eh, fuck it…you're one crazy son-of-a-bitch," he said. He lit the cigar and released a mouthful of grey tobacco smoke.

"Maybe I am," he said. "But unless you have a better idea, let's get to it."

"You're seriously using yourself as bait?" Lisa said. She was still in disbelief. The Colonel was intentionally having himself lowered into the water, where he would create a sensation to attract the beasts and draw them up. And if successful, he would be at the pilots' mercy to pull him out in time, not just to avoid getting devoured, but out of the way for Raven Two to unload its missiles at the creatures.

Salkil accepted the weapon back from Hendricks and chambered a round. "You said so yourself, these things prefer live targets. And we don't have time to goof around. Who knows, maybe I'll be eaten." He attached the cable to his harness and put a finger on his mic. "Alright, let's act fast. After we kill these things, we need to hurry up and complete the last part of the mission. Then we'll extract."

"Colonel!" Rick shouted over the hum of the blades. "Remember, we need to collect samples of the creatures! We need to confirm the original is dead."

"Yeah, yeah, Doc. We'll have it taken care of," Salkil said. "Alright, let's go!"

The helicopter lifted off the pad, and the rappel tether uncoiled. Salkil grunted as the harness tightened around his waist and chest, and he was lifted up into the air. He looked down at the water beneath his feet. It seemed so calm, aside from the mild swells from the tide. But he knew, beneath that calm was a vicious storm.

Rick and Lisa watched for a moment as he was carried away. They heard footsteps approaching, and they turned to see Forster and Nelson walking up to them. Both looked back with puzzled expressions. The Chief noticed the portable radio in Rick's hand.

"What the hell is going on? You guys kiss and make up?"

"He's trying to draw them up," Rick said. "When they come up after him, the other chopper will rain hell on them."

"Ballsy," Forster said. "So, what's the other part of the plan he was talking about?" Rick's expression grew melancholic, which worried Forster. "What's he going to do?" Rick looked past her toward Nelson.

"We're gonna have to evacuate Felt's Paradise."

The Huey glided to the targeted position and stopped. The main pilot turned it around until it was facing toward the *Pyramid*. Salkil could feel himself gently swinging from side-to-side. The harness dug into him, being most irritating on the insides of his thighs. He shouldered his weapon, pointing the muzzle at the water. He knew it wouldn't do any good against the sharks, but he didn't care. He figured if he were to go out, it would be like a bad-ass. Otherwise, he'd literally be nothing more than bait on fishing line.

He looked ahead at the Corvette, eyes focused on the outside view of the bridge, envisioning everyone in place.

"Keep your eyes on that monitor," he said into the mic. "Raven One, take me down." The descent began with a sudden jolt, as if the helicopter was hit over the top with a hammer. After that, it was a gradual lowering. Salkil watched the water. The downdraft created an uneven distortion on the surface, almost giving the appearance of sizzling water. He went in feet first.

"Alright, that's good!" he said. His timing was perfect, as when the chopper stopped, he was up to his chest. Rippling water splashed his face. He spat out some bitter tasting drops of saltwater. He looked down below him. He could only see down a few feet. The rippling disturbance didn't help. Essentially, he was blind to anything lurking below. "Any changes in their position?"

"*Negative, sir.*" The sonar monitor asked. Another voice blared through the ear piece. It was Rick Napier's.

"*Colonel, you'll need to splash around a little more. Gain their attention.*"

"You almost sound hopeful I'll get eaten," Salkil joked. He kicked his legs and splashed his weapon over the water. He took his left hand off the barrel grip and slapped it down repeatedly.

"*Targets are moving,*" the sonar tech reported.

"Care to elaborate? For all I know, that means they're doing the tango."

"*They're moving up. They're moving slow...okay now one's stopped, but the other is still slowly approaching.*"

"*Raven One, this is Napier! Pull up! These things attack with quick bursts of speed. They'll be on you before you're clear.*"

"*Sir?*" the pilot said to Salkil, unsure of what to do. Salkil suddenly felt himself growing nervous, a feeling he rarely experienced.

"Bring me up," he said. His demeanor was calm and collected, until he saw the shape emerge beneath him. In the blink of an eye, his brain analyzed that he would not be lifted in time. "Pull forward!" he yelled. Luckily, the pilot didn't hesitate or question. He pushed forward on the controls, dragging Salkil to the north, just out of the way of the open jaws. The hybrid shot upward, inches past the Colonel. It twisted into a spiral. Its nose bumped against the tail.

Warning lights flickered throughout the cockpit. Raven One spun out of control. The pilots fought for control, yelling commands over each other. Hendricks fell into a seat while the gunner felt his support straps struggling to keep him in place. Salkil soared against the air as he swung about with each rapid spin of the chopper. He felt the blood draining from his head from the forward momentum. To keep from passing out, he tensed his legs and abdominal muscles to execute the Hick maneuver.

The pilot yanked up on the stick to keep the Huey from splashing down. He looked through the windshield. The surrounding scenery of blue sky and water passed by in one large blur.

The Raven Two's pilots watched the chopper climb while still zipping out of control. It zagged in every direction, then tilted heavily to the left. It leveled out and accelerated uncontrollably right toward them.

"Shit!" the pilot called out. Raven Two ascended, barely avoiding collision as Raven One passed inches underneath. Raven One zoomed forward for several seconds, and the pilots finally managed to steady the aircraft.

Salkil managed to work the nausea down after the spinning finally stopped. He felt like an astronaut pilot having gone through centrifuge training. He took a deep inhale through his nose.

"Status...on targets?" The redistribution of blood in his body made breathing...and talking...difficult. He even had difficulty hearing the radio response, which sounded like a muffle. Salkil pressed the side of his helmet tighter against his ear. "Say again."

"*Bogies have descended,*" the sonar tech repeated.

"Alright," Salkil said. "Let's try again."

"*Sir, perhaps we can try another...*"

Salkil cut Hendricks off. "We're trying again. Raven One, commence procedure now."

Rick ran through the corridor, listening to the transmissions on his radio. Right behind him were Forster and Lisa, and way behind them was Nelson. The Chief cursed as he struggled to keep up as they made their way to the bridge. Forster looked back at him.

"Just go on. I'll catch up," he said. *They need you more than me.* After witnessing the near collision in midair, the group decided to hurry to the bridge. Even from the top deck, they could not get any visual of the hybrids under the water and needed to see the sonar images.

"Colonel, another bit of advice..." Rick said.

"*Spit it out,*" Salkil answered.

"After the chopper lowers you down, have it drag you across the water," Rick said. "I think only the one came up last time, but if you're moving, they'll probably race to come at you."

"*You really do want to see me eaten, don't you?*"

Maybe.

"I'm entering the bridge now," Rick said, literally passing through the entrance as he spoke. He and Forster stood on both sides of the sonar technician, wedging him out of the way. Rick studied the screen. Two green blobs flashed on the grid. The reading indicated that they were over two dozen meters deep. Rick recalled Salkil's remark. "Don't worry, I'll tell you when to pull up."

The Colonel's feet dipped back into the warm Atlantic, and the chopper stopped when he was about waist deep. Next came the dragging sensation as he was pulled against the water.

"I'll never look at fishing the same ever again," he quipped. The chopper dragged him toward the east, while Raven Two kept pace, positioning its rockets on Salkil's position.

"*Raven One, make sure he's down to his chest,*" Rick said. "*They need to hear his heartbeat.*"

"Great," Salkil said. The chopper dipped slightly, nearly putting the Colonel under completely. He was up to his neck, spitting out mouthfuls of seawater after each swell.

God, this better work.

Rick and Forster watched the blips slowly move toward the surface. At the top of the screen was a distortion indicating Salkil's presence. The blips gradually followed it.

"Rick, they're about to move," Forster said. Rick hesitated, allowing the blips to move closer. He could envision them preparing to make their run. He agreed with Forster.

He raised his radio, "Raven One, pull up now!"

The pilot yanked on the joystick. The harness bruised Salkil's waist and chest as it seemingly tightened around him. The chopper lifted high into the air. In a pained voice, he yelled against the wind. "Raven Two, fire!"

Raven Two's co-pilot depressed the trigger. Half a dozen 70mm rockets ignited and soared the short angular distance to the water. "It's away," the pilot said.

The timing was perfect. One of the large cone-shaped heads had just emerged to breach the water where Salkil had been a moment prior. In another instant, it was blanketed in an enormous explosion. It was an immediate confirmed kill for at least one of the creatures. Bits of shell and innards showered the ocean around the ball of flame. Fragments small and large mostly sank into the depths, while some of the more buoyant bits floated along the surface. A twister of smoke lifted into the daylight sky. There was no recognizable carcass to be seen.

"Boom!" the pilot yelled triumphantly.

Salkil barely had a glimpse of the beast when the missiles had rained down on it. He was pleased at the spectacular execution. The only problem was the visual was inconclusive as to whether they had destroyed both hybrids.

"Bridge? Napier? Any more readings?"

Rick tapped on the screen. The image was fuzzy. The force of the blast seemed to have disrupted the transceiver circuit. Probably one of the reasons the ship was decommissioned, the computer system was out of date. Worse, he couldn't read any of the instructions to help improve the frequency.

"Hang on, we're having technical difficulties," he said. Whenever the image cleared, it showed multiple objects. Rick shook his head, unable to make sense of them.

"They're debris from the missiles and the shark," Forster said. "I can't see if the other one's still alive."

"Nor can I," Rick said. He spoke into the radio. "Colonel, we're inconclusive." The mercenary took his place and attempted to check the circuit.

"Shit," Salkil said. There was no immediate way to know if they got both of the sharks. He hoped the sonar would function properly. "Hold tight," he said.

In Raven Two, the two pilots looked to each other. They were growing impatient, and slightly on edge. The Navy was on approach, and time was dwindling.

"Sir, we'll go down for a better visual," the pilot said. Salkil felt his pulse flare.

"Raven Two, negative! Hold fast."

Ignoring his instructions, the pilots lowered the Huey down to the surface. The landing skids scratched the water, just outside the huge field of carnage. The water was blood red, with entrails and shell floating about. The gunner stuck the M60 out the bay door and scanned the water. Aside from the gruesome visual, the sea had settled until being as calm as a summer breeze.

"Nothing," he said. The pilots looked to each other, bearing beer-stained teeth as they grinned ear-to-ear in celebration of their new kill.

"Sir, I think we can say there's no more sharks," the main pilot said. He started his ascent, turning the nose toward the *Pyramid.*

A burst of water sprayed the windshield and flooded the main compartment. A set of jaws clamped down on one of the skids. Six thousand pounds of mass pulled the chopper down. The gunner nearly fell backwards, held on only by the safety belt on the mount. He found himself staring right into the eyes of the red shark.

The weight caused the chopper to pitch heavily to port. The gunner found nothing but ocean in his line of sight. The pilots struggled with the controls, but it was useless. The chopper crashed into the Atlantic in a horrendous display of metal and water being flung about in every direction. Rotor blades splintered into large fragments as the blades chopped the water. The engines flooded and died, and the Huey settled, buoyant, leaning to port.

The gunner was entirely submerged. He opened his eyes, ignoring the sting of the saltwater as he tried to undo his safety belt. A trained mercenary, he kept calm and relaxed, careful to retain the little air he had. He found the clip and pressed the button to release himself.

He looked up from the harness right into the dark eyes of the hybrid. It stared back at him, teeth bared from its jaws. The training suddenly had no meaning. His tranquil composure turned into fright, and for the first time in his professional life, military or contract, he screamed in pure terror.

Rows of teeth pierced his torso, front and back. His head and shoulders were inside the creature's mouth entirely. Like two-inch daggers, they mangled flesh and bone. The beast yanked him from his gunner's seat, then turned away and raced along the surface with its prize.

Salkil could see the mercenary's legs kicking from the corner of the creature's mouth. After a few bloody chomps and shakes, the kicking stopped. The hybrid raced into the distance, leaving behind a red squiggly trail of blood.

"It's heading out to sea," he said. "*Pyramid!* Position the Melara! Don't let the bastard get away."

An alarm sounded on deck as the weapon system went online. Rick, Forster, Lisa, and Nelson looked out the forward window on the bridge, and watched as the 76mm cannon lowered its barrel, then rotated its base. Chatter echoed through the radio frequencies as the mercenaries communicated the creature's position.

"Rotate starboard, seven-point-zero-five degrees," the leading mercenary said, watching the dorsal fin through a pair of binoculars.

"*Seven-point-zero-five degrees,*" the merc in the weapon control room confirmed. "*In position.*"

"Fire away!"

A burst of grey smoke surrounded the muzzle as the Melara fired off several shots. Traveling at the speed of sound, the shells reached their target.

The hybrid never knew what hit it. In less than a second, it disappeared inside a series of huge explosions. Bits of shell and guts sprayed into the air like bloody fireworks, crashing down in tiny fragments into the thrashing ocean.

The bridge became filled with the cheers from the hired guns, ecstatic about their job well done. Rick blew a sigh of relief, as did Forster. At least these creatures would not get away and spawn new hybrids. All that was left was to salvage a specimen from each one, in hopes of discovering which one was the original.

Forster looked to the port window in the bridge. She wasn't feeling victorious yet. The captured hybrid would have to be destroyed. It wasn't over yet.

Hendricks and the gunner pulled Colonel Salkil into the chopper. He quickly ripped off the harness, his body feeling the relief from the tight nylon letting free. He looked at the former Lieutenant.

"Let's get this mess cleaned up," he said. "Get some Zodiacs out there. Time to finish the job."

CHAPTER
41

Mercenaries hurried about the ship's deck as they busily moved containers of gear to the surface. From afar, they appeared like a small colony of ants swarming about their fortress. Three Zodiac boats emerged from the lower hangar. The crew inflated the tubes, giving the boats a full length of twenty-five feet.

Forster stepped outside, watching the mercenaries go to work. Crates of supplies were wheeled out on dollies. She watched the men open the crates and remove large nylon straps. Within every inch on these straps was a rectangular black pouch, and each one was full. The men loaded these straps into the nearest zodiac.

"What is this?" she asked a passing mercenary. He only answered with a snide glance and continued walking away. She turned around, hoping to see Rick or Lisa, but they were still inside the bridge. Nelson limped from the hangar, still relying on his crutch to get place to place. A group of mercenaries gathered around the Zodiacs and began lowering them into the water. Forster looked into the nearest metal crate and pulled a strap. The mercs would likely snatch it back once they saw her with it, but she didn't care. She opened one of the many rectangular patches. Inside was a solid object, like a simple block. A metal piece had been pressed into it, the exposed tip only extending a few millimeters. The tip was blinking red. Nelson looked at what she had, then leaned back.

"Holy crap, that's a C-4 explosive," he said. His gaze turned to the portside as they lowered the boats into the water.

The drone of the Raven One Huey grew louder. Mercenaries cleared the way, and the chopper touched down. Salkil was still dripping wet as he stepped off. He had removed his helmet and secured a portable radio.

"Alright, hurry it up! Pilots are waiting. And we don't have all day. Make sure the chopper is fully fueled and ready to go," he said to the men as he walked by. He slowed his stride after seeing Forster and Nelson examining the explosive. "Didn't your mothers teach you not to play with other peoples' things?" He snatched the strap out of Forster's hands and replaced it in the crate.

"C-4?" Forster said. "Your guys are loading it onto the boats. What are you up to?" Salkil looked to the downed aircraft by the rocks in the distance.

"Unfortunately, we had not planned on losing a chopper in our mission. Unfortunately, there had been no reports of stolen military aircraft to fit the cover story," he said.

"You're gonna blow it up?" Forster said.

"You're using an awful lot of explosives for one chopper," Nelson said.

"Yeah?" Salkil said. *Your point?* Nelson understood the tone. There was no intention of having any recognizable trace of the Huey remaining. Salkil continued walking. He could hear Forster's footsteps as she followed him.

"What's the cover story, exactly?" she said. Salkil kept walking, entering the shade from the overhead hangar. She grabbed him at the shoulder and spun him to face her. "What do you mean, stolen?" He stared at her, almost puzzled.

"Have you not been paying attention to the news?" he asked.

"I've been busy chasing down your fish," she said.

Salkil looked past her at Nelson. "You think she'd show more gratitude. First, I save her life…well all of your lives actually. Then I kill the other hybrids. Yet, she accuses me of creating the problem." He spoke to the Chief as if they were buddies in a bar—like *he* should agree with his sentiment. Nelson didn't respond. Like Forster, he wanted answers. Salkil didn't care. He turned and entered the hangar.

Nelson dug his phone out of his pocket. He tried to access the internet. The signal was weak and the smart phone took an eternity to access the news app. Forster stood at his side, waiting for any results. They watched the loading circle swirl endlessly, until the screen went to white, and finally, the first headline flashed as the page slowly loaded.

Militant group steals decommissioned Emirates Navy Corvette.

The rest of the page came into view. *Terrorist group who claimed responsibility for oil rig bombing has reportedly seized control over the recently decommissioned Navy Corvette, the Pyramid.* Nelson looked at the time and date of the article, then at the time on his phone.

"This news just came out," he said. He put the phone away. "Jesus, they didn't get this thing from the black market. They actually stormed an Arab Nations Navy port and stole it."

Rick looked around at the bridge. The mercenaries had left in a rush, leaving him and Lisa alone for a few minutes. He looked out the main window and watched two of the Zodiac crafts cruising toward the downed chopper. Each Zodiac carried at least four men.

"That's an awful lot just to rescue two pilots," he said aloud. Footsteps approached from the corridor. He and Lisa turned around as Salkil entered the room. The Colonel stopped and looked at them for a brief moment, then stepped further in.

"Well, your advice worked," he said. Rick nervously tapped his fingers against the sonar board.

"So, what now?" he asked.

"We're going to finish the job," Salkil said.

"He means with us," Lisa said. Salkil tilted his head up, mouth slightly agape. *Oh, I see.*

"Honestly, I hadn't thought about it," he said. "You guys weren't part of the plan. I did you a big favor by rescuing you off your ship. I was hoping that, in return, the four of you would live your normal lives, and never speak a word of this." Rick was somewhat relieved to hear that proposition. He still hated that the dirty lie would still endure.

"Don't know how you're gonna get away with this anyway," he said. "There's no way you'll get this thing out of local waters before the Navy reaches you."

"I'm not planning on it," Salkil said. Rick and Lisa heard the squeaky sound of rolling wheels coming from down the corridor. They grew louder until several mercenaries entered the room with stretchers. The dead soldiers from the morgue were piled on them like bean bags. Rick and Lisa felt sick as the mercs moved the bodies and positioned them throughout the bridge. They looked at Salkil with disgust.

"What the hell..." He put the pieces together in his mind. "Oh my God...you never expected to get away in this ship. You're *expecting* the Navy to blast this ship to oblivion. And when it's done, these guys here will take the fall for you."

"Congratulations, Detective," Salkil said. "Like I said, I tried to kill these things, and everybody got in the way. This was the only way to ensure that these things never see the light of day again."

"No, this was the only way your name would remain cleared," Rick said. "If you cared as much as I did about the truth, you'd face the heat. You wouldn't care what it did to your name."

"Oh, like you did?" Salkil said. "Making all that money didn't seem to bother you."

"It bothered me a bunch," Rick said. Lisa nodded in agreement, staring the Colonel down with blazing eyes. "I only took the deal because you threatened my daughter! Remember that?"

Salkil began to regret his spur-of-the-moment decision to rescue them. He wasn't sure if he could trust them with his secret. There wasn't much time for a choice.

He clicked his radio transmitter, "Let's get ready to get underway. Zodiac units, after you set your charges, go to the rendezvous. We'll collect you there." The order also served as a stall for Salkil as he brainstormed the current predicament.

A new blip on the sonar screen drew his attention. In three large strides, he crossed the room to the unit. Rick and Lisa looked at each other, then stepped near him. They saw the blip. Something was approaching from the south.

"Whatever that is, it's big," Lisa said. She restrained a grin. "Navy ship, maybe?"

Salkil looked through the window. Besides the mercenary crew gathered near the chopper, there was nothing but ocean. He grabbed his radio.

"Hendricks? We're getting a new reading from the south," he said.

Hendricks stood up at the bow of his Zodiac and scanned the horizon. There was nothing but a thin line separating the sky from the ocean.

"Nothing so far, Colonel," he said. "Let us move around the rock a bit for a wider view."

Hendricks' Zodiac was the third and last to approach the chopper. The other two zodiacs, each carrying four mercenaries, had just arrived. The pilots inside had made their way to the bay doors, ready to be picked up. The mercenaries handed them the C-4 to plant inside it. The merc driving his boat steered to port, giving them a view around the atoll.

"No visual," he said through the radio. "Don't tell me we've got another shark out here."

"No, this reading indicates something larger."

Hendricks felt a sudden apprehension at the description. "Oh shit. Navy submarine, most likely."

Salkil shook his head. The object slowly approached, never coming to a complete stop. It moved around the atoll in a crescent-shape trajectory. *Maybe.* Its approach was slow, much like a submarine's would be in this instance. Yet, it didn't add up.

"It's too small for a submarine," he said... "but too big to be a whale." He looked at Rick and Lisa. "How deep is it around here?"

"To my knowledge, between three and four hundred feet around the atoll," Lisa said. Salkil shook his head again.

"A submarine wouldn't run so shallow for a mission like this," he said. His eyes returned to the screen. "Jesus..." he picked up his radio. "Hendricks, it's shallowing. Its now to the west and closing..." the blip suddenly increased speed. Every person in the bridge hurried to the window.

On deck, Forster and Nelson saw the few remaining mercenaries climbing to the upper deck. Curious, they followed. Climbing inches behind the last mercenary, she heard the radio chatter. Something about a large object closing in.

They stood with the few mercs by the radar tower. The bow was now facing the rock. They saw the chopper, and the two Zodiac boats bobbing near it, with a third several meters to the east.

To the west, a mountain of water rose.

Hendricks ordered his Zodiac to be slowed, and he lifted his binoculars to his eyes.

At the chopper, every hired gun ceased what they were doing, and looked to the enormous approaching swell, unable to see the mass behind it. Breaking through the top of the mountain was a triangular object. Red in color, it had a height of ten feet. The mighty swell split in two and peeled from the center like theater curtains. Behind it was a cone shaped head, containing two black eyes, each the size of a twin bed, and an open set of jaws large enough to fit a city bus.

Hendricks lowered the glasses. He didn't need them, as the beast was so massive. He felt his blood stirring. This was like the other hybrids, but it was colossal. More massive.

A Behemoth!

The mercenaries erupted in sheer panic as the enormous hybrid shot toward them. A swing of its tail caused tidal waves, as did its enormous girth as it cut across the surface. One of the Zodiacs sped out of the way, leaving the pilots behind in the chopper. The other Zodiac was about to do the same until the beast came down on them.

Thirteen-inch jagged teeth pierced the hull of the chopper with ease. The monster's nose smashed into the nearby Zodiac, sending it clear out the water.

The boat flipped several times, throwing its occupants from its deck. Two of them hit the water, skipping like stones before settling. The other two landed on the rocks, smashing their brains all over the granite.

Water filled the chopper, the rushing current forcing its way down the gullets of the two pilots. The crushing jaws clasped further. The steel sides, floor, and ceiling screamed as it crumpled in the organic vice, crushing the two pilots into mush.

"What in the name of CHRIST!" Salkil yelled. Rick and Lisa were in equal shock. The beast was a hundred-and-fifty-feet long at least! Salkil looked at the crew behind him, each on the brink of panic, a rarity for them.

"Man the guns!" he yelled. He grabbed his radio and ran out the door. "Get the chopper started! I'm on my way to the deck!" He ran at a full sprint through the corridors.

The mercenaries scattered to their positions. One took the helm while the others hurried to the armament chamber.

Rick and Lisa looked back to the window. The enormous beast raised its head again, throwing the scrap metal that was the Huey from its mouth. His heart pounded and sweat began to soak his recently dried clothes.

"I think we found the original," he said.

The escaping Zodiac lifted and fell with the huge waves pushed by the hybrid as it smashed its head into the water. It moved along the surface, taunting them with its enormous dorsal fin. Both boats focused their fifty caliber machine guns on the girth.

Bullets smashed against the solid shell, as Hendricks predicted. It didn't matter. The creature moved in a semicircle. He watched the dorsal turn toward the other Zodiac. The .50 cal. blazed, pounding the snout with dozens of rounds in just a few seconds. The beast rammed the boat, tossing everyone aboard into the water. The tubes burst, and the steel hull crumpled. The shark whipped its head back and forth, chomping the tiny human tidbits. One bite took two of the mercs at once. One was impaled at the center torso by one of the teeth, which severed him in half as the jaws closed down. The other one was fully intact and clawing against the soft leathery flesh of the tongue as he washed down the creature's gullet.

The other two mercenaries splashed about in the water, struggling in a fruitless attempt to get away. They were on opposite sides of the shark. Hendricks directed his Zodiac to draw closer to the beast. Bouncing in the waves, it raced towards it, eventually turning to travel parallel. They were thirty feet away from it. The machine gun blasted away. With his one arm, Hendricks pulled a grenade from his vest. He bit the pin away with his mouth and spit it out. He counted to three in his mind and threw the explosive. It exploded just as it hit the rigid shell. The smoke quickly cleared, revealing zero penetration. The smallest spines were even still intact.

The shark turned swiftly, intrigued by the small challenger. Its tail creased the water in a huge swipe, smashing the fleeing mercenary as it turned. Its nose was pointed at the last mercenary. The water lifted him, hauling him overtop its head. Through the terror, he found an optimism as the creature passed inches beneath him. Perhaps it would not eat him, and he could swim to safety.

The thought ended, as did his life, when he found himself run through by a huge spine on its back.

"Move!" Hendricks yelled. The Zodiac zipped out of the way just as the creature opened its jaws. It missed, but quickly turned to pursue. Hendricks snatched another grenade and pulled the pin. He looked up, just as the snout rose again. He threw the grenade, which exploded atop its head. The beast didn't even feel it.

With another swipe of its tail, the creature was on them. Jaws bit onto the Zodiac, slicing into the bow. It reared its snout toward the sky, spilling the four mercenaries inside into the back of its throat. Hendricks saw nothing but black as the jaws slammed shut like bay doors. He reached for anything he could grab, but there was nothing except the wet, slithery flesh of its throat. The beast that swallowed his arm three years prior had finally finished that meal.

Salkil watched the creature spit the smashed Zodiac vessel. It was a déjà vu of the worst sort. Once again, he was inside a chopper, watching the hybrid weapon do battle against three Zodiac crews who were no match for it. Only this time, the beast was a hundred-fifty-feet long, and with its incredibly thick shell, it had to weigh close to a million pounds.

"We need to hit it with everything we've got," he said. He clicked his transmitter. "Aim the Melara and smoke this thing!" He then put his hand on the pilot's shoulder. "Fire the rockets when ready."

The pilot pointed the chopper at a downward angle. The shark moved gradually, sizing up the *Pyramid*. Unlike three years ago, it was not going to be intimidated by the large mechanical enemy.

Missiles whooshed from the pods. Balls of flame erupted along the shark's back. The pilot continued firing. More missiles rained down, finding their target below.

The *Pyramid*'s gun fired off several shots, sending shockwaves through the deck. Explosions rained all over the huge shark. Salkil stuck his head out the open bay door. He could see the hybrid through the billowing smoke. It was moving, unfazed by the bombardment. The shell was completely intact.

The creature felt nothing other than pressure and heat from the assault. Its senses were heightened. It had studied the larger, artificial 'creature' in the water. The vibrations from the cannon going off was like a heartbeat. The beast considered it a challenger and an enemy. Its tail pounded the water, launching it forward. Its eyes rolled back.

"Brace for impact!" someone yelled on the bridge. The warship shook as it was knocked back several meters. Everyone on the bridge fell to the floor. Emergency lights flashed.

The leading mercenary scrambled to his feet. "Keep firing!"

Rick and Lisa both lay on their stomachs. They looked to each other. They thought the same thing. They sprang to their feet and ran out of the bridge. As they ran through the corridor, the ship was hit again. The impact came from the starboard side. The hallway rotated to the left, and suddenly Rick and Lisa found themselves running at the corner between the wall and the floor. The hall rotated back as the ship settled.

They exited through the hangar doors. They looked around for any lifejackets. Water sprayed on deck as the Behemoth grazed the stern with its left pectoral fin. At first, Rick saw the creature circling the ship in a tight pattern, possibly exercising a strategy of slicing an enemy with its spines. Then he saw the caudal fin cocked back, like the hammer to a revolver. As if a trigger was depressed, the tail swung back, slamming into the side of the *Pyramid*. The warship went into a spin, and the Napiers were once again on their hands and knees.

The Huey fired a rocket, landing a shot right overtop the creature's head. A cloud of smoke briefly consumed the landing pad and hangar. When it cleared, Rick could see the creature hooking back, trying to get at the chopper. It wasn't hurt, but it was frustrated, unable to snatch the aerial opponent.

It lifted its head, unable to gain the height it needed. The Huey went in reverse. Another missile was fired, landing directly on its nose. The beast shook its head, getting the burning smell of smoke out of its nostrils. The shell was undamaged.

The warship settled, with the beast now being on the starboard side. Rick and Lisa looked at the huge red creature as it chased Salkil's chopper. They looked at the crates, believing them to hold supplies. Before they stepped forward, two life jackets landed on the deck in front of them, as if dropped by the heavens. Rick and Lisa turned and looked upward. Standing on top of the hangar were Forster and Nelson, both wearing lifejackets and equally convinced the *Pyramid* would not survive the assault.

The whirring mechanical sound of the Melara cannon screamed through the air. The weapon turned on its rotator and fired off a burst of six blasts. The shells hit the creature along its back, doing nothing more than gaining its attention. It turned around, smashing several rocks with a swipe of its tail. The cannon rained more hell, raining shots on its head.

The beast gained speed. Water rolled in huge swells as the creature heaved its mass toward the enemy.

Forster saw the huge mass draw close. She sucked in a breath, just as the creature's snout punched through the steel hull. Barely maintaining his balance, Rick shoved his wife up the ladder. He secured the clip on his lifejacket and swiftly followed her up. Looking to the starboard side, he could see the swirling water to the starboard side. The shark had pulled away, and the ocean was racing to fill the breach. New alarms rang throughout the ship.

Watertight doors activated, sealing off the lower compartments, while pumps got to work on reducing flooding.

As Lisa stepped up onto the upper deck, they felt the Melara gun blasting away again. The shark rammed the bow. The bow heaved as the ship was forced backward. A surge of water flooded the landing pad and lower decks. The shark moved away, leaving the bow of the ship crunched. Water raced through the new breaches, forming small rivers traveling through the ship. The deck had upheaved, pressing thousands of pounds of steel into the Melara gun. Gears groaned as the rotator tried to turn, but it was wedged in place. The aiming mechanism was disabled.

The *Pyramid* rocked to and fro. Mercenaries abandoned their stations and started climbing toward the upper deck. Forster looked at the waterline. It was steadily climbing.

The port Rheinmetall MLG machine gun blasted the water. Forster followed its aim, seeing the Behemoth making another run at the ship, coming in from a hundred yards out.

It submerged, leaving behind a mountain of settling water. The mercenary ceased fire, losing his visual of the target. He stood up from the mount for a better look.

A wall of water skyrocketed. The Behemoth breached the water, completely airborne. Its huge body cast a shadow over the ship for less than a moment before it came crashing down. The gunner let out a scream before being smashed by the creature's rigid underside. Steel splintered all across the ship. The radar tower smashed, and the whole middle of the ship bent inward into a V-shape. The force of the landing catapulted everyone standing atop the vessel several feet into the air.

Forster landed on her side in a fetal position. Her shoulder and hip ached. Fighting through the pain, she lifted her head. Rick and Lisa had landed several feet toward the center of the deck. Less than thirty feet away was the enormous red mass. Its eye opened, revealing a black circle the size of a boulder. She froze at the very sight of the creature.

The Behemoth lay across the ship. Its tail swung in midair, past the edge of the ship. It lifted its head, allowing space for its front legs to unfold from its underside. The pointed tips at the end of the legs pierced into the deck, and the hybrid propped itself up.

Forster stood up, scanning the deck for Nelson. He was nowhere to be seen. Rick and Lisa hurried to the ladder, ready to climb back down to the helideck. They stopped after seeing it was completely flooded. The weight of the beast was pushing the already sinking ship further beneath the waves. The waterline was halfway to the upper deck and climbing.

"Joe!" Forster called. Her voice was lost in the chaotic uproar of yelling mercenaries, exploding bulkheads, swirling water, and smashing steel.

"Over here," his voice called out. She scanned the deck again, still not seeing him. She hurried to the side, finding the Chief getting tossed about in the thrashing waves below.

"Oh god!" She got on her stomach and extended her hand. "Grab onto me! I'll pull you up!"

Rick and Lisa gathered by her. The downdraft of the chopper drew his attention behind him. The Huey had descended. The rocket pods, half empty, were aimed at the creature's head.

"Actually, we don't want to be up here!" he said. He grabbed Forster by the vest, tossed her into the water, and immediately splashed down behind her. Rockets exploded from above. Protected by the bulk of the ship, all four of them floated to the top.

The shark torqued its body, no longer interested in the defeated foe. It tucked its spider-like legs underneath its belly. Its tail swiped the ruins of the ship, sending several mercenaries into the air like golf balls. It slid into the water like a snake. Water rolled away, making way for the huge mass that re-entered.

Forster sucked in a breath. The surge swept her and her friends away. She felt herself lifted, then smashed down as the wave rolled. In seconds, she was twenty feet down, twisting about in the water.

The Huey hovered to the north, keeping its nose pointed at the target. Staying many dozens of meters ahead of it, the pilots backtracked the Huey.

Salkil stood between the pilots, never taking his eyes off the monster. "How many missiles do we have left?"

"Ten in total," the co-pilot said.

"Keep it following us," he said. "We must draw it to the north. The Navy will be moving in from there. Get on the radio and contact the USS Carnahan and USS Donovan and inform them of the situation. The co-pilot clicked a few switches. He fumbled with the radio dial.

"Sir, they're operating on a secure frequency," he said. "We don't have their channel." Salkil hissed. His anger was directed at the situation, not the merc. There was only one way to contact the Navy; to place a direct call to the Naval Command Center in Georgia. Doing so would confirm his presence at the scene, a scene at which he was not supposed to be present.

But the Navy was looking for a warship and had no knowledge of the hybrid. They had to be warned, or else many sailors would certainly perish.

"Alright, Napier, you win," he said. He made the call.

CHAPTER
42

Whirlpools twisted around the ship where water was filling the interior. Random bursts occurred as enormous air bubbles ruptured, making space for more water to make its way in. The alarms died as water fried the circuits. Only the red interior emergency lights functioned, casting a red glow beneath the waves.

Forster broke the surface and inhaled a deep breath. She had never been so grateful for lifejackets any more than this moment. Being thrashed about in the waves left her exhausted and disoriented. Resting her head on the shoulder of the lifejacket, she rested calmly, rising and falling with each wave. One grew gentler than the last, as the source had moved north. After she caught her breath, her ears detected the sounds of screaming all around.

She lifted her head, seeing the bubbling water in front of her. The ship had completely submerged. A huge echoing thud thundered beneath her. The *Pyramid* had hit the bottom. A few mercenaries splashed about, three at the most. The dead ones floated in the distance.

Scanning the water, she saw a hand waving at her. It was Nelson, floating maybe two hundred feet away. She summoned what strength she had and began paddling. Her muscles burned with each stroke, but she eventually reached him. Nelson was waving in another direction. Forster stopped for a moment and saw Rick and Lisa swimming over from different directions.

They gathered together in a tight group. Thunderous metal creaks continued reverberating down below. Forster clung to the Chief, partially out of sheer exhaustion.

"You alright?" he asked.

"Yeah," she said. She noticed his pained wincing. "You?" It was suddenly obvious. The saltwater was seeping in through his bandages and stinging the hell out of his leg wound.

"I'll be fine," he said. He looked around. Bits of debris floated about, but nothing buoyant enough to hold an adult. He looked to the rocks. "Well, I don't see any choice but to swim toward the atoll."

"Can you make it?" Rick asked.

"Only if a couple of you won't mind dragging me along," he said. Rick and Forster each tucked an arm under him, and started paddling, with Lisa leading the way. They only made a few strokes when Lisa stopped, perking her head as high as possible.

"Hey, honey...we don't have time to…"

"Hang on, Rick," she said. He heard it too. A boat engine. He looked toward the island. Two fishing boats raced toward them. They raised their hands in unison.

The first fishing boat came to a stop nearby. The Captain quickly stepped to the starboard side of the stern deck. He kneeled at the ladder and extended his hand.

"Swim on over!" he called out. They hadn't bothered waiting for the invite. Forster climbed up first. She stood on wobbly legs, yanking off the life vest. She looked at the man to thank him but paused after recognizing him. It was the bearded man from the bar last night. He smiled. "Hello ma'am. Glad to see you again," he said.

"*You're* glad?" she said with a smile. Rick and Lisa helped Nelson up on deck. All of them collapsed to their knees, the energy seeping from their bodies. The other boat pulled up alongside theirs. Forster recognized the fisherman aboard. It was Jeffrey.

"You folks alright? What the hell happened?"

"Long story," she said. Her eyes went to the surviving mercenaries struggling in the water. "Hey, would you pick them up?" Jeffrey gave a thumbs up and throttled his boat. Forster turned to the fisherman with the long grey beard. "I never got your name."

"Phillip," he answered.

"Well, Phillip, thanks."

"Don't mention it," he said. "Gee, when you said you were shark hunting, you weren't playing around."

"You saw it?" Lisa asked.

"Are you kidding?" he said. "The whole side of the island had to have seen it. What the hell is that thing?"

"*Isurus Palinuridae*," Rick said as he stood back up. "Think of a shark with the shell of a lobster, only bigger and meaner. A lovely gift from our government, meant to be used as a weapon."

"Only this one's a hell of a lot bigger!" Nelson said. "Now we know what happened to those fishing trawlers. How the hell is it so huge?!"

"My guess, they used an accelerated growth process. Probably a new experimental one. And it just never stopped. As the hybrid remained hidden for the past few years, it kept growing."

"Yeah, and obviously its shell thickened in the process," Forster said. "Explosives didn't even scratch it."

"Hot damn," Phillip said. "Well, this isn't the kind of fishing I'm familiar with. How do you kill something like that?"

"Who knows? I'm still getting over the fact that the other ones we were dealing with all this time were BABIES," Nelson said. "Hell, killing them was damn near impossible. Don't know how anyone will manage a friggin' fifteen story shark."

Jeffrey's boat started back toward them after picking up the three surviving mercenaries. He passed Phillip's boat on his way to shore. "We'll meet you at the harbor," he said.

"Wait!" Forster called out.

"Yes?"

"Let's go over there first." Forster pointed to the Raven Two helicopter. Though smashed, it managed to stay afloat. "They loaded it with C-4. If we can get it out…"

"Wait…what are you thinking?" Nelson said. "Even if you could explode it on the shark, it wouldn't penetrate the shell."

"Yeah, but what it we detonated it from inside the shark?" she said. Rick realized what she was thinking. He recalled using the fuel barrel inside the baby hybrid's mouth at the atoll to explode it from within.

"The soft tissue inside it would be unprotected," he said. He looked to the mercenaries on Jeffrey's boat. "Hey! How much C-4 is on that chopper?"

"Enough to level a building," one of them said. "But don't think we're going anywhere near that shark!"

"I'm not asking you to. Just help us get the explosives, and a detonator!" After a brief hesitation, the mercenary nodded. It was the least he could do.

****

The three-hundred-seventy-foot littoral combat ship USS Carnahan was three quarters of a mile from the west peak of Pariso Marino. On the stern deck was a helipad, containing two Seahawk combat helicopters. Navy sailors prepped the choppers for launch while others manned the armaments - four fifty caliber II chain guns. The Bofors 57mm cannon was armed, ready to fire on the reported hostile warship. Navy Seals boarded the Seahawks, ready to attempt a boarding mission aboard the Pyramid. The green light had not yet been given, as there was no sign of the target.

Captain Reece Danaher stood in the pilot house. New orders were being received from Vice Admiral Griffin onboard the USS Donovan. The orders were to locate a Bell UH-1N Twin Huey, black in color. On board this chopper was an Army Colonel, who reportedly had new intelligence regarding the threat.

What the hell is he doing out this way? Danaher thought to himself. He looked to the radar tech. "Do we have a reading on the Bell?"

"Affirmative, Captain," the tech said. On the nearby sonar console, another technician stared hard at his screen, while pressing his ears into the headphones.

"Sir? I'm picking up a reading," he said. Captain Danaher approached, looking at the screen. The computer indicated a large mass near the island coast.

"That can't be the ship, can it?" he said.

"I don't think so, sir," the tech said.

"We have a visual on the Huey. One thousand meters off the port bow," a voice rang through the comm. Danaher looked through the front pilothouse window. The helicopter looked like a small insect buzzing in the distance. He lifted binoculars to his eyes. There was no sign of the ship.

"Make communication with that aircraft. Have the SEAL team on standby."

****

The enormous shark continued its pursuit of the chopper. The Huey flew in reverse, keeping an altitude low enough to maintain the beast's interest, but out of range in case it breached. The Behemoth was mostly submerged, except for the tip of its dorsal fin. Its girth appeared like a red cloud beneath the huge swells it pushed aside, as if hell itself was traveling within the shallows.

Finally, to gain a new visual on its target, the monster lifted its head above the water. Its dull black eyes gazed unblinkingly at the chopper.

"Fire another," Salkil ordered the pilots. With a press of the trigger, a rocket fired from the starboard pod. It exploded on the creature's nose, doing nothing other than to fuel its desire for pursuit. "Good, keep pissing it off."

A voice came through the radio frequency, "*This is Captain Danaher of the USS Carnahan. Please acknowledge this transmission.*"

"Captain Danaher, this is Colonel Richard Salkil of the U.S. Army." The Colonel looked to the northwest, seeing the cruiser approaching in the distance. "I have a visual on your ship."

"*Colonel, what is the status of the situation?*"

"Are you carrying Seahawks aboard your vessel?"

"*Affirmative.*"

"Dispatch them at once," Salkil said. "Have them approach our position."

"*Colonel, what exactly is the situation? Where is the Pyramid?*" Salkil bit his lip. He knew he was going to sound like a lunatic, but it was essential for the Navy to know what they were up against.

"Captain, the *Pyramid* has been destroyed with all hands," he said. "There is a new threat lurking near the island, and it is imperative that it is eliminated. The target is a colossal organism. A giant shark." Radio silence followed. He could envision everyone on the bridge to be staring at each other in confusion. Laughter was possibly even breaking out. Who the hell knows. But one thing was for sure, they certainly thought he was crazy.

"*Colonel, please repeat last.*" What the Captain omitted was, "Did I hear you right?"

The impact of another missile turned into a burst of heat against the creature's snout. It remained uninjured, but increasingly frustrated. It reached up with its head, but the small mechanical enemy was still out of reach. The shark splashed its head down and submerged again.

As it pressed forward, new vibrations were picked up on its lateral line. They came from different directions. Some of the vibrations came from the northwest, indicating that something larger than it was on approach.

Simultaneously, there were new vibrations coming from the east. These sources were much closer and spontaneous, much more like that of prey. Unable to catch the airborne challenger, the Behemoth decided the pursuit was no longer worth the effort. With a swing of its massive caudal fin, it launched itself forward, zipping underneath the chopper.

"Sir, it's increasing speed!" the co-pilot announced. Salkil looked down, seeing the rolling water as the shark passed under them. It had picked up speed, but not in a manner of retreat.

"Keep after it," he said. The pilots had already turned the chopper around to pursue. By the time they rotated, the creature was already several hundred meters ahead of them. He pressed his headphones back to his ear. "Captain, do you still have a sonar reading on that mass?"

"*Affirmative.* It's moving toward the shore, along the west peak of the island."

"Make sure your choppers are armed with Hellfire missiles," Salkil said. "Alert the rest of the fleet to do the same. Deploy all units."

****

Captain Danaher's jaw was slack, visually representing his bewilderment. The Colonel sounded insane. A giant shark? And even if it existed, Hellfire missiles? A few good bursts from an M60 should do the trick. But Salkil was a well-respected commanding officer, and he wasn't going to openly challenge his advice.

Danaher opened up communications to the approaching Naval Destroyer, *Donavan*. "We are dispatching Seahawk units to identify a new target. I request additional aerial units for support."

"*What is the target?*" the Captain of the *USS Donavan* asked.

"According to the Colonel, the target is a colossal organism. A shark," Danaher knew how he sounded, and scrunched his eyes shut with slight embarrassment. "His words, not mine."

****

After collecting the surviving gear from the helicopter and the ravaged Zodiac boats, Phillip brought the group into the harbor. Once there, they boarded his truck. Luckily, the airport was a short drive away from the harbor, and speeding double over the limit did much to reduce drive time. Screeching tires brought the truck to a halt as they burst through the front gate. As the truck skidded, everyone was already boarding out the doors.

"Thanks, Phillip!" Forster waved at him.

"Don't mention it," he said, and waved back. They hurried toward Lisa's yellow and black R44 helicopter. Lisa and Rick took the front seats, while Forster and Nelson sat in the back. On their laps were large bags resembling duffle bags. Luckily, the mercenaries were able to salvage most of the explosives. Just as importantly, they located a triggering device in the console of one of the Zodiacs. On the way to port, they gave a crash course on how to detonate the explosives.

Nelson was growing increasingly nervous. "Can we be sure this'll work?"

"It'll work," Forster said. Her assurance unfortunately did little to help.

"Let's think about this. First, we're gonna draw the little one up, and sedate it in the mouth with a needle. Then second, when it's conked out, we're actually gonna try and rig these explosives on the little hybrid…" thinking of a twenty-four-foot creature as "little" was overwhelming in itself… "and then we're gonna try and use it to lure the big one?"

"They don't seem to have any qualms about eating each other," Forster said. "We need to give it the enticement of blood. We'll attach a tracking device on the harness. The sedation will wear off quickly, and when it does, we'll release the bastard out into the water. Best case scenario, his mom will gobble him up and we'll blow them both up. Worst case scenario, the big one doesn't eat it, but we still can blow up the little one."

Rick looked back at the open duffle bag Forster held. In addition to the C-4, the mercenaries were kind enough to give them some spare grenades. With a little luck, they could use them to kill the little one while keeping its body mostly intact.

Lisa started up the chopper. The cockpit shook as the rotors gathered their momentum. After reaching the required rotation, Lisa yanked up on the stick, causing the chopper to lift rapidly. Nelson grabbed his seat, swallowing hard. Even Rick tensed from the rapid ascension. Lisa sped the chopper to the north toward the resort.

****

The rollercoaster zipped down the hundred-foot slope and sprayed water as it grazed the ocean. It continued up, twisting into a loop-de-loop. As it went, another car started loading passengers, ready to start cranking up the incline. Further up the peninsula, the gaming docks were packed with visitors. With the increase in visitors, many of whom had arrived to see the new attraction, the park was packed for the first time in months.

"Hell no, I'm not shutting the place down!" The volume in William Felt's voice could be heard down the hall as he argued with Dr. Tucker. The biologist was still in shock after witnessing the creatures devouring the skier. The two aides had resigned on the spot, disgusted with Felt's seemingly deliberate lack of understanding.

Word had spread like wildfire when the foreign warship had passed by. People could see the Air Force jets passing overhead, providing reconnaissance of the situation. Then the news reports hit the airwaves, informing the public of a stolen decommissioned Navy corvette stolen by a group claiming responsibility for the oil rig bombing.

William Felt could not be bothered with any of the concerns. As long as people brought their wallets to the resort, he wasn't going to do anything to reduce their interest.

"Sir, there's something going on! Didn't you see the ship? It might be in everyone's best interest if we got everyone off the water," Tucker argued.

"I didn't bring you along over here to advise me how to run my resort," Felt said. "You're here to study the hybrid." Dr. Tucker shook his head. He didn't care about the hybrid anymore, especially after narrowly escaping the other one.

"You know what, Felt?" he said. "I'm catching a flight back and informing the board to keep their funding." He turned around and left.

Oh shit. Felt stood up from his desk and followed him out the door. Despite the booming business, he still couldn't afford any drop in funding.

"Oh, give me a break! You can't be serious…" Felt stopped in his tracks as soon as he entered the hallway. Everyone had hurried out, rushing outside.

Chatter could be heard, both in and out of the building. He peeked out the nearest window, looking at crowds of people along the docks and shoreline. Everyone was looking out into the bay. He looked further out into the horizon. At the far end of the peninsula, there was some sort of disturbance in the water. His first worry was a possible tsunami, but the swells weren't quite large enough for that.

He hurried downstairs, eventually running all the way to the front of the aquarium. There, he joined a crowd of his customers as they witnessed the rolling water in the distance rise into a huge mountain of ocean. At the top of this mountain, a ten-foot dorsal fin emerged.

Terror struck the docks. People turned and ran over the narrow pathways, knocking each other over to get to shore. Employees abandoned their assigned posts and joined the exodus.

Drawn by the numerous vibrations on the gaming docks, the Behemoth propelled into the shallows. Its huge bulk cut through the surface, plowing it through the furthest section of dock. Huge fragments of wood and metal sprayed the air, joined by the bodies of those unlucky enough to be standing on it. The beast thrashed its body in the shallow area, biting into the water. With each mindless chomp, the shark scooped up mouthfuls of debris and visitors.

Madness and panic struck the shoreline. Many people turned and ran inland, screaming for dear life, while many others desperately searched for separated loved ones. There was no sense of direction. Security rushed into action, but upon seeing the enormous shark, they joined the chaos.

Felt couldn't help but stare in a combination of disbelief and horror. The shark, a gigantic version of what he had in the exhibit, was destroying his resort. It smashed the rest of the docks, then rammed the empty pen nearby. Large fragments of steel and glass swished in the bay as the shark passed through.

In the madness, the rollercoaster technicians abandoned their posts, not bothering to hit the emergency brake. The car had just reached the top of the incline as the shark made its attack. It fell down the slope, and the screams that followed were not thrills. The car splashed into the water in the usual routine, drawing the attention of the Behemoth.

It sprayed ocean as it shot toward the slope. Its belly scratched the floor, and it used its legs to push itself up. Reaching with its head thirty feet high, its jaws clamped down on the arm of the rollercoaster. The whole structure shook from the tension. The shark yanked back, breaking off the entire initial slope of the rollercoaster. Thousands of pounds of metal came crashing down, creating a domino effect for the rest of the rollercoaster as the weight distribution became uneven. The car, having made two-thirds of its run, fell off the rails with every soul aboard.

The shark spat out the inedible portion of metal and began to climb inward. Its tail extended into the bay, thrashing back and forth in a natural motion. People lucky enough to survive its initial attack were swiped from the water by the enormous caudal fin. Thick metal splashed on shore and the bay as sections of the rollercoaster came apart.

The Behemoth planted its two front legs onto the shore, looking inland toward the abundance of prey that ran about.

"Follow my lead," Colonel Salkil spoke into the radio, communicating with the four Sikorsky SH-60 Seahawks that followed him into the bay. He felt his face flush when they entered the area. The shark had moved completely inland. Only its tail was in the water.

Commander Rivado, who piloted the lead Sikorsky SH-60, found himself dumbfounded. He was looking at an honest-to-God giant shark...with lobster legs.

"We have a visual on the biologic," he said, communicating with Captain Danaher. "Target is moving inland. We are seeing multiple casualties and are moving in to engage."

"All units, prepare to fire Hellfire missiles on target," Colonel Salkil said.

"Negative, Colonel," Commander Rivado said. "There are too many civilians in the blast zone. We must draw it out into the water with the M60."

"If you do that, all you're going to have is a giant pissed off shark with an impenetrable shell," Salkil said. "We can't allow this creature to escape."

Commander Rivado ignored the Colonel. His orders were from the Navy, and he was not going to fire explosives where civilians were present. "Unit Two, descend to fifty meters with me. Units three and four, hang back two hundred meters and be ready to hit this thing with missiles. We're gonna draw it out."

The two Seahawks hung back while the two leads descended. Hovering just over a hundred feet above the massive shark, they turned to allow the starboard machine guns to protrude outward. Both gunners opened fire, sending a barrage of bullets onto the shark's back.

The creature continued climbing inland, not even feeling the gunfire.

Raven Two circled inland. Salkil watched the operation and was now growing angry at the Navy ignoring his instructions. The shark took another step on land. He had no idea how long it would last without an oxygen supply, but if his military training and experience had taught him anything, it was to prepare for the worst.

He tapped the pilot on the shoulder. "We have what, five missiles left?" The pilot nodded. He didn't bother waiting for instruction. He turned the Huey toward the beast. They passed several meters above the Seahawks, being sure to keep them out of the line of fire. The co-pilot pressed the trigger, raining three of the five rockets onto the back of the shark's head.

The wave of heat and pressure caught the Behemoth's attention. It swung its body around, seeing the helicopters hovering over the water.

Commander Rivado was about to shout into the radio at the Colonel's interference. But the smoke cleared, and his anger turned to astonishment when he saw that the creature was unharmed.

"Holy..." he said. He studied the surrounding area. "Does anyone have a visual on any civilians near the target?"

"*Nobody that's alive,*" answered Unit Three's pilot. Rivado took a breath.

"Alright, Unit Two, on my command, launch Hellfire missiles." Rivado flicked a switch, arming the missiles.

"*Standing by, Sir,*" Unit Two said.

"Fire," Rivado said. Two missiles launched from both Seahawks. The entire side of the shark erupted into a huge explosion. Both pilots backed their choppers away from the ball of fire. What was left of the rollercoaster was now in flames, as was much of the artificial shoreline.

A huge red mass broke through the huge wall of smoke. The Behemoth lurched toward the choppers, frustrated from their assault. Its shell was completely intact, with some minor scarring and burns. Nothing that wouldn't be fixed over time.

"It's still alive!" a pilot yelled over the radio.

"Colonel Salkil, what the hell is this thing?!" Rivado said.

"Keep hitting it," Salkil responded. The beast crawled back into the water, the resulting surge sweeping the shore. The choppers proceeded out of the bay, followed by the shark.

Two more Hellfire missiles struck the Behemoth near the dorsal fin. Another huge explosion followed, as did the same result. The beast kept coming.

****

Dead silence struck the cockpit of the R44 Helicopter as they approached the resort. Forster and Nelson leaned in between Rick and Lisa to get a better view of the horrific devastation. The park was demolished. Smoke billowed from the shore and water. The wrecked remains of the dock and rollercoaster filled the shoreline, and bodies lay adrift. Further out into the bay, they could see the shark in pursuit of several military helicopters. Flashes of orange lit up in the water as they continued hitting it with missiles.

Forster closed her eyes and silently counted to ten. It took that long to calm her nerves. The resort where she had worked had become a warzone.

Lisa began the descent. "Okay, help me keep an eye on the pavement below. Don't want to set down on anybody." The chopper slowly came down in front of the exhibit. Water gushed from the edges of the shark pen. Forster watched the turmoil taking place inside. The hybrid's sensory system was overwhelmed by the overabundance of vibrations and smells from the giant and the military bombardment.

The chopper touched down, and they all stepped out. Rick and Forster both took a few steps toward the pen, only to stop short. The hybrid had smashed into one of the walls, then doubled back to attack the other side. "Oh, shit," Forster said. "This'll be harder than I thought."

Nelson saw a police car pull up. He ran over to the officer, who appeared shocked to see him arrive in a helicopter.

"Chief! Where have you been?"

"That's a story in itself," Nelson said. "What's the status of the situation? Is the Navy sending additional forces?" The officer shrugged.

"All we know is they were responding to reports of a hijacked ship," he said. "Then this...shark...it just came up and started attacking."

"Just proceed with evacuating everybody," Nelson said. "Oh...and do you have a spare radio?" The officer tossed him one. "Thanks."

Nelson rejoined the others several feet away from the pen. The bay shook as several more missiles struck the giant. The baby hybrid struck the wall again. Metal groaned as it dented outward.

"Are we sure we'll be able to sedate it?" Lisa asked. Forster remained silent, and gradually approached the ledge. She saw the beast going berserk inside.

"We have to try," she said. She turned toward the aquarium and ran inside. In the stairwell, she took strides of three steps at a time, hurrying upstairs.

****

The littoral combat ship passed by the west peak. The towers of smoke were visible from the furthest reaches of the bay. Captain Danaher ordered all weapons stations be manned. As they cleared the peak, he lifted his binoculars to his eyes. First, he saw the cloud of smoke in the middle of the bay, then the Seahawks. Then there was the huge mass pushing through the water. The dorsal fin was unmistakable. The Bofors 57mm cannon on the bow rotated to take aim.

"Fire!" Danaher commanded. The gun shook the deck with each recoil. Balls of fire and water burst around the target.

"Sir, target is still on approach!" the sonar tech said to Danaher.

"Then keep hitting it!" he yelled.

The creature pushed forward, ignoring the impact from each explosive. Signals surged through Ampullae of Lorenzini. It detected the *Carnahan* in its path. The fact that its new enemy was over twice its size meant nothing to it. The Behemoth knew no fear, nor did it understand the concept of retreat. It added intense pressure to the swing of its tail, generating a huge burst of speed.

"Target's speed has increased. Distance is closing rapidly!" the tech announced.

"Keep firing!" Danaher commanded.

The cannon was only able to fire off two more rounds. With each added meter, the Behemoth gained momentum in its approach. It was a million-pound projectile jetting over a thousand meters of distance. Thick protective lids covered its eyes.

It struck the starboard bow. The ten-inch thick hull imploded, leaving a forty-foot hole. The *Carnahan* swung heavily to port. Alarms rang out through the cruiser. Sailors on deck clung for dear life as the ship rocked violently. Watertight doors sealed throughout the ship, but the huge inflow of water had almost instantly flooded the lower compartments.

The machine gun armaments on the starboard side fired into the water.

Raven Two maintained an altitude of three hundred feet above the ship. Colonel Salkil watched through the bay doors. Its head was completely lodged inside the ship. Like a hundred-fifty-foot worm, it wiggled about to free itself, thrashing its tail left and right. The effort sent the *Carnahan* spinning in place. Several sailors lost their footing and ended up in the water, soon to be lost in the turbulent waves.

Finally, the shark yanked its head free and started swimming into the distance. It was clear that it was preparing to make another collision run at the ship. The breach was a deep one, and had created worse damage than a torpedo.

"They can't take another hit," Salkil said. He watched the swells caused by the huge beast.

Looking to the horizon, he saw the Naval Destroyer *Donovan* rapidly approaching. From the southwest, several Coast Guard vessels were now in view, operating in a joint response. Salkil no longer felt relieved by their presence. Rather, he wondered how many of those ships would still be afloat once the conflict was over. How many more lives would be lost?

This beast was a weapon of the worst kind.

Damn you, Dr. Wallack. I hope you're burning in Hell.

****

Nelson pressed the bottom of the syringe pole tightly against the end of a broomstick. Rick tightly wrapped duct tape around the two ends, allowing for more reach. Rick ripped the tape free, and Nelson held the extended pole by the tip of the broom handle. It gave about eleven feet of length; still not enough to ease his nerves.

Before he could voice his concern, Forster snatched it from his hand and filled the syringe with ketamine. After tossing the empty vial away, she glanced at the others to make sure they were ready. Rick and Lisa were standing by with the large harness, normally used for securing whales. Strapped to the harness were several blocks of C-4 explosives.

Another smashing sound echoed through the pen. The shark had rammed the door. Forster could see the gap forming in between the two sliders. Another hit, and the shark would be free.

"Alright, let's do this," Forster said in a confident voice. She moved over to the side of the pen and stepped out onto the deck. It slowly cruised along the far side, possibly dazed from smashing its head against the doors. Forster knelt down, keeping her eyes on the fin. She tapped the water.

"Here, fishy-fishy!" she said. The shark turned, but then turned back toward the doors. Forster slapped the water again. "Come on, don't you want us to take you to your mommy?" The shark redirected itself toward her distortions.

"Julie, be careful," Nelson said. She glanced back at him.

"Just be ready to go with that--"

"LOOK OUT!" Nelson yelled and pointed. Forster whipped her head around and screamed. The hybrid was breaching, jaws fully extended. When she looked away, it had made its run.

The jaws snapped shut inches from her torso, just as she fell backward onto the pavement. She hit the concrete hard, and the pole rolled away from her grip. For a moment, the breath had left her lungs. The world was spinning around her. A pain throbbed in the back of her head.

She felt the familiar sensation of water splashing her feet. She looked up. The hybrid was climbing out of the pen, its jaws merely inches from her legs. She kicked against the pavement, pushing herself backward. Each backward push was matched by a forward step from the pursuing hybrid.

Nelson prepared to throw a grenade, but couldn't, as Forster was in the kill zone. Ignoring the pain in his leg, he ran toward the creature, waving his arms in hopes of distracting it.

The plan worked a little too well. Propped up on all six legs, the beast swung its head toward him. He jumped back, narrowly avoiding being snatched up.

Forster rolled to her side and grabbed the pole. She stood up, holding it like a lance. The hybrid spotted her, and it viciously turned toward her. As it did, its tail swung in the opposite direction, striking Nelson in the chest. The Chief hit the pavement hard, and the grenade rolled free of his grip.

"Joe!" Forster yelled. The creature turned completely toward her, baring two-inch fangs. Holding the makeshift pole, Forster jabbed it toward the shark's mouth. As she did, it dipped its head. The needle struck the rigid shell on its nose and broke in two.

"Shit!" Forster tossed the pole to the side. There was no hope in sedating the shark anymore. Her eyes turned toward Nelson. Rick and Lisa helped him to his feet, and were rushing him to safety...

...leaving behind the grenade he had held.

The hybrid perched on its legs, ready to scurry toward her. Forster turned to her left and dashed. The beast, unconditioned to hunting on land, was not fast enough to seize her in its jaws.

Forster snatched the grenade and tightened her finger around the ring of the pin. The shark started after her again. She pulled the pin, and released the lever, triggering the five-second charge. Three of those seconds had passed when she chucked it. The grenade bounced against the shark's snout and was mid-way toward the ground when it discharged. Forster covered her face, feeling the intensity of the shockwave.

As she looked again, she saw the creature through the grey smoke. Its lower jaw was completely gone, as were portions along the side of its face. It crawled toward her, still intent on eating her. Blood spilled from its mouth, leaving a thick red trail. Forster shrieked in horror and backed away.

The hybrid stopped. For a moment, it seemed to blankly stare at her. Its legs shook, and then buckled under its weight. The hybrid crashed down, slumping against the pavement. After a few muscular twitches, it lay perfectly still. Dead.

Forster caught her breath, as Rick ran over to her. "Gosh...you alright?"

"I'm alright," she said. The sounds of explosions in the bay drew their eyes to the water.

"So much for our grand plan," Rick said in a defeated tone. Forster stood silent. She looked toward the employee docks. The maintenance vessel *Fairbanks* was still there. It was banged up, but operational, and equipped with a towing cable.

"Maybe not," she said. "Strap the explosives on it. I'll be right back." She ran toward the vessel.

****

The Seahawk units followed the beast as it moved away from the ship. Leading the chase, Commander Rivado checked his armaments. He only had one Hellfire missile remaining. Judging by the recent experience, he knew it wouldn't stop the creature. There was only one other option.

"All units, form up on me," he said. He ceased his pursuit, just as the creature made a turn to circle back. He adjusted his position, lining up with the shark trajectory. The other choppers lined up beside his. "All units, target the biologic with your AGM-119. Stand by, and be ready to fire," he said, arming the trigger.

"*Unit Two, ready.*"

"*Unit Three, ready.*"

"*Unit Four, ready.*"

"Fire!"

From underneath each chopper, a nine-foot long anti-ship missile dropped from each Seahawk. After descending several feet, each missile's afterburner ignited, sending it cruising toward the Behemoth. Each one hit their mark, exploding over the creature's head and neck.

They saw its bulk driven downward from the force of the blast. Rivado watched for its mass to reappear, but the smoke clouded his vision. "I no longer have a visual on the creature," he said. "All units, spread out. Watch for any signs of..."

The water exploded and the Behemoth leapt, hurling itself at the aerial attackers. Its body smashed against Units One and Four, which broke apart midair before splashing down. Units Two and Three elevated rapidly, and the Behemoth crashed back down. As soon as it hit the water, it continued its run at the *Carnahan.*

It crashed into the portside, penetrating several meters into the hull.

****

Lisa and Rick tied the harness around the dead creature's body. Nelson ignored the tightness in his chest and ribs as he helped secure the triggering devices. Each one had to be set properly in place in order for each block of C-4 to explode.

Forster opened the pen doors and backed the *Fairbanks* inside, all the way to the ledge. Once docked, she got out and jumped onto the ledge, holding the towing cable. She secured the cable tightly around the hybrid's caudal fin.

"Wait a minute...this is insane!" Lisa protested.

"Julie, it's too dangerous to go out there!" Nelson said. He pointed to the *Carnahan* in the distance. Its bow was completely submerged. The alarms echoed throughout the sky. "It's a warzone over there. It's not safe."

Forster touched his face with both hands. "I'll be fine." She jumped into the boat. He tried following her, but his cracked ribs nearly sent him doubling over. Rick chased after Forster, stopping at the ledge where she leapt back into the Fairbanks.

"Julie, this is crazy!" he said.

"It's been a crazy week," she said, then started the engine.

"Good God, Julie…what are you doing?" Rick said.

She looked back at him. "Bettering humanity."

The engine roared. Rick shut his eyes. *Damn you, Rick, you always want to do the right thing.* He jumped onto the boat with Forster.

"What are you doing?"

It was a question shouted simultaneously by Forster and Lisa.

"You'll never be able to unhook the cable while avoiding the creature. And who's gonna detonate the explosives while you're speeding away?" He looked over at his wife. "I'm in trouble, aren't I?" She nodded, but did not withhold a loving gaze. She understood.

Forster throttled the boat out of the pen, quickly pushing it to full speed. The cable went taut, and the dead creature's carcass slid into the water. Covered with a black harness loaded with explosives, it towed behind the *Fairbanks*, trailing a river of blood.

"Hopefully the big one will still smell the blood despite the chaos," Rick said.

Raven Two circled inland as the Naval and Coast Guard reinforcements began to enter the bay area. Colonel Salkil waited for the inevitable bombardment, which proved more and more unlikely to stop the beast.

"Oh great," the co-pilot said. Salkil approached the cockpit.

"What's the matter?"

"We have a civilian craft entering the kill zone." He pointed at the twenty-foot vessel. Salkil looked closely.

"What's that?" he said. The boat appeared to be towing something behind it. "Take us closer to it." The pilots looked at each other, shrugged, and followed the order. As they neared, the trail of blood came into view. The bulk of the cargo bounced along the waves. The Colonel fixed his gaze on the people on the boat, recognizing Napier and Forster. He looked back at the dead shark, seeing the explosives strapped to it. He suddenly realized their plan, and burst out a huge laugh. "Damn, that's ballsy!"

"Sir?" the pilot questioned.

"They're gonna try and explode it from inside," Salkil said. "Take us closer to the big one."

"SIR?"

"We have two more missiles," Salkil said. "That'll get its attention. We need to help lure it to the boat." The pilots hesitated, thinking of what happened to the Seahawks. "DO IT!"

"Yes sir," the pilot said. The chopper descended, zipping toward the sinking cruiser. The shark dislodged itself from the second breach, and started to swim outside of the bay.

They fired the first missile, which struck the caudal fin. The Behemoth turned around.

"Alright, good," Salkil said. "Start working back like we were doing." The chopper gradually flew backward, maintaining distance between it and the creature.

Salkil looked back, gauging the distance the *Fairbanks* needed to clear. "Keep going," he said to the pilots.

The creature started turning away, losing interest. The pilot fired the last missile, striking the creature along the gill line. It dipped heavily, as if enraged. Salkil looked back, seeing the massive thrashing that took place. The beast dove, and bounced along the seafloor, then angled upward. Its tail swept against the water, pushing the creature upwards. "Pull up!" Salkil said.

It was too late. The Behemoth shot clear of the surface, right at Raven Two. Its jaws clamped down on the entire front of the aircraft. The teeth on its upper jaw smashed through the windshield, coming down on both pilots as the jaws tightened.

Salkil hit the floor, feeling weightless as the chopper smashed down into the bay in the Behemoth's grasp. Less than a second later, he was underwater. The Behemoth shook the helicopter in its mouth, slamming it into the seafloor.

Salkil cursed to himself, his voice muffled by the water. It was the first time he endured defeat. And the last.

The hybrid smashed the chopper again, crushing it completely, and all those inside.

The smell of blood turned its attention to the surface. The creature rose to the surface, savoring its strength.

"There it is," Rick said. The fin emerged several hundred feet from the starboard bow. It cruised in a straight line, then slowly turned toward them. "It's studying us."

"Be ready to disconnect that cable," Forster said. She slowed the boat, allowing the beast to hone in on them. The water rose into huge mountains as the creature accelerated toward them.

Rick held his breath.

"Now!" Forster yelled, and maxed the throttle. Rick detached the cable. Liberated from the extra weight, the boat whooshed out of the way. The creature passed by their recent position, snatching up its own offspring in its jaws. The taste of blood was timely, as the creature required sustenance to supplant its spent energy.

It swallowed its meal whole, and its body demanded more. The creature splashed the surface while it changed course to pursue the small boat.

Rick held the detonator in his hand, ready to press the button as soon as they gained a safe amount of distance.

"Oh shit," he said. Forster turned, seeing the creature in chase. Its cone-shaped snout was quickly closing in on them. Rick hurried beside her, and grabbed her by the shoulders, forcing her to her feet. "We gotta jump!" he said. There was no other choice, and no time to hesitate.

They leapt as far as they could over the starboard gunwale. They hit the water and were immediately swept up by the current caused by the passing Behemoth. Both Rick and Forster rolled head over heels in the water.

Rick steadied himself and swam to the surface, still clinging to the detonator. He took a breath, just as the shark smashed the empty boat. Forster emerged several feet away.

The shark detected the rapid heartbeats of the two targets, and quickly turned toward them. Rick and Forster looked at it, then at each other.

"Well, hope this thing's waterproof," Rick said. The sudden downdraft turned his gaze upward, as Lisa's yellow R44 helicopter quickly descended.

With the shark approaching, she didn't have time to measure distance. She splashed the landing skids into the water, inches from her husband. "Come on!" she yelled, seeing the mass quickly approaching.

Rick and Forster wrapped their arms around the skids. "GO!!!" Lisa lifted the stick, and the chopper quickly rose. The creature raised its snout, literally grazing the bottom of Rick and Forster's feet as they rose out of reach.

Holding on tight, Rick maneuvered the device in his hand into a proper grip. He looked down to the Behemoth as it thrashed in the waters below him. "Last time," he said. He pressed the button.

Pressure and heat expanded from within, and the Behemoth heaved in unknown pain. It opened its mouth, as a ball of fire and blood expanded in a ghastly display. The creature smashed down, blood trailing from its mouth and nose. Its body spasmed and turned, until finally it lay motionless at the bottom of the bay.

CHAPTER
43

Lisa slowly touched the chopper down, allowing Rick and Forster to set foot on the pavement. Forster let go, and immediately saw Nelson approaching.

"Oh, thank God, Julie…you're alright." he said. She ran to him, hugging him tightly and pressing her lips to his. "OH!" he groaned. Forster pulled back, remembering his cracked ribs.

"Oh, shit! I'm sorry," she said.

"Eh, don't mention it," he said, embracing her with another kiss.

Lisa switched the rotors off and quickly climbed out of the helicopter, embracing Rick in a similar manner.

"You're crazy," she said.

"Yeah, well…" he kissed her again.

The four of them walked out of the lot, passing a dumbfounded William Felt, who stood silent as he gazed upon the ruins of his resort. Several cars arrived, unloading a flood of reporters who came rushing around them. Forster and Nelson ignored the questions, using his injury as their excuse to hurry through the crowd. As they walked, Forster looked to the clear sky and thought of her father. For the first time, she felt he was smiling down at her.

Rick and Lisa kept pace behind them. Reporters bombarded them with questions, most of which they ignored. Suddenly, one reporter raised her hand and pointed at him.

"I know you! You're Rick Napier!" she said. Rick stopped at the mention of his name. The reporter continued, "You were the one who spoke about the creature attack at Mako's Center three years ago!"

"Wasn't that a hoax?" another reporter asked.

The first reporter spoke louder. "You being here…as this strange shark attacks the island…it can't be a coincidence." Rick looked around. To his surprise, the crowd had quieted down, waiting for him to speak. He looked back at the female reporter. She awaited his response. "Well?"

He thought of his friends at home. He thought of the lost sailors in the bay. The world deserved to know the truth.

"It's all true," he said. "All of it. The hybridizations, the cover-ups, it all happened."

The press erupted with questions and comments, many labeling the group as heroes. With his arm around Lisa, Rick followed Forster and Nelson out of the lot. Cameras flashed, and questions hollered.

The dark-haired reporter shouted over the others.

"Rick Napier, could there be any more hybrids out there?!"

The crowd eventually spread out all over the area, turning their attention toward surviving victims and military officials. That final question repeated itself in Rick's mind. As it did Lisa's. As it did Nelson's. As it did Forster's.

Did we get all of them?

All four of them turned their eyes toward the view of the ocean. The Atlantic was blue and calm, reaching out for eternity. It seemed so peaceful.

Deceptively peaceful.

The End

CHECK OUT OTHER GREAT
DEEP SEA THRILLERS

THE BREACH
by Edward J. McFadden III

A Category 4 hurricane punched a quarter mile hole in Fire Island, exposing the Great South Bay to the ferocity of the Atlantic Ocean, and the current pulled something terrible through the new breach. A monstrosity of the past mixed with the present has been disturbed and it's found its way into the sheltered waters of Long Island's southern sea.

Nate Tanner lives in Stones Throw, Long Island. A disgraced SCPD detective lieutenant put out to pasture in the marine division because of his Navy background and experience with aquatic crime scenes, Tanner is assigned to hunt the creeper in the bay. But he and his team soon discover they're the ones being hunted.

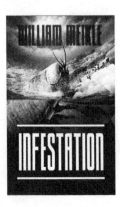

INFESTATION
by William Meikle

It was supposed to be a simple mission. A suspected Russian spy boat is in trouble in Canadian waters. Investigate and report are the orders.

But when Captain John Banks and his squad arrive, it is to find an empty vessel, and a scene of bloody mayhem.

Soon they are in a fight for their lives, for there are things in the icy seas off Baffin Island, scuttling, hungry things with a taste for human flesh.

They are swarming. And they are growing.

"Scotland's best Horror writer" - Ginger Nuts of Horror

"The premier storyteller of our time." - Famous Monsters of Filmland

CHECK OUT OTHER GREAT DEEP SEA THRILLERS

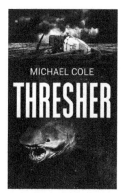

THRESHER
by Michael Cole

In the aftermath of a hurricane, a series of strange events plague the coastal waters off Florida. People go into the water and never return. Corpses of killer whales drift ashore, ravaged from enormous bite marks. A fishing trawler is found adrift, with a mysterious gash in its hull.

Transferred to the coastal town of Merit, police officer Leonard Riker uncovers the horrible reality of an enormous Thresher shark lurking off the coast. Forty feet in length, it has taken a territorial claim to the waters near the town harbor. Armed with three-inch teeth, a scythe-like caudal fin, and unmatched aggression, the beast seeks to kill anything sharing the waters.

THE GUILLOTINE
by Lucas Pederson

1,000 feet under the surface, Prehistoric Anthropologist, Ash Barrington, and his team are in the midst of a great archeological dig at the bottom of Lake Superior where they find a treasure trove of bones. Bones of dinosaurs that aren't supposed to be in this particular region. In their underwater facility, Infinity Moon, Ash and his team soon discover a series of underground tunnels. Upon exploring, they accidentally open an ice pocket, thawing the prehistoric creature trapped inside. Soon they are being attacked, the facility falling apart around them, by what Ash knows is a dunkleosteus and all those bones were from its prey. Now...Ash and his team are the prey and the creature will stop at nothing to get to them.

CHECK OUT OTHER GREAT
DEEP SEA THRILLERS

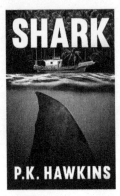

SHARK: INFESTED WATERS
by P.K. Hawkins

For Simon, the trip was supposed to be a once in a lifetime gift: a journey to the Amazon River Basin, the land that he had dreamed about visiting since he was a child. His enthusiasm for the trip may be tempered by the poor conditions of the boat and their captain leading the tour, but most of the tourists think they can look the other way on it. Except things go wrong quickly. After a horrific accident, Simon and the other tourists find themselves trapped on a tiny island in the middle of the river. It's the rainy season, and the river is rising. The island is surrounded by hungry bull sharks that won't let them swim away. And worst of all, the sharks might not be the only blood-thirsty killers among them. It was supposed to be the trip of a lifetime. Instead, they'll be lucky if they make it out with their lives at all.

DARK WATERS
by Lucas Pederson

Jörmungandr is an ancient Norse sea monster. Thought to be purely a myth until a battleship is torn a part by one.

With his brother on that ship, former Navy Seal and deep-sea diver, Miles Raine, sets out on a personal vendetta against the creature and hopefully save his brother. Bringing with him his old Seal team, the Dagger Points, they embark on a mission that might very well be their last.

But what happens when the hunters become the hunted and the dark waters reveal more than a monster?

Made in the USA
Monee, IL
10 May 2023

33468909R00163